Sheila Turner Johnston was born in v
childhood in different counties the le
as the family moved wherever her fat
Queen's University, Belfast, and apart from managing -- g
against all her expectations, one of her best experiences was reading
her poetry to an audience that included Seamus Heaney, who was also
one of her lecturers.

Sheila has won prizes for both fiction and non-fiction, and has
written many articles for both local and national publications. She
and her husband Norman founded the publishing stable Colourpoint
Creative Ltd, which is now owned and managed by their two sons.

Healer of My Heart is her second published novel.

Sheila can be contacted at sheilaturnerjohnston@gmail.com

Web site: www.sheilaturnerjohnston.com

Also by Sheila Turner Johnston:

Maker of Footprints Colourpoint, 2nd ed, 2019

The Harper of the Only God Selected poems of Alice Milligan (as
    editor) Colourpoint, 1993

Alice, a biography of Alice Milligan Colourpoint, 1994

The Middle Ages (with Kathleen Gormley) Colourpoint, 1997

History In Close-Up: The Twentieth Century Colourpoint Educational,
    2010

History In Close-Up: The Medieval World (with Norman Johnston)
    Colourpoint Educational, 2011

HEALER
OF MY
HEART

Sheila Turner Johnston

SHEILA TURNER
JOHNSTON

HEALER
OF MY
HEART

COLOURPOINT

Published 2020 by Colourpoint Books
an imprint of Colourpoint Creative Ltd
Colourpoint House, Jubilee Business Park
21 Jubilee Road, Newtownards, BT23 4YH
Tel: 028 9182 6339
E-mail: sales@colourpoint.co.uk
Web: www.colourpoint.co.uk

A catalogue record for this book is available from the British Library.

Extract from *Aubade* by Philip Larkin is reproduced by kind permission of
Faber and Faber Ltd.

Designed by April Sky Design, Newtownards
Tel: 028 9182 7195
Web: www.aprilsky.co.uk

Printed by CPI Group UK Ltd, Croydon

ISBN 978-1-78073-284-8

In loving memory of my husband Norman,
for whom all things have been made new.

Let me not to the marriage of true minds
Admit impediments. Love is not love
Which alters when it alteration finds,
Or bends with the remover to remove.
O no! it is an ever-fixed mark
That looks on tempests and is never shaken;
It is the star to every wand'ring bark,
Whose worth's unknown, although his height be taken.
Love's not Time's fool, though rosy lips and cheeks
Within his bending sickle's compass come;
Love alters not with his brief hours and weeks,
But bears it out even to the edge of doom.
If this be error and upon me prov'd,
I never writ, nor no man ever lov'd.

William Shakespeare
Sonnet 116

1

THERE ARE SOME memories that scar the soul so brutally that they can – must – be buried deep, deep, deep in everlasting ice. That ice must never melt, never run cold through the canyons of daily life, never jab the present or the future with a single frosted tentacle. Never even lie liquid and still in a cool dark pool.

Life goes on. Sometimes, against all expectation, all hope, it's good. Sometimes events go with the grain, smooth and unhindered. Sometimes there is even laughter and a way to see the next day, the next week. Month even.

But it's there. Down, down, down deep in the ice, the ice that must never melt. Else we drown.

But it's there.

But if a flame comes near, warm and dangerous and loyal and persistent and patient and inextinguishable?

Well then. That's trouble.

If Robyn Daniels could let herself go back even for a second, which of course she couldn't, she would recognise that the rime began to crust across her spirit when she was fourteen years old. She was sitting on the edge of her bed when the first icicle grasped and grew.

She was home. She had survived.

No, that wasn't right. She hadn't survived. She'd been dragged back, kicking, scratching, fighting every inch.

Depression was a terrible thing, they had said in the hospital as they checked the graphs, felt her pulse. Especially when it hit someone just on the verge of her whole life. Of course, she's at that awkward time. Fourteen years old. Hormones kicking in. They shook their heads. Fussed about.

Still, everything to look forward to, they said. How could you do this to your Mum and Dad? Look how upset they are.

Her father was upset all right. He was so upset his eyes bored into her, dared her, threatened her, scorned her – all in one gimlet gaze.

But it would stop now. It wouldn't happen again. Not ever again. She just knew it. She rubbed the bandages that still patched her forearms. At least she had achieved that. It was over. Not ever again. With anybody.

She hit the mattress with her fist. Anger was taking root, growing, spewing into her very soul.

Not ever again. Ever.

She crawled into bed and curled into a tight ball.

Her mother knocked on her door. Mummy didn't know. Did she? Anyway.

The chair was wedged under the door handle. Neither of them would get past that.

Let's just leave it at that, shall we? Take it from here. See what happens.

See how we get by.

Eight years later, almost to the day and the minute, Robyn Daniels was laughing.

Newly qualified as an English teacher, she was ironically thankful for the process of procreation for she was relieved to have at last secured a temporary post – her first – covering a maternity leave. The school was prestigious and large. Still rather nervous, she would get lost if she had to cover, as now, in an unfamiliar classroom. But if she didn't totally mess up, these few months were going to look good on her fledgling CV.

She pulled another exam paper towards her. She was taking

a relaxed approach to this class to catch up on some marking. These were the most senior students, mature, intelligent and no trouble to supervise for a colleague called away to help with preparations for the end of term sports day.

One, who she thought was called David, was perched on a desk in his shirt sleeves, large feet on a chair. Five of his classmates surrounded him. Four of them were girls. He was telling a joke, which he was illustrating with hand gestures and funny voices. He told good jokes. They were genuinely funny. At the punchline, as Robyn's sudden laughter danced across the desks, David glanced round and smiled at her, a flick of complicity, there and gone like a breath smothered.

She always remembered that.

She snagged one heavy curtain of brown hair behind her ear and checked the glass pane in the door. Yes. Chloe, David's girlfriend, was already outside, waiting. Keeping an eye on her territory.

What is it like to feel that way about someone? What is it like to want somebody, to be jealous, to lose sleep over someone? She had no idea, but it didn't matter. It wouldn't happen. Ever. Unconsciously, she rubbed her wrist.

As David put his feet to the floor and stood, one of his audience, a pale, thin girl with a baggy jumper and creased tie, put a hand out to touch his arm. He took a quick pace to the side and avoided the contact. Turning, his eyes caught Robyn's again. He looked away. Sombre now, apart. A chameleon, she thought.

Robyn sat at a table in the staffroom trying to finish some work while comments zipped around her.

Edith, head of Home Economics, was staring into her mug, aghast. "Somebody has used my mug! *Everyone* knows the one with the cats on it's mine."

One comment was so close to her ear that Robyn couldn't ignore it. "So how about dinner once term's over?"

The transparent eyes of the young Geography teacher, Angus Fraser, were fixed on her, unblinking.

She sighed. "Give up, Angus."

"Come on, Rob. We're bottom of the heap here. We've got a lot in common. How could it hurt?" He put on a comic face. "The summer's a-comin' and we could have some fun, merry maid."

She tucked her hair behind her ear. "Stick to Geography, Angus." She nudged her chair a few inches away from him. "I've to head back home for the summer anyway."

He laughed, a scoff in the tone. "Running back to mummy already?"

Robyn gathered her papers. "My Dad's not dead a year." She stood up. Something about him made her uneasy. "I'm not running back. I'm going back."

After school Robyn stayed at her desk, chipping away at paperwork. A twinge of hunger made her stop and stretch. The beat of a drum vibrated through the soles of her feet as she locked the classroom door in the deserted upper corridor.

The Holy Huddle Hooley. They were rehearsing for next Thursday's end of term gig when the Christian pupils said they were going to prove, loudly, that the devil did not have all the good music.

It was the first time it had happened. David Shaw, the joke teller, had arrived at the school just before Christmas. The two facts were connected.

Robyn liked some of the Holy Huddle – the less pious ones. The gym looked strange as she entered. Desks marched in rows occupied earlier each day by those taking examinations. It was impossible to move without causing the ching and clunk of metal legs and wood that seemed to Robyn to be a trademark noise of schools everywhere.

Edith, seemingly recovered from the trauma of the mug incident, stood to one side, by the climbing bars. Robyn joined her, leaning on the bars to watch the group round the drum kit and keyboard on the slightly raised stage. Billy Dobbin, the boys' games master, wandered in, track suit bottoms sagging round his thighs.

"Bit of a racket," he said, and lounged his bottom onto a desk, causing it to shift and ching against a chair leg. He blew a bubble with his chewing gum and burped.

Another senior, Tim Thompson, was on keyboard, his red curls tossing to the beat of his chubby hands as they pounded out a heavy rhythm. The stool strained valiantly beneath the gyrations of his ample behind. David was fiddling with the sound desk and Chloe was studying a sheet of paper in her hand.

Occasionally, David stopped everyone to go over a few bars again. A chap with a guitar arrived, puffing. David motioned him into place impatiently.

Billy popped a bubble and sucked it off his cheeks.

"Cocky bastard, isn't he? Rich mummy and daddy, moved into a big house on the Malone Road, long legs and a pretty face. Just about got it all."

They listened for a few moments and then Edith said: "I don't think he's cocky. I think it's just that he knows who he is and he's comfortable with that."

Billy waggled his brows sceptically. "And how would you know, Edith? He doesn't cook in your kitchen, I'm sure."

"I knew the family in Enniskillen."

Billy chewed some more. "Sprung fully formed on an unsuspecting school. Female hormones sloshing over the tops of our shoes. Then they found out he was a Jesus freak. What a waste of testosterone!" He grinned and waggled an eyebrow. "Or maybe not?"

He stood; the desk slid. His trainers made his stride soft on the wooden floor as he loped away. He turned back.

"Watch out or the bloody bugger'll convert you!"

"Billy!" said Edith, "Language! This is a decent school!"

Billy grinned again and chewed. The gum appeared, poking between his teeth.

"Yup," he said. "It's bloody posh." The gum changed sides. "D'you think it's only the plebs who swear? Wash your bloody ears out and bloody listen, Edith baby."

"Wash your mouth out, Billy Dobbin," said Edith.

He left. Robyn looked at Edith and tried to contain her chuckle.

Robyn's flat was just two streets from the school. She turned her key in the lock and slipped inside. It was above a dental practice, on the first floor of a tall Victorian terrace house in one of the elegant streets off Belfast's main artery to the south-west. She had lived in this flat for several years. It was important to her.

When she moved in, Neil, a friend from childhood, had said – in what was a rare moment of wit – that it wasn't a flat at all; it was a cupboard with ideas above its station. He hadn't been in it since.

The tiny hallway had three doors, two on the right and one straight ahead. First on the right was the bathroom. Next was the kitchen. Robyn could stand in one spot and prepare a meal, reaching everything from hob to sink without moving a foot.

Straight ahead was the sitting room. The light was flashing on the answer-phone perched on the edge of the stuffed bookcase. Robyn put the kettle on and got a ready-meal out of her small freezer before pressing the button.

"Hi Rob, it's me. Why won't you get a mobile, you dinosaur?" Robyn smiled. Neil's sister Gemma hadn't changed since primary school. "So you've only yourself to blame that this is short notice. I'm on a late tonight so how about tea in town? I've got an hour from six."

Robyn put the ready-meal back in the freezer.

Over salads, in one of the city's trendy snack bars, Robyn relaxed as her friend chattered. Despite Gemma's blonde beauty and outward sophistication, she talked with her mouth full just as she had in nursery school. She had a new hot boyfriend. He was called Jack. Robyn listened patiently. This happened every so often. Gemma had met him in the library when she had dropped an armful of books on the stairs. He came to the rescue. Just like a White Knight. Gemma's eyes had a misty moment. Then she waved her fork.

"I'll be so glad when the school term's over. All the pupils and students in the city are coming to blows over seats in the library. Honestly, don't the universities have enough space of their own?"

Robyn extracted the piece of coleslaw that had flown from Gemma's fork to visit the sugar.

"Exam time. Nearly over, though."

"They were queued at the door before we opened this morning. Nearly knocked me down." Gemma tackled a button tomato. "And then we have your lot. Seniors mostly. In fact there was a big guy in yesterday evening looking for some lit crit on Heaney or somebody. I asked him if he knew you and he said he did, but you weren't one of his teachers."

"I wonder who that was."

Gemma waved her knife. Robyn moved the sugar.

"Over six feet – wavy black hair. If I hadn't just met Jack I might have been tempted to explain the Dewey Decimal system to him. Slowly."

Robyn smiled, mug paused on its way to her mouth. "There's a guy like that in the other English group. Might have been him. I think he's a bit older than the others."

Gemma tore a piece of roll with teeth all the whiter for the frame of her scarlet lipstick.

"Neil's still pining after you, you know," she said, words muffled round the bread. The gutsy staying power of Gemma's lipstick was a constant source of puzzlement and wonder to Robyn.

Robyn rolled her eyes. "I've no idea why. I've never led him on. Your brother needs to get over his obsession with me and get on with his life."

"I've told him that." Gemma slumped back in her chair, her eyes following a businessman in a suit weaving his way through the crowded tables to the door. He was gripping a paper cup and a folded newspaper, all in the fingers of one hand.

Robyn followed her gaze. "You do see the wedding ring on his finger, Gem?"

"Yea. Bollocks." Gemma's attention returned to her plate to skewer another tomato. "Anyway, Neil would put one of those on your finger."

"Tell him to get lost." Tension turned Robyn's voice brittle. "I won't ever get married. I won't ever be…" She hesitated. "…with anyone."

Oblivious of a change in her friend's mood, Gemma grinned. "So you've said before. Well, Neil would be…" She mimed quotation marks with the free fingers that weren't still holding her knife and fork. "…with you any time."

Robyn looked at her watch. "It's nearly seven. You'd better get going or you'll be late."

Robyn walked back to her flat, a brisk half hour in the evening light. The city's day was on the turn. The workers had gone home, the players preened for the night ahead.

There was only one armchair in her little room. She sat with another mug of coffee in her hands and thought how Gemma, dear old man-crazy Gemma, didn't know it all, didn't understand. Robyn didn't want anybody. She didn't know how to want anybody.

Darkness fell before she roused herself and got ready for bed. She carried a chair to the hall and wedged it against her front door.

Friends weren't always a help. More often they were just a pit-stop. She plumped her pillow, tucked the duvet under her chin and curled up, hoping there would be no nightmares this night.

You can try to get by. But maybe, sometime, you will run out of road.

A couple of days later Robyn returned marked exam papers to her excited junior class. She had finished them after midnight and she was tired, but she had promised to have them by today.

The last weeks of term brought presents from some of the pupils. Even though she had not been at the school for long, Robyn received a number from senior boys who suffered the agonies of having a crush. Some were accompanied by excruciating verse and some by quotations considered apt by the devoted pupil.

After school, Robyn popped the latest offering into her bag – a copy of Heaney's translation of Beowulf. She sat to ease off the shoes that had been hurting her all day. When the family shoe shop was in business, she had never had to think of buying shoes. She had first pick of any new stock. Now she had to shop like everyone else. These red open-toed creations were Gemma's idea.

"Just you, Rob," she'd gushed. "You look great in red and these'll match your red dress. Look, they're almost exactly the same shade. Oh, go on! You can break them in."

Robyn stretched her legs and flexed her crushed toes. The shoes were breaking in her feet. She leaned back and rested her head against the wall behind her chair.

Angus Fraser locked his room at the far end of the upper corridor. His last class had been boisterous and difficult, but he didn't care. The easiest option was to let the little buggers riot until the bell went and then get rid of them as fast as possible. At the central stairs he paused and looked along to the English rooms. It looked as if Robyn Daniels' door was open. He frowned. No-one turned him down as many times as she had. He was starting to get annoyed.

Treading softly, he reached her door and peered round. Robyn was seated at the desk. Her bare feet were tucked up and partially hidden under the hem of her red dress. Her head was propped against the wall and her hair cascaded over the heart-shaped neckline and brushed along the creamy skin of her arms. She was sound asleep.

Lust hit Angus so hard he gasped and gripped the door jamb. By God, he would have this one! The thought possessed his brain as, eventually, he backed away, the sight of her imprinted on him, branded, hot and deep.

David Shaw leapt up the stairs three at a time, passing Fraser on his way down. He greeted the teacher, but Fraser seemed preoccupied. David walked quickly to Miss Daniels' room, hoping she was still there. He knew it was her habit to work on after school. Seeing her door open he pivoted on the door frame and swung in.

He had taken a breath to say her name when he saw her and stopped. His smile unfolded quietly. He was looking at a pose that his friend Tim Thompson would love to paint. The angle of the head, the exposed throat, the full red dress, the bare toes – it was the stuff of dreams. He backed out silently, wondering what could have made her so tired.

He had a question for her but it would have to wait.

2

IN THE STAFFROOM at lunchtime on Friday, a telephone call came for Robyn. She had been hoping for peace in the company of a cheese and pickle sandwich and a mug of coffee. She picked up the receiver reluctantly. It was Neil.

"Hi," he said. "Got you at last. I tried twice this morning to get you but the damn office wouldn't put me through to you."

"I've told you. The office won't put a call through when classes are on."

"Well, I have to deal with calls when I'm working. It's part of the job."

"It's school policy. Nothing to do with me." There was a short pause.

"Or get a mobile, for God's sake."

"So how're things?"

"Fine, fine. I'm in Belfast at the moment. I had to come up to see a client. I could bring you back down to your mother's for the weekend. I can call at your place after you finish. Gemma's not coming, this is her Saturday on."

"I was going to stay up this weekend…"

"Oh, come on, Rob. It'll save you a bus fare and I can take you straight to your Mum's door. Besides, I called with your mother two days ago. She's lonely. She'd like to see you… and so would I."

He was always glad to see her, tiresomely glad. Equally tiresome was her mother who never missed an opportunity to praise him, such an enterprising young man.

"A business of his own, Rob," she would say. "He's always

been very fond of you, you know. Sure, he isn't perfect, but then no man is."

There would always be a bitterness in this. No, Neil wasn't perfect but he had been an unwavering support when her father had died. Begrudgingly, her brother Stephen had come over from Canada for the funeral. He came the day before and left the day after. She had heard from him only once since. He didn't want his new life sullied by memories of the past one.

"I'll be home for most of the summer...", she began.

Neil sighed. "Don't you want to see your mother?"

Oh hell. She said she'd be ready at six and hung up. As she swallowed the last of her sandwich, Angus approached the empty chair beside her.

"There are some great movies on at the moment."

"Give me a rest, Angus. I'm not going to be about this weekend anyway."

Ignoring the empty chair, he sat on the arm of hers. A tide of alarm rose in her without warning. The buttons of his cream jacket brushed her shoulder. She fumbled to screw up her sandwich wrapper and stood up abruptly. Her hand was shaking as she set her mug down by the sink. It rattled on the ledge. Angus was watching her with a thin smile and raised brows. He stood up lazily.

"I don't think I've ever had that effect on a woman before."

The bell shrilled the end of lunchtime.

When Neil rang the doorbell for her flat that evening, Robyn put her weekend bag on the landing and went back for a folder of papers. She had promised one of her junior classes that she would have their exam marks for them on Monday. They had to be done, so they would just have to take a trip to Tyrone with her. She checked her purse for her key and slammed the door.

By day the street door was open for patients, but after 5.30 it was locked. As she struggled through it, Neil reached in to help her.

"Here, let me take that."

She handed over her weekend bag, shouldered her handbag and tucked the folder under her arm. Neil pulled the door after her.

"Honestly, you'd take two trips up and down to get out rather than let me help."

He was right; she would, and had.

His BMW was double parked. He opened the door for her and put her bag and folder in the boot. His dark blond hair curtained his cheeks as he bent. He wore it too long and parted in the middle. Robyn knew he thought it made him look trendy. It didn't.

"Good to see you, chicken."

Undeniably, it was so much better traveling in a comfortable car than alone on the bus with the prospect of a walk to her mother's house – a short walk made long by the addition of a weekend bag. For the first fifteen minutes Neil concentrated on negotiating the tangle of traffic. As soon as he had eased his way off the sliproad onto the rush hour motorway and they were cruising west, he jerked his head towards the back of the car.

"That looked suspiciously like work in that folder."

"That's just what it is, I'm afraid. I'll have to find some time to do it."

He was silent, his disapproval wrapping round her. For as long as she could remember, she never quite did the right thing. She tried diversionary tactics – something she was practised at.

"So what's all the news from the homestead?"

He was in process of tailgating a Peugeot that was going too slow in the fast lane. He flashed his lights and the driver moved over.

"Thank you!" He glared at the driver as he surged past. He

answered her previous question and related various bits of news, most of which she had heard from her mother already.

He flicked an indicator and veered to overtake an articulated lorry. Robyn stiffened and reached for the grab handle on the door. He noticed and laughed.

"Don't be a wimp, Rob! Honestly, if you ever took up driving you'd take forever to get anywhere."

"Actually, I was thinking I might take a few lessons. I've enough to put a deposit on a car."

He looked across at her, eyebrows raised. "What brought this on?"

"Independence, convenience. The usual things."

He drove silently for a while, frowning.

"Well, you must do what you want, of course."

The purring of the expensive engine and the comfort of the seat sent her into a doze. She was startled awake as the car turned suddenly to the right and racketed over a cattle grid. As she sat up, she saw that they had just passed through the cemetery gates, a mile from the town.

"Neil! Where are you going?"

"Sweet dreams?"

"Why are you going in here?"

"It's on the way and I knew you'd want to visit your father's grave." He grinned triumphantly. "The headstone was put up last week. I didn't tell you because I wanted it to be a surprise."

He drove slowly up the central pathway between older graves, to the derelict church which straddled the centre point. Newer headstones nestled on ground that gently sloped down behind the church to a thorn hedge. Pigeons churred in the light breeze of the flawless evening.

Robyn hated it. Neil jumped out of the car and waited for her to follow. She forced her legs to move and walked round the church to the gleaming black marble of her father's grave. She felt physically sick.

An urn containing long-stemmed pink carnations was placed in the middle of white gravel. In gold lettering the headstone proclaimed her father's name, his dates of birth and death. At the bottom of the stone there was the line: "Safe in the arms of Jesus".

Robyn drew in her breath sharply and pointed at it.

"Who chose that line?"

"Well, I suppose I suggested it to your mother. She liked it." He sounded slightly aggrieved. "Why? Don't you like it?"

"Not really, no."

"Your father was a good man. People still miss him."

"I just wish you'd both consulted me."

Robyn turned away and walked down the bank towards the hedge, skirting the fresh flowers covering two new graves. The voices of evening golfers drifted through the leaves from the other side. There was a gash in the bank giving way to a patch of gravel. She jumped down and sat on the grass with her feet on the gravel.

She threw a pebble with such force that it scared a small storm of sparrows into flight. As if it were possible to be safe in the arms of any man. Neil probably thought she was taking a moment to gather her thoughts, to pay her respects in silent reverence. He would approve of the way she was lovingly remembering her father.

She wasn't. She was thinking of what line she would have had engraved on his headstone. Just as Neil came up behind her, she settled on one:

"Rot in hell, Dad."

3

IRRITATED, NEIL COLLINS watched Robyn. He had been planning this surprise for weeks. Her mother, Anne, had left all the arrangements to him and he had given many hours of thought to the right and proper monument to mark the resting place of Matthew Daniels, one of the town's most respected businessmen. Not that he had been in business when he died. First he had sold the shoe shop and retired. Then, after several years of denial, he and his family could no longer escape the doctor's diagnosis of dementia.

As Neil walked slowly to where Robyn sat with her head bowed, he felt a flash of pity for her. She still wasn't over it, poor thing. The years of watching her father waste away to an incontinent skeleton had been very hard. He had been there for the family – "the son I should have had", as Anne was fond of saying. When Stephen left for a job in Canada not long after his father's diagnosis, Anne Daniels had dealt with the blow by not missing him and not needing him. Stephen became an acquaintance who phoned occasionally, and came over every few years to fulfill his obligations. Neil thought he probably only did that because his new Canadian wife insisted.

He kicked aside a nettle and checked to make sure there were none nearby that Robyn might carelessly put a hand on. He stood and looked at her bowed head for a moment, appreciating how, even in the setting sunlight, there were natural copper highlights glinting in her long hair. Her Irish rose colouring had matured over the years from pretty schoolgirl to striking student and now to this enchanting young woman.

A jag of anger stabbed him. What was so wrong with him that she could never see him as anything other than a family friend? He stooped and touched her shoulder. Her start of fright as she jumped and spun round, almost overbalancing, startled him.

"Sorry," he said.

She waved a hand dismissively.

"It's OK. Graveyards – you know. Anyway, let's get going. Mum'll be wondering where we are."

The Daniels had lived in this avenue for almost as long as Robyn could remember. When she was four years old they had moved from a terrace house near the town centre. The move was always spoken of with great pride. It was the moment when her father had declared that he was Somebody. No longer a small fish, he housed his family in 'a most desirable residential area', as the estate agent had boasted on the sales brochure. He had become a Councillor; he was elected onto local committees; he was asked to be a judge at fêtes.

Yet Robyn recalled playing on the footpath outside the little house on the hill on one of the town's backstreets as if it were a golden age. At the back of her brain there was a nugget of knowledge that she had been happy then. Happy to be tucked in at night and fall fast asleep in innocent, unthinking security.

No memories like those attached to this house, this suburban bungalow in a tree-lined middle class avenue, where everyone's grass was manicured and all the flowerbeds were trowelled into submission whatever the season. No memories like those at all.

Her mother gave her a peck on the cheek and hugged Neil warmly.

"Thank you for persuading her to come, Neil."

Anne Daniels was an immaculate woman. She was tall and slim and her greying hair was styled to perfection into a becoming bob which just skimmed the pearl studs in the lobes of her ears. Her friends admired the way she had coped with the illness and death of her dear husband; how she had refused to decline into sorrowful widowhood.

The delicious smell of a lamb roast permeated the house. Robyn returned from leaving her weekend bag in the smallest bedroom, the room she always occupied on her visits home. It had been her brother Stephen's room. Her mother had reinvented the bigger room, the room of her teenage years and it was now the spare room, a riot of cream and green, with pink roses sprawling over the twin quilt covers. The room it had been was obliterated.

"Where's Onion?"

"I put him out. The meat smell was driving him mad. He's probably huffing under a bush somewhere, washing a paw. Mash the potatoes for me, will you? I'll just check the lamb."

"Honestly, Mum. Sausages would do. Do you eat like this when I'm not here?"

She opened the back door but Onion wasn't in sight.

"Of course not. But I have to make an effort some time. Anyway, did you never see that programme about how they make sausages? I haven't eaten one since."

Neil was reading the paper. He lowered it for a moment.

"Quite right. Offal you don't want to know about. Stick to good plain food. Never go wrong."

He resumed reading. Robyn reached for the potato masher and thought that he sounded just like her father.

After they had eaten and Neil had left, Robyn shut the door of the dishwasher and turned to her mother, who was still finding ledges to wipe and cloths to rinse.

"Mum, why didn't you tell me that Dad's headstone was up?"

Anne smiled brightly. "Oh, didn't I tell you? Did Neil take you to see it on the way past?"

"Yes, he did."

"Do you like it?"

"It's very… civilised. You could have left out the pious text, though."

"Neil thought it was very appropriate."

"But Neil doesn't know that Dad was a manipulating bastard, does he?"

"Robyn!"

She fought to keep her voice calm. "And Neil doesn't realise that you have thrived like a flea on a dog since the day and hour he went into that home."

"Your poor father! What he suffered…"

"He didn't suffer enough, Mum, and you know it. He was a twisted rat. Are you rewriting your marriage? My God, don't you remember?"

Her anger burst through its restraints, howling like a storm banging a door back on its hinges.

" 'Safe in the arms of Jesus'! Were you ever safe in *his* arms? Were you?"

She was frightening her mother but she didn't care.

"But Rob, that's all over. We have to forget it and move on."

Robyn's words came out on a snarl. "Well, I'm glad for you, so glad that you can do that. You're the woman who could never cook meat the way he liked it; you never had the tea ready on time. You couldn't even have the house tidy when he brought a visitor home. Remember the day you fancied changing the furniture round in the sitting room? Remember? Remember how he made you put it all back the way it was because you hadn't asked his permission to do it? Stephen and I had enjoyed helping you do it too. But Dad made us watch you put it all back by yourself and he didn't lift a finger to help you!"

Anne put her hands over her ears.

"Stop it, Robyn, stop it! He's gone. It's over."

Furiously Robyn pulled up her sleeves and thrust her upturned wrists into her mother's face.

"But what about the scars? What about the scars? They're not gone, are they?"

Anne ran from the kitchen. Robyn heard her slam her bedroom door.

As if a plug had been pulled, anger drained out of Robyn and she felt very, very tired. It wasn't fair, what she had said to her mother. She was right, after all. Why should she not grasp what remained of her life and celebrate freedom and independence and all those things that she had forfeited by marrying a middle-aged narcissist when she was too young to know what the word meant?

With a chair wedged under the door handle of her bedroom, Robyn curled up under the quilt on the little single bed. She woke with a cry about three in the morning, shaking and sweating. She knew it was only the nightmares returning, as they always did in this house. She was not really being suffocated, terrified by a patch of blacker black in her room. But it was a long time before she slept again.

Her mother was in the kitchen before her in the morning, calm and neat. Her face showed signs of strain, her eyes still slightly puffy, but she tried to sound cheerful when Robyn appeared.

"Let's go shopping this morning,' she said. "It would do us both good."

Robyn poured a bowl of cereal and sat at the kitchen table.

"Mum, I'm sorry…"

"Please don't talk about it again." Anne turned away to the sink to rinse some dishes, hiding her face. "It doesn't do any good."

"But what will, Mum?" Robyn asked quietly. "What will help?"

Anne swung round, agitated. "Help? Who needs help? We have the rest of our lives. We make what we want of it. Let the past go. Forget it."

She put down the dish mop, snapped off the yellow kitchen gloves and sat at the table opposite her daughter.

"Robyn, please make a fresh start. Maybe try giving Neil a chance? No, listen to me. He'll help. He'll take you. He's been smitten with you since he was at school. He's had a few girlfriends but he always drops them. He's a good man, he'd look after you; I know he would."

Robyn waited while the words, "He'll take you", circled round her mind and settled in the place where all the other words were kept. Then she looked at her mother's earnest expression.

"Do you still think there's such a thing as a good man, after all that happened to you?"

"Robyn, please, I want to see you settled with a family. Once you have a family, you'll have a future. It'll keep the depression at bay. Make a new life, a happy life. Do it right, not the way I did. I want that for you so much." She reached out and tried to take her hand.

Robyn stood and brought her bowl to the sink.

"Where do you want to go shopping?"

4

Later that day they went for a walk in the local park. Robyn wasn't surprised that they just happened to run into Neil. Anne's "What a surprise!" wasn't even passably spontaneous. Neil lightly touched the loose, crocheted sleeves of Robyn's pink tunic. Her hair bounced over her shoulders, rippling like a cape in the light breeze.

"You should have brought a coat, Rob. It might rain later."

"Don't fuss."

The town's park was as familiar to each of them as their own houses. They had played here as children, daring each other to go higher and higher on the swings – although usually Neil's sister Gemma won because she was so fearless. They strolled past the slide and Robyn remembered her childhood fear of it. Once, Neil had persuaded her to climb the ladder by promising to climb behind her and catch her if she fell. But when she was nearly at the top, nerves had overcome her and she insisted on climbing all the way down again, trampling down past him and past six other impatient children who were waiting for her to take her turn. He had been embarrassed and furious.

"I said I'd catch you!" he yelled.

"You might have dropped me," she yelled back.

Her brother Stephen, almost a teenager, snorted. "Girls are stupid."

Today, the sunny afternoon had brought a new generation of children to riot round the brightly coloured playground. Anne swerved to a bench and sat down.

"I'm a bit tired. I think I'll just people-watch for a while." She waved a careless hand. "You two go on. I'll catch up in a few minutes."

This was so planned. But it was a lovely day and Neil's challenge – "Come on, race you to the boat!" – was tempting.

She was fast and he was not as light as he had been. It was no contest. She was over the wooden side and sitting on one of the planks across the hull when he climbed in beside her, panting.

She laughed. "You're getting tubby!"

He waited till his breath steadied. "I want to talk to you."

Instantly all the joy of the day left her and apprehension made her head drop. He took her shoulders and pulled her round to face him. At his touch, a sleeping nugget of panic deep within her tensed and trembled.

"Look at me. Look at me!" He shook her until she met his eyes. "You know how I feel about you. I know you do. I've never seen you show an interest in anyone else." He gave a bark of frustration. "God knows, I've tried to get you out of my head but you're stuck there even though I know the…" He stopped, looked away for a moment, changed tack. "…even though I've tried to be with other women. Damn it, Rob, we could be married by Christmas."

She remained still through this speech. Then bit out through clenched teeth, "In what charm manual did you read that proposal?"

He released her and stood, throwing his leg over the plank in front and the next and the next until he reached the prow. By the time he turned, the spark had left her. She felt flat, spiritless. He raised his voice.

"My God, woman, here I am, a man who'll look after your every need for the rest of your life and you… you look depressed!"

She looked up slowly. "I'm a bit of a failure at relationships. I'm afraid."

"But you've never really tried!"

He spread his hands in a gesture of helplessness. A clutch of children barrelled up the slope, intent on a game in the boat. The leader jumped in, swinging on the mast, brandishing an imaginary sabre and yelling directions to his pirates.

Neil was furious.

"Hey, get lost! The boat's occupied."

The chief pirate, a street-wise youngster of about ten, eyeballed Neil before leading his marauders away sullenly.

"We could have moved on, you know." Robyn said. "This is meant for children."

"They can come back later."

With a quick snarl of frustration he strode back. He took both her arms and pulled her towards him. Her arms came up to his chest to push him away with a strength fuelled by panic and anger. Over the side and running. She reached a fallen tree trunk and in one swift movement had climbed it, back against a jutting branch and knees drawn up to her chin.

Neil heard giggling and looked around. The pirate gang were hiding in a bed of shrubbery, convulsed with laughter. Furious, he strode across the grass to the tree trunk.

"Thank God we're out of sight of your mother."

Her right arm hugged her knees; she was rubbing the heel of her left thumb rhythmically against a rough piece of bark near her foot, shredding the skin until blood showed. Her voice was slow and deliberate.

"Don't ever try that again."

"For God's sake, Robyn!"

He walked some paces away and back again to give himself time to cool down. Slowly, she uncurled and dropped beside him.

Unexpectedly, she leaned forward – he was only an inch taller – and kissed him full on the mouth. She stood back, her eyes closed for a moment as if she were wine-tasting. When she opened her eyes, they were unreadable. A waiter would not have known if the wine had pleased.

"Friends, Neil," she said, "or nothing."

He looked at her hand. "Look, you've cut your hand by this silliness. We'll have to go back and get a bandage before it gets infected."

5

On Monday evening, finally back in her flat after staying late at school as usual, Robyn poured a mug of tea, winkled a biscuit from a new packet and took it to her chair by the window. She thought about what she had seen as she had walked down the drive after school earlier. A low wall topped by tall railings ran along the perimeter of the school grounds. At the end of the school day, these railings disappeared behind the crowds of pupils waiting for lifts, buses; gossiping, arguing, flirting. Later in the afternoon, there was rarely anyone around. So Robyn was surprised to see two figures seated low on the protruding ledge.

The pale thin girl from David's class was talking earnestly to him. David was looking at the pavement between his feet, his hands clasped loosely between his knees. His attention was so totally on the girl – Robyn remembered her name was Penny – that he did not seem to hear Robyn's footsteps as she passed a few metres from them.

David might have some explaining to do if Chloe heard about that tête-à-tête.

The ironing board slouched behind the kitchen door. Extracting it was one of the few activities that reduced Robyn to swearing. She pulled, the board swivelled – and the open packet of biscuits shot from the ledge to the floor. The jarring of the doorbell interrupted the scene. Mood rather threadbare, she stepped over the pieces of broken biscuit and went down the stairs to open the street door warily.

It was a large yellow teddy bear. "Hello, Rob," it said.

Neil's head appeared around its ear.

"What are you doing here?" Robyn asked, heart sinking.

"For you." He thrust the bear at her.

She took it and squeezed its tummy. "Thank you."

"The weekend... well." He spread a hand. "We're still friends at least." She rubbed the bear's nose while he fidgeted. "Look, do I have to just stand here? I've something to tell you. I was going to talk about it at the weekend, but.... Can't I come up?"

She looked up at the sky.

"I don't think it's going to rain for a bit. Let's just take a walk. But only half an hour or so. I've stuff to do. And you still have the drive home."

She went back up for her jacket and door key, leaving him on the step.

"So what 'stuff' have you to do?" he asked. "School's done half way through the afternoon and you're only filling in for somebody anyway."

They were strolling towards the city. Robyn kept a distance that ensured they wouldn't touch.

"You haven't a clue, have you?" she said. "I had lesson plans to do at the weekend. It didn't happen. Remember the folder I brought with me? The folder in the boot?"

It had been an almost silent drive back to the city. He must have stayed in the city overnight.

"Oh that."

"That."

"What are lesson plans? Don't you just..." he shrugged, puzzled, "teach stuff?"

She couldn't be bothered to reply. There was something in her shoe. She kicked it off and shook it. It was a piece of biscuit.

They sat in the window seat of a coffee shop and Robyn spooned the froth on her cappuccino. Neil flicked his hair back with one hand.

"I'm moving to Belfast."

Surprise made her freeze momentarily, spoon in mid air.

"What?"

He smiled at her expression. "I'm moving to Belfast." He sat back and spread his hands wide. "Congratulate me. At last I've signed a deal on new business premises. I signed on the dotted line today. It's perfect, designed for a technology company."

Carefully she set her spoon in the saucer, tipped her head back, hitching the dark curtain of hair behind one ear. "How long have you been thinking about this?"

"Quite a while. But I didn't even tell Gemma."

"Goodness."

"I suppose it was seeing the new office blocks going up that started me thinking." He nodded at her hand. "Why have you taken the bandage off your cut? You should have kept it on for few more days."

"It's fine."

He lifted his cup. "You really need someone to look out for you." He took a sip. "When I move up here I'll be able to do that."

"But what about your staff?"

"What about them? They'll be fine, they'll get other jobs. Some of them have interviews already."

"You mean the staff know about this already? And you didn't say anything even to Gemma? You've always told Gemma everything."

His bark of laughter made her jump. "Oh, there's things about me that even Gemma doesn't know."

In that moment, Robyn didn't like him at all, not at all. There was a shadow of nastiness in his tone. In a sudden change of mood he clattered his cup down and sat back.

"It's so perfect, don't you see?" He waved a hand earnestly towards her. "I'm going to buy a house, the first house of my own. And House of Collins will have a whole new image."

Robyn lifted her cup and sucked down the last of the froth. "It'll be quite a move."

"I'll show you round as soon as I get the keys. There's a bit of money business to sort but I've been told it'll be fine."

"Your mum and dad will miss you. And so will my mother."

"Oh, your mum's thinking of moving up too. Didn't she tell you?"

She choked on a swallow. "Quite a cabal, you two, aren't you?"

The frost in her tone passed him by. "What's a cabal?"

"Never mind." She reached for her jacket. "I must get back."

On the street at the door of her flat he put one hand on her shoulder. He ignored her instant tension, brought his lips close to her hair. His hand moved to her chin, finger and thumb. *Close. Too close.*

"Think about it. We could be good together. I know we could. Just *think* about it."

She pulled away but he gripped her chin tighter until she felt the hurt. His voice became hoarse.

"Please, Rob."

She felt his breath and her own fear all in the one moment, snakes twisting round each other. It was going to happen again. No matter what Neil did now, it was going to happen again.

He let her go so suddenly that she staggered. He stepped back and spread his arms wide. "OK. Friends. I know." He turned as if to go, spun round again. "You know, if you would let me, there's nothing wrong with you that I couldn't cure." He spun away from her. "I'd better get on the road. Give my love to the bear. Tell him he's a lucky teddy."

He walked quickly towards his car, buttoning the jacket of his grey business suit. Behind him, Robyn fled.

Neil put the key in the ignition but didn't fire the engine. After a few moments he hit the steering wheel and swore. He'd just made a big mistake, but damn her! Frustration and humiliation brought high colour to his cheeks. He turned the key and shot into the traffic, careless of the near miss and horn blast. At the end of the road he usually turned left to head west out of the city and home. Without hesitation, he flicked his right indicator.

In a narrow street near the city centre, a woman answered a knock on her front door. She raised her eyebrows.

"Oh, it's you. It's a bit early." She looked again and read his expression with the experience of years. Her hand came out and took hold of his tie. She pulled him through the door. Business was business.

Robyn tried to surf the panic. She really tried. But the wave broke over her.

She sank to the floor and crawled behind her chair. She wrapped her arms tightly around her head and body, pressing herself into the gap between the window and the bed. Incoherent fear took over, banishing reason to a far away place. When finally she stopped shaking, she lifted one arm and looked round the room, grasping for reality again. Anchor points.

On the couch, the bear lay where she had left it. Deliberately, she rose and took a pair of scissors from a drawer. She cut through the red bow round the bear's neck. As the bow fluttered to her feet she sat down with the bear on her knee. First she ripped open its stomach and pulled all the stuffing out onto the floor. Then, methodically, she cut the floppy remains into tiny pieces until the carpet was covered in lumps of yellow. When the eyes landed amongst the remains she stopped suddenly. Dropping the scissors, she lay down on top of the covers and curled into a ball.

I'll get by. I'll get by. I will. I must. But I'm tired.

In the tiny kitchen the ironing board still stooped over a scatter of broken biscuit.

David Shaw straightened his tie as he waited at the staff room door. Finally Miss Daniels appeared.

She looked terrible. The sleeping beauty he had seen before looked strained and tense as she came out into the corridor. There were black rings under her eyes. She didn't speak, merely looked up the length of him, waiting to see what he wanted.

"I saw you at our rehearsal." He paused but still she didn't respond. Not a flicker. This was uphill. "Two of the people who were going to help out on Thursday night – you know, at the Holy Huddle gig – can't come now. And anyway, I really need to be sure that there'll be enough staff at it. And I just wondered if maybe you were coming? Or would come?"

She turned away and he thought she was just going to leave him standing there. Over the few months they had both been at the school, he had gathered that she was liked and respected. It was why he was here now. He had never seen her like this. She turned back.

"David, I'm not a good person. Why on earth would you want me at your gig?"

He decided she must be making a joke.

"There'll be a few worse than you there."

"I don't think so."

Her tone was flat, dispirited. He decided to keep climbing the hill.

"Thursday night; it starts at seven-thirty, but we need to be there by six to check all the mics and stuff like that. Could you make it? Please?"

He finished on such a hopeful note that she gave a half smile. She walked to the window and stood for a moment, slightly turned away from him. It struck him that today every line of her was dejected and even the clothes she had chosen were dull and unflattering, such a contrast to that vivid red dress. He chewed on the thought as he waited.

"I'll make a deal with you." She gave a little toss of the head as she turned back, hair shadowing her face. The ghost of herself was in it. "My store needs reorganised. It's a total mess. I need to sort it out before term ends. If you'll help me with that, I'll help you at the Hooley."

"It's a deal. When would you need me?"

"Are you free after school today?"

He thought quickly. Nothing that couldn't wait. "I'll come straight round."

That girl has problems, he thought as he walked away. But he had achieved his objective. Now no one could say he didn't have enough staff attending. The Hooley was on!

The store opened off the classroom, and Robyn had already made a start when he arrived. He had discarded his tie and opened his collar. The sleeves of his shirt were rolled to the elbow. She organised him briskly, wanting the job done. When her instructions were clear, some kind of conversation seemed necessary. She asked him about his other subjects.

"I'm doing RE and Geography as well as English lit." He lifted a pile of Shakespeares. "But literature's really a lot of other subjects put together anyway."

"What do you mean?"

"You're really studying people, aren't you? It's about human psychology." He searched for an example. "Trace Lear's journey to self-awareness." He shuffled some books along. "Or *Lord of the Flies*. Is Golding right that that would happen in that particular set of circumstances?"

Immediately she took his meaning. "Yes – or should Catherine Earnshaw have followed her head or her heart?"

He pointed to a pile of texts. "Do you want those over here?"

"Yes, but further up towards the corner."

"She should have followed her heart."

"Why?"

He landed the first pile of books with a thud. "Because Heathcliff loved her."

"And Edgar Linton didn't?"

"Linton loved possessing her. Heathcliff just loved her. And that's better."

"Move them a bit further up… yes, that's fine. But Edgar gave her so much. She had a comfortable life and the devotion of a good man."

With the side of his fist he thumped a stack into neater order. "If that's all she wanted then maybe she did do the right thing. But she settled for black and white when she could have had colour."

After a moment Robyn said, "Well, at least she had the choice." He looked puzzled. "Between black and white and colour, I mean. Sometimes colour isn't an option."

His face creased around a grin. "Oh, there's always colour! We find it or mix it ourselves."

They worked on in silence. Robyn slid books onto the ledge above the storage cupboards and David put them where she wanted. She could sense through his quick movements that his thoughts were still bubbling. The chameleon was sociable today. She waited, wanting him to say more. When he didn't, she prompted.

"Where do we look for it?"

His eyes skipped to her, rested briefly. Then: "There's colour in words."

"Roses are red, violets are blue," she rhymed.

He laughed. An easy, adult laugh. "How about: 'They go the fairest way to Heaven that would serve God without a Hell.' Count the colours in that!"

She stopped in astonishment. "Where on earth did you hear of *Religio Medici*? I didn't come across that till university."

"I found it in one of the bookshelves at home. I think it's my mother's – she's a doctor. I can't remember who wrote it, though."

"Neither can I." She watched as he worked, his long back flexing easily. "Are there a lot of books in your house?"

"Stuffed shelves in every room. I went from pulling them out and throwing them around, to loving the feel of them and the covers, to actually starting to read them."

"Didn't you have your own books?"

"Plenty." He paused, resting his hand on the ledge. "I suppose I was lucky really. My parents never stopped me reading anything. If I wanted to go from Roald Dahl to Dickens and back to Winnie the Pooh or Asterix, they never said I shouldn't."

"So what's your favourite Dickens?"

"I don't like Dickens."

"Sacrilege!"

He stood back to glance up along the top shelf and pointed. "You see that stack? If you put them in this corner, piled a little higher, you would get all these on the floor into that space up there."

She pondered for a moment, eyeing the possibility.

"Let's do it."

In one quick movement he was on the ledge and started handing the books down to her, his head bent against the ceiling.

Curious, she said, "What do you not like about Dickens?"

"He's bleak; depressing."

"But he was drawing attention to social evils. And he did believe in happy endings. Look at Scrooge, redeemed in the end!"

He was quiet for a moment, working a pile of books forward to where he could lift them. "But that's not real life, is it?" he said finally. "Depressing things can stay depressing. Not everyone's redeemed."

For Robyn at that moment, it was as if the very tip of a little

44

finger had lightly touched still water and sent the merest ripple across the dead surface. She would not have it.

"Don't go all religious on me, Shaw."

He looked down at her suddenly and on her upturned face she felt the breeze of his sudden flash of impatience.

"Religion or reality. Why on earth do you think they're not the same thing?"

It wasn't the same after that. They finished almost in silence. Politely, he reminded her of her part of the deal and then left.

She stood in thought looking out over the playground, her hands steepled over her nose and mouth. David must be an exceptional student. He would probably lift a first class honours degree in a few years without breaking a sweat.

He and Chloe Masters emerged from a door below her and crossed the playground jauntily. Chloe was short and lightly made; she fitted three steps to David's two. As they turned out the gate, Robyn saw Chloe say something. David threw back his head and laughed, his hand resting lightly on her shoulder as they walked.

Robyn turned back to her desk, lifted her bag and keys and took a last look around the empty classroom. Her head ached and the world had become black and white again.

6

A COLDNESS HAD entered Angus Fraser. Rigid, implacable, irresistible. He moved restlessly in his desk chair as the picture of Robyn Daniels with a man looped in his brain.

He had known roughly where she lived. Now he knew exactly. Having spotted her walking with her man friend last night, it had not been difficult to drive round the side streets, coming out onto the main road every few hundred yards, keeping them in his sights. Watching them on her doorstep, he was amazed that the man did not go into the house with her. Businessman probably. Suit, flash car. After he had gripped her face, Robyn disappeared fast. Not even a goodnight wave. The guy wanted to stay. He must have. She must have led him on and then told him to get lost. There were names for women like that. Every one of them needed taught a lesson.

Around him his class rioted. They could go to hell. He bent over his desk, the coldness tightening like a frost.

Gemma was showing an elderly man how to use the online catalogue. He thanked her with a smile. Robyn, seated at one of the research tables, watched her with admiration. Gemma was good with people. She sent a 'see you in a minute' gesture to Robyn, and dealt with another query before managing to drop into a chair across the table.

"Some difference in here now. No problem getting a seat," said Robyn.

"Isn't it lovely? Libraries would be heaven if there were no people."

"Just like schools with no pupils."

"I can't get out this evening. I'm stuck till nine. Somebody took sick and had to go home, so I'm covering." She looked at Robyn more carefully. "You look a bit uptight. Anything wrong?"

"I'm OK. I just fancied a walk, that's all."

"That's not all, Rob. I know you." Gemma looked around, checking the enquiry desk and the other tables. Empty enough to keep talking. She cocked a groomed eyebrow across the table and waited.

"Honestly Gemma, you *have* to get Neil to back off." Her brief laugh was brittle. "He even said at the weekend that we could be married by Christmas!"

Gemma's mouth dropped in an exaggerated gasp. "Typical man! How on earth could you manage that? You'd get no hotel free at this notice. Besides, you'd freeze. You'd have to have fur bits on your dress, for goodness sake! I fancy a drop shoulder sleeveless bridesmaid's number." She posed dramatically, one arm held out gracefully, the other hand behind her head, pushing up her hair, scarlet fingernails peeping through her blond bob. "I hope you told him next summer would be the earliest."

Robyn pulled a tissue from her sleeve and fiddled with it. "You're still seeing Jack the White Knight, are you?"

"Oh yes! I'm not letting this one go. I'm seeing him tomorrow night." She arched her head sideways, "Anything might happen."

Robyn tore the tissue in two.

"You'll sleep with him." Robyn fired the comment like a pistol shot. Gemma blinked.

"If you want to keep someone, you have to put logs on the fire." She paused then added: "Besides, I want to. He really turns me on." She dropped her voice further and leaned across the table, eyes dancing mischievously. "He's a great kisser! – one good smooch and I'm putty in his hands."

As if they belonged to someone else, Robyn watched her own fingers squeezing and tearing the tissue. "Neil's moving to Belfast," she said.

"Yes! He told me this morning he'd finally signed the lease. It's a great site. He showed me round it last week." She checked the enquiry desk again and turned back, eyebrows raised teasingly. "You dark horse! And he's looking in all the right places for a house. Right roads going to all the right places. Neil says that was your idea."

A woman approached the enquiry desk. Gemma pushed her chair back and grinned across the table as she stood.

"Oh go on, Rob!" She tossed her hair. "Loosen up! Put a log on the fire and see what happens. You'd have some fun and you'd make him a happy boy! You could always dump him later."

She ducked as a crumpled tissue flew across the table. Robyn lifted her bag and strode out onto the echoing stone landing, clattered down the wide stairs, past the imposing book cabinets on the half landing. Gemma caught her in the foyer before she reached the revolving door. At the hand on her arm, Robyn spun round, her hair flying.

"Rob? Take a joke, for God's sake."

There was a display of book cover designs in the long hall and some browsers turned, curious at the noise. Robyn's ashen face showed two scarlet spots on her cheekbones. She hissed through gritted teeth.

"The first I heard of Neil moving to Belfast was last night. And I'll never make him a 'happy boy'. I wish you'd get that through his stupid hair into his stupid skull!" She took a few rapid steps backwards and cried. "Fire's burn, Gem. Fires burn!"

Then there was just the door, spinning crazily on its pivot.

Neil drummed his fingers on the steering wheel impatiently. No sign of her yet. Where the hell was she? When he had phoned her and said he would be here, she had said very little, but she certainly hadn't said she had to be anywhere else. Where else would she go anyway?

He looked at his watch. Seven-thirty. This wouldn't do. It was undignified. Matthew, her father, had been right. One evening years ago, when Robyn had flounced off in a huff about something he had said, Matthew had slapped him on the back. "Whatever you do, don't apologise, Neil. Fatal mistake. Show who's boss."

Shortly after eight he saw her. Her head was down as she turned into the street and crossed to where he waited outside her door. As he slammed the car door, she looked up, startled. He could see from her face that she had forgotten all about him calling.

"I've been waiting for ages. Where have you been?"

He thought he saw a flare of distaste, but it was gone before he could be sure.

"Walking."

"Why didn't you wait for me? I told you I'd be calling."

She turned away and then back again. "Actually, Neil, I haven't just been walking. I went to see Gemma in the library."

A light rain was starting to fall, speckling the pavement, tapping on the roof of the car. Robyn turned her face up, letting the droplets gather on her cheeks and lashes. He opened his mouth but she spoke first.

"You're a liar, Neil. You've lied to your sister and you've lied to me."

"Don't be ridiculous! When did I ever lie to you?"

"Gemma knew you were moving up here. She saw the place last week. And I bet you were going to tell me that you'd spotted a nice house and you'd made an appointment to view it. Oh, and by the way, Gemma, it was *Robyn's* idea." There were three steps up to her door. She turned on the top step, her key in her hand.

Her hair shone in a gauze of rain. "That puzzles me. Why would you let Gemma think I knew about your plans?"

He put his foot on the first step. So she wanted to know, did she? Then he would tell her. He jabbed a finger at her face. "She laughs at me. Do you know how that makes me feel? Have you any idea? She's known how I've felt about you for years, but she doesn't know that you actually cringe when I touch you." He didn't notice her recoil. "She doesn't know I have a bit of work to do yet."

Robyn's back was pressed against the door, her expression horrified. "You have a bit of work to do?"

Neil put his foot on the next step. She pushed him hard and he staggered back.

"You bastard!" she spat. "Your sister also knows how *I* feel about *you*."

The rain was getting heavier, flattening her hair and separating it into limp strands. He felt his anger rising, caution overwritten by long frustration.

"Yes, I lied! I lied to make you look normal so that I wouldn't feel so…!" He spun out onto the pavement, turning with his fists clenched in irritation. Looking back at her, breathing heavily, he decided to go on, careless of who would hear, "Damn it, Rob, count your blessings. I'm willing to watch the knives and the pills. Who else would have you? "

Robyn' hand covered her mouth in shock, her eyes staring at him. Then she lowered her hand.

"You haven't listened, have you? You've never listened, Neil. And that's your fault, not mine." Her voice rose to a shout. "I don't want to be had at all!"

She spun round, inserted her key and in one swift movement had slammed the door behind her. His body sprawled onto the heavy wood a split second after it closed. It was minutes before he stopped hammering it.

A stranger could have found the hall by following the jumble of voices and out-of-tune guitars. It was transformed.

"Hello, Miss Daniels!" Three girls from her junior class grinned a greeting as they wobbled along a line of chairs with a bunch of balloons. The balloons seemed destined for the top rung of the climbing bars, if they lasted long enough to get there. There was a loud bang and the tubbiest of the trio squealed and fell off a chair.

Robyn decided to intervene. "Here, let me reach them up now you've got them this far."

She climbed the first few rungs and tied the string at the top.

"Thanks Miss," they said in unison and ran to the stage, looking younger in jeans and jumpers than they did in school uniform. "Hey, David. We've done that. What can we do now?"

Edith appeared, bottom first, through the fire door beside the stage. She was dragging a table. From the colour of her face she had pulled it all the way from the HE rooms. Robyn lifted the other end.

"Right over to the foyer, Robyn. He wants it for the bouncers."

"Bouncers?"

"I think that might be you and me."

"Do I look like a bouncer?"

Edith raised her brows. "Do I?"

On the stage, Tim Thompson and David Shaw were hunkered down beside sound equipment, twiddling knobs. Chloe was in a corner, eyes closed, humming softly to herself and beating time with her finger.

Only her strong desire to keep her word had made Robyn leave her flat this evening. A call had come for her in the staffroom at lunchtime on Wednesday. The receiver was left off the hook, waiting for her. The person who answered had confirmed that the caller was a man. It had to be Neil – who else would it be? –

and she had quietly replaced the handset without speaking. She had heard no more from him, although she had walked home quickly each day. Getting by. Still getting by.

By eight o'clock the Hooley was at maximum volume. Leaving Edith by the door, Robyn circled the edge of the noise. The juniors looked younger out of uniform, the seniors looked older. The school's own Holy Huddle group had kicked off and a full hall of young people waved their arms in rhythm to a loud song about Elijah and trumpets.

Now, a visiting gospel group was rapping around the stage, the lead singer spinning on his toes. Robyn cocked her head to listen. She had never heard Christian rap before. She looked for David but couldn't see him. This had to be his influence. Back out in the foyer, Edith sat reading a novel.

"Music's not bad," Robyn said. You should go in for a bit. I'll keep an eye here."

Edith was unmoved. "Not unless they sing 'Shall we gather at the river?'"

"I don't think that's in their songbook."

"Neither do I. I'll keep reading. You go back in if that's your thing. I'm fine here. Sure what's to keep an eye on anyway?"

Back in the hall, the lead singer was waving his arms now and clapping his hands above his head. The audience was waving back and stamping feet at the same time. The floor as well as the walls shook.

Angus was surprised to be quite enjoying himself. The rhythms were good and there wasn't a uniform in sight. The middle school pupils were the funniest to watch. No matter how low their necklines or tight their jeans, they still had a skimming of immaturity. His lip curled. Kittens swaggering like cats and still tripping over their tails.

Senior girls were another thing entirely. The full fresh feline. If he met some of these in a club down town he wouldn't be going home alone. As it was, even he wasn't stupid enough to risk his job by coming on to a pupil. His radar picked up Robyn's re-entry into the hall. He shifted to keep her in sight.

Robyn found the drinks machine. David Shaw was beside it, head back, Adam's apple making short work of a Coke. His eyes lit on her when he dropped his chin.

"Sir Thomas Browne," she said loudly.

He cupped an ear towards her. "Sorry?"

"*Religio Medici*. It was written by Sir Thomas Browne. I looked it up."

"Ah! Rings a bell all right."

He threw the can into a waste bin. For something to do, she gestured at the machine and mimed empty pockets. He searched his jeans and found some change. He held it out to her. She hadn't meant him to do that. She hesitated. He pointed to the buttons on the machine and raised his brows in question.

She shrugged. "Orange."

The can rolled into the drawer and he handed it to her.

"Enjoy." He nodded, crooked a corner of his mouth, and walked away.

Robyn pulled the ring. Money's no object to you, I suppose.

She checked in with Edith who seemed to be at a crucial point in her book. She merely grunted when Robyn spoke. Robyn read the posters on the wall. "Don't start any fires you can't put out." This was superimposed over a picture of a flaming orange bonfire against a black sky. Underneath written very small, was a reference: James 3.

The next poster had a large picture of the top of a slim leg wearing a pink frilly garter. "No lap dancing clubs – Belfast has suffered enough."

At Robyn's snort of laughter Edith looked up. "Good, isn't it? I don't know who put that one there," she said.

"Probably the same person who put the other one there. They're an original bunch."

Edith kept her place with a finger and closed her book. "Indeed. It's a bit like Tim Thompson's style. Quirky sense of humour." She stretched her free arm and yawned. "Some of them look great, even to a rusty old maid like me."

"Nothing rusty about you, Edith." Robyn sat down beside her. "David Shaw's groupies are out in force."

"Yes, well, his designer stubble has a start on everyone else's."

Robyn frowned. "What do you mean?"

"He's eighteen already. In fact I think he's nearly nineteen."

"Is he? So why hasn't he done his A levels already?"

Edith opened her book again. "Oh, I think he missed a year of school along the way or something. I don't really remember." She turned a page.

Robyn nodded at the novel. "Sure you don't want to go in for a bit?"

"I'm fine, honestly. I'm just at the 'boy loses girl' bit."

Clearing up was going to take a while. About ten o'clock Robyn decided to see if the caretaker's room was open. There was an endless supply of black bin bags in there. A headache was stalking her. She went out into the dusk. It was calm, quiet, only the distant base thrum of percussion finding its way out through the corridors and walls. She inhaled the fresh air deeply. The lights of the city paled the stars which were just beginning to glimmer in the summer evening sky. Thin clouds, like teased wool, drifted lazily. Across the quadrangle there was an area of grass and trees. Not so long ago, this grass had been strewn with pupils revising for their exams in the sunshine. This evening it was deserted, leaves trembling in the hint of a breeze.

Stopping in front of a copper beech, Robyn leaned her forehead against the rough bark and closed her eyes. Unconsciously, she rubbed the inside of her right wrist. Now, alone, the blackness was rolling close. She was getting so tired of fighting it. Tired of being odd. Tired of being lonely in a city of people. Tired of being an actor on a stage. Tired of looking beautiful and feeling ugly, dirty. Neil's shout was a rebounding echo still. "I lied to make you look normal! Who else would have you?"

She turned her back to the tree trunk and looked up through the branches. So are you rotting in hell, Dad, or are you waiting for me? She shivered.

A twig cracked. David Shaw was standing less than three metres from her, his cream shirt in low relief against the dusk.

"Are you all right?" His voice was sharp; no courtesy title given.

She straightened. "Of course. You startled me." He continued to look at her, eyes slightly narrowed. She said: "Shouldn't you be inside, bossing or something?"

He relaxed and grinned. "Or something. In a minute." He gestured to the sky. "I just wanted to say thanks for a great night."

"I forgot. God's a pal."

He ignored that. "Thanks for helping."

"I said I would."

"Did you enjoy it?" He had come closer and seemed really to want to know. She struggled. It was unfamiliar, being asked for her opinion as if it mattered.

"You made a lot of people happy for an evening." She thought of Penny. "Bit of a temporary fix for some, I'd say."

He reached up and a branch rustled as he pulled a leaf. "Nothing wrong with temporary fixes. It's the principle behind Elastoplast." He ripped the leaf and dropped it on the ground, glancing down to scuff at it with his foot. "There are some unhappy people in there. If they've been happy for an evening then – great."

She shrugged. "I suppose so. Anyway, I should go. That hall has to be spotless in the morning."

She began to walk away across the grass. Without meaning to, she found herself slowing. Slowing. Coming to a stop. She turned. He hadn't moved. Sometimes she was also tired of the very new stresses of being a teacher, so different from familiar student life. This was time out. Off the record. Step off the stage.

She spoke quickly, harshly, with an anguish in her voice that she had not intended but could not disguise. "But what about all the unhappy evenings to come and to come and to come and never to end?"

There was a moment of total stillness. Then he walked slowly out of the shadows towards her.

"You didn't answer my question. Did you enjoy this evening?"

She sensed that there had been a subtle shift and that, briefly, it was time out for him too. "Yes," she said.

"Then you can feel happy sometimes. You know you can. And it's better to be happy sometimes than never to be happy at all."

Her mouth twisted. "So it's down to practice."

"Works for me. Keep smiling till your brain believes your face." She smiled. He lifted a hand triumphantly. "See?" He thought for a moment, becoming serious again. "We're not puppets; we can make our own choices."

"Like Catherine Earnshaw."

"Yes."

She was ahead of him, travelling along his thought. "And you chose colour?"

His reply came after a heartbeat. "Eventually."

A light blazed briefly and went out. Across the quadrangle someone had come outside. Chloe's voice called anxiously. "David?"

He glanced over his shoulder and then back to Robyn. He gave a little mock bow. "Shalom," he said softly.

"Shalom, David."

Chloe appeared by his side and took his arm possessively. She saw Robyn and without addressing a word to her, pulled David's elbow.

"Come on," she said. "Everyone's in a panic about where you are. You've to do the epilogue, and then the Head wants to do his 'behave yourself on the way home' speech." With another silent look at Robyn she steered David back to the building.

Robyn walked away. I just hope you appreciate him, Chloe, although I doubt it. A cool night gust lifted her hair. As she crossed to a door into the corridor, a shadow hunched itself off the wall.

"Hello," said Neil.

7

S HE HANDED HIM a bin bag. He held it between his finger and thumb, dangled it like a malodorous dead rat. She strode back up the corridor, fizzing with anger. How dare he come here, specially after their last encounter? He was like a piece of sticky tape that she couldn't flick off her finger.

He caught up with her, bag trailing. "I drove all the way up here after work this evening to talk to you. You weren't at your place so I came here."

She kept walking. "Well, where else would I be?"

"So tell whoever needs to know that you have to leave now and we'll go somewhere."

She stopped and faced him. "Thank you for your interest in what I do, Neil. Perhaps I should explain. This is an end of term gig. It's been really good and they're a courageous, energetic bunch of young people. I've enjoyed helping them this evening, and I'm going to finish what I promised to do, and that means helping with the clearing up."

He looked a bit smaller than he usually did. And why did he keep his hair in that floppy style? Tonight it was more irritating than usual.

After a moment Neil straightened, rustled the bag into a ball and dropped it on the floor. "OK. I'll wait."

Around them, young people were fooling about in bunches of laughter. Exhaust fumes filtered in as the cars of parents nosed round the quadrangle. Robyn passed some more serious clusters, deep in discussion of some of the challenges and issues which had surfaced during the evening.

The hall was quickly returning to normal. Chloe pushed a brush with a wide head in methodical sweeps. One sweep came very close to Robyn, causing her to hop sideways. Chloe moved on, not looking up. Neil's arrival had caused a little stir and Robyn could feel the speculation humming round the hall. He stood by the door, hands in pockets looking awkward, cross, and out of place.

Tim Thompson was packing up the drum kit, but she couldn't see David Shaw. Edith waited until they had got the table through the fire door into the deserted back corridor.

"So who's that?" she asked.

"Who?"

"That guy."

"Just someone from home. He gives me a lift sometimes."

Edith's eyebrows waggled. "That all?"

"Yes."

"Looks like a businessman?"

Shut up, Edith. "He has a graphic design business," Robyn said, just to say something.

She was feeling a great need for this evening to be over, to retreat into herself and be alone, safe in her hideaway. Reaching the hall again, she had a hand out to push the door when a slight movement caught her eye. Further down the corridor, David Shaw was standing with his back to them, legs planted apart, fingers thrust into his hip pockets. Facing him, perched on a radiator, was Penny Woodford. She was smiling up at him, lashes fluttering and legs emerging thinly from a pink hem.

Robyn pushed through the door without comment. Edith looked for a moment longer before following. She sounded anxious.

"I've seen them talking before. Funny. She's not his type, to put it mildly."

Robyn sidestepped some stray balloons. "Every girl in this

school wants to be his type. Can't blame her for trying."

"She'll not get anywhere though. Not with him." Edith picked up a couple of spent party poppers. "Not a girl like her surely?" She sniffed. "That young man has *standards*."

"He's male, isn't he? If she's got it and he wants it…" Robyn tailed off. Neil was coming towards them, jaw fixed.

"Right Rob, let's go. It's late enough."

"Neil, this is Edith Braden, the head of Home Economics. Edith, Neil Collins."

Robyn watched Neil dredging for politeness. A voice at her shoulder made her turn.

"And I'm Angus Fraser, not head of Geography. Pleased to meet you." Neil took a longer look before silently taking the hand Angus held out. Angus turned to Robyn. "Good night, wasn't it, Rob?"

Neil's fingers dug into Robyn's arm. "Come on, let's go."

"Oh, do you have to go?" Angus sounded desolate. "I was going to treat you both to a drink." He leaned confidentially towards Neil. "She's not long here but already she's a favourite."

A left-over junior pupil had climbed too high on the climbing bars. Edith went to stop him from hanging himself. Robyn's mood pivoted on a sudden cusp of mischief and retribution. She smiled warmly at Angus.

"Another time maybe. Neil has a long drive home tonight so he's anxious to get on the road. Aren't you, Neil?" Neil's eyes bored into her. "Goodbye. Safe home," she said.

Neil flicked his hair with one hand. Looked from one of them to the other. She could see him assessing whether to make a scene.

"I'll be in touch," he said finally, and strode away.

Angus looked disappointed. "Pity. But perhaps I can give you a lift home?"

Neil might still be in earshot. "That'd be great. Thanks," she replied loudly.

She turned. And met the steady brown gaze of David Shaw. He was in the doorway behind her, shoulder against the wall, his eyes resting on her thoughtfully.

Angus was well pleased. He had been careful to ask for directions as if he had no idea where she lived. He congratulated himself on his vigilance. That poor bastard Neil. She was making a fool of him.

He eased his Alfa onto the main road, pleased at how steady his hand was on the gear stick. She told him where she lived and not by one turning did he betray that he already knew. When she flicked the black cascade of her hair over her shoulder as she turned to thank him and left the car, his self-control was absolute.

One wrong move and it would all be to do again.

"See ya!"

The door of the small green hatchback slammed shut and David Shaw did a three point turn in the cul-de-sac where Tim lived. Just Chloe to drop off and then home. Chloe's folk lived in a sixties house not far from the teacher training college.

He hoped she wasn't going to want a big goodnight scene. He was tired, feeling the aftermath of weeks of planning and anticipating problems, of persuading people to see the same visions he saw. God knew he wasn't good with people. God knew he had trouble with his tongue and his temper. Why didn't God give him something to do on his own, where the only person he had to be angry with was himself? He was good at that.

He stopped the car and Chloe turned expectantly. He couldn't kiss her; he really couldn't. He brushed her cheek with a finger.

"Thanks Chloe. You were great tonight. See you tomorrow."

"Yeah." She waited. "Last day of term. Half day then."

"Yeah."

She gathered her dignity and got out. "See you then."

"See you."

David drove back. He passed the College and wondered if that was where Robyn Daniels had done her teacher training. Or had she gone to England like so many students did, shaking the dust of this country off their feet. If she had, at least she had come back, hadn't stayed to become pseudo-English. He turned into the tree-lined avenue where he lived. Quitters thought they were leaving problems behind. From what he knew of England, he suspected they were migrating to a lot worse.

Was the man who had appeared briefly this evening the reason she was miserable? David frowned as the memory came back to him; a figure in the dusk, something perilously close to hopelessness clinging to her until he had spoken. He recognised it because he had seen it before.

He crunched the car between pillars tucked into branching lilac bushes and parked some way down the side of the house. His parents' cars were parked side by side at the front. The light was still on in the den. He locked his car and paused momentarily to inhale the mingled scents from the large secluded garden. His parents looked after some of it themselves, but they also had a gardener. Walking round to the back of the house, he passed a weeping cherry tree and paused to put a hand gently on its slim trunk.

"Good night," he whispered.

An outside light blazed suddenly, and the back door opened. He loved his parents very much, but it was time to move out. But hey! how ungrateful can you be? He fixed a smile and went in.

Excitement and fear duetted within Robyn as she wedged the duvet under her chin. She had accepted a lift from another man; she had made a choice. She trembled slightly with the thought of her own audacity. As Neil and Angus had regarded each other, something in her had changed, timorous but real, and there was exhilaration in the change.

She turned restlessly, pummelling her pillow. As soon as she closed her eyes, Neil's furious face bloomed across her eyelids. She tightened her lids, splintering his image into fragments.

Screaming. Three o'clock in the morning and someone was screaming. Robyn had thrown the duvet to the floor and leapt out of bed before she realised the nightmares had returned and the screams were from her own throat. Crouching on the floor, she hunched backwards against the bed. Her hands wove together, each gripping the other wrist. She tucked them up and hugged herself tightly. It was always about three in the morning, when everyone else was asleep. Three o'clock in the morning was the bad time.

All the earlier exhilaration had vapourised into the night. It would always be like this. No change of mood, no exercise of choice, would take the devils away. Why did she keep hoping? What was she holding out for? Normality? She could stop or go on. She gripped her wrists tightly. The demons took over her brain. In the blackness of night, stopping seemed the easiest option. She was right out of courage.

The full packet of pain killers was easy to find and there was a glass of water beside the bed.

She sat in her chair and set the packet of tablets on the arm and moved the glass of water to the floor at her feet. After a few minutes she reached down for the glass. Stopped, startled. A man's voice had sounded as clearly as if he had spoken across the silence of fresh snow. She stood up and spun round, knocking over the water. Her room was as empty as it always was.

He had said just one word: "Shalom."

She stood still for a moment, then picked up the packet of tablets, turned it over in her hand as if she couldn't understand why it was there. She dropped it to the wet carpet. Wrapping the duvet tightly round herself, she lay down again. The demons had fled for tonight.

Shalom. Somebody had said that to her recently, but she was asleep before she remembered who it was.

It was Gemma who made the first move. She suggested this full blown dinner for two in a warehouse bar in the Cathedral Quarter, not far from where she worked.

They had eaten their starters almost in silence, discomfort stubbornly lounging between them. Restraint did not suit Gemma. Her opening gambit was softened with an awkward laugh as she toyed with her fork.

"Look Rob…" She waved a hand. "He's my brother, you know."

"So?"

"Well, we understand each other in a way. We're very similar. I remember you used to say that, when we were growing up. You used to say that it was no use asking my opinion on anything because it was always the same as Neil's."

"Neil was always your hero. But that was when we were children. Even when we were teenagers Neil chose the films we'd go to see, even where we'd sit. And you always backed him."

Gemma was scoring the table cloth with the prongs of the fork. She smiled at a thought.

"In primary school I used to drag you up to people and tell them you were the person my brother was going to marry. We were just children but maybe Neil started to believe it himself. Maybe that's when his obsession started."

"Some bride. Dirty knees and two front teeth missing."

"Only in P2," Gemma corrected. "Your teeth were perfect after that."

"No, they weren't. Don't you remember the classy brace? My teeth were going their own sweet way until my father …"

She stopped. Until her father had seen a possible flaw in his princess and had personally taken her to a private orthodontist. Long drives to the dental clinic. Long, long drives. Robyn's hand trembled slightly where it lay beside her glass. Gemma spoke softly, misunderstanding.

"I know you must miss him terribly. He was a really good man." She squeezed Robyn's fingers. "But life goes on. He wouldn't have wanted to go on the way he was." She paused. "And he wouldn't have wanted you to take so long to get over his death. He would want you to be happy."

"Would he?"

"Of course he would! Don't be so daft."

Beside them, a young couple were shown to their table. Robyn watched them. The girl was wearing a large diamond on her engagement finger. She said something and laughed. The man pretended to disapprove and then kissed the tip of his finger and placed it on the end of her nose. She bit his finger lightly and then they settled to their menus, discussing and pointing.

Gemma pushed her plate. "Let's give up on these and go for dessert. I've just seen something so wicked passing by it could have horns and a tail."

Gemma got her wicked dessert, but became thoughtful again. Robyn watched her fork chasing a cherry through a swathe of fresh cream. Finally she skewered it and looked up.

"I think," she said, "that Neil's trying to help you. He's worried, because of… what you did before."

"Did he say that?"

"Sort of. Look… " She was picking her words carefully. This was so unusual that Robyn was almost amused. "We know you had a bad time as a teenager. You were unlucky in the way the hormones hit you. We all want to get you past that once and for all." Gemma looked sideways at her. "Because it still hangs about, doesn't it? The blues?"

"I'm fine. I don't need anybody to worry about me."

"Yes, you do." Gemma's fork was suspended momentarily. "I don't suppose you could at least *think* of Neil as more than a friend?"

"You sound like my mother."

"Yes, well." Suddenly she became impatient. "For God's sake, Rob! You've never been anyone else's."

"Can't I just belong to myself?"

Gemma looked momentarily puzzled, then tossed her head. "Oh, you know what I mean. Remember that holiday in Scotland just after our A levels? Louise and Tanya and you and me? Our first major break for freedom?"

"I remember the posh hotel we stayed in. We could afford just one night. Waiters in kilts and private chalets in the grounds. Then it was back to B and Bs. What about it?"

"We got chatted up in the hotel bar."

"Oh yes. That was when Tanya disappeared for the night and never would tell us where she'd been."

Gemma tapped her nose. "Or what she'd been doing."

"Anyway?"

Gemma thrust a finger at Robyn. "You disappeared to your room. Half the bar was lusting after you and you took an early night!"

Their coffee arrived.

"What was wrong with that? I was probably tired."

Gemma rolled her eyes. "Oh Rob, you're such a serious case! There was a bar full of talent, we were young, free and single and –" she paused for effect – "you wouldn't even have a bit of a lark."

Robyn cradled her coffee cup. "How's the White Knight?"

Gemma blinked at the sudden change of subject. "He's fine, great, in fact."

"How would you feel if you discovered Jack had lied about you?"

"I'd be…" Gemma tailed off. She took a gulp of coffee. Like a cat licking its paw after a fall, thought Robyn. She watched as Gemma's mind changed tack.

"Hey, let's stop being so heavy!" Gemma giggled. 'My poor brother. He's just a man."

"Maybe that's his trouble." Robyn pushed back her chair. "My brother, right or wrong," she said, crumpling her napkin.

At the taxi rank Gemma got out a compact and redid her lipstick. She snapped it shut.

"So. Are we OK?"

Robyn put a hand on her shoulder. "Thanks, Gem. You really mean well. I know you do. But I just need to be left alone."

There was one message on her answer phone. She listened to Neil's first three words and then pressed delete. After wedging the chair behind her door, she lay awake for a long time, looking into the dark.

8

THE BOTANIC GARDENS, an oasis of green parkland between the Ulster Museum and the Victorian grandeur of Queen's University, were close enough for Robyn to escape into them occasionally. She knew every corner as a student swotting on its lawns and benches.

But this morning it tasted different. As Robyn walked past the ice cream seller with his cart and under the arch of the wrought iron gateway into the Gardens, she knew she had all summer to enjoy this, at any time of the day she chose.

She walked between the trees along the pathway to the great glass bulk of the Palm House. This sunny July afternoon the population of the park was a cross-section of the city. There were families playing, children squealing, toddlers crying, teenagers loitering, older people strolling or feeding the pigeons.

Robyn found an empty bench by the large roundabout of flowers opposite the door of the Palm House. She had brought Heaney's *Beowulf* with her but it lay unread in her lap. She loved flowers and they were everywhere, from the beds of pink begonias to the urns at each side of the entrance to the Palm House. Ivy trailed gracefully from the planters and, as they had for decades, the old double doors squeaked every time they were opened.

She had made a decision. She was not going back home this summer. She was going to have one summer away from the memories, the places, the people. It was her Elastoplast, the temporary fix David Shaw had spoken of. She didn't know what the cure was. But this was a 'getting by'.

A young man with a ponytail sauntered past, his arm draped around a thin blonde girl in jeans and a skin-tight T-shirt. He whispered in her ear and she giggled. Everywhere Robyn looked she saw couples: happy couples, laughing couples, besotted couples.

Had she the courage to keep on getting by? She certainly had the opportunity. The few people who cared about her seemed to see a way for her so clearly. They meant well. They really did. They would not, could not, understand. How could they, when it was impossible to explain?

She looked at a mother and father who had spread out a rug on the grass. They were obviously enjoying the first steps of their little boy. He was running unsteadily between them, from one pair of arms to the other. Robyn smiled as he bumped down on his round bottom and chuckled.

But the few who said they cared about her knew only some of it. They didn't know it all. They wanted her to settle into safety, have children. They didn't know that the very thought made her sick.

Deep down, the anger still squatted, an impassable boulder. Crouching, invisible, silent, potent. Deep frozen, covered in smiles, disguised in excellence.

She decided to walk across the grass towards the Museum.

Two things happened at once. A frisbee flew past her ear and something soft but heavy collided with her legs. Steadying herself, she looked down into the one good eye of a yellow Labrador, who bounced on happily and tumbled onto the frisbee in a heap of paws and ears.

A voice that she knew was quick to apologise. "Sorry. He's got only one eye and he doesn't always judge things right."

She waited while he came up to her. He looked fresh, bright in denims and a short sleeved checked shirt.

"It's OK," she said. "What happened to his eye?"

The dog had dropped the frisbee on the ground and was panting hopefully beside it. David picked it up and spun it away again before answering.

"We don't know. He was abandoned as a pup in a cardboard box on our doorstep one night. The vet tidied up the eye, but the sight was messed up for good."

The dog came back and held up the frisbee again. Robyn bent to pat him. "What's his name?"

"Manna."

"Manna? What sort of a name's that?"

"It's the stuff the Children of Israel were given to eat in the desert. You know – manna."

"I've heard of that manna. But a dog's name?"

"They found manna on the ground and nobody knew what it was. Same as him." He nodded at the dog.

"Ah! I see. Very apt then."

They stood for a moment. Robyn waited for him to move on but he seemed reluctant. He looked over her head and asked: "So. How are you? Now?"

She started walking again, back across the grass the way she had come. She should not have let down her guard that night. She reached the path and discovered he was still beside her. She tried to sound dismissive.

"I'm fine."

"Good."

She glanced up at him and caught his eye. His sudden smile turned a key. A calm settled on her as he fitted his steps to hers and stubbornly stayed with her.

"I'm trying the Elastoplast idea," she said.

"Is it working?"

"It's only just been applied."

David threw the frisbee. A cluster of pigeons scattered and gathered again. One pigeon seemed to bob more than the others as it walked, hobbling on one foot. The other leg ended in a stump.

Robyn nodded at it. "I wonder what happened to that one."

"No-one can warn the pigeons."

She looked at him questioningly. He explained.

"I heard an ambulance driver once. He was retired and talking about his work in Belfast in the '70s." They had walked on a few paces before he continued. "One day he was called to a street where a bomb had turned a shop full of people into a pile of rubble. He was digging with his bare hands. He lifted a pile of bricks and there was a pigeon, covered in dust and plaster. Its head was a bloody pulp." He paused again. "The man said it was weird. He was looking for pieces of people and still he could get upset that a three minute warning is no good to a pigeon."

She was silent. There was nothing to say to that. Then tentatively, she asked, "Did your family lose anyone in the Troubles?"

He shook his head. "No. Yours?"

"No relatives. Some friends."

"Anybody close?"

"No, but…" Thoughts were flowing. "Sometimes I feel as if I'm hurtling through space and there's a meteor shower all around me. I'm flying along with these rocks and boulders whooshing past. And I think: one of these is going to hit me soon. It has to."

She had never said that to anyone before. When she sneaked a look, he was nodding slowly as he walked. He had a quietness about him, she noticed, turning things over, taking his time. It was rare, the knowledge that you don't always have to say something.

They would reach the gates soon. She sat on a bench. With a moment's hesitation, he sat also. Manna settled at his feet. David tapped the book that she set down beside her.

"I bet I know who gave you that. He doesn't do English, right?"

"No, he doesn't."

There was a silence. The calmness had not left Robyn. Then he said: "You're popular, you know."

"Is this another piece of Elastoplast?"

He grinned. "Why not?"

"OK. But tell me why somebody like me is popular? Hard to believe."

"Who's 'somebody like me'?" She didn't answer that, although he waited, watching her. Then he said: "You care. You care about what you're teaching. And you care about who you're teaching." He rubbed the dog's side with his foot. "It shows."

"I… get by, I suppose."

"Chloe told me about you doing Fire and Ice with her class."

"Robert Frost."

"Great poem. It hisses and spits."

On the grass opposite, a father was stooping to hold his wriggling toddler while he wiped the remains of an orange lollipop from her cheek.

"That's a great description," said Robyn. "You should steal it and use it in your exam."

He smiled. "OK."

A group of girls in their early teens came along the path, bunched in gossip. One, with a beaded red strand in her hair and a nose stud, nudged the girl beside her. The group slowed to study David. His gaze skidded across them unseeing. Elbows on knees, he pulled at the Labrador's ears absently. He was still gnawing at some thought. Then:

"I think ice is good after fire. It stops the burns hurting. It's like an anaesthetic." He gestured with one palm upwards, "But it has to hurt again."

"Not if we stay in the ice. Remember the last lines?"

He sat up then and turned towards her. "But you can't heal

while you're frozen. You have to let yourself hurt again."

Where did the 'you' come from? She looked around, the calmness sucking away like the sea before a tidal wave. All of a sudden, she was amazed that she was having this conversation, in this place and with this person. The tidal wave crashed in and made her sharp.

"How would *you* know? You should get a bit of experience before you start handing out the medicine."

He bent his head. Sinews rippled along his forearms as his fists clenched. A cloud passed and the sun danced across the waves of his hair. It needed cut, she noticed. Dark tufts just grazed the collar of his shirt. His deep set eyes were in shadow as he stood. The dog bounced round him, overjoyed.

"Indeed. Enjoy the rest of your afternoon." He turned and walked quickly towards the park gates.

Damn! Damn! Damn! She hit the bench in a fury at herself. Why did she do that? Why did she spoil it? She stood abruptly and took two steps after him.

"David!"

At first she thought he hadn't heard her. Then he slowed for a few paces before turning, planting his feet apart in a posture like a challenge. She searched for words, his puzzled anger palpable across the space.

"I suppose your dog…" She swallowed. "Manna. I suppose you take him for a walk every morning?"

Pigeons fussed along the path between them. A skateboarder chopped through and they flapped and scolded in annoyance. She waited.

Finally he said: "Most days."

Then he turned his back and walked away.

Sweat sprang out on Angus Fraser's temples. Easy does it. He moved the mouse carefully. Click that. Select that. OK.

A breath stopping moment and then a photograph filled the screen. Ah! lovely. He had caught her in mid step, the full gypsy skirt – reds, greens, blues – brushing her calves as she walked.

Click. Even from the rhododendron bank, he had captured her, three-quarter face, head and shoulders. She was looking to her right, at the big Shaw guy who had appeared out of nowhere. God help him. She would chew him up and spit him out when she had finished with him. Except she wouldn't risk her barely started career by doing something so stupid.

He magnified the left side of her face. The camera had caught the porcelain cheek, the soft jut of the high cheekbone, the exquisite quality of her dark hair. He had never seen hair like it. He touched the screen with the back of his fingers, stroking down the image of the long strands. This was beautiful; heavy, shining like a mirror.

He had taken some more distant shots of her sitting alone after the big guy and the dog had gone. Just as he considered approaching, she had shouldered her bag and walked away briskly. He had decided to let her go – for now.

The Shaw household was quiet. David lay on the sofa in the den, his extra length ending in bare feet draped over the padded arm. The TV remote lay on his stomach and he jabbed it fitfully, channel hopping. He was alone in the house. His mother had been called to the hospital and his father was at a church leaders' meeting.

There had been a minor scene earlier. David appreciated the fact that the scenes in this house rarely went beyond minor. He knew from the stories his friends told that his own home environment was a comparatively peaceful one. While his relationship with his father could be uneasy, he had nevertheless been brought up with a combination of logic and reason, where points of view, including his own, were respected. They could be hotly debated, and often were. But they were always respected. He was fortunate in where he had been placed on this earth. He felt very far from deserving it.

He swung his feet to the floor. His mother had not wanted his father to go out tonight.

"You know you must ease up on your commitments, Vincent," she had scolded as she folded a pile of towels, clean from the dryer. "And I want you to go for a check-up." She was petite, her movements quick and precise.

"Elizabeth, stop fussing," her husband replied impatiently. "You prodded that stethoscope of yours over me and that's enough. I'm married to a check-up."

"No, you are not. I'm not a cardiologist." She waved a hand in his direction. "You're an economist – do I ask you about ancient monuments just because they come under the Civil Service too?"

He tried to pacify her. "I'm as fit as a fiddle. Honest!"

David remembered how his mother had kissed his father and rested her head on his chest.

"It's just that if anything should happen to you too…" Her eyes caught her son's and had followed him as he left the room without a word.

David gave up on the television and turned it off. He threw the remote onto a chair. Then he retrieved it and put it on the coffee table to forestall a comment from his father about it getting lost down the side of the cushion. Restlessly he paced to the window and pulled the curtain aside. The weeping cherry was still visible in the dusk.

Before she had left for the hospital earlier, his mother did exactly as he knew she would. She found him in his room and suggested what he could have for supper. Then she had added, pretending it was an afterthought: "We're very proud of you, David. You know that, don't you?"

He dropped the curtain and turned back into the room with

its mahogany bookshelves lining the walls and its air of deep, soft comfort. Despite this luxurious house, he was longing for a place of his own. He was ready for it, moulded by background and experience to a maturity beyond his years.

Manna was sound asleep on the rug. His nose twitched slightly and his paws trembled as he let out a little woof. Chasing the frisbee again in his doggy dreams. David stepped over him and sat down again. Something else was nipping at his consciousness. He pulled one ankle across his knee and put his head back, deep in thought.

He conjured up the sight of the student teacher (or was she qualified now? He wasn't sure how the system worked) walking across the grass in the park. There was something wrong with her and he was curious to know what it was. He was still stinging from the end of their encounter. He closed his eyes. He was used to articulating his thoughts, but he could not get a grip on this. He could pray for her; he would pray for her. But he had discovered that prayers are flighty bubbles of air unless they are anchored in action.

Manna snored and, without looking, David gave him a gentle dig with his foot. A memory amused him. The dog might have had an excuse for colliding with her. But did she really think he would throw a frisbee that close to her without meaning to? The dog had only one eye, but there was nothing wrong with his own two.

His mobile sang briefly. It was a text message from Chloe; she was going away on holiday in two days. Could they meet up for a coffee before she went? He punched out "OK", sent it and forgot it.

9

A PASSENGER FERRY was slipping across the water. Robyn watched its progress, wishing she was on it.

She and Neil were sitting on a bench at Groomsport, where the coast formed the southern sweep of the mouth of Belfast Lough. To her left, the far side of the Lough was blurred by a slight haze. Looking ahead, out to sea, the green humps of the Copeland Islands jutted beyond the next headland. The tide was coming in, washing rhythmically over the rocks on the other side of the sea wall. A large gull eyed them lopsidedly from its perch on the top stones before heaving itself up into the light breeze. The air was flavoured with the tang of seaweed.

It was ten days since they had had their confrontation on the street. Business commitments and then a trip to a new and potentially important client in Dublin had kept Neil away. Besides, as he had just pointed out, he expected her back at her mother's house any time. The fact that Robyn had snubbed him at the school and evaded all his attempts to contact her by phone, only annoyed him more.

Her eyes on the shrinking superstructure of the ferry, Robyn recalled his surprise when she had actually phoned him and asked to meet. The whole length of the bench was between them, their backs to a wooden picnic table.

"You're not coming home this summer?" Neil's hair blew across his eyes and he brushed it away angrily. "But you always spend the summer at home."

She sighed. "Not this year. I've told you. Belfast is my home now."

"Well, maybe in a way…" He kicked a pebble. "With everyone moving up here, Gemma already here…" A thought fed his indignation. "But I was counting on you to help me pack up and organise things for the move. There's a lot to do and you're a good organiser." His tone was tinged with petulance. "I thought we were" – he mimed quotation marks – "friends."

She looked at him in surprise. "You're moving so soon?"

"I'm in from the first of August. I need to have all the preparation stuff done in the first two weeks and be back in business by the middle of the month."

Robyn stood and went to the sea wall. She knew this was going to happen some time. How strongly she did not wish it to happen at all.

The sea licked the bottom of the wall below her. She searched for the ferry but it was now just a grey square on the horizon. She didn't have much of a life of her own, but any that she had was here, away from her family, away from anything to do with her past. The thought that her past could follow her wherever she went appalled her.

Neil came up beside her and put a hand on her shoulder. She pulled away, her hair tangling across her face. He thumped the wall.

"I don't understand you. I have looked after you and your family ever since your brother left home and your father took ill. What more can I do? I've cared about you almost all of my life." His voice became almost plaintive. "What more can I do, Rob?"

"You can't do anything more," she said impatiently. "I've told you before. I'm not good at… being with people."

"But why? What's *wrong* with me?"

"Neil, listen to me. *Listen!*" He stayed quiet, grumpy while she continued. "I wanted to see you today to make you understand." His mouth opened again and she shouted, "Damn it, Neil, shut up!" He closed his mouth. She took a deep breath and went on.

"You know how I was depressed? At school? I was in hospital?"

He waved a hand impatiently. "Of course I do! But you're years beyond that now. It's past." He frowned, cross. "Time to realise that."

She tried again. "But there was more. You don't…"

"All sorts of things happen to us when we're children! They don't have anything to do with us now," he snapped. "You can't let some adolescent moodiness spoil the future! It's in the past. Forget it!"

Adolescent moodiness?

With the old familiar feeling of going limp in the face of something she could not control, her shoulders sagged as she gave up. She stood still, thinking of fire and ice. Melting was impossible; much, much too painful. She would prefer to stay frozen for the rest of her life than touch the fire ever again.

It seemed to be the summer of decisions, choices. This one was made before they had met today. But he had just shot the bolt home more firmly. Deliberately, she searched for another personality within herself that could deal with the situation. She decided to become Miss Daniels, rookie teacher.

She returned to the bench and patted the seat beside her. "Come and sit down." He allowed himself to sit. As he opened his mouth again, Robyn lifted a hand to stop him. "We won't meet up for a while, even as friends."

For a moment he said nothing, just looked amazed. "But I need you this summer. This summer of all summers. There's so much happening. So much is coming together for me. How could you be so selfish?" He gave a little laugh. "Don't be such an idiot. What would you do without me?"

"Maybe I'll find out. And you'll find out what life would be like without me. You must stop this obsession with me, Neil. You *must*. I'm not good for you. It's *you* who needs to move on."

He shot to his feet. "It's that other teacher, isn't it? The one who came up to us that night. Have you been seeing him?"

Bloody hell. "No, I haven't seen him since that night."

He didn't seem to be listening. He grabbed her arm and pulled her to her feet. Angrily, she tore her arm out of his grasp. Some walkers passed them and their curious looks made him stop. The walkers moved on, heading towards the beach. A yellow Labrador trotted after them. Robyn checked its eyes. Two good ones. She turned back to Neil.

"I know you've been a friend for a very long time. I really want you to be happy; you deserve…"

"That's all I am to you, even yet. A friend." He lunged at her, brought his lips down hard on hers. Her stomach heaved. She clenched her fingers into knuckles and hit his cheekbone with all her strength. He released her and she flung round to lean over the sea wall, lean into the seagulls squalling round the rocks near the beach.

Shit! Take deep breaths. Steady. It can't happen here. It just can't. For several moments she fought the panic spinning and whirling, attacking the inside of her head, punching her brain. When the storm began to recede she turned, cold as the ice inside her.

"I swear, Neil, if you *ever* do anything like that again, I'll report you to the police. In fact maybe I should right now."

He raised his hands quickly, palms out. "Sorry, sorry, Rob." He seemed to calm himself. He even looked a little ashamed. He took a step towards her.

She backed away. "Where you want to go, I can't go with you."

"Can't or won't?"

She met his eyes. "Can't and won't."

He looked out to sea briefly and then his demeanour changed. He straightened his shoulders in a gesture that reminded Robyn of someone brushing off an unpleasant stain on their shirt.

He was discarding this whole conversation, discarding it like crumpled rubbish.

"You're overwrought. I'll take you back now. Come on." He turned to go back to the car. "How about dinner out somewhere tonight? We'll make an evening of it, eh?"

With quick steps Robyn crossed the grass away from him and headed for the main street where surely some kind person in a shop would believe she didn't have a mobile phone and would call a taxi for her.

She paid the driver and ran up the stairs, slammed the door of her flat behind her. By the sea she had successfully fought the panic, but little aftershocks began to shake her body. Keeping tight control of her movements, she went to the space between her chair and her bed and went down on her knees. Then she stretched full length on her stomach, arching her arms along the floor around her head. Gradually her eyes closed. She heard the ghost of a voice she knew breathe from the walls, sighing like a gentle memory:

"Shalom".

Emotionally exhausted, she dozed where she lay, the shadow of a smile surprising her mouth.

At five to seven that evening, Neil strode down the street to Robyn's door. Pink ribbons curled in his wake, streaming from the bow on the large bouquet of flowers that he carried.

He bounced up the steps and rang the doorbell for her flat. He would make up for another damn mistake this afternoon. Curse his clumsiness! Surely her face would brighten into a smile when she opened the door and saw what he had brought her. He straightened the bow; tweaked the cellophane; dusted his shoulders.

She can't have heard the bell. He pressed it again. It was all a silly fuss over nothing. He would charm her tonight, make her laugh. It was all a silly misunderstanding. Well, with her history he should expect some tantrums. He'd help her deal with them in time.

He straightened his tie; nodded to a passing girl who cast an envious glance at the flowers. Oh no, these aren't for you. These are for my girl.

Often when he called he would hear her footsteps on the stairs. He put his ear to the door. Not a sound. Frowning, he bent and peered through the letterbox. The hall was empty.

He pressed the bell again. Checked his watch. It was useless to go back onto the pavement and look up. Her flat was at the back. He hammered the door with the side of his fist. Still no sound of her feet on the stairs.

She can't have meant it. She can't. He hammered again. Then he jabbed the doorbell and held his finger on it for a full thirty seconds. Finally he dropped his hands to his sides, the top of the grand bouquet trailing the ground. He turned and leaned his back against the door. She can't mean it. Maybe she has gone out somewhere and forgotten the time. Or she's got held up somewhere. He checked up and down the street, willing her to appear.

But that wasn't going to happen. In the pit of his stomach he knew it. For a moment he experimented with hating her. Tried to banish her coldly, to throw out the line, "Well, if that's the way you want it."

His knees buckled as he dropped the flowers and slid down until he was hunkered at the bottom of the door. He put his arms across his knees and buried his face, feeling the tender spot where three knuckle-shaped bruises straddled his left cheekbone. It was no use. He couldn't hate her. He didn't have that way out. She had always been by his side, part of his life, child and adult. She was an obsession. He knew that. Ambition, money, status, he was obsessive about them all. The excision of Robyn from that tight ball of desires would be a wound that would bleed. He clenched one hand, feeling the silk of her hair as if it bunched in his fingers.

Her mother; he would have to face her mother. Briefly he considered turning all this into a towering anger and taking it to the one place where he was able to indulge in madness and empty his rage into someone whose job it was not to complain, someone who took the monster in him and left him free until there was another dragon to slay. But this time the thought of the dark terrace, the upstairs landing with its brown doors closed on the duty of business inside, was repugnant.

He loved her hair. She should never cut it. A single tear ran down the side of his nose, hovered for a moment and then dropped to stain the step between his heels.

10

THE GUEST HOUSE wasn't far away and Robyn walked back to her flat the next morning. It had been the only thing to do. Desperately she needed to follow, insist on, and reinforce her own choice. She had decided to remove herself from the situation. Carefully she rounded the corner and checked the street. Although even he wouldn't have stayed there all night.

It was after nine-thirty and the dental surgery was open. In the hallway Robyn called hello to the receptionist who was almost hidden behind a huge vase of flowers.

Robyn exclaimed. "Is it your birthday?"

The girl peered through the confection. "No. These were on the footpath outside when we opened up this morning. Imagine! Not the kind of thing you'd just drop and not notice." She arched an eyebrow. "Nothing to do with you?"

Robyn made her laugh light. "I should be so lucky!"

Her telephone was ringing as she put her key in the door. It was Gemma, in explosive mood.

"Where the hell have you been, Rob? I've been trying to get you for hours."

The answer phone wasn't blinking. "You didn't leave a message."

"No, I didn't. I didn't want to say this to a bloody machine. Neil's at my house. He had an accident last night on the way home. Went off the motorway into the embankment."

"My God! Is he hurt?"

"Cuts and bruises and badly shocked. He spent the night in A and E and they X-rayed just about every bone in his body, patched him up and let him go as long as he stayed with me."

"Has he said how it happened?"

Robyn could hear Gemma's intake of breath. "He's told me about yesterday. He was really upset. He wasn't thinking straight." Her voice was sharp with stress. "Come over here and see him, Rob. He's in a state and he wants to see you. I know he can be a pain, but did you have to be so blunt with him?"

It was one of those typical summer days: a pot-pourri of sunshine, clouds and rain. There had been an early shower and the streets were dotted with puddles, their edges retreating now in the sporadic sunshine. In the Botanic Gardens, Robyn walked restlessly past the white plinth of the statue of Kelvin at the gate and rapidly covered a circuit of the front of the park. She was wearing a light hooded showerproof and had intended to walk through the park and out the back gate to Gemma's. When she reached the fork in the path, she turned away, unable to go on.

Overwhelming relief that Neil was not badly hurt was mixed up with huge self-reproach. She had been too harsh. What if he had been killed? How could she have lived with that?

She was passing under the trees again. The benches were filling with people, not so many today because of the showers. Her emotions had been shocked into a somersault. Go round the path again. You haven't even decided what you're going to say. Should I give in? Just give up? Why not? It would please so many people. I have been horrible. I'm a bad person.

The frightened, damaged little girl was fighting her way up again, throttling everything that she had begun to hope to become. Then the whispers started, like worms in her head.

Daddy's little girl. But this is our secret. Just between the two of us. She put her hands over her ears. *If you tell anyone, everybody will know what a bad girl you are. Bad girl you are. Bad girl. Bad girl.*

She came down the hill towards the statue again, her footsteps tapping the refrain faster and faster. Inside the main gate she stopped suddenly and a middle-aged man almost collided with her. She took several deep breaths, hands tight over her ears, eyes squeezed shut, willing the whispers to go away. She straightened and started along the path again. *Bad girl.* This time she would go through the back gate and walk the half-mile to Gemma's.

Something nudged her leg. It was a one-eyed yellow Labrador, wagging his tail, offering her a frisbee and managing to pant loudly, all at the same time. She bent to take the frisbee and slowly raised her eyes. He was sitting under the trees. His back was into the corner of the bench seat, one ankle pulled across his knee and his hands clasped behind his head. He was watching her.

He must have seen her little fight with herself. He must. She stalled by making a fuss of the dog, keeping her face turned away from the level gaze. It was only a few days since she had snapped at him. *Bad girl. Bad girl.* What did she say now? She had to go past him. Finally she met his eyes. After a moment, he gave the slightest of nods. She might have imagined it. Then he clicked his fingers and Manna trotted back to him, leaving her holding the frisbee.

"You can't have been there long," she said lightly as she walked towards him. Manna took the frisbee from her hand and lay down to chew it.

"I haven't."

"Aren't you going away this summer?"

"Not till August."

"Ah."

He was taking no chances this time, it seemed. He would hardly speak to her, never mind start a conversation. The planes of his face were still, shuttered. Not even the kind of smile you would give to an acquaintance. She began to feel silly standing there. What was she expecting? He had talked to her and found her out; found that she was weird and unpredictable. Not worth the bother. Who was she, compared to the packed court of King David?

The sense of failure, like a ball and chain, dragged her heels as she walked on. There was one person who would put up with her. One person who would have her. One person who would tell lies to make her seem normal – for the rest of his life if necessary. Another way to get by. She was a bad girl, bad girl, to have treated him so badly. Maybe her mother didn't know yet what she had done. Maybe she need never know. *No, mummy mustn't know. We won't tell mummy.* She headed down the path to the back gate, defeated again.

At the top of the slight incline, the doors of the Museum opened. Angus Fraser stepped out and made his way down the path, pausing behind each tree trunk. David Shaw was still sitting where Robyn had paused briefly. This was awkward. He didn't want Shaw to see him trailing Robyn, but if he didn't follow her now, he would lose her.

Angus stopped and watched through branches. The dog was chewing something while his master shifted restlessly, glancing along the path after Robyn. The guy lowered his head for a moment. Angus sneered. Ha! a holy Joe. Probably praying she'll find him irresistible. He had been waiting in his car to catch her leaving her flat this morning. Except that she didn't leave. She arrived. With an overnight bag.

Bitch! Photographs and fantasies were all very well, but he'd want the real thing very soon.

Great – the guy was leaving, walking away. No, he's stopped. Turned round. Turned back. Hunkered down beside the dog and rocking on his toes. Make your mind up, boy! Damn. He had snapped a lead on the dog and finally set off in the direction Robyn had taken.

Now what? A surge of annoyance made his head hum. But this might be interesting. He set off to follow the boy, just catching sight of him as he rounded a corner.

The river was quite fast today, despite it being the summer. Nestled at the feet of mountains, Belfast was rarely short of water. Hands thrust into the pockets of her coat, Robyn wandered aimlessly along the embankment. Where had the person she had been yesterday vanished to? What was the good of making decisions for yourself if someone was going to come along and say: Sorry, that won't do – you have to do this instead. Why bother trying to be anybody? Why bother at all? Why be happy only sometimes if you could stay frozen and never have to feel anything, happy or sad?

Several seagulls bobbed on the water. On the far side, a union jack flew from a lamp post. She walked along in the direction of the flow, the rippling motion almost hypnotic. This wasn't the way to Gemma's house. It was back nearer the bridge. She stopped and put a hand on the railings, willing herself to turn, go and be a decent, civilised person and tell Neil how glad she was he wasn't badly injured; tell him… She started in surprise. David Shaw was leaning on the railings beside her.

"Do you make a habit of materialising suddenly?" she said.

"You just didn't hear me. Or him," he nodded at the dog, "which is more surprising."

Manna's pink tongue hung from the side of his mouth, shaking in time to his yellow sides, which were heaving like bellows. After one quick glance at her, David didn't make any attempt at conversation, just stood there looking across the river.

"I've a cat," she said. What a stupid thing to say.

"Him or her?"

"Him. He's called Onion."

His mouth twitched. "Onion. I like it. How do you manage

to keep him alive in Belfast? Must be a cat graveyard."

"He's not here. He's at my mother's."

"Are you not from Belfast?"

"No. I'm from way out west!"

Somehow she had settled her arms on the railings beside him and the silence was OK now. A racing canoe sliced up the river, the rowers straining rhythmically. It reminded Robyn of something.

"I wrote a poem about this river once. For my school magazine."

"Remember any of it?"

"It wasn't any good. In my last year at school we were bussed up here for the University open day. Some of us went exploring before the bus took us back, and we ended up here. Almost exactly here in fact."

"You went to Queen's?"

"Yes."

He looked round at her then. He seemed pleased. "That's where I want to go."

"I think the Head will want you to go in for the Oxbridge exams."

He snorted. "He can want all he likes."

"Don't you want to have a crack at it?"

"I want to stay here." He looked across at the gable end of a block of flats where a paramilitary mural glowered over the street below. The eaves above it were painted red, white and blue.

"Do you? Will many of your friends stay?" she asked.

"A lot of them want to go to Scotland; Dundee, St Andrews."

"Why don't you want to go too?"

"Because I want to stay here. It's my home."

After a moment, she said: "Funny." He raised an eyebrow. "It's just," she explained, "that I know a few people who went to university in England. And they haven't come back. But I feel just like you said. I'm sticking with it." She nodded across at the mural. "To hell with them all! This is my country too!"

He turned round and leaned back on his elbows. "Sounds like a toast. 'To hell with them all!' "

She laughed. "A great toast!"

Manna had decided to lie down and David dropped the lead. His mobile bleeped. He pulled it from his pocket, glanced at it and put it back again.

"Any career plans?" she asked.

"I'm not sure yet. Nothing definite."

"Waiting for the Damascus light?"

"I could wait for worse," he replied.

"Seriously though?"

He spoke carefully. "I'll do my best with what I'm given, where I'm put, who I'm with." He shrugged. "God knows the rest."

Robyn was sure the careers master had never had a reply like that on one of his forms.

"I wish I had your confidence," she said.

His mood somersaulted suddenly and he grinned. "Yeah, sounded good, didn't it? I wish I had my confidence too!"

A jogger pattered down the cycle path that bordered the road. A tin can floated by, not far from the bank. Robyn looked around and found a pebble. Her aim was good, but not good enough. David found a stone but just missed the can, ripples dissipating in the flowing water. It was going further away and he had a last try. This time there was a thunk and the can spun and settled again.

Robyn applauded. "Bull's eye!" They stood again in silence, leaning on the railings. Then she said: "I used to do that from a bridge when I was a child. It was great when the river was high and fast. We used to walk home from school that way and it was great fun. Have you heard of a game called Pooh sticks?"

"I've read Winnie the Pooh, remember."

She stretched over the railings and wrestled a twig from a bush. She intended to throw it into the water but when she turned back, David had walked several metres away and was still walking.

"David?" she called. He turned suddenly and walked back.

"Cramp in my foot," he said.

"Oh." She threw the stick. "Next stop Scotland."

"Next stop that clump of grass hanging over the water." They watched. The twig caught, jerked and stuck.

"Hey, you're a prophet as well," she said. A thought niggled at her. "David, what does 'shalom' mean? I mean, really mean?"

"You're the language expert."

"Not on that."

He thought for a moment. "It's a deep word. Lots of layers to it. It means peace, but not just peace. It's not just absence of trouble. It's the presence of something special. When you say 'Shalom' to someone, you're wishing them to be whole in body and spirit, to be at peace with themselves." A seagull wheeled over the far bank. She knew by his voice that he had turned his head towards her. "Shalom aleichem means: Peace be unto you."

"Is there a reply?"

"Aleichem shalom, I think. Unto you be peace."

She straightened slowly. "What a beautiful thing to wish for someone."

"Yes. And it's a word that should never be said without really meaning it."

His brown eyes were steady when she looked round. "And you meant it?" she asked shyly.

"Oh yes."

Another racing canoe sliced past.

"Hey, what about your poem? The one you wrote for your school mag?" he asked.

"I told you. It was no good."

"Tell me a few lines and I'll write an essay on it."

"I could call your bluff."

"Go on."

"It was called The River," she said defiantly.

"Original title."

She almost thumped him and then remembered just in time who he was, and who she was. It was so easy to forget that. "Give me a moment to think." She searched her memory but couldn't remember all of it. "Actually, it's a bit depressing."

"Go on. I can take it," he challenged, his voice light, humorous.

She took a deep breath and recited: "Solid city race-boat, Cutting quickly through, And the glassy, oily surface, Heals itself like new." She stopped, checking to see if he was laughing at her. He was listening, head bowed.

"Go on."

"Heavy, heavy heartbeats Throbbing by the side Of the river that's so lucky It can't feel like human-kind."

Her embarrassment grew with his silence. Then he said softly: "I stood beside a river once, feeling just like that."

Robyn was silent.

His mobile rang and he swung away to answer it impatiently. "Yeah, yeah, yeah. I'm on my way." He pocketed the phone. "I have to go. I was to meet up with some of the guys. And I have to get this mutt back home first."

Manna had recovered from his forced march to the embankment and stood readily enough, his eye searching his master's face for clues. Robyn pulled the dog's ears and patted him.

"OK."

He turned to cross the road. "Bye."

"David," she called as he reached the far side, next the brightly coloured swings and slides of a children's playground. He turned. She waited for a lorry to pass. "The word 'shalom'. The way you explained it means it's a holophrastic word."

"Holo… what?"

"Holophrastic. Look it up!"

His laughter reached across the traffic and she could see the smile still on his face as he jogged away, the dog bouncing along in time to his steps.

11

THE FOUR YOUNG men were on a high as they arrived at McDonalds in the middle of Belfast. Friday teatime and the city was packed. David loved it, loved the feel of it, loved the way it fitted him like an old shirt. He had heard about the black years when the city centre was hollow and dead at night, fear lurking at every corner and in every doorway.

But late night shopping and clubbing were back and Belfast was a buzz of activity. He had adopted the city with zealous determination. Their move from Enniskillen was explained by his father's promotion, but David knew that in reality it was his parents' fervent wish to leave the town.

Two of the friends pounced when a table became free while the others ordered their burger meals. Tim Thompson wanted an apple pie as well. Tim always did. There was a shuffling and sorting of straws, chips and the ridiculous pile of paper napkins.

Mumbling round his first urgent mouthfuls, Mullan asked, "So where were you that you were late, Davey boy?" He was an aggressive type with spots and a stiff retro overhang of gelled hair.

"Busy."

"Chloe-type busy?"

"Chloe's in Lanzarote," said Tim quickly.

"Eyeing the waiters, no doubt." This was Meekin, a suave fair haired lad with fine features slewed by a crooked nose.

Mullan crowed. "They'll be doing more than eyeing her if they get the chance."

David knew he was being baited and didn't rise to it. He

calmly bit his cheeseburger and diverted a descending dollop of sauce with practised ease.

"I know where he was," said Meekin smoothly.

"Where?"

"Round at Penny Woodford's house. Didn't get his trousers zipped in time."

Only a slight hesitation in David's jaws showed that this one had brushed closer.

"Wise up, Meekin," said Tim. "We're not all like you, dickhead."

Meekin wiped his fingers on a napkin fastidiously. "No, we're not all like me indeed. I don't pretend to be a saint, unlike some. Some of us," – he looked at David – "were born old."

Mullan leaned forward. "Is she as up for it as everybody says, guys?"

Meekin raised a blond eyebrow. "You mean you don't know? You pathetic sod."

David put down his burger carefully. "Leave Penny Woodford alone, Mullan. You're the last thing she needs."

Mullan lifted his hands and waggled his fingers mockingly. "Oooooh! I'm so scared. Going to thump me with your Bible, eh?"

"I'd need a bigger one for your skull."

"Penny's a big girl now." Meekin sighed and paused patiently for Mullan's sniggers to subside before continuing. "She can look after herself – and whoever else she wants."

"I said leave her alone." David's look was steely. Meekin didn't read the warning signs.

"Bit late for that, Shaw. Was she wearing red frilly…" David's long fingers shot out and bunched the neck of Meekin's shirt in his fist. He bent Meekin across the table, onion scraps and sauce smearing down his shirt as his crooked nose arrived in close proximity to David's.

"Keep your filthy mind in the sewer where it belongs, Meekin."

Tim leapt up and pulled David's shoulders. "Hey! Chill, man. We'll get thrown out."

Slowly David released Meekin who slid back into his chair. His face flushed, he took several napkins and brushed his shirt.

"Temper, temper. I was only winding you up. Old man."

"So. Any plans for next week?" said Tim desperately.

Conversation moved on with determination to the local ice hockey team and what films were showing. David's attention wandered until Mullan said:

"I saw Robyn Daniels in town a few days ago. Walking along past Marks."

"Daniels isn't easy to miss," said Meekin.

"I thought she would head off home in the holidays." Tim said. "Chloe said she said something about it in class one day when they were talking about Benedict Kiely. She said she was from the same town as him." He licked his fingers. "She went home from the Hooley with Fraser, did you notice?"

He opened his apple pie and blew on it before taking a bite. The other three paused in unison to watch as the apple filling burst out the other end and headed for his trousers. David handed him a bundle of napkins before it landed. This was routine.

"Tim," said David patiently, "that doesn't have to happen every time, you know."

"S'pose not."

"I don't like Fraser." This was Mullan.

"Maybe she does," said Meekin.

"Lucky bugger," growled Mullan, and burped.

David shook his last chip out of the box. So why was she still in Belfast?

Gemma's sitting room was large and bright and had once been two rooms. Now it ran from front to back, with a door to a small kitchen that fitted into an extension into the yard. Robyn turned in from the hall and stopped in shock.

"Neil!" she exclaimed.

Neil lay on the couch. Bandages laced his forehead and cheek. Stitches stood proud of a long cut rising upwards from the right side of his mouth. His right arm was held in a sling and he wore a neckbrace.

Her instinct to go to him was curbed by the tableau that he and his sister made. Gemma had answered her knock without a word and preceded her into the room, leaving Robyn to close the front door herself. Now Gemma was standing beside Neil, her arms crossed.

"Gemma phoned you ages ago, Rob." Neil's aggrieved tone was clear even though he spoke with care through one side of his mouth.

"I was held up." Robyn moved into the room and sat on the arm of the couch, at Neil's feet. "Gemma said you had no broken bones. Is your arm sprained?"

Gemma's voice had an indignant edge. "I'm supposed to be at work an hour ago. I thought you'd stay with Neil when I had to go."

"I'm sorry. You didn't say."

"I didn't expect to have to say."

Gemma was definitely hostile. It was blood versus water. Robyn glanced at Neil. He was fussing with his sling, his chin creased over the neckbrace as he tried to look down.

"Is it very sore?"

"Of course it's sore. He's sore all over. And this is your fault."

Robyn stood up again. "Actually, no, this isn't my fault. I don't know what he's told you. This is Neil's fault for driving when he was upset. He should have known better."

"You'll have to get a mobile," mumbled Neil. "I mean, who hasn't a mobile nowadays?"

"Why don't you just microchip me in the scruff of the neck? Probably be cheaper in the long run."

"Don't be like that. I don't like it."

Neil reached out his good hand and after a moment Robyn took it reluctantly. He fidgeted. "When I was in hospital last night, I gave them your number to call first. The nurse told me there was no answer." He looked up. "Were you not at your place overnight?"

Robyn dropped his hand as if it was a burning coal. By the way he winced, his ribs were bruised.

"Then they contacted me," Gemma snapped. "And I couldn't reach you till this morning."

"You're seeing somebody, aren't you?" Neil tried to turn his head up and winced again.

Robyn felt surrounded by pressure, poked and prodded. She had tripped into a snakepit. A familiar feeling bloomed inside her as her personality heeled over, pivoting yet again on a point of strain.

"Of course I am. In fact I see quite a few others. I have a double life as a prostitute down an alley. Didn't you know?"

The effect on Neil was electric. He swung his legs to the floor and then collapsed backwards in pain. Gemma fussed to his side but he thrust her away with his good arm. With considerable effort he pulled himself to his feet. He thrust out his hand and gripped Robyn's chin roughly.

"Neil..." It was Gemma, alarmed.

He spoke as clearly as he could, twisting Robyn's skin till she gave a cry of pain. "Don't talk about yourself and those whores in the same breath." His voice rose to a shout and spittle showered her face. "Do you hear me?"

"Neil! Let her go!" Gemma pulled him back and he released

her, falling back onto the couch.

Gemma put a hand out to Robyn. "Are you OK?"

Robyn felt the blood going from her head as she turned to the door. Her hand shook. She closed her eyes and steadied herself on the wall. She was suffocating, gasping. *You're being a bad girl again, aren't you? Just as well only Daddy knows.* She felt Gemma's touch her arm.

"He's very stressed. He doesn't know what he's doing."

"Yes, he does, Gemma. Oh yes he does. They all do." Robyn took several deep breaths and straightened. A boiling anger was rising in her and she really didn't want it to spill over just now, just here. She looked at Neil, lying pale and exhausted.

"I'm sorry for you, Neil. One of the reasons I was late was because I was thinking hard about what I said yesterday. I thought maybe I was wrong. But you know what? I was right. I don't want to see you *ever* again." She turned to go, then turned back. "I really hope you get better soon," she said. "But you're such a black and white person. I just never realised it before." She went out into the hall. "And get your hair cut, you look stupid!"she yelled and slammed the front door behind her.

Through the window, Gemma watched her walk away down the street.

"Now who's going to look after you tomorrow?" she said.

There wasn't any name she could put to this anger. It welled up from somewhere very deep, very black. It mushroomed until it covered the entire world around her and she was in the middle of it, throwing punches and hitting air.

She walked back to her flat and was reaching to push the street door open before she realised someone was approaching, saying her name.

"Well, Robyn Daniels! How are you? You are still about."

Angus Fraser was the last person she expected to see.

"Angus. What are you doing here?"

"Actually, I was just ringing your doorbell. I was calling to see if you'd gone home yet."

She was distracted, fidgety. "Why?"

He shrugged. "Just wondering."

"I'm tired, Angus. This isn't a good time."

"How about tomorrow then? I was thinking of going for a drive up the coast and I thought it'd be much nicer with company. And I thought of you – unless you've other plans, of course."

A hand on the door, she answered over her shoulder. "Thank you, Angus. But no thanks."

"Sure?"

"Absolutely."

"But you'll be going back home soon?"

"I'm staying up this year."

"Ah. Another time then."

He smiled and walked away.

Robyn stood in the middle of her room. Her anger had subsided, been tucked away. Despite what had happened afterwards, it had something to do with her meeting with David Shaw. In a way she didn't understand, his company and calmness were empowering, and his influence was still gentle on her when she had entered Gemma's house. Indeed it had not entirely dissipated even yet.

Her shock when she had looked at Neil this afternoon was not just at the state he was in, but at how she felt. This was the person who had been around through almost her entire life. He had been there in crises, in family events, in bereavement, at Christmas, at Easter, at weddings, at every corner and at every straight.

He was a small, fussy, arrogant dictator. Being around him was to be constantly on the defensive, waiting to be found out, for the next inadequacy to be blazoned in lights.

She sat down suddenly. She should have seen before. He was exactly like her father. No wonder the two of them had got along together so well. A memory. She was just a teenager and had been helping her mother in the kitchen. She had been about to return to the sitting room when she overheard her father:

"I hope it works out for you, Neil. I couldn't hand her over to a better person. You'll know how to handle her."

You bastard. You wanted to hand me over to another man. Look after the goods, boy.

Deliberately, consciously, she called up the peace she had felt beside the river and said aloud – "I don't have to belong to anybody. I'm me. I can choose for myself. I can choose my friends, my job, my home."

They were only words in the air but at least she had said them.

Later, her telephone rang. She let it click to the answer phone and turned down the music to listen. It was her mother. I've just heard about Neil's accident. How terrible. You must be terribly upset. Ring as soon as you get in, no matter what the time. You are so lucky he's still around. I hope this will bring that home to you, Robyn.

Aha. Mummy doesn't know yet.

Energy surged through her. She vacuumed the floors, cleaned the window, dusted every surface.

Her sleep was sound and dreamless.

David Shaw sat cross-legged on the floor of the study, in front of his mother's shelves of medical books. He took each one in turn and checked the index. Some were irrelevant, some too advanced; some he flicked over a few pages and ran his finger down the lines. One was more use and he read several pages, motionless in concentration. Manna nuzzled him and whined. Getting no response, the dog planted a huge paw on his shoulder.

His mother came into the room and he slammed the book shut.

"David! Everything all right?"

"Fine. Just checking on something."

"Is something wrong?" His mother's face took on its familiar look of anxiety.

David unfolded himself and stood up. "No, Mum. I'm fine." His voice was patient, used to allaying fears. He gave her a quick peck on the cheek. "I wouldn't want to have any of the horrors described in those books. I think I'll go back to the Mr Men."

She smiled. "Much nicer reading. Shouldn't you be at the church?"

"Five minutes ago. See you." He pointed at Manna. "Hang onto him while I escape."

Despite being late, he decided to leave the car and jog to the church. A shower of rain had cleared and the trees along the avenue glowed with the sheen of freshly washed leaves. The air smelled warm and green.

What he had read had confirmed his suspicions. It also scared him. Earlier, when Robyn Daniels had reached over to pull a branch from the bush by the river, he had seen a scar running down the length of the inside of her wrist. It was very pale; it wouldn't be noticed unless her arm was close to you and you were looking straight at it. Shock at the realisation of what it was, in all probability, had made him want to run away. It was instinctive. Get out of here. You can't handle this. This is deeper than you can cope with. No-one has all the answers and you have fewer than most.

He stopped and crouched to tie a lace on his trainer. That this girl was troubled was evident. To find out how much those troubles had affected her and for how long – that scar was old – frightened him. Instinctively he had walked away from her, hardly knowing he did it. He remembered saying in his mind:

"No. Too heavy! Not me."

Then she had called his name, and he had turned and walked straight back to her side.

As he turned in through the wrought iron gates of the church he remembered something his father had said years ago in a voice choked with tears: "A day at a time, child. A day at a time. It's all we can do. We have to get by."

David paused outside the door of the church hall. Soon he would be surrounded by the exuberance of the members of the youth group, pulling at him, calling him, the younger ones wanting piggy backs, the boys wanting him to play football, the girls teasing him, hoping that he would tease them back. As he pushed the door, the youngest of the children inside let out a whoop of delight and rushed to clamp himself around his leg.

David sent up a quick prayer. "A day at a time. Still. For her. And for me."

12

THREE ANGULAR PEGS threatened to poke the eye of any unwary customer trying to get a view in the full length mirror of the claustrophobic fitting room. Robyn tried a pirouette, flicking her hair out from the neckline of the green dress. It suited her and she knew it. It wasn't trendy, it was classically elegant. It had everything: lace, delicate cap sleeves, a wide pale green lace band circling the fitted waist, stitching detail on the gently flared gores of the graceful skirt.

This was the fifth shop she had visited this morning, and she had bought something in every one. She had intended to look for clothes suitable for school – *if* she managed to get a job when this temporary post finished. But this dress was a sheer indulgence. She didn't know where she was going to wear it, but a new life needed new clothes. She'd wear it when she'd worked out the life. She took it off with care. This would have to be the last.

She debated whether she could comfortably have lunch in town with so many bags to manage. Eventually she gripped a sandwich and a bottle of orange juice long enough to reach a table in a coffee shop.

She kicked off her shoes and stretched her toes. Shoes! She should get some new shoes. The orange was cold and refreshing. This was the first major shopping trip that she had undertaken without either her mother or Gemma being with her. Why had she suddenly found faith in her own judgement? The feeling was good in a scary kind of way.

A short walk away, at the side of the City Hall, she was just in time to catch her bus. It was still early on a warm afternoon. She planned to hang up all her new clothes and then take a book to the Botanic Gardens.

As the bus turned a corner, an unmistakable figure stood out from the shifting currents of people on the pavement. David Shaw was guiding Penny Woodford to a pedestrian crossing. Penny's denim jacket was frayed and she had dyed her hair bright purple. The stud on her chin moved in time to her jaws as she chewed. Just as the bus moved on, blocking them from view, they turned slightly to dodge through to the kerbside, and Robyn saw David put out an arm and his hand almost touched the small of Penny's back.

It wasn't a day for the park after all. Robyn stood in the middle of her room with a black bin bag in her hand and all her old clothes in a heap on the floor. The doors of her empty wardrobe yawned behind her. Carefully she lifted and judged each item. The pink tunic with the crocheted sleeves was the first to go into the bag. Even though it was new, she would never wear it again.

When the reprieved clothes were back in the wardrobe, or carefully folded, Robyn unpacked and hung her new clothes. She shook out the green dress. It seemed even sillier now. What a waste. Only a good day and a good occasion would be the time for it, and when was that going to happen?

That night the black bag was wedged beside the chair at her door, ready for the charity shop.

At three o'clock in the morning, she woke. The black fog was coming back. She felt the dread of it digging deep. She threw back the quilt and stood up. Motionless in the middle of the room, she looked into the dark and waited. No sound. No voice. Nobody wishing her to be whole in body and spirit; to be at peace with herself.

She woke in the morning stiff and cold, curled in a ball in her chair.

Edith Braden waved across the snack bar, smiling broadly.

"This was a great idea, Robyn. I'm finding the holidays a bit of a bore."

"Great to see you, Edith. Have you been away anywhere?" Robyn settled herself at the table, relaxing at the prospect of company.

"Not possible, I'm afraid. My mother's a dear old soul, but there was just no respite care available. So I'm stuck."

"It's not great travelling just now anyway. Terrible queues at the airport."

Edith looked at her appraisingly. "You look a bit pale. What have you been doing with yourself?"

"I spent a lot of money yesterday. Enough to account for the pallor."

"Great pastime. What on?"

"Clothes."

"More? You're the best dressed person in the school."

Robyn bit her sandwich. There was mustard in it. She hated mustard. She raised a teasing eyebrow. "Well, I want to stay that way."

"I don't believe you. You're not the vain type. It's the man in your life, isn't it? Need to impress him."

"There's no man in my life."

"So you said. Where's the guy from the Hooley?"

Robyn took her sandwich apart and scraped the mustard out. "Still on the planet somewhere, I assume."

Edith cocked an eyebrow. "No story there then?"

Robyn smiled but said firmly, "There's no story. End of."

"He seemed a solid type, just what you need."

"What do you mean – just what I need?"

Edith looked down. "Well, I mean that you seem..." She hid behind a mouthful of egg and onion sandwich.

"What, Edith?"

" ... you seem a bit lonely sometimes."

Robyn squashed her sandwich together again. "Well, I'm here talking to you!"

"You are indeed. Don't mind me." Edith lifted her teapot. "I just thought you were maybe going to settle down to a normal life in suburbia."

There was that word again.

"Normal? Getting married would ensure I had a normal life? I didn't think you of all people would have that idea." Immediately, Robyn regretted the words. She reached over and touched Edith's arm. "I'm sorry. That was..."

Edith calmly poured the last of the tea from her teapot-for-one.

"I'm more than twice your age, Rob. Believe it or not, I was in love once. Jackie, a lovely Fermanagh lad. Farmer's son. But I thought I'd play hard to get. String him along. He wanted to marry me and I said well, I'd have to think about it. Make him wait."

She sipped her tea, holding the cup in two hands in front of her mouth as she spoke, her voice slow. "Finally I decided it was time to say yes. He was to call for me that evening and we were going to the pictures. He was late." She stopped talking for a moment. Robyn waited. "My father phoned his father. They had just found Jackie's body in the lane. There was a booby-trap on the gate. Blew his head off when he touched the bolt." She put her cup down. "It was meant for his father. He was in the Reserves."

"Oh Edith. I am so sorry."

Edith made a quick dismissive gesture. "Don't waste time on being sorry. It was a long time ago. The only reason I'm wringing your heart with history is to explain I'm not single by choice.

It can be a very lonely row to hoe. Regret isn't good fertiliser." She looked at Robyn keenly. "I may be wrong, but I don't think you're the type to go through life happy to be alone."

"As you say. You may be wrong."

"So no hope then?"

"Nope."

"Good solid businessman." Edith mused.

Robyn kept her tone light. "Let's change the subject. Another pot of tea?"

When she returned with the refilled teapot and another coffee for herself, she said gently, "I hear what you're saying, Edith. But your choice was forced on you. I've made my own."

Edith sighed. "He wasn't all that bad looking. Looked at in a certain light."

A change of subject was urgently needed.

"Tell me about the Shaws."

Edith looked puzzled. "What Shaws?"

"David Shaw. I think you said you knew the family in Enniskillen."

"I did. Vincent's a good bit older than Elizabeth, but they were so obviously besotted nobody thought it strange."

"David's their only child?"

"Elizabeth didn't seem to conceive easily. They were married a good few years before he came along. Even then she nearly lost him. She had to lie in hospital for two months to make sure he went to term. I visited her then. It was very hard for her; she was such an active, intelligent girl."

"So why did they come east?"

"Vincent's something very important in the Civil Service. I think he was promoted. I've lost touch with them really. I left Fermanagh years before they did."

"Did you know David as a child?"

"I met him occasionally. Saw him in church, of course, and

at church things. They're a nice family. I mean, *good*, you know? Down to earth." Her eyebrows rose. "Why the interest?"

Robyn shrugged. "Oh, I had a chat with David after school one day. He seems a bit, well, different. Quite a serious guy. Older than his years in a way."

Edith didn't speak for a moment. Then: "Yes, I could believe he's grown up that way. There was always a depth to him. Even when he was four years old he was a thoughtful child."

"Loneliness certainly isn't something he suffers from anyway."

Edith put her cup down. "I wouldn't be so sure."

"Oh? What do you mean?"

Edith looked at her watch. "I really must go. I left mother with a neighbour and promised I'd be back by half two. I can only afford help in term-time." She hooked her bag from under the table. "Let's meet up again. I enjoyed getting out for a chat."

The colour printer hummed a sheet of photo-quality paper into the tray. Angus had spent all morning following her. She was getting inside his head; he needed to see her; wanted to see her everywhere he looked. There was a buzz in his head. Sometimes it hurt.

He had pictures of her walking through the city streets, distant shots slipped between traffic, a nearer image as she bent slightly to shift the weight of her shopping bags from one hand to the other. He had caught her profile as she looked into the window of a mobile phone shop. Her look was thoughtful, her hand up to the side of her head, frozen in the act of brushing her hair from her eyes.

This was the one he had decided to print.

He picked the paper up carefully, sat for five minutes examining every line, every hair. He pinned the picture of her to the wall beside his bed. Along with the others.

Robyn had promised herself that she would take a day in school. The head of her department had decided that he wanted to change the texts for the junior classes and she needed to do a bit of homework. It would be penance for the shopping safari.

Instead of turning towards the school gate she was drawn towards the Botanic Gardens. Lunchtime would be time enough to be at her desk. There were fewer people about.

In an uncultivated corner, beneath some trees, four tall foxgloves swayed elegantly out of the undergrowth. Two pink and two white. She stopped. Just at this spot, a riot of orange nasturtiums twined and tangled through the railings and tumbled over the edge of the path. The rhythmic clicking of a dog's paws made her look round quickly. A woman in a track suit jogged past, her red setter waving the feathers of his jaunty tail.

On the steps of the Museum she stood and looked out over the grass and the shrubbery, across to the main gate. Back outside the Palm House, she sat for an hour, reading through some notes. The park was so quiet, almost eerie. She looked up and down the path. It was lunchtime, time to grab a bite and get to work. She shouldered her bag and walked towards the school.

At the gate, she looked back, looked around. Nevertheless, she thought, it is a lonely row to hoe.

That night her mother rang. She was annoyed.

"Poor Neil. I've talked to him. He says you don't ever want to see him again. Surely you could have been a bit kinder? He's devastated and look what's happened. He could have been killed!"

Robyn let her talk, answering none of her questions, but learning that Neil was still at Gemma's house. He wasn't fit enough to make the journey home.

"You know of course," Anne continued, "that his accident

will mean difficulty for his business. You didn't have to be so blunt, Robyn."

"I don't know what he's told you but I'm sure it was colourful. I didn't make him have the accident."

"You upset him so much."

Robyn took a deep breath and tried to change the subject. "So will you be coming up to look at houses soon?"

"What's the point? Poor Neil can't do anything at the moment. Anyway, you'll be down when he manages to get back home, I'm sure. We'll talk then."

Another person wasn't listening to her. Anger broke through.

"Mum, don't you get it? I won't be back. He'll be fine as long as he has you. *You're* bloody besotted with him."

There was a silence and then Anne, furious. "How dare you? That man has done more for this family than any man ever has and well you know it."

"I thought he was helping us. Not buying us."

"I love you, Robyn. But I don't think I want to see you for a while."

"Fine by me."

Robyn slammed the phone down and flung herself on the couch. Finally she crawled into bed. Under the duvet, she rubbed her right wrist. She would not go back. She was in control of her own life.

She was.

It was just a bit harder than she had imagined.

13

NEXT MORNING SHE left her flat early and sat outside the Palm House again. *Beowulf* was open on her lap but her concentration was fitful. At last she smiled, her face hidden by her hair, as a voice spoke behind her.

"Holophrastic. Adjective." A long leg was thrown over the back of the bench. "From the noun holophrase." The second leg followed and he vaulted onto the seat beside her. "A single word expressing a whole phrase or combination of ideas."

"Go to the top of the class," she said.

"How about a gold star?"

She glanced round. "Where's Manna?"

"At home with an enormous bone. Dad said he'd take him out later."

She closed her book and sat back. "Do you often jump over park benches and land beside strange women?"

"Only the really strange ones."

"And without your guard dog? Risky."

"I live dangerously."

Yes, he did. This was dangerous. Reckless. Easy. So, so easy.

He leaned forward, restless, and lifted her book from where she had set it. He flipped the pages. "You haven't got far through it yet."

"How do you know?"

"Because you turned one page in ten minutes." He stood and took a turn to the far side of the path and back, drumming the book between his fingers. He was in jeans and a faded denim shirt. There was a hint of agitation in the quick glance that he flicked to her face.

She stood up. "The roses should be in full bloom at the moment," she said. "I think I'll check them out. Of course," she mused, "you could come with me, unless it would damage your image to be seen walking round rose bushes."

He turned into the rhythm of her steps. "I'll issue a statement on the evening news. It wasn't me. It was a look-alike. Honest."

"That should sort it. Except…"

"Except what?"

"Nothing. Can I have my book back?"

He gave it to her and she tucked it into the large bag that she carried slung across her body. There were more pigeons than people. David still seemed rather restless, turning to walk backwards for a few steps every now and then, scanning the park. Two magpies bustled across the grass some distance away.

"Two for joy," she said automatically.

"Good omen."

"I didn't think you'd believe in omens," she said.

"Sometimes I do. Maybe not magpies. Do you?"

"Not magpies anyway. There are too many single ones about."

They turned a corner and the trellises of the rose walk came into sight. Around it were the rose beds, great arcs of red, yellow, pink, gold and all hues between. Robyn stopped and inhaled deeply. The breeze strengthened momentarily and the air was thick with scent and the hum of insects.

"This is our country. Where beautiful roses grow," she said.

David said nothing, simply waited for her to move on. She led the way across the grass and wandered between the flowers, bending to smell a great head of pink petals.

"Smell that. It's powerful."

The name of the rose was written on a wooden peg at the front of the bed. He stopped and turned his back to it, hiding it from her. "Guess the name of it."

She laughed. "Don't be silly. I've no idea what it's called."

"That's why it's a guess."

"Pink something. Pink lady."

"No."

"Pink slipper."

"No."

"Give me a clue."

"It's one word."

"Pinkness."

He grinned. "No."

"Another clue."

"An Irish river."

"Lagan."

"Too far north."

"Lee."

"Too far south."

"Liffey."

"Too far east."

"Shannon."

He moved away to let her see the sign. "Got it in two hundred and forty-seven."

She moved along to a bed of yellow roses and stood in front of the name board. "OK smart guy. What's the name of these ones?" He came too close and she motioned him away. "No peeking."

He tapped his chin and pretended to concentrate.

"One word?"

"No."

"Two words?"

"Maybe."

"Is it yellow something?"

"Possibly."

"Yellow peril."

"This is a *rose* here, not a disease."

"Yellow … sunset."

"Better. No."

"Clue time."

"OK. It's a book. A big book."

He walked in a circle, thinking. "Yellow pages."

She revealed the sign. "Got it in… I think I lost count."

Robyn was feeling light-headed. This was fun. This was thoughtless, stupid, idiotic, pointless fun. They wandered on, taking turns to guess, making up the most hilariously unlikely names. Then David stopped by a sea of deep red, where exceptionally large flower heads swayed gently, each on a single stem.

"You'll never get this one," he said.

She shook her hair back over her shoulders. "One word or two?"

"Two, but you'll not guess it."

"You just want me to give up."

"Why should I? There's no prize."

She came a bit closer. "Actually, I think I might know that one. Is it Uncle Walter?"

His brows rose in surprise. "It is. How'd you know?"

"We had some roses in the garden at home." She hunkered down and brushed one of the great flowers against her cheek. "I just happen to remember this one." She took a quick look round, then twisted and pulled the rose. "Look into it. It's so intricate, so beautiful." She held it up so that he couldn't avoid doing as she asked. "Folds within folds. A master design. Look right into the heart of it. I remember someone once saying roses were God's origami."

She glanced up, knowing he would smile at that. He did. She explained: "One of these roses grew just beside the back door and I used to sit on the step wondering why something so beautiful had no scent. It just seemed pointless to me. What good is beauty if it leaves no trace of itself in the air around it? Beauty can be very dead, very selfish."

David went back to the bed of pink roses where they had started the game. He chose one and plucked it without hesitation. "Don't judge a whole species by a bad example." He held out the pink rose. "This is a rose too."

She took it, smelling the scent instantly. "I wasn't judging the whole species. Just some of them." She put the two blossoms together. " 'Red darkness of the heart of roses.' "

"Rupert Brooke," he said.

She looked up, delighted. "Yes! Can you go on?"

"Not really. Something about 'unnameable sightless white' and all the colours that lie between darkness and darkness."

"I can just remember the next line. 'Red darkness of the heart of roses, Blue brilliant from dead starless skies.' "

She wandered round to the rose walk, where tall stone pillars formed a long arcade, roofed at intervals by wooden cross beams. Tendrils of fine rose creepers twined and tumbled wherever they could seize a grip. He strolled beside her, following wherever she wanted to go. A young couple came from the other end and passed them with a polite nod. Suddenly she gave a yelp and dropped the red rose. Blood ran between her fingers. He chuckled.

"No scent, but it has some bite!"

She sucked her palm. "Are you always so sympathetic?"

"No. Sometimes I can be an unfeeling bastard."

She examined her hand where the thorn had pierced the mound beneath her index finger. They were about half way up the rose walk when he said: "Speaking of wounds, how's the Elastoplast fix working out?"

She hesitated, not sure she wanted to revisit this. She shrugged. "Getting tugged a bit. But it's still there."

He was quiet for a few steps. Then: "What's going on under it?"

"I don't know." She dodged a dragon fly. "I'm afraid to look."

He nodded. "I know."

She frowned, her mind tilting away from his tranquillity, his certainty. His ability to reach through her carapace and circle dangerously close to the ice at her centre was a threat. A sudden headlong rush of anger broke.

"You know? You think you know. You know damn all!"

He swung round on her instantly. "Don't do this again! Not with me." Every line of him had tensed, voice temper-strong. "You have no idea what I know about anything."

"You know nothing about me!" She had raised her voice and hated herself for it.

His eyes sparked, deference nowhere in sight. "I know a hell of a lot more than you know about me."

Robyn spun away from him and paced quickly to the end of the walkway. Alarm began to edge out anger. What was she doing? There was enough conflict in her life without having a row with someone she would have to face in school in a few weeks. Yes, they knew each other already. But not like this. Yes, in any other circumstances they could banter, bicker like friends. But not in these circumstances.

There was a line he should not cross. She took some deep breaths to calm herself. It was a pity, but the lessons she had learnt were true. There is no such thing as a good day without a reckoning. There is no such thing as free fun. The price will always be asked, always paid. Better to stay hidden, expect nothing and don't be disappointed. She sucked her palm. Roses have thorns. Don't forget it. Better still, don't go near the roses.

She turned, sure that he would have walked away, given up on her for the last time. He was still there, feet planted solidly apart, hands by his sides, his face dark and tense.

Still there.

Slowly she walked back. She couldn't blame him. He hadn't

crossed that invisible line alone. She had stepped over it too. Indeed, maybe she had been the leader. When she was two pillars away from him, she hesitated. A gust of wind blew her hair across her face and she brushed it away. A bee, heavy with pollen, bumbled slowly from one blossom to another. David looked at her with an expression she could not read. He lifted one hand slightly and she heard him repeat, in a tone now devoid of anger:

"Don't do this again. Not with me. There's no need for it with me."

She studied the trellis above her head for a moment, watched a butterfly. Life held its breath, hesitant and trembling at a turn in the road. She took a few more steps towards him. "I'm afraid I'm not… very good at people."

His lips curved into a slow smile. "No-one said you had to be."

They wandered to the building housing the Tropical Ravine, with its banana trees and controlled ecosystems. Inside it was heavy with humidity.

"My mother remembers the old building, the one that used to be here," said David. "She said she used to love watching the big koi swimming though the water lilies in the fish pond that was in the old Ravine."

It was so warm and oppressive inside that they didn't stay long. They sat on a bench outside and Robyn wave a hand to cool her flushed skin.

"That Rupert Brooke poem was about a fish, wasn't it?" said David.

"Yes, it was. And that's reminded me of another line. 'Red darkness of the heart of roses, Blue brilliant from dead starless skies, And gold that lies behind the eyes.' "

His mobile bleeped the arrival of a text message. He ignored it, and she could see he was in what she was beginning to call his 'thinking mode'. She waited.

"I envy people who can express their feelings in words like that. Do you think," he asked slowly, "that we can purge ourselves of the past simply through words? Simply by saying – and being – sorry?"

"I suppose *being* sorry is the important bit."

"You have to say it too." He was emphatic.

A pigeon churred contentedly in the depths of a chestnut tree.

"If you can, I suppose." She looked at his still profile. "But saying sorry, or having it said to you, isn't always possible. And then you just have to live with it."

For several minutes, he was silent. It was OK to be with him and to be silent. Easy. So, so easy. In one of his quick changes of mood, he swung round and said: "Hey, it's hot. How about somewhere cooler?"

His mobile phone rang. With a frown of annoyance, he turned it off without looking at it. Robyn bunched her hair away from her neck and fanned her cheeks.

"Sounds good. I'm a puddle here!" she said.

He seemed to find that very funny.

"Ssssh!" He put out a hand to stop her, a finger to his lips. They had wandered round a secluded patch of shrubbery, away from the tarmac, where the paths were earthen soft with layers of leaves. Silently she followed his look. A plump song thrush stood statue-still under a bush, his speckled breast fluffed and proud.

"He's a beauty," she breathed.

In one quick twist the bird was gone, vanished into the deeper undergrowth.

"Looks good for an accident of random molecules," David said.

"Look here." Robyn squatted beside a flat stone at the edge of the path. He hunkered beside her. "This is the thrush's anvil.

See these pieces of snail shell? He's been smashing his dinner here."

He lifted a piece of shell and turned it over. "Cleaned his plate." They dusted their hands and walked on. "Do you know a lot about birds?" he asked.

"Very little. My father took me and my brother camping once. He showed us a thrush's anvil in Gortin Glen. He was a keen ornithologist. He used to write articles for the local paper sometimes."

"Used to?"

"He died about a year ago."

"I'm sorry," he said.

"David?"

"What?"

He was sitting on a branch above her, one leg drawn up and the other dangling by her ear as she leaned against the trunk.

"How's Penny?"

She noticed a definite delay in his reply.

"Penny's Penny."

She shifted slightly. At least he hadn't said "Penny who?"

She got to the till first and he didn't make a fuss.

"Now we're even," she said as they settled at a table in the busy Museum café.

He pushed her orange juice across the table. "Even?"

"You bought me a drink at the Hooley, remember?"

His can spat as he pulled the ring. "I remember the Hooley very well."

She looked away from his quick glance. The old café had been on the upper floor and had a view of an ancient cemetery, nestled like a secret beside the Museum. She remembered a grey morning when she had looked down on an ivy-covered mausoleum, crumbling at one corner. Drunken grave slabs surrounded it, some completely flat, some doggedly hanging on to their crazy angles.

"Do you remember the view from the top…" she began.

He took a gulp of his drink. "Don't say anything about graveyards."

His intuition startled a smile from her. She wrinkled her nose. "Oh, just a line or two?"

"Not even one," he warned.

" 'Unresting death, a whole day nearer now…' "

He slammed the can on the table. "No!"

"OK then." She sat back, puzzled at his vehemence. "But you should read *Aubade*. Phillip Larkin. In fact, if you're going to Queen's, you really must read some Larkin. He was a librarian there in the fifties. And you won't like what he says about death and religion."

He fiddled with the ring-pull. Then he spoke with a sudden rush of intensity. "I know *Aubade* very well. Larkin says 'Death is no different whined at than withstood.' And religion is just a 'vast moth-eaten musical brocade, Created to pretend we never die.' "

She closed her eyes. She had been holding on so long, coping day by day, inch by inch. Her highest ambition was to get by; her greatest achievement was a night with no terrors; her most alluring temptation was to give up and let herself fall. Now here was this amazing young man who was punching his way through steel armour with an effortless grace. He was stirring the surface of the still water and spangling it with colour. And he had no idea of any of this.

She knew she was being unprofessional, way out of line, but she had gone too far beyond the bounds for that to be redeemable. She could accept this friendship, or slip into an even greater loneliness for having known it. That was the choice.

When she opened her eyes he was watching her, a slight smile hovering around his mouth. She held his look. Held it. And felt the decision being made.

Made. Communicated. And agreed.

She held one hand upright, palm open towards him. "Shalom aleichem, David Shaw."

His voice was soft as he lifted his own palm in response. "Aleichem shalom, Robyn Daniels."

14

THE EVENING WAS still bright when Robyn turned the key in her door just after seven o'clock. She dropped her bag on the floor and sank onto the couch. The room seemed dull, the evening sun not reaching in through the small window. The usual feeling of gaining safe harbour was not with her. Far from it. It was more like landing on an alien planet.

Her book had slipped from her bag and she reached down to lift it. Pink rose petals spilled on the carpet. She had forgotten that she had tucked the flower into her bag. If it had still been a flower she could have put it in a glass for a few days. But it was crushed, ruined and only fit to discard. She gathered up the petals and tossed them in the wastebasket. Later, when she was going to bed, she found another one in her slipper.

David loved words; loved playing with them, rearranging them. He loved the way writers could weave words into a tapestry, could use the way they sounded to mean more than their definitions. He had never really thought about a word as ordinary as 'delight'. Yet it bounced round him as he walked home, having a life of its own. It inhabited the creases of his quiet smile; it was in the twig he absent-mindedly twirled as he walked; it circled with the cat who appeared at his feet asking to have her ears scratched.

As he went through the gateway of his home, he jumped for a high branch of lilac and sent it twanging into the air. Before he could go down the side of the house, the front door opened.

"David, where have you been?" said his mother. "I was trying to get you. Dad's not well." She looked stressed and annoyed.

"Why did you switch your phone off?"

Her stethoscope hung over the lapels of her blouse.

"What do you mean – not well?"

"His secretary drove him home. He's lying down."

David had taken the stairs three at a time before Elizabeth had closed the door.

Angus paced round his house trying to work off his frustration. Frustration was bad. Sometimes it made things happen that he did not want to happen.

He had been enjoying the morning in the park. In fact he was about to approach Robyn and chat to her. He might have been able to persuade her to spend some time with him.

Then that holy bastard had showed up – materialised beside him like an angry genie; asked him what he was doing. Angus thumped the kitchen worktop at the memory. For a religious type, Shaw could look remarkably threatening. He had towered over him, watching through narrowed eyes as he slipped the camera into his pocket. His excuse – that he was taking some natural history photographs for the juniors next term – sounded pathetic even to himself.

How long had Shaw been watching him? And why? Shaw had stood, rooted, until Angus had turned and walked away. But Angus had worked his way back down another path in time to see Shaw meet Robyn. It looked almost like an arranged meeting. The two were obviously comfortable with each other. Angus kicked a door. He hadn't risked following them any further.

If she had decided to have a fling with a pupil, then she was an idiot. His head began to hurt. God help Shaw. Either she'd ruin him – he picked up a ceramic planter from his hall – or *he* would. Pieces of smashed pottery skittered from the front door to the back.

"No, the Home button!"

"I did press the Home button."

"You must be the last person in this country to get a mobile. It's unbelievable!" David took the mobile from Robyn and patiently explained it again, pointing as he spoke. "Home button, e-mail icon, messages."

They were scarcely visible in the afternoon crowds in the Shopping Centre. Heads together, they had found room on a long curved bench just inside the main doors as Robyn tried to understand her new phone. She took it back.

"Right. Let me try ringing someone now." She thought for a moment, and realised that there wasn't anybody she wanted to ring.

David took it back again and tapped. Then he held it up so she could see what he was doing. "Watch carefully," he instructed. "I'll be setting a homework on this."

"Yes, sir." She paid elaborate attention.

The public announcement system blared over the noise of shoppers. Mouth close to her hair, he gave a running commentary. "Phone book." He raised an eyebrow questioningly. "OK?"

She nodded. "With you so far."

"You've got one phone number in there."

The letters DS appeared on the screen along with a number. She was puzzled. "Who's DS?"

He handed the phone to her. "Tap the number." She tapped it. After a moment his phone began to ring at his belt. He answered it. Her eyes danced as she looked at him looking at her, both with their phones to their ears.

"OK! I like this." She opened her bag to put the phone away when a thought struck her. "But what's my number? I need to know my number."

He showed her the screen on his own mobile. "That's your number."

"I didn't say you could have it." That was the old Robyn

talking. Damn, she was still in there somewhere. But David merely leaned forward, elbows on knees and grinned back over his shoulder at her.

"Nope."

She stretched her legs and waggled her toes inside her shoes. New, comfortable, walking shoes. The curved bench was thronged with people. Further along, two teenage girls, deep in conversation, were ignoring a little boy who seemed to be in their charge. The toddler pushed himself away from the knee he was leaning on and, dummy pulsating vigorously in his mouth, tottered towards David. He didn't quite reach him, toppling forward at his feet with a bump. The dummy fell out, the little mouth turned down and the chin crumpled for a yell. David reached out and lifted him.

"Hey, don't yell," he said gently. The child looked up at his broad smile and put the protest on hold. "You're not really hurt, are you?" David retrieved the dummy and his fingers cradled the side of the child's head protectively as he stood, lifting the child into his arms. He walked over to the two girls who were still engrossed in conversation. The toddler gazed down from his shoulder with interest.

"Hey," he said. They looked round, mouths open. "I eat children. Fortunately for this one, I've eaten enough for today. Although," – he prodded the striped T-shirt stretched over the chubby tummy – "he might do for supper." He stooped and handed the child over to one of the gaping girls. "I'm joking," he said. "Somebody else might not be."

Three pairs of round eyes followed him as he returned to Robyn who had been watching, fascinated.

"That really annoyed you, didn't it?" she said.

"Responsibility for another human being is heavy stuff." He swivelled round. "Right. Homework. See if you can phone me again."

Concentrating, she tapped and waited until his phone rang. She cancelled the call with an air of triumph. He was pleased.

"You're a quick learner." His phone rang again and this time he answered it. While he spoke, Robyn looked past him to the two girls with the toddler. The nearest one held the child firmly on her knee while they glanced occasionally at David and muttered to each other. They were discussing him. Robyn looked at his profile as he held the phone to his ear. He was worth discussing.

He was still talking on the phone. "No, I'd better stay in tonight. Mum's still a bit shell-shocked... Sure, next week. Chloe's back then, she could come too."

When he finished, Robyn asked: "What about your Dad now?"

He leaned his elbows on his knees again, tossing his phone from one hand to the other. "He's home. They only kept him overnight. He'll be off work for a while though," – he smiled – "which annoys him."

"Still, he'll need to rest." She watched a middle-aged man and woman lightly kiss goodbye and turn in opposite directions. "I'd better go," she said, not getting up. "I've to call in the library to see someone."

"Yeah. I'd better go too. I said I'd meet Tim," he said, not getting up.

She looked at her toes. "David?"

"What?"

"Of all the girls you could have, why Chloe?"

He looked round in surprise, momentarily speechless. "Why not?"

She thought for a minute. "She's too small for you."

He gave a slight laugh, his brows drawing together. "Maybe she'll grow a bit more."

"I didn't mean height," she said.

He was quiet for a minute, studying his thumb. Then he

retaliated. "That man who called for you at school that night." He must have felt her tense. "Are you… in a relationship with him?"

She blinked. A week ago she would have cut him to pieces for that. Now she said, "No."

He nodded. "He isn't right for you."

"You know that? After one sighting?"

"And things you've told me." His gaze was jumping sightlessly across the racketing crowds. Robyn heard only his voice as if the two of them were in an empty room. "You've been very unhappy. For a long time, I think. Even as a friend, does he notice?"

She had almost stopped breathing. "Not in any way that matters."

He said no more, just looked at the tiles between his feet, knowing he had made his point.

Robyn ran up the imposing stairs of the library, determined to do this, to be a decent human being and enquire after a friend. In the first floor reading room, she selected a periodical and sat in an easy chair in full view of the enquiry desk. She had come this far. Gemma could do the rest.

After half an hour, a chair was pulled up beside her and Gemma's voice said: "Hi."

Robyn folded the magazine and looked up. Gemma looked immaculate as ever. The blonde hair still swung round her ears, the fingernails were still scarlet, not a chip visible. Matching toenails peeped from blue strappy sandals. It was hard to read her expression and Robyn didn't feel like small talk; like pretending nothing had happened.

"How is he?" she asked.

"He's walking better now but the bruised ribs'll take some time to stop hurting. The stitches on his mouth are out, and his arm's out of the sling. His wrist's just strapped now."

Robyn moved to stand. "Glad he's coming on. Give him my regards."

Gemma's hand restrained her. "Is that it?"

Robyn sat back again and regarded her old friend. "He hurt me, Gemma. Nobody does that to me again. And I told him that."

"He scared me too for a minute. But he's really, really sorry. Honestly. You have to believe me."

"I don't believe he's sorry for anything."

Out of habit, Gemma reached from her chair and tucked the magazine back on the stand. She said: "Neil said you were cold. I believe him."

"You've always believed him."

Gemma sat looking at her clasped hands. "There isn't any point in us having a row, Rob. I really don't want to. Surely we have too much history – all three of us." She looked up. "I was going to ring you tonight."

"And what were you going to say?"

"Neil's still at my place. He couldn't travel yet. I was going to ask you round. Give him a chance to say sorry."

"You must be joking! I won't go into your house again until he's left it. And anyway, why can't *he* ring me to apologise?"

"He knows you wouldn't speak to him."

That was true. Unusually perspicacious of him, Robyn thought. Fleetingly, she wondered if David would know the word perspicacious. Guessing the meanings of words was becoming a bit of a running game between them. She didn't always win it.

"Give me one good reason why I should go back on what I said."

Gemma thought for a moment. "Surely he's still a friend? I mean..." She threw her hands up in bewilderment, "...after all these years. Say we had an old school friends' reunion, we'd all be there, wouldn't we?"

"Well…"

Gemma had a sudden idea. "I know! I'll take him down the road to the Botanic Gardens in the car and help him walk in a bit, to somewhere you could meet him. The rose walk maybe. He needs to be walking more and getting some fresh air anyway."

"Definitely not."

"Oh, come on!" Gemma sounded exasperated. "Give him a chance." As Robyn looked up at her quickly, she pressed the point. "Everyone should have the chance to say sorry." She looked at her scarlet toes. "And maybe you could say sorry too."

Robyn gasped. "Me say sorry? What on earth for?"

"Because you upset him and he nearly got killed."

"I'm not responsible for that!"

"OK. OK. Of course you're not." Gemma's tone became placating. "Don't go running off down the stairs again on me." She softened this with a smile. "How about I walk with Neil down to the embankment tomorrow and you meet him there. Just for a few minutes. It's only a hundred yards from the house."

Robyn stood and walked round a book shelf, struggling with the decision. Finally she said: "All right. Eleven o'clock. Just down from your house." She raised a finger for emphasis. "Two minutes, Gem."

She tensed as Gemma reached out, gave her arm a squeeze then looked back at the desk. "I must get back to work. By the way," she lowered her voice, "things are hotting up with Jack." She grinned conspiratorially. "I've got a few nicknames for him now. But none I could tell you!"

"I'm so happy for you," said Robyn, leaving.

Curled up in her chair with a mug of coffee, Robyn looked around her bedsit. For the first time the feeling sneaked up on her that it was a bit small. It was also very dark and isolated at the back of the building. Restlessly, she considered the furnishings and colour scheme. It was too dark red and grey. Yellow. It needed some yellow. That would bring a sunnier feel to it. Curtains and cushions would be a start.

Her mother would just love coming with her to look for them. Briefly she considered phoning her, but decided against it. It was too soon. Had those who knew her back home noticed that she wasn't there this summer? She had one or two acquaintances who might, but probably they wouldn't wonder enough to enquire after her. Friends had never got emotionally close. And never stayed. She was sure Gemma stuck around only because of Neil.

She uncurled and went into the kitchen for a biscuit. At least she had proved to herself that she could make a friend outside her family. She had proved something with David Shaw.

She gave a wry smile. But then, how long would he stick around? He was a stepping stone. Once the new school term started, reality would impinge on this slightly unreal summer world and she would go back to finish the last few months of the maternity leave she was covering. These holidays were still time out, transitional. She bit her lip. There would hopefully be some job interviews too but, unlike the number of students qualifying, posts were not plentiful.

Rattling the side of her mug with her nails, she thought about Angus Fraser. Hmm. Maybe if he appeared again, she'd go for coffee or something. Just check him out.

Later she sat in bed and explored her new phone. She remembered most of what David had shown her. When she had checked out most of the icons, she fixed her pillow and lay down on her side to sleep. Her eyes kept straying to the outline of the phone on the table beside her bed.

After ten minutes she reached for it. Her cheek still on the pillow, she lay and typed 'Look what I can do!' There was still only one number stored in her phone. She hit 'Send'.

The phone lay silent beside her pillow. Eventually she went to sleep.

In the pitch black of the night, the room filled with a piercing noise. Robyn woke with a start, her heart racing. The phone. She must have left it set to loud. One message. 'go 2 top of class!'

She peered at her watch. It was half one. Where was he at half one in the morning? And who was he with? She speculated for a moment then rolled over and went back to sleep.

15

ANGUS FRASER WAS puzzled by what he was seeing.

There wasn't enough cover for him to get too close, but he had been able to duck under the slide in the children's playground just at the back gate to the Botanic Gardens. From there he could look along the embankment to the other side of the road, towards the bridge.

The traffic interrupted his line of sight but he recognised the man who walked slowly to meet Robyn. It was her man friend. She seemed to be keeping some distance from him. Any time he tried to narrow the gap between them, she lengthened it again by taking a pace back along the railings.

Angus watched patiently, then cursed as cramp gripped his leg. He stood to flex it. When he looked again, she seemed to be agitated, gesticulating, waving her hands wildly. She was easy to see in her light red jacket and denim jeans. A lorry obscured his view momentarily. When it passed, Robyn was spinning away from the guy, her hair flying like a cape. Despite seeming to be in some pain, the man followed her and grabbed her arm. In an instant Robyn turned and smashed the flat of her hand into his face. The guy staggered against the railings, both his hands to his face.

Robyn ran past him and came towards Angus' hiding place, slowing to a brisk walk as she approached. She took something out of her pocket – it was a phone – and stabbed at it. She was ringing someone. No, she wasn't, she had dropped her hand to her side, still holding the phone. She was crossing the road, hardly paying any attention to the traffic. He pulled back out of sight. She passed him and hurried up the path to the park.

He came out of hiding and swung round to look back towards the bridge. A blonde woman was with Neil, her arm supporting him; with her other hand she was dabbing at his face with a tissue. Angus looked over his shoulder in the direction Robyn had gone. Then he turned back to the couple by the railings. After a moment's thought, he quickened his step and went towards them.

"Are you all right? Need any help?" he called.

A light breeze was making the pages flutter as David studied the rules and regulations of the camp in Florida where he was going as a helper for three weeks in August. He was looking forward to it. This would be his first major trip abroad alone and he was more than ready. He stretched, then caught a sheet of paper just as it slid off his knee. The garden bench was in an alcove of lawn in the back corner of the luxuriant garden. The sun came round to it in the afternoons, but on this dry summer morning, it was a pleasant retreat.

His mother was at work and his father had taken Manna with him to visit neighbours. David was heartily glad because his father was a poor patient, fretting and restless, impatient with idleness. David swivelled and put his feet up along the bench. Wedging his papers under his knees, he threw his head back to look up through the branches above him. Tufts of cloud floated across the bright blue sky. David spread his hands and raised his arms high, feeling that he was smiling up into the face of God.

Three weeks and then back to the final push to exams. It would be a crucial year, and he was determined to do well. When they had moved east, he had wanted to go to the Further Education College to finish his exams, but his parents wanted him to qualify from a prestigious school. Eventually he had given in although, older that his peers, he felt out of place. RE would be the difficult one, but he found it fascinating. He was fairly confident of English. His lips curved in a slight chuckle. Did she know she put her tongue between her teeth when she was concentrating? As for Geography, he would probably be OK there too. His thoughts darkened. Fraser made him uneasy. Had be been watching Robyn in the park?

His phone bleeped. One message received. 'Where r u?'

He swung his legs to the ground. It was sent from Robyn's phone. Puzzled, he replied: 'home. you?'

After a moment the message came back: 'r u busy?'

David thought for a moment. Then he thumbed: 'where r u?'

'park'

'c u there'

He waited a moment but there were no more messages. As he passed the green car in the drive, he considered taking it, but decided that he'd probably be quicker on foot. You don't have to look for a parking spot for your feet.

Jogging through the gates of the park, he looked around for the red jacket he was fairly sure she would be wearing. He found her pacing up and down the path by the Palm House. She was in a fury. Without even saying hello, she launched into a tirade.

"Who the *hell* do they think I am? They really do think they own me! They really do." She rounded on him, making him take a step backwards. "How dare they? How *dare* they?" She paused for breath then stormed on. "They want me to go back with them. They have it all arranged. A friend of Gemma's is coming up tomorrow and he's so happy to take me and Neil back with him!"

David recovered from his initial shock and held his hands up. "Hey, calm down. I haven't the faintest idea what you're talking about."

This only incensed her more. "Calm down? Calm down! Why the hell should I?"

David made a mental note never to say that to a woman again. He stayed quiet, hoping that her anger would eventually run into sand.

"Why does no-one believe me?" She stormed away and whirled round on him again. "Am I invisible? Do my feelings not matter? Just because something is my opinion, it doesn't mean it's no opinion at all. And he didn't say sorry."

People were staring. David took a quick look round and realised just how public this was. Aware that some of the observers could be pupils or the parents of pupils, he took her arm firmly and steered her to the Palm House. He moved so fast she stumbled on the steps but he pushed her ahead of him through the squeaky doors and almost into the middle of the foliage of a tall plant with spindles of bright red flowers.

She swung round on him and the edge of his eye caught the movement of her right hand as it streaked towards his head. His arm shot out and caught her wrist. She was stirring his own temper. He tightened his fingers. Anything to shock her out of this fit. Because that's what this was. Some switch had been thrown. He raised his voice.

"Robyn! Whoever you're angry with, it isn't me. Stop this now."

She blinked, seeming to come out of whatever madness had taken hold. He waited a moment, then pulled her wrist down and opened his fingers, letting her arm rest on his palm. The white imprints of his fingers scored across the faint scar. With his other hand, he traced a finger down the line of it, stopping where the pale mark met the crease at the base of her thumb. His gaze was transfixed on the vulnerable translucence of her inner wrist.

Desire hit him like shrapnel.

She was watching his movements intently, her voice a whisper.

"I'm sorry, David."

He dropped her arm, feeling shaken, dizzy. He took a deep breath, fighting his way back. "I should hope so. You were so cross, you might have knocked me out."

She smiled slightly, embarrassed. "I don't think so somehow."

"Tell me," he said, "if I hadn't come, who would have suffered instead?"

Her shoulders sagged wearily. "Same person as always. No-one."

He stooped to look into her downcast eyes. "Bet I'm better than him."

She looked up then. "Miles better."

Pretending that he had no idea what had happened at the railings, Angus put a solicitous arm under Neil's and helped him along.

"I think we've met before," said Angus. "Aren't you a friend of Robyn Daniels? You called at the school one evening at the end of term."

Neil, breathing heavily, gave him a black look. "That's right."

They reached Gemma's house where Angus lowered Neil carefully onto the couch. Gemma disappeared briefly and returned with a plaster.

"The wound's opened again, but I don't think it's too bad." Neil held up his face as she tapped the plaster onto the corner of his mouth. "That should do it."

Angus studied her bottom appreciatively as she bent over her brother. He looked away quickly as she turned.

"Thank you very much for your help."

Angus called up his most charming smile and held out a hand. "No problem. Angus Fraser."

Gemma shook his hand. "Gemma. Neil's my brother."

"Ah, so you're not two-timing our gorgeous Robyn then, Neil," he joked.

"Can I get you something? Coffee? Coke?" said Gemma quickly.

"A coffee would be nice."

When she left the room, Angus sat easily in an arm chair and beamed across at Neil who was lying with a face like thunder. "I remember the evening at the school. You called for Robyn and she wasn't ready to go. You left without her." He crossed his legs. "I took her home."

Neil watched him from under lowered lids. "There's no need for us to detain you, you know."

"Oh, not at all. I'm delighted to meet you again – and your delightful sister." Angus made an expansive gesture. "She's quite a girl, Robyn, isn't she? I'm not surprised you were a bit mad at me."

"I wasn't mad at you at all. You're hardly her type."

Angus' brows shot up. "Whatever you say." He looked nonchalantly round the room then back at Neil. "What happened to you?"

"Car accident," said Neil.

"Shit. Still, at least you're alive to talk about it."

Gemma returned and handed Angus a mug. She sat on a low stool, angling her legs sideways and crossing her neat ankles.

"So do you teach with Robyn?" she asked.

"Just the last month or so. She's just in subbing for a maternity leave. She's very young and inexperienced, but extremely popular." He paused, took a sip of his coffee. "Very popular. With both teachers and pupils."

"That's interesting," said Gemma. "She's always been a bit of a loner. She never seemed that easy with people when she was growing up. She was always the shy one. We were at school together," she explained.

"Really?" said Angus. "Isn't it amazing how people change?"

"She has changed." Both Gemma and Angus looked round at Neil in surprise. He shrugged. "Damned if I know why. She was always very reasonable, was able to see things from my point of view." He thumped the back of the couch. "Now she seems to have a mind of her own and it's making things bloody awkward."

Even Angus was startled by this little speech.

"Well," he drawled, "maybe she just wants to spread her wings a little. She's in new company, first job, new colleagues." He swirled his coffee thoughtfully. "She's not that much older than some of her pupils either. Takes a while to remember you're not a student any more. Some of the older boys lose sleep over her."

Gemma smiled. "Schoolboys with crushes! Yeah, I can believe that. It happens everywhere."

Angus put his mug on the fender. "Indeed. Most teachers, of course, don't encourage it." The room went silent. Angus stood up lazily. "I must go. I hope you're on the mend, Neil. Perhaps we'll run into each other again some time." He made for the door, then turned back. "Plenty more fish in the sea, mate." He winked broadly and left.

The bronze statue, Woman in a Bomb Blast, sat on a low plinth in the middle of the dark atrium at the far end of the original museum building. David had brought Robyn here because of its tranquillity. He came here alone himself sometimes. The bronze exhibit was new; he had never seen it before. It was about half life size, and depicted a woman blasted almost horizontally backwards. Her blouse was blown up over her face; her legs flew upwards, twisted and helpless. Her arms were flung out in desperation. Her right arm ended in a hand contorted into a claw. Her left arm reached behind her, hand flailing. One of a series by FE McWilliam, it had been cast in 1974.

Perched on a long stool in a window embrasure, her jacket rolled up on the floor, David listened as Robyn told him about Neil; about his obsession with her; about trying to get him to leave her alone.

"It's as if he's a child throwing a tantrum because he's not getting what he wants." She clenched her fists and shook them. "And it makes me so angry. And then I feel angry with the whole world."

"I noticed."

She put a hand quickly, lightly on his arm. "But you get mad sometimes too? I know you do."

"I've been very angry with myself and with some people. I don't think I've blamed the whole world for everything yet."

"I have."

The bitterness in her tone jarred with him. "Why?"

"Because it's a bad place full of bad people. And we live in a spectacularly good example of it." She gestured at the bronze.

David studied the statue. "That's not the only way to get screwed up."

She looked at him. "You know that too?" she asked after a moment.

He looked down, away from her eyes. "I know that too."

They were silent for a while. Then she said, "I was born on an anniversary of the Kings Mills massacre. My mother always said it was a bad omen."

"She said that? To you?"

"She did. Do you know about it?"

"I've heard of it, that's all."

"There was a bogus checkpoint set up. Twelve armed men stopped a minibus with ten Protestant building workers in it. The driver was a Catholic. They told him to get lost, then they lined up the workmen and shot dead all but one. The survivor had eighteen bullets in him."

"Quite a birthday," said David.

"I was born on a bad day. It's made me feel like a bad person all my life."

She started as he thumped his hand down on his knee. "Don't

be so bloody ridiculous! You're smarter than that."

"Language. What would your minister say?"

"He can say damn all. I've never pretended to be a typical northern Prod."

"You're not a typical anything, David."

He reached out and took her left arm, turning her wrist upwards. As he suspected, there was a faint scar on it too. Not quite as long as the one on her other arm. Like a penance, he made himself trace this one also.

Softly he said: "Across for an ambulance. Up and down for a coffin." She was motionless, dropping her head so that her face was hidden in her hair. "You didn't mean to survive this, did you?" He waited, still holding her wrist. His impatience grew and he raised his voice, gripping her harder. "Did you?"

Her head spun round and she cried: "No, I didn't!"

"But you did! That makes you a survivor." His temper finally got the better of him. He flung her arm away and stood up, turning to confront her. "You're a survivor. For God's sake act like it!" As he turned to get as far away from her as he could, he couldn't help adding: "If I can do it, so can you."

He got as far as the main door before he calmed down. He stood still, breathing deeply. He was mad at her, but he was punishing her because he was mad at himself. Mad at what he had felt; what he still felt. Shaken because looking into her mind was like looking into a mirror. Confused because having known her properly for a few days was like having known her for ever. And that couldn't possibly be. And it certainly wasn't safe.

He walked back slowly. She had put her feet up where he had been sitting and was curled into a tight ball, her back against the window frame. He put his hands in his pockets and, feet planted apart, stood looking down at her. Slowly she raised her head and her hair fell away from her white face. Her eyes meeting his were enormous.

"Want to tell me about it?" he asked.

Her voice pleaded for him to understand. "I can't."

He took a deep breath and studied her for a moment longer. Then he held out his hand. "Fancy a sandwich?"

She tucked her hair behind her ear. "Ham? No mustard?"

"Ham. No mustard."

She uncurled and stood. "OK then."

She picked up her jacket. And took his hand.

16

BAREFOOT, DAVID PADDED into the kitchen where his mother was peeling potatoes. He propped himself against the ledge and picked at some freshly chopped carrot in a bowl. Elizabeth glanced up and smiled briefly. "What have you been up to today?"

"This and that."

"Sounds fascinating." She set a peeled potato in a saucepan and lifted another one. "Oh, can you do the reading at the morning service tomorrow? Dad was supposed to do it, but I don't want him to feel under pressure to go out if he feels tired."

David threw a piece of carrot into the air and caught it in his mouth. "No problem."

Manna's claws clicked on the tiles as he wagged his way off the carpet and over to where food was being thrown around. David tossed him a piece of carrot and Manna bounced up and crashed into the kitchen table, aware that his favourite food was airborne in the vicinity. David straightened the table and helped Manna by pointing to the carrot on the floor.

"If we have to have a one-eyed dog," he complained, "why couldn't we have a smaller one? It would cause less havoc."

Elizabeth laughed. "Poor Manna. He can't help being that size." She looked up at her son. "Just like you can't help being that size!"

He darted behind her and bent to put his arms around her waist. Lifting her with ease he swung her round and round. "And just like you can't help being this size!"

"David! Stop it – I'm holding a knife!"

He propped her back against the edge of the sink and patted her head. "Midget," he teased.

Manna had finished his carrot and was watching with his ears flopping forward and his head nodding from side to side in puzzlement. Smiling, Elizabeth resumed peeling. David became serious. He perched against the ledge again and picked at the carrots.

"Do you see many people who have tried to commit suicide?"

Elizabeth looked surprised. "Thankfully, no. Not many. Some, of course, but not many."

"What do you look for if they have?"

"Well, I would usually listen to them, and talk to their families. You have to try and find the reason. You have to listen. Very often it's just a cry for help."

David chewed silently for a moment. "Help for what?"

His mother turned to face him. "Where is this coming from? Don't tell me you've picked up another stray? Honestly, you attract people with problems like wasps to jam."

"Don't exaggerate. Help for what?"

Elizabeth shrugged and carried on peeling. "Oh… depression. Abuse. Very often there's a lot of anger inside. Sometimes it's a hangover from a trauma in childhood…" The knife stopped, hovered for a moment. "Of course, not everyone reacts to childhood trauma in the same way."

It was a moment after she had finished the sentence before she looked round. He was looking down at Manna, fondling the silky ears. When he didn't speak, Elizabeth put the knife down and reached her arm clumsily around his waist, hugging him sideways. "David, we love you. You must never question that."

"I don't question it." He hunched away from her with a bleak smile. "But there's forgiving and forgetting. Forgetting's the harder part."

He watched as his mother's eyes filled with tears. "But how could we ever forget?" she said.

She brushed her eyes. When she looked again there was only Manna, his head turned to the hall door slowly swinging closed.

David checked on his father who was watching television in the den and then went up to his room. Sitting on the chair at his desk he swivelled round. A small television sat on the chest of drawers at the bottom of his bed. Posters covered the walls – musicians, travel scenes. A large picture of an orange sky as the sun rose over a mountaintop. Words blazed across the bottom: "We are an Easter people and hallelujah is our song." A large wooden cross hung over the head of his bed. Beside it was a calendar of Garfield cartoons.

The black quilt on his bed was rumpled the way he had left it when he had got up this morning. The sliding door of the fitted wardrobe wasn't quite shut on the rail of clothes inside. Plenty of clothes. Good clothes.

He swung back to his desk and leaned on his elbows to look past his laptop and out the window. His room looked over the front garden to the laurel hedge and the trees in the avenue beyond.

He had to move out. He had to. Yet he knew he couldn't do that just now. He couldn't leave his parents just as they dealt with the anxiety of his father's frailty. But by next summer, even if university was just down the road, he promised himself he would get a place of his own.

He dropped his chin into his hand and twirled a pen round on the desk. It snagged on his mobile phone where he had set it down when he came in. A sudden longing to talk to Robyn again washed over him.

It had been a crazy afternoon. They had both reacted to the release of tension by going slightly mad. After a feast of sandwiches in the café, they had wandered round the exhibits in the natural history gallery. She doubled up with laughter at his impression of the fury of the wildcat who fought a perpetual battle with a stuffed eagle in a glass case. They squabbled about the correct pronunciation of the word 'Echinoderm'.

At the display of molluscs, they marvelled at the huge bivalve, a shell almost up to David's knees in height. They speculated on whether the world would have ever heard of Jonah if he had been swallowed by a bivalve instead of a big fish. She had turned away in disgust from a Giant Japanese spider crab, all of five feet across. David had turned his hands into claws and pursued her.

They wandered on to the geology gallery and on a huge wall map of Ireland she pressed buttons to light up areas of different rock types. She didn't let him see which buttons she pressed and gave him marks for how many he guessed right – after she'd checked the answers herself.

Finally they had arrived at the park gate. She thanked him shyly, hesitated, and then skipped lightly away across the road to walk back to her flat. Her red jacket swung over her shoulder, half hidden in her curtain of hair.

He smiled at the memory. On an impulse he lifted the phone and thumbed: 'u ok?'. Within seconds a message came back: 'fine!'

He set the phone down. If only she could unpick the knots of her own past, he suspected that she was the one person in the world who would be patient with his own.

Later that night, Tim phoned him.

"I want to talk to you, man," he said.

"Talk."

"Not now. Tomorrow afternoon. My house."

"OK. What about?"

"Tell you then. Cheers."

Gemma set the salad bowl in the middle of the table and sat down.

"There. I think that's everything."

Neil tried pouring a drink for Anne Daniels who was sitting opposite him. A stab of pain went through his ribs and he set the jug down. "Sorry, Anne. Still a bit stiff." He pushed the jug towards her.

"You poor thing," she sympathised. "Still, you're not as bad as I thought I might find you. Give yourself a week or two yet and you'll be fine."

She looked great, he thought. The drive up to Belfast had not tired her at all. She was wearing well. If genes had anything to do with it, it boded well for her daughter.

"Much traffic on the way up?" he asked.

"No, it was a fairly smooth run. It's not nearly as bad as in the days when the army was here. Some of their road blocks weren't easy to see in the dark. I came round a corner once and only just saw the red light in time. If I'd driven on they might have shot me!"

"That would have meant a public enquiry!" Gemma, to whom the Troubles were history, grabbed the mayonnaise bottle and pretended to be a television reporter. "Anne Daniels, supposedly upright citizen, is actually a loyalist arms smuggler, it has been revealed. She was discovered this evening with a boot full of rifles and detonators. Police are checking her car for further evidence."

Neil was aghast. "Gemma! don't make a joke of it."

She sulked. "Why not? It's the only thing to do." She passed Anne the bread. "Have some Semtex – I mean bread."

Neil took a deep breath and tackled the subject they had all been avoiding.

"Have you seen Robyn recently?"

Anne took a delicate bite of ham, chewed and swallowed before answering. "No. I haven't. I spoke to her last at the beginning of the week. We were both a little fraught." She cut a finger of bread. "Have you seen her?"

"Yesterday morning. She's being very stubborn."

Anne raised an eyebrow. "What do you mean – stubborn?"

Neil waved his fork irritably. "Well, she won't go back home. She says she's going to stay in Belfast."

Gemma looked from one of them to the other as if she were watching a tennis match. She said conversationally: "We met one of the guys who teaches with her. He says she's really popular with the pupils. He wasn't bad himself. Hidden depths, our Rob."

"Shut up, Gemma," said Neil.

Gemma calmly buttered a piece of wheaten bread. Anne turned back to Neil. "It's all very strange."

Neil searched for words grumpily. "She was always supposed to be mine." Even he knew this sounded petulant. "I mean, who else would have her? She's as odd as two left shoes."

"Maybe she doesn't want to be anybody's," said Anne.

Neil looked at her in surprise. "I thought you were on my side."

Anne shrugged. "She may just want to work something out of her system. Have a fling before settling down."

Gemma broke in again. "That reminds me of something Rob said to me once. She said 'Can't I just belong to myself?' "

Anne folded a piece of lettuce and skewered it with her fork. "She's her father's daughter. Wilful and stubborn."

"Poor Matthew," said Neil automatically. Then he banged the table. "But she didn't used to be! Now thanks to her, I have to put off moving up here. It's damn awkward. The new office is sitting waiting and I have to start paying rent on it in two weeks."

Anne set her knife and fork down deliberately, waving her hand in refusal of Gemma's offer of another drink. "Actually, Neil, I've been thinking. Perhaps you should see if you can extricate yourself from that contract."

Neil's voice went up a note. "Why on earth would I do that?"

Anne spoke carefully. "When I considered investing Matthew's estate in your business, I hoped I was investing in a secure future for my daughter." She wiped her mouth with a napkin. Gemma stopped chewing. "It doesn't seem as if things are going to work out like that."

Neil spoke in disbelief. "You wouldn't do this to me. You wouldn't! Not after all I've done. All we've been through."

Anne lifted her knife and fork and cut a tomato. "Believe me, I don't like this any more than you do." She paused with the fork half way to her mouth. "But if Robyn has changed as much as she seems to have…" – she raised an eyebrow in his direction – "…we're not related, are we?"

That night, Neil lay in bed and swore into his pillow. Two weeks ago he didn't think he could hate Robyn. But he was working up to it.

The chime of the doorbell made Robyn look up from her book with a start. Who on earth would be calling at this time on a Sunday afternoon? As she went down the stairs to the hallway, she hoped it wasn't Neil. But it was Angus who leaned round the door jamb, face very close to hers as soon as she opened the door.

"Hello, Robyn," he smiled. "You did say maybe another time?"

"Angus!" She controlled her surprise, her hand still on the door latch. "Another time for what?"

"A drive. We never did go on that drive yet. The weather seems settled. How about tomorrow?"

"I think it was you who said 'another time'. Thank you, but no thank you," she said.

Angus put his hand on the door. "What about dinner then? Just down in the Square. Ten minutes from here."

Conflicting fears and desires wrestled in her head. She had

even briefly speculated about this. To go out for dinner sounded attractive, even normal. What would be wrong with it? But she wasn't attracted to Angus Fraser, not one bit. In fact he still made her nervous. But wasn't that because for so long she had been afraid of life in general, wrapped up in a cocoon of iron protection? For a reason she didn't understand or analyse, something new was present, making her able to consider possibilities, to understand that she had a right to options.

It's just dinner. Oh, what the hell? Make an effort. Just once.

"OK. But not late."

His smile flashed. "Great. I'll have you back before ten. I'll pick you up about six thirty. Till tomorrow."

As he walked away she closed the door on his pale eyes and leaned against it. It was just dinner. And just down the road. She could manage that.

David held the steering wheel on full lock in an even sweep round the turning circle at the end of the cul-de-sac. When he pulled up at the familiar blue gate, Tim was already on the footpath. He climbed into the passenger seat, red curls twisting over his freckled brow.

"My folks are in this afternoon, including my sister," he said. "It'll make her week if you come in. But you're not going to."

"Am I not? I thought you wanted to talk."

"I do, but not with an audience, man. Drive."

With a puzzled shrug, David eased the car into gear and drove. He turned towards the city centre and pulled up in a side street. Tugging the handbrake on, he slid round to face Tim, propping himself against the door and hitching a knee in front of the steering wheel.

"So? What's the big deal? Woman trouble?"

Tim grimaced. 'I should be so lucky." Then his tone became challenging. "You're the one has the woman trouble, man.

What's with you and La Daniels?"

David's eyebrows bunched. "What?"

"You know how I have to fill art portfolios with sketches before September? For my art presentation?"

"I do."

"I was in the Museum yesterday. Fossils and stuff are great things to draw."

"So?"

"Don't be so innocent, Davey! When you arrived at the café…" he poked a finger, "I swear she was holding your hand."

David kept his voice level. "Where were you? I didn't see you."

"I bet you didn't! You weren't paying too much attention to anyone else. I nearly said hi, but then I decided staying out of sight might be more interesting. And it sure was!"

David shifted his back against the door, his black hair crinkling on the glass. "You didn't see anything much."

Tim thumped David's large foot where it rested beside the gear stick. "What's going on, mate? That wasn't an English lesson."

David turned back into his seat suddenly and fired the engine. "There's nothing to talk about. Is that all you dragged me out for?" When he reached for the handbrake, he found Tim's hand there before him, holding it firm.

"Listen to me, I'm a mate. OK? Is she fooling with you?"

David leaned over the steering wheel and drummed his fingers on the rim. He didn't look at Tim. "We just happen to have run into each other a few times over the holidays. That's all. She's OK."

"She's more than OK, man. She's the dream lay of half the sch …"

"Don't!" David's head spun round in one of his sudden spurts of anger. "Not even you, Tim. Don't talk about her like that. It's gross."

Tim went quiet. Then he said slowly: "You just told me enough." He looked away, out the side window. "Chloe's back on Wednesday, isn't she?"

"So?"

Tim shrugged. "Just checking." He became thoughtful. "You know, you and La Daniels looked good together. You've no idea how jealous I am."

Very deliberately, David turned to face him. "Before God, there is nothing going on between us, I swear. How could there be?"

"You don't need to swear, Davey. You're an honest old Prod." He tilted his head and looked quizzically at his friend. "But get it out of your system, man. If you don't, you'll get hurt and that'll put you in a foul mood and I'll get the ass end of it." David half-smiled, but Tim raised a plump finger. "One other thing. Her career's hardly started. Do you want to see her on a professional misconduct charge?"

David hit the steering wheel. "How the hell could that happen? There's been no misconduct. I've told you."

"I believe you. Keep your hair on! But I saw you both, remember." He thought for a moment. "Your minds are together, even if nothing else is. Yet."

"Pillock." David sat still, watching a slight spit of rain patter the windscreen. Then in a few sharp movements, he swung the car out into the street. "I've a youth group tonight and nothing prepared yet. I'd better get back."

They didn't speak until he pulled up at the blue gate. He looked across at Tim, then punched him on the shoulder. "You're OK. But just let me go to hell my own way."

Tim jerked the door handle and heaved himself out. The rain had got heavier. As he slammed the door, David heard him say, "No chance, man. No chance."

As he prepared to swing into the gate of his own house,

David's eye caught a movement further up the avenue. A girl with no coat, purple hair and a chin stud stepped out from the hedge. She was soaked through. He pulled the car past the gate and stopped. Reaching over, he pushed open the passenger door.

"Get in," he said. "You have to go home."

17

ROBYN WAITED FOR the doorbell. She had dressed carefully in navy trousers and a short-sleeved top. Her red jacket lay ready on the table beside her bag. She felt good, confident. Taking a deep breath, she promised herself that she would enjoy herself this evening. Allow herself to relax, to have a good time. She didn't know why, but something had loosened inside her. She felt cleaner, lighter. She pummelled one of her new yellow cushions and sat down. Her mobile phone bleeped. She had told no-one else she had it. She hugged it like a secret, a convenience for herself alone. And one other.

'Walk this evening?' said the screen.

She smiled and thumbed a message. 'Sorry. Got a date!'

There was quite a pause before a message came back: 'Who with?'

She thumbed: 'Mind your own business!' and softened it with a winking emoji.

Angus transformed himself into the perfect companion. He could do it effortlessly. He thought that Robyn looked more enticing than he could ever remember seeing her before. He watched her bouncing down the steps to his car. Her clothes hugged her figure as she slipped into the seat beside him. He couldn't help his eyes tracing down the V of the neckline to where a strand of her hair was caught. He realised that she had seen where his eyes had wandered and smiled quickly.

"OK. Let's go find a menu."

He turned the conversation to holidays and weather, trying to make her relax. He would make sure she was even more relaxed by the time the evening was over.

The restaurant wasn't very busy and they were seated in a booth near the window. And then, damn it! she wanted apple juice. Apple juice! On the other side of the wooden partition, American accents were discussing their hotel.

"Lots of tourists about," said Angus casually.

"There are." Robyn turned her menu over, scanning it. "There are accents from all over the world here now."

"Ever been to America?" he asked.

"No. I haven't travelled very far at all, I'm afraid."

And so it continued. She seemed to stay distant, wary, and it irritated him. She ate very little. Over dessert, he watched her left hand settle beside her plate as she lifted her fork with the other hand. He tried reaching for her fingers but they vanished onto her lap as if he approached with fire. The quick dart of her glance to his face tightened the pressure in his head.

When she crumpled her napkin and said, "Well, I think I should get back," he slid from the booth so fast he saw the little startle he caused. He cursed himself for the slight alarm. He reached to grip her arm, to pull her up. Stopped himself. Not yet. Not yet. Let's go. Time to get this done. Time!

His hands were greasing the steering wheel when Robyn sat forward and looked round.

"Angus, you've passed my street."

"But I'm bringing you back to my place for a drink, remember?"

She frowned. "No, I don't remember. We were heading back."

"And so we are. Back to my place." He pulled off the main road, drove down the street to his own two-storey semi and pulled into the drive. His mouth was dry. He put his hand on her knee and felt her go rigid.

"You said just dinner," she said tersely.

"Come on, Rob." She was beginning to make him angry. He could feel his head starting to pound again. "Just a drink."

She shifted away from him, back against the door, hand reaching round to pull the handle. "I'm going home now, Angus. I'll walk."

His eyes narrowed. Briefly he reached over and gripped a strand of her hair. Then he turned and flung himself out of the car. She was out before him, backing towards the street into the view of the traffic and the neighbours.

She held her bag and jacket in front of her. "I don't think I'm your type, Angus!"

He held up his hands in a pacifying gesture. "It's been a great evening. Can't blame a man for trying!" He indicated the still-open passenger door. "Come on, I'll drive you home. I promise."

" 'On your honour' I bet! No thanks." He took a step towards her. "*Don't touch me!*"

Her low snarl mildly surprised him. He brought a hand up to take her hair again. The next second, he had staggered back against the car, doubled up and gasping in pain. The bitch had fired her knee into his balls!

"You don't even understand a two letter word!"

The disgust in her voice drenched him as she vanished into the evening. Inside the house he lay on the sofa until he could breathe again. Then he knocked the ornaments off the mantlepiece in one sweep. He was as mad with himself as he was with her. Stupid bastard! He should have managed that so much better. She was laughing at him right now. He just knew it. He flung himself up the stairs and went into his bedroom. He lifted a mirror off the wall and hurled it across the room. Glass shards went everywhere, just missing the picture of her at the shop window.

He sat on the edge of the bed, his breathing erratic. A piece of glass glittered beside his shoe. He picked it up and turned it over. Cool down, cool down. This isn't over yet. Not by a long way. He'd get her in the end, and when he did he'd make her suffer. His head throbbed so hard he pounded his temple. He tossed the glass into the bin. *Cool down. Cool down. Think.*

Pale and tired, Robyn sat at her desk in the upper corridor of the almost empty school. It had been a bad night. The devils had come out in force. And the voices. She stood to fetch a book from the store and winced as her shoe hurt where her heel had rubbed raw. It had been a long walk home last night. She could have called a taxi, but she had too much anger to work off. She even thought of calling David, but dismissed the idea immediately. She had her pride. She had told him she was going on a date. She didn't want him to know the near disaster that it was. From the moment Angus had picked her up, she was uneasy. There was just something about him…

Had her father put a curse on her? She sat at her desk again and buried her head in her folded arms. His large face loomed in front of her. She could feel his hand on her chin, turning her face this way and that, studying it in the light, the same light that caught on the hairs curling from his nose.

As the memory took hold, coalesced into still living horror, Robyn sat back in her chair and hugged her arms tight around herself as she had then. The the day went dark as his face closed in on her mind, to obliterate the world. *"Daddy's little girl."*

She flung the book at the wall. Then regretted it because the cover tore from the spine and there weren't enough copies as it was. Pacing up and down between the desks, she fought back. Damn you, I have every right to leave you behind, you bastard. You will not spoil my life. You will not. You're dead. Dead. Anger threatened to choke her again.

There was a faint sound from her bag. Her phone was ringing. "Hi," he said.

"Hi," she said.

"How was last night?"

"Fine. OK."

Pause. "Good." Pause. "Where are you?"

"I'm in the school. Sorting a few things."

"Need some help?"

She didn't. "Well, yes, OK. If you're about."

"See you in fifteen."

She was in the storeroom when footsteps approached. She turned, the smile already on her face. "That was quick. It's only ten…" Her smile froze as Angus walked in.

"Hello," he said.

"Get out, Angus."

"Don't be like that. I've recovered, as you see." He came closer, pulled up a stool and sat. She turned back to the shelves.

"You're pathetic," she said.

His pale eyes studied her, unblinking. "You've got me all wrong, Rob. I'm really quite a nice guy. It was all a misunderstanding. I thought we'd just have a nightcap, like normal people. You've got spirit. I like that."

She snorted. "I don't see why. It was painful. I hope."

He spread his hands. "Let's forget about last night and start again." As she looked round, her face loaded with scorn, he put on a pleading expression and joined his palms in front of his chest. "I misjudged you. Forgive me?"

"Get lost. I'm sure there's some poor woman out there who might be warped enough to think you're attractive. Beats me, though."

His face darkened at her undisguised contempt. "What's so wrong with me?" He stood and stepped towards her, lowering his voice.

Robyn backed against the window ledge as he came closer. She felt her stomach start to heave as a thick gold chain round his neck glinted on his pale flesh. Reaching round, her hand found an old window pole propped in the corner.

"The Headmaster will hear about this when term starts," she hissed.

"I did nothing…" Angus began.

Robyn turned slightly and her eyes darted past him to the door. Angus swung round. David Shaw filled the doorway. He was leaning his back against the door jamb, arms folded, ankles crossed across the gap, biding his time. How much had he heard? Robyn saw his deep eyes narrowed in warning as, without moving, he said evenly, "She said get lost, Fraser."

Angus said smoothly: "Ah, the toy boy." He turned back to Robyn. "I forgot, of course. You do have other fish to fry." He went up to David. "She'll have finished with you soon, Shaw. Moved on to the next one."

Robyn held her breath. She knew what David was thinking as if she were inside his head. Don't hit him, David. Please don't hit him. David flicked a glance to her as if he had heard. Then he moved his feet aside.

Angus turned back to Robyn. "Message received." He pushed roughly past David and they listened to his footsteps fading in the empty corridor.

Still propped in the doorway, David looked at her from under his brows. "Great evening was it then?"

She shrugged. "Yes, well. Maybe not that great."

"Want to get out of here?"

She propped the window pole into the corner. "Definitely."

She had never been in his little green car before. His music was a mixture of pop and gospel. There was a Newsboys album playing as he nosed onto the motorway and headed east across the city. Terrific beat. Great lyrics. On the back seat was a rolled up jacket, a book of choruses with guitar chords, and an unopened bag of liquorice allsorts. She looked across at his profile, his expression one of concentration as he negotiated a roundabout. He must have felt her gaze because he looked across momentarily.

"You OK?"

"You don't apologise for who you are, do you?"

His brows rose. "Wait till I've stopped driving before you ask me questions like that."

She hardly noticed where they were going, tiredness dulling her senses. He drove for miles, finally leaving the city and heading along the coast. At one point a train kept pace with them, rising high on an embankment between the road and the sea. Finally, he pulled up on the main street of the village of Groomsport.

She looked down at the harbour, and over to the right, past the Harbour Master's house to the sea wall where she had told Neil she didn't want to see him again. They were standing quietly side by side. Robyn looked out over the lough.

" 'The wrinkled sea beneath him crawls…' " she began.

" '…And like a thunderbolt he falls,' " he finished, not missing a beat.

They looked at each other, delighted. Then, taking their time, they strolled across the grass past the play area and found a seat near two restored fishermen's cottages that sat, whitewashed and proud, at right angles to the sea.

A middle aged couple went past, pushing a girl in a wheelchair. A child in a mauve dress skipped along, then stopped to take off her shoe and shake a stone out of it. She replaced the shoe and did a few experimental hops before running on. On a flat area near the road, several youths in baseball caps and T-shirts with numbers on the back, noisily kicked a football about. Two girls in jeans leaned against a lamp post, licking lollipops, resolutely unimpressed.

Without speaking, David pointed to the sky. A kite swirled above their heads, its long orange ribbon of tail twisting and dipping in the wind. Out to sea, a speed boat bumped over the creases of the surface, its wake as white as its own hull. Nearer the land, small orange buoys bobbed in the harbour, rising and falling to the gentle rhythm of the small waves that lapped their lace edges onto the shingle.

Five minutes must have passed as Robyn looked about, feeling quietly, deeply, peaceful. Without looking, she knew he was feeling the same. A little dog, grey, hairy and snub-nosed, scampered by, trailing a lead. His owner puffed after him, whistling in vain.

Finally David said: "What did you ask me in the car?"

"It was more of a statement. I said you don't apologise for who you are."

"Of course not. Do you?"

She tugged her hair out of her eyes and said, surprising herself, "Not any more."

"You mean you did?"

"All the time." The breeze was laden with the salt smell of seaweed. She turned to him. "Angus frightened me. But I just … despise him." She gave an impatient gesture, trying to find words to explain. "And he's right, he didn't actually *do* anything. But I might report him in September. I think, for the first time, there's no-one blaming me. And I'm not blaming myself."

"I think," he said slowly, watching a gull ride the breeze to twist onto the thatched ridge of one of the cottages, "Fraser might be a little bit nastier than normal."

"He's no different from any other man." She couldn't help the bitter edge to her voice. It made him turn his head, a question in his eyes.

"Are you afraid of me?"

She laughed at the absurdity but his expression didn't change. He was waiting for an answer. "Of course not. But you're…"

She frowned. He waited. "You're a friend." He leaned forward and reached between his heels for a tuft of grass. She was still frowning, thinking, as if somehow she hadn't quite got that right to her own satisfaction. "You shouldn't be. But you are."

He was quiet, dropping the grass between his fingers. Suddenly he sat back and in one swift movement his arm went round her. Startled, she stiffened.

"You said you weren't afraid of me," he challenged.

She felt the crook of his arm curled round her shoulder, his fingers descending to cradle her elbow. She turned her head into his shoulder and looked up. Tentatively she raised a hand and slowly traced the edge of his fine jawline. Then she pulled her hand away, watching his brown eyes darken behind his lashes. She drew her legs up under her and turned her whole body towards him, feeling him grip her tightly as she tucked herself into his side. Fitting her cheek to his shoulder, she closed her eyes.

"I'm not afraid of you at all," she said quietly.

She kept her eyes closed, her mind a scramble of confusion. What am I doing? Why does it feel so easy, so good? This is so right and so wrong all at the same time.

David looked down at the top of her head, at the glossy strands that escaped his arm to settle across his collar bone and tangle with the buttons of his shirt. He felt nothing of desire. This was quite different from that fiery, transient surge. There was a deep peacefulness in this. He tightened his grip on her slightly and looked across to the far side of the lough where a slight haze blurred the edges of the mountains.

"Right, Lord," he said in his mind, "you'd better have a good reason for this. Because I think I'm in big trouble unless you know what you're doing." He tilted his cheek onto her head. "And keep her safe."

Uneasily, he recalled how he knew that you don't always get what you pray for, however fervently.

He was still holding her when he saw Angus Fraser standing at the seaward side of one of the cottages, hands in his pockets. Fraser looked directly at him, then turned and disappeared.

18

THERE WERE THINGS she wanted to know. Things she wanted, needed, to know now. It was as if a heavy shower of rain had washed away a layer of mud and exposed the corners of long-buried shards. For the first time, Robyn contemplated these jagged edges; looked at them without instantly wanting to push them back out of sight again.

On Friday morning she caught the express bus. On Friday afternoon, she was sitting at the kitchen table in her mother's house, mug between her hands and Onion on her knee. As always, everything in the kitchen shone. There were no dishes waiting to be washed. The hand towel and drying cloth were folded precisely over the rail. The ceramic hob looked as if it were straight out of the showroom. An asparagus fern wound its way across the wall towards the window, every frond neatly supported on a small hook. Even the fridge magnets were arranged in straight lines.

Anne smiled across the table. "It's funny how long you can be away and yet Onion still treats you as if you'd never left." She reached over and touched Robyn's hand. "I'm so glad you came down. I did go to see Neil in Belfast, but I thought maybe you needed to bide your own time."

"Where's Neil now?"

"He's back. His own car was repaired at last and he drove down himself. It was very brave of him."

"Indeed."

"And anyway, he couldn't leave his office for any longer. And … he has a lot of thinking to do now that…" she waved a hand in the air.

Robyn stroked Onion, provoking a crescendo of purring.

"I hope he does well, but as you say..."

Her mother looked at her for a minute and then sighed. "I hoped you would have been well settled with a husband and your father's money would have meant you would have had a comfortable start."

Robyn stared at her, mug half way to her mouth. "What do you mean, 'My father's money'?"

Anne looked surprised. "The money I said I'd invest in Neil's business. Neil must have talked about it." Robyn continued to stare at her as she went on. "How do you think he was going to finance the expansion and move to Belfast? What was going to pay for the new building?"

Robyn put her mug down carefully. "This is complete news to me."

"You mean Neil didn't tell you about it?"

Robyn stood up, tumbling Onion to the floor. "You were going to give my father's money to Neil?"

"I've told him that I won't be investing now."

Robyn kept her voice under control with difficulty. "Why didn't you discuss this with me? Why didn't you tell me yourself?"

Anne put her hand to her forehead. "Please don't get mad, Rob. I wanted to do what was best for you. Neil's a good organiser. He looks after things like that. You'd got your first job..." Her voice trailed off.

Anger was surging through Robyn, rushing in waves in front of her eyes, blurring the sight of her mother sitting at the table, twisting the gold and diamond rings on her fingers. She smashed her hand down on the table, making her mother jump.

"Neil was going to look after that! Neil was going to look after me! Neil was going to look after the goods! Neil was going to take over! Wasn't that the plan? Wasn't it?"

She threw the rest of her coffee into the sink, only just

managing not to hurl the mug in after it. Onion pawed open the kitchen door and, with a flick of his ginger tail, slid away into the hall. Anne turned in her chair and looked up pleadingly.

"I still want you to have the money, Robyn. Even if you take up with someone else."

Robyn looked at her and realised that her mother didn't know her at all. She hadn't a clue. Or had she, and was she trying to assuage some guilt? Robyn came back to the table and sat down. Unconsciously, she began rubbing her right wrist.

"I wonder is there anything else I haven't been told? In fact, I came here today because I wanted to ask you something, Mum. Something I should have asked you years ago. Why didn't you leave Dad?"

Anne fiddled with the pearls she wore even in the middle of the afternoon. "Leave your father? How could I do that? I was completely dependent on him. Besides, we had a good position in the town. Your father was a fine figure, people respected him. He gave a lot of money to the church." She shrugged as if she simply couldn't understand the question. "And then, when he became ill, well, I had promised to be loyal in sickness and in health."

"I was baptised, wasn't I?"

"Of course you were. You were beautiful even as a baby, except that you cried all through the christening. That was embarrassing." Her eyes clouded. "Dad blamed me. He said I hadn't fed you. But I had."

"So you made promises about me too. Didn't you?"

"Of course."

Robyn felt the old fetid bitterness spewing out of her, unstoppable. "Promises about keeping me safe. Bringing me up in a Christian home. Not putting any stumbling block in my way. Stuff like that."

"Yes."

Robyn closed her eyes. "Do you," she said, "remember me asking you to leave him?"

"Yes." A whisper.

"Do you remember me pleading with you to leave him?"

"Yes." Still a whisper.

Robyn opened her eyes. "Another question. I didn't think I could ask this one, because I didn't want to have to deal with the answer. But here goes." Robyn moved her head to fix her mother's eyes with her own. Slowly and deliberately, she asked: "Did you know just how bad he was?"

She watched this one sinking in. Her mother looked grey, the skin on the backs of her hands wrinkling like tissue paper as she wound her fingers together. Her voice was low, almost frightened. "What do you mean?"

"I mean, did you think he was an autocratic hypocrite who made your life hell? Or did you know he was a pervert who was even worse than that?"

Anne looked up, pleading. "Rob, there is no point in raking up the…"

Robyn found herself shouting. "Oh yes, there's every point! It matters now, every bloody day, to my life!"

Anne leapt from her chair and ran to the living room. Robyn sat for a moment, breathing deeply, calming herself. But she felt relentless. Her mother had sat in an armchair, her hands over her face. Robyn circled and sat opposite her.

"I'm telling you it matters. I'm entitled to know, and I want to know now. Did you know what he was doing to me? Yes or no."

She thought her mother wasn't going to answer, but then Anne removed her hands and said hoarsely: "Your brother knew. He told me."

Robyn's eyes widened in shock. "Stephen knew?"

"He said that he used to hear his father in the middle of the night. He saw what he was… where he was…" Anne looked up and said quickly, with a defiance that struck Robyn as grotesque: "It affected Stephen too, you know."

Anger was making Robyn's whole body shake. Her shoulders quivered, her legs trembled. Her voice rose again. "My God, Mum!" She flung her arms wide. "And your promises to your husband, your desperation to keep up appearances, were more important than any responsibility you had to your daughter?" She leaned forward. "Someone said to me recently that responsibility for another human being is heavy stuff. The person who said it is about a third of your age, but for some reason he's ten times wiser than you could ever be."

Anne was weeping now. Slow tears of helplessness tracked down cheeks become old. But Robyn hadn't finished.

"And when you found me on the bathroom floor, my arms sliced open and blood soaking through to the floorboards? Fourteen, wasn't I, when I did that? Not even then?" She became reflective. "I wonder are the marks still there, on the floor. Is the wood still stained? And I wonder how you explained that to the fitter who laid the new flooring."

Unexpectedly, Anne said, almost proudly: "Your Dad did it himself. He was good that way."

Robyn ignored this. The statement, and the tone in which it was said, betrayed too much to take in just now.

"I nearly died, didn't I? I nearly managed it."

"Yes. But your Dad got you to the hospital very quickly."

"Bully for him. But then, if I'd succeeded, the questions for a respected citizen might have dug a bit deeper, mightn't they? An inquest would be harder to hide from."

Anne held out a hand. "Please, Robyn, it's all in the past."

Robyn leapt to her feet. "No, it's not in the past! Don't you see?" Frustration made her pace around the room, ornaments rocking as she passed. "Oh, he never touched me again after that. But I was on medication for two years." She mimicked a concerned tone. "Poor Matthew. The time of it he has with that daughter. He's been so good to her. How could she possibly suffer from depression, coming from such a wonderful family?" She turned and jabbed a finger. "He nominated Neil as his successor, didn't he? Neil was going to take me on, and you went along with it. You're *still* going along with it."

Anne spread her hands wide, tears still fretting down her face. "That's why I wanted you to marry him. To give you a normal life, children. Forget the past. And the money – I wanted it to make up for what he did."

Suddenly energy drained out of Robyn and she sat heavily in the chair. She explained patiently: "That won't do it, Mum. That won't do it at all." She studied the pattern on the carpet for a minute. Then she looked up. "You just said you wanted me to have the money no matter who my partner is. But don't you understand? How could I inflict myself on any man? The very thought of anyone touching me like that ever again makes me want to throw up." She leaned forward, speaking slowly, emphasising every word. "Am I being clear enough?"

She sat back, not feeling an ounce of remorse at the sight of her mother's wretched face. "I could never respond to Neil. Although I don't believe he knew the reason. He thought I'd get over it. But I woke up in time. I have the power to say no." She was almost patient as she explained: "If someone truly loved me, I don't think I could recognise it. That's why it matters. It's not in the past at all. It's not just in the present either." She looked out the window, her face bleak. "It's all of the future too."

After a silence, she got up wearily. As she passed her chair, Anne thrust out a hand to grip her daughter's. "Robyn, forgive me. Please," she said hoarsely.

Robyn looked down and said sadly: "Can anything you do to a child, or allow to be done, ever be forgiven?"

Then she went back to the kitchen and lifted her bag.

Opening the cloakroom in the hall, she lifted out her jacket. Anne followed her, tissue crumpled in her hand, jabbering, imploring.

"You can't go now. You'd get back far too late. When you phoned earlier, I made up your bed. Stay overnight at least. Don't go like this. Let's go shopping tomorrow."

Robyn found Onion curled in a perfect circle on her mother's bed. She lifted him and hugged him, burying her face in his soft side. The pressure of her arms squeezed spasms of purrs from him as he nuzzled her face and licked her nose. Gently, she set him back on the bed and left him with a last pat. In the hall, she opened the front door and stepped outside.

Looking back, she said quietly: "Goodbye, Mum."

Then she slammed the door.

19

ON SATURDAY AFTERNOON, the land line rang in the flat. It was Neil.

"I've just called at your mother's. She said you were here yesterday. The poor woman looks as if she's been crying all night. What on earth did you say to her?"

"Ask her, Neil."

There was a pause. "Why didn't you tell me you were down? You always tell me when you're coming." Another pause. "She told you I'm back home?"

"Yes." She took a deep breath. "I hope you're feeling better."

"Physically, yes."

"Good."

"I think you should know that I've had to cancel plans to move to Belfast. I believe you know why."

"I do."

"I was very lucky that there was another tenant ready and willing to take the building I wanted." She noticed the stress on the last two words. "So now I'll have to drive past it and see someone else's sign up on it."

"That's too bad."

His irritation began to shake loose. "Yes, it is too bad! And this is all because of you. You can't blame me for making plans when I thought everything was clear."

"Absolutely nothing was clear to me, Neil, as I have discovered. But then maybe that didn't really matter. You were going to take care of everything."

"Of course I was!" he exploded. "There's no need for any of

this. You're going to regret this sooner or later anyway." She listened to his struggle to calm himself. "So let's forget this ever happened. Let's meet and sort things out. Fresh start." He added brightly: "I think they're building more units further along on the same site."

"Neil?" she said softly.

"Yes?" he said hopefully.

"No," she said clearly, and hung up.

It had been four days since he had seen her and he had not heard from her either. David was only half listening to his father who was wandering round the garden explaining what he wanted to do before the summer was over. Manna padded along beside them, snapping at flies and missing.

"See here, where these hostas are?"

"Mmhm."

"It's too sunny for them. I'd like to try strawberries here. I never managed to grow strawberries successfully in the last place. Either the soil or the weather; don't know which." Vincent smiled ruefully. "Or maybe it was just me."

Perhaps he should phone, just to make sure everything was all right.

Vincent pointed. "Those loganberries are doing fine growing up the back of the garage. So I don't see why strawberries wouldn't be OK."

He had been busy of course. There had been a meeting to do with going away next month. Then he'd had to put in some work on assignments and coursework.

Vincent was still considering. "And then here, this mallow has got much too large. It's going woody. I'll have to cut that right back."

And then there'd been Chloe. The big scene with Chloe. Pretty as the mallow flower and tanned as shoe polish after her holiday.

172

He thought he'd chosen his words well. He'd certainly rehearsed them for long enough. What had she called him? A pagan. A cad (that was a posh word for Chloe). A bog-trotting clod (more like her). An unfeeling two-timing something-or-other. At least he'd been able to argue that the last one wasn't true.

"In fact, son, would you get me the clippers and I'll lay into some of this jungle now."

David heard that. "No, Dad, I'll do it later, maybe tomorrow."

"Tomorrow's Sunday."

David didn't reply to this, remembering his mother's strict instructions. His father was not to be upset, or drawn into any of their frequent heated debates. It was hard to do, because they both rose to an argument. The pros and cons of sabbatarianism would have to wait. Vincent staggered slightly on the steps up from the lawn. David steadied him.

"Come on. Inside. Or would you like a chair outside for a bit? I can get one from the conservatory."

"Don't pamper me! I'm fine. I'm going to the study. I need to look at some reports the office sent over. I'll be back at work soon, and I need to be up to speed with what's been happening."

Manna sat in the doorway and scratched an ear enthusiastically. Cream hairs floated past the weeping cherry, carried on the warm air. David eased the dog out of the way and Vincent disappeared into the house.

David went to the back corner of the garden and stretched out on the bench seat, dropping a hand to fondle Manna's ears as the dog flopped beside him with a sigh.

When Robyn had stirred and eased away from his arm, she had smiled up at him briefly, stretched and stood up. She had been quiet in the car, preoccupied, saying only a brief goodbye when he left her at the door of her flat. When he went to bed, he found one of her hairs on his shirt.

David knew that Robyn attracted attention. He was also sure

that she could handle most come-ons. It must have happened to her before. But Fraser bothered him. David didn't care that Fraser had seen them together at Groomsport. Not for himself anyway, although Tim's warning had given him pause for thought, until he reasoned, rightly or wrongly, that anyone could do what they liked in the summer holidays. And anyway, she was only subbing for a few months. She was almost still a student herself.

But Fraser must have followed them. In his car. And had he just happened to be in the school at the same time as Robyn, or had he followed her there too? He swung himself upright and hooked his phone from his pocket. He started to tap out a message, but cancelled it. He chewed the corner of the phone in thought. He got up and walked round the seat, absently tossing and catching the phone in one hand. He sat down again. He started another message. Cancelled it.

What was wrong with him? Something had changed inside himself, making him hypersensitive, nervous of doing the wrong thing. Impatient with himself, he jabbed through to her number and called it. She answered quickly.

"Hi," he said.

"Hi," she said.

"Are you all right?"

"Fine. Why?"

"Just checking."

"You OK?" she asked.

"Of course. What would be wrong with me?"

She gave a slight laugh. "Oh, I don't know. Choked on a dictionary or something."

He smiled at the hedge, not knowing what to say.

"Are you at home?" she asked.

"Yes. Why?"

"Just wondering."

He bent to pick up a stray twig and swung it in one hand.

Neither of them said anything for a moment. Then he said: "Fancy a chat some time? If you're still not afraid of me, that is."

He had said this lightly, but she replied: "I think you should be more afraid of me."

"Sounds like a competition. Let's form a Frightened Society, with an annual prize for the most frightened person of the year."

She sighed, an amused sigh. "You're a nutcase."

He gripped the phone tighter. "I want to see you."

There was total silence for so long that he began to think the connection had been cut. Then she said, very low: "Yes."

"Tomorrow afternoon?"

"OK."

"Walk or drive?"

"Drive."

"I'll be there about two?"

"Fine."

"And Robyn?"

"What?"

"Shalom."

He heard the smile as she replied. "Shalom."

The little green hatchback approached slowly. Robyn wondered how David fitted into it. It wasn't new, but somehow it had character. Or maybe that was to do with the driver. Why was he going so slowly? She went to the edge of the footpath. He was studying all the cars on each side of the street as he drove along. Several cars crawled impatiently behind him, but he ignored them.

He double parked and reached over to open the door.

"What's wrong?" she asked. "The drivers behind you are not amused."

"And they'll stay that way till we're out of this street."

He crawled the rest of the way, looking from right to left.

Once onto the main road he relaxed and smiled across.

"Just looking for someone."

"Who?"

"Doesn't matter."

She dropped it.

The weather was uncertain, breaks in the clouds alternating with the threat of rain. But a burst of sunshine illuminated the view from the great sandstone tower of Scrabo on the hill above the town of Newtownards, to the south of Belfast. Half way up the rough track from the car park, a bench nestled in the scrub of the hillside.

"Want a rest?" he asked.

"Don't be cheeky!"

At the top, they caught their breath and walked round to the side overlooking the town and across to the airfield. A microlight was making a careful approach to the runway, dropping over the edge of the town. Beyond, to the south, little islands punctuated the waters of Strangford Lough in dots and commas.

Robyn dropped her coat onto the grass and sat on it, mesmerised by the view. She pulled her knees up to her chin and felt David hunker beside her.

She spread her hands wide. "Freedom!"

"You sound like an escaped convict."

She smiled crookedly. "I feel like one. Escaped just before being hanged at dawn."

They looked out at the town spread like a map below, silent and content. Then he said: "Robyn?"

"What?"

"Fraser. In your storeroom. As I was walking up the corridor I think I heard him say 'I've recovered', or something like that. What did he mean?"

She buried her face in her knees and then looked sideways

at him, a grin forming. "Well, I had to… be forceful when he stopped being a gentleman."

He tilted his head and raised an eyebrow enquiringly. "How forceful?"

"I kneed him in the balls. Hard."

It started as a small chuckle in his stomach. Then it rose, bubbled, grew until he was throwing back his head and roaring with laughter at the sky. He overbalanced and fell from his heels. Flat on his back on the grass, his whole body convulsed.

When he could speak, he said: "Brilliant. Priceless. I wish I could have seen that. Just don't do that to me."

She looked at him lying beside her, his face full of humour, his crisp black hair tufting through the grass, hands spread wide behind his head. She said: "I'd never have to."

He twisted his head to look at her. "You'd never want to, I hope."

She shook her head and reached over to pull a piece of grass from his hair. "No, never."

She told him she wanted to learn to drive. He found a large shopping centre car park and got out. He came round to the passenger side.

"Shift over. You drive round the car park."

"Don't be daft!"

"No time like the present. I'll show you where the brake is and it's a doddle from there."

She shuffled over to the driver's seat. "But there are cars around. The shops are open."

He settled beside her and tapped the steering wheel. "That's what that's for. Don't worry. You'll miss most of them."

She adjusted the seat, moved the mirror and gripped the wheel. The next half hour involved kangaroo petrol, stalling, a fierce argument, grinding gears, and one near miss – the cause of another argument.

Eventually she rolled into a parking place near where they had started. He opened his door and looked down.

"Hey, you're between the white lines! Imagine that."

She thumped the steering wheel, her eyes alive with achievement. "I think I could do this."

They swopped seats. "I think you could too," he said, easing the seat back. "But next time I'll bring the travel sick tablets."

Inside Down Cathedral in Downpatrick, they walked slowly through the entrance under the tower, past the tourist shop and through the great wooden screen into the choir. There were a few other visitors, the echoing nave magnifying each quiet conversation. David opened a door to one of the dark pews at the back and they sat together in the quietness, looking towards the sanctuary and up at the great east window.

After a moment she glanced round. He had his eyes closed. She stayed quiet until he said, "I love places like this."

"So do I. That notice on the door on the way in – did you see it? It hoped visitors would find a sense of eternity in time."

He took a deep slow breath and looked high up to the branching ribs of the vaulted ceiling. "Eternity in time. People have been worshipping on this site for hundreds of years. Eternity meets time. And creates places like this."

They were silent again.

"David?" she whispered.

"What?"

"Are all your family Christians?"

"Most of them."

"It must be great to be so certain of things."

"Some things. But…" He stopped.

"But what?"

"I think there are more things I'm not certain about."

She thought for a minute. "But the bit you are certain about is the bit that matters."

"Exactly."

She leaned forward and put her chin on the back of the pew in front. "Some religious people are hypocritical bastards."

"I know." She looked round, surprised. She had expected him to be defensive. He asked: "Where did you meet yours?"

"I'm related to a few."

"So being a bastard is in the genes then?"

"Doesn't it show?"

"Only when you're cross."

While they had been in the cathedral, the sky had darkened and a thunder storm had broken. They waited in the porch of the tower. The light had shaded to steel. The storm passed directly overhead. Lightening ripped across the sky, followed by great rumbling crashes of thunder.

"There goes the wardrobe," said Robyn.

"Come again?"

"It's what my mother used to tell me when I was frightened during a storm. It's just furniture tumbling down the stairs."

He was looking at an illuminated display board on the wall, reading the history of the Cathedral Hill. He must have sensed something in her voice for he turned. There was another massive rumble and a crash that reverberated through the building. She was standing near the wooden door, looking out, and couldn't help a little jump of fright. He was beside her in two strides, his arms going round her gently, one hand stroking her hair, his chin resting on her head.

"It's OK," he murmured. "It'll be over soon."

When the last spatters splashed on the flooded car park and a beam of sunshine broke through the trees over the grave of St Patrick, he pulled his head back to look down at her face.

She knew he would see the tears pooling in her eyes. His hand cupped the side of her head and she felt his thumb move lightly across her cheekbone.

"Hey, look at that." he whispered. "The ice is melting."

"Your mobile hasn't rung once this afternoon," she remarked.

It began to ring.

"You had to say that, didn't you?" he said, reaching for it. He checked the caller and a look of annoyance crossed his face. He swung away across the car park.

Robyn leaned her folded arms on the roof of the car and watched the steam rising from the tarmac and from the trees and grass and buttercups. In the strong heat after the thunder, the roof of the car was already dry. The day was blanketed in fragrance: wet earth, warm damp leaves, the scent of meadowsweet. All of this was mixed with a chorus of birdsong and the hum of insects. It was early evening and all the other visitors had gone, leaving the Cathedral Hill quiet and serene.

She heard David's voice and looked round. He was over by the cathedral wall, pacing in uneven circles, phone to his ear and gesturing angrily. She heard the word 'no' repeated with emphasis. She looked away. When she glanced again, he was phoning someone else. He caught her eye and winked, turning away again when his call was answered.

She had gone along the path to the great granite boulder marking the grave of St Patrick when he came to find her.

"Everything all right? Not your Dad?" she asked.

"Everything's fine." He walked away a few paces and came back. "Do you have to be back for anything?"

"No."

"Are you hungry?"

She put her head on one side and considered. "Yes, I suppose I am."

"Let's eat."

"But look at the time. Don't you have commitments on a Sunday night?"

"Usually. But someone else can take over for once. In fact, I've just checked out for the evening."

Sitting on a bench seat with tubs of chicken wings and chips, David pulled out a small guidebook that he had bought in the cathedral shop.

"Did you ever hear the word 'narthex'?"

She licked sauce off her fingers. "Don't think so."

"Apparently we were in one today."

Robyn bit a piece of chicken. Flicking her hair over her shoulder she half-turned to study him as he read and chewed. His Adam's apple bobbed with each swallow; his lashes moved slightly as his eyes scanned the page. Suddenly, his mouth full of chicken, he turned his head to catch her watching him. His voice muffled, he said "What?"

She bit a chip and felt a smile growing, spreading, a recklessly happy grin.

"I was just thinking of my last meal out."

He swallowed. "I hope this day won't end like that one."

Suddenly serious, she said, "This day has been ten times better than that one. And this meal is a banquet."

He closed the booklet and sat back. She felt his arm slip round her shoulders, his hand come gently round to her cheek. His fingers burrowed through her hair and traced the edge of her ear. That was all. Yet a sudden sensation arrowed through her, sliced down like the lightening had sliced from the sky. It settled somewhere deep within her. And slowly faded. She had never felt anything like it before.

Shaken, she looked up at him quickly, her head resting on his shoulder. He wasn't smiling. He was gazing at her with great concentration, his brown eyes become almost black. The panic began to gather, to rise to her throat. She saw a great shadow come at her, making her want to scream, to beat it away. Her hands became fists and she twisted to push David's chest as hard as she could. Instantly, he moved away. Her breathing was coming in gasps.

"Robyn, what is it?"

She was fighting it, forcing it down. She put her hands over her face, control returning slowly. "It's not you."

Her eyes wide, she stretched out and, just as he had done to her in the cathedral, put her hand to his face. It felt slightly rough to her palm. He stayed motionless as her fingers touched the short black curls at the nape of his neck. She traced the side of his nose; on down past the corner of his mouth.

Her voice was a whisper. "This has to stop, David. For all sorts of reasons this has to stop."

It was summer-dark when he pulled up at her door. She said all the right things and left the car quickly. She turned to the steps, her key already in her hand. To her surprise, he arrived beside her.

His voice strained he said: "I just want to make sure you get in safely."

"I'm fine. Look." She pointed. "Door. Key. Me."

It lightened things a bit. He watched until the door slammed and she was gone. Then he turned on his heel and, ignoring his car, walked rapidly back up the street. In a shadowy doorway, a figure lounged against the wall, the street lamp shining on the tips of his shoes.

David took the steps in one leap and stopped a few inches from him. Angus shifted himself upright.

"Ah! It's Holy Joe. I thought she might be with you." His lip curled. "Have you been showing her heaven then?"

Angus wasn't short, but he was slight compared to the youthful power bunched in David's tense frame. David raised a hand, finger a centimetre from Fraser's nose. His deep eyes pinned him to the wall. His voice was low, threatening.

"If you touch so much as a hair on her head, I'll show you what hell's like, Fraser."

"Threatening me, are you?"

"Crawl back under your rock." He raised his voice. "Now!"

Angus moved slowly round him, and went down the steps. He walked backwards for a few paces, keeping David in sight, and then went towards his car, further up the street.

"Oh, Fraser," David called. Fraser turned warily in the lamplight. "How are your balls today?"

When Fraser's car turned out of the street, David went back to his own and settled down to wait. After a moment, he phoned home. His mother answered.

"Mum. I'll be home soon. So stop worrying."

She hadn't said she was, but she didn't have to. After keeping watch for half an hour, David eased the car out from the footpath.

It was going to be a sleepless night.

20

A T ONE O'CLOCK in the morning David pushed the quilt back and slid out of bed to sit at his desk looking out at the moonlit garden. The flowers and leaves were garnished with silver, a faint breeze stirring the lilac and the tall fronds of the pampas grass. There was a movement at the hedge next the road. A fox emerged and snuffled silently along the flower bed, stopping now and then to capture a titbit, to push under leaves, to lift her head to listen intently, her paw frozen in mid-air. She trotted to the pampas grass, her luxurious brush slicked with moonlight.

David watched, fascinated. She circled the clump of pampas and then stopped again. She looked to left and right, then her head turned and she looked straight up at David's window. He felt her meet his eyes. For a long moment they looked at each other. Then the fox dropped her head and disappeared the way she had come, like a beautiful ghost.

Tiredness, concern and the night were doing funny things to his brain. He leaned on his elbows and put his hands over his face. He tried to pray but no words would come. It didn't worry him. He let his feelings speak instead, letting them swirl from him in an inarticulate tide.

When he opened his eyes again, he knew he was not going to let this person go. He didn't understand what was wrong with her. He just knew all that was right with her.

The pictures almost completely covered two walls. Angus lay on his bed and pondered the framed print of a rustic bridge and apple trees on the third wall. Who had given him that rubbish? It would go in the bin and leave the entire expanse beside the window free for the next pictures.

He held up the latest photograph he had printed. It was one he had taken at Groomsport, just before David had seen him. Shaw's arm was around Robyn, his expression calm but otherwise unreadable as she leaned against him, her feet tucked under her and her eyes closed. Around them, the sights of the seaside in summer had been frozen in the moment.

If she spoke to the headmaster about what had happened, it was her word against his. And this photograph could be very useful. He smiled. He wasn't going to go near her for a while. Just let her relax. He would be the soul of civility.

On Thursday, Robyn saw a notice in the window of a charity shop. She walked in and volunteered to work two mornings a week till the third week in August to help out when the regular volunteers took their holidays.

On Thursday night David phoned.

She talked to him briefly, pleasantly, telling him about the shop. He sounded pleased. After a minute or two, he went quiet. Then: "Robyn, what's changed? I know something happened, but I don't know what. Tell me."

"How's your Dad keeping."

"He's going for a check-up tomorrow. Don't change the subject."

"I really must go. I hope your Dad gets a good report tomorrow."

She hung up. Sitting on the edge of her couch, she waited. It was stupid, but she waited. And yet, knowing him so well, she knew he wouldn't ring back. That night, she started sleeping in a tight ball again.

In the next fortnight, she saw him only once. On the way back from the shop one lunchtime, she bought a sandwich and took it into the park. Walking to her favourite spot in front of the Palm House, she stopped suddenly. On the bench where she had once sat with him, he was with a girl. It was Penny Woodford. Her knees showed through slashed jeans and the roots of her purple hair were showing. David was frowning; Penny was chewing vigorously and seemed to be arguing with him.

Robyn took a different path, away from them. But although she hadn't noticed Manna, Manna had seen her. After a few steps, his body brushed her leg as he misjudged the final bound he made to reach her. A rush of affection came over her when she recognised him. Out of sight of his master, she dropped onto the grass and let him bounce joyfully round her. She squeezed his cheeks into creases; rubbed his ears. When he rolled over, she scratched his creamy tummy until his panting tongue lolled out the side of his mouth and touched the grass. Even upside down, his body wagged from the waist down.

He ate one cheese and tomato sandwich, and she ate the other. She pulled it into pieces for him and then had to help him locate the bits. She expected him to go back to find David again, but he stayed beside her. She finished her own sandwich and then reached sideways to circle the warm barrel of his body with her arms. She put her cheek to his plump side and held him tightly. He gave a slight whimper.

David was looking down at them, his feet planted solidly apart, his fingers pushed into the pockets of his jeans. He was alone. Robyn looked up the length of him and thought that, even in denims, he looked like he came from the Malone Road.

"At least you're still speaking to my dog," he said.

She stood up, rubbing grass and hairs off her hands. "Well, you can't hang up on a dog, I suppose."

It was a poor response and she knew it. He'd had his hair cut.

"I'm leaving for Florida next week." He didn't change his stance. Just stood solidly in front of her. "I would really like to see you properly before I go." He looked away. Back again. "In fact, I need to."

His cheekbones had got the sun. "You don't mean that..." she began.

"Don't tell me what I mean!" he flashed, making her blink in surprise. "You said I was a friend. Do you treat all your friends like this? Is this how you treated that other guy, the one who made you so angry you nearly hit *me*?"

"I don't have many friends..." As soon as it was out she regretted it.

"Why doesn't that surprise me?" The scorn in his voice was unexpected, cutting. He clicked his fingers and Manna trotted to him.

Temper etched across his face. She scuffed the grass with her foot and then looked up. "What day do you leave?"

"Early Saturday."

She took a deep breath. "Friday then maybe? I'm in the shop in the morning."

"Right, I'll call there at one," he said and walked away.

She gathered up her sandwich wrapper carefully, her fingers feeling weak as she crushed the paper.

Not knowing what to expect when she first volunteered, she found herself enjoying the work. It was so different from school. The other volunteers accepted her without question, and she had begun to look forward to the variety of people who entered the shop, and to discovering the variety of reasons for them being there.

At one o'clock exactly, the bell on the door chimed and David walked in. The other volunteer on duty nudged Robyn.

"Hey," she said under her breath, "toss you for that."

Robyn arched her eyebrows. "Sorry. He's booked for today."

She was still enjoying the memory as David set their tray

down on a table in a café at the side of the City Hall. He sat opposite her. She opened her salad roll.

"Not risking mustard today, I see," he said.

"No way. Loads of mayo, though."

"You like mayo?"

"As much as I hate mustard."

A corner of his mouth twitched. "That's a 'yes' then."

She watched his fingers as they curled round the wrapper on his own roll and tugged it apart. He lifted the teaspoon and stirred his cappuccino slightly. She watched him lick the spoon and set it in the saucer again. His left hand rested on the table between them.

Robyn felt as if time had slowed down and she was in a film being played at half speed. The fine hairs on the back of his hand were pale, but darkened and lengthened towards his wrist. His fingers were long and fine. His middle finger was quite a bit longer than the others. His thumb was slightly turned under his hand as it rested on the table. At its base there was the faint mark of an old cut. The tips of his fingers were oval, the nails cut short. Her eyes moved on to examine his wrist where the hairs became darkest just as his skin disappeared into his cuff, the silver edges of the links on his watch strap just visible. His hand moved slightly, just a little shift as he lifted his cup with the other hand.

Without warning, she felt the arrow hit her again as it had the day they visited the cathedral, a sharp stab that quivered, settled deep inside. She looked down quickly, not knowing what it was. He was looking at her as he set down his cup, saying nothing. A slight cream of froth fringed his upper lip. His tongue darted out to flick it away.

"So," she said suddenly, "I'm sure you're looking forward to America. Not long now."

"Do you have a chain on the door of your flat? I mean the door onto the landing of the house."

"What?"

He repeated patiently: "Do you have a security chain on the door of your flat?"

"I don't."

"I think you should. Is the door wooden?"

"Yes."

"Would you let me fit one?"

"What for? The door to the street is locked at night…"

"But not during the day. When the dentist's is open. Right?"

"Well, no."

"I want to fit a chain on your door."

There was a stubbornness in his voice.

"A chain," she said, collecting her scattering thoughts. "A chain on my door. But I've no tools, no screwdriver, or whatever you'd need."

"My car is parked in your street and I've a toolbox in the boot."

"You think of everything, don't you?"

It was almost like before. She held the screws, rummaged in the toolbox when he wanted a cross-head screwdriver, put her fingers in her ears when he used the drill. Scolded mildly when he swore as the head of a screw began to shear as he turned it. Got out the dustpan and brush to sweep up the sawdust.

Finally it was done. He went onto the landing and Robyn closed the door. She put the chain in place and opened it again. David rammed his shoulder into the door and looked satisfied as the chain held easily. She let him in again. He reached into his pocket and brought out a small object.

"That's for you too."

She examined it. It said 'Triple action personal alarm' on the side.

"Put that in your bag now, and promise me you'll not go out without it."

"David, what's all this…"

"Just promise me."

"OK. How does it work?" She fiddled with it.

"Don't!" he said quickly. "If it goes off, we'll both be deafened and I'll be arrested! Here, there are instructions with it." He fished them out and gave them to her.

He filled her little hallway. She dropped the alarm into her bag, then folded her arms tightly round herself as he walked into her tiny sitting room. He stood beside the chair, the chair where she had been sitting in the deep night when she had heard his voice say "Shalom" so loud and clear. The night of the Hooley. The night he had saved her life.

"I think," she said, "you're the only other person to come in here in almost five years."

He nodded slowly. "This is your hiding place, isn't it? This is your burrow." He sat in the chair. "This reminds me of a song about hiding in your room where no-one can touch you. You're like a cold rock.' "

"Stone doesn't feel pain." Her voice was low, almost a whisper.

She sat on the couch and he leaned forward, took her right arm. Turning it over, he pushed back her sleeve and traced the faint scar. "It's to do with this, isn't it?" She watched his fingers move slowly over her skin. "Something happened to you." He watched her carefully. "Something that was so bad, it's still with you. Still crippling you." He waited but she said nothing. "Tell me," he urged softly. "Robyn. Tell me."

She pulled her arm away. "I can't! I've told you I can't."

"Why can't you? Why is there something you can't tell me?"

She raised her voice in desperation. "Because you would hate me!" Her voice tailed off. "And I couldn't bear that."

Momentarily, he looked stunned. "Hate you? Robyn, there's nothing you could have done that would make me hate you." He tilted his head thoughtfully. "Could you hate me?"

"No."

"I might remind you of that some day."

Unusually, she found herself searching for words to express herself. "I let people down. I mustn't hurt you too." She sounded pathetic, even to her own ears. She tried being defiant. "I don't need anyone. I mustn't need anyone. Specially not you."

He flung his hands wide in anger. "To hell with that! Don't be so ordinary."

"David, you can't just dismiss who we are." She put her hands out, pleading. "It just isn't on. The summer holidays are not the real world."

"In all my life," he said slowly, deliberately, "I have never felt anything so real."

Panic began to nibble at her heels. She pulled her legs up onto the couch and wrapped her arms round herself again. She couldn't cope with this; didn't know how to cope with it.

"I think you should go now," she said, her voice tight, strained. "You must have a lot to do for tomorrow."

He slid from the chair and sat on his heels in front of her, hands clasped loosely between his knees.

"Most things are done. I've just to stuff a few things in a rucksack." He looked down. Thinking mode, she thought automatically, despite herself. After a minute he looked up. "You could survive without me. I could even survive without you." His mouth crooked at the corner. "We're survivors after all. But I want to do more than survive. This is a good world, Robyn. Whatever happened to you, whatever happened to me, those were aberrations, things we have to deal with, maybe for a long time. But they certainly don't make us who we are, or who we can be. Or who we're meant to be." His hand came up and she felt his fingers brush her cheek. "No comment?"

"No comment," she said, her voice shaky.

"One more thing before you throw me out." His voice

became soft, almost a caress. "You are a lovely, lovely person. What you were told and what you feel about the day you were born is so wrong. No matter what awful thing happened that day years before, someone very beautiful was born on that date." He moved her chin gently so that she was looking at him. "You were the good news; you were not part of the bad news." He stood up and went towards the door, opened it. He looked back. "Take care."

Then he was gone, his steps echoing on the stairs.

She knew. Suddenly she knew. She moved her arms lower, to circle her abdomen. This is what it feels like. Longing, yearning, wanting. And this is what it feels like to hear him walk away. Cold, lonely, bereft; and yet still longing, yearning, wanting.

His complete, absolute, unwavering faith in her; his obdurate refusal to become like any other person she had ever known; his instinctive understanding that the past cannot be neutered just because we want it to be; it made her breathless, dizzy.

She closed her eyes and pictured him again, every line and muscle of him.

21

THE DAYS OF August spun past and the summer holidays accelerated. Robyn's thoughts were never at rest. Yet it was not the restlessness of dissatisfaction. Far from it. She felt like a new butterfly trembling on its discarded chrysalis: wings still damp, sun still strange, danger lurking, but ready to try now, ready to fight. Both her body and her mind had been touched, and there was a healing of the heart in it. She could feel it.

She realised that Angus had done her a favour. Because she knew what she definitely, emphatically, did not want, it freed her to contemplate what she did want.

Looking back, she could see that in fact she had managed to slip away as she lay on the floor of her parents' bathroom, her blood soaking the floor while desperately she tried to die. Although she had not died, she had not really lived again either. She had become an observer of her own life, the audience of her own play.

She recalled the day she had confronted her mother and said what she had never before given shape and form. Now she could control her own life and say that no-one would ever again have power over her, make her hurt, make her despise herself.

One night as she got ready for bed, she stretched her arms high over her head, watching her waist lengthen, her breasts swell, her stomach flatten across her pelvis.

"I am a lovely person," she said deliberately, defiantly. "I am. Someone has told me so."

Even so, she wedged the chair under the door handle before she went to bed.

Robyn booked two driving lessons a week. She had a good instructor, a man in his thirties who encouraged her and told her she was a quick learner. They moved into the easy and humorous relationship of instructor and learner. She checked her savings. Enough for a car. A small one, a second-hand one.

Her fourth lesson passed without her stalling the car once. She made herself a toasted sandwich and grinned at a memory. Travel sick pills indeed!

She was walking home past the University one afternoon when she became aware of a dog panting insistently at her side, the panting punctuated by a whine. It was Manna.

"Hello you!" she said, delighted to see him. Manna was ecstatic, leaping around her, wagging his tail, his ears bouncing as he tugged on his lead. Robyn looked up quickly. A distinguished man with a thatch of thick grey hair was holding the lead, a look of puzzlement on his face. Instantly, Robyn knew who he was. He had given his son his fine features, his strong jaw and his deep set eyes. When he spoke, Robyn recognised even the tone and timbre of his voice. But his son had grown past him by six inches at least and had nothing of his frailty. This man was pale, his cheeks slightly hollow, and the slight stoop of his shoulders was all his own.

"My dog seems to know you?" he remarked, a slight smile underlining the gentle question.

"Mr Shaw?" she asked, her hand on Manna's head.

"Yes. But I'm afraid, unlike my dog, I don't know you, young lady."

"Robyn Daniels. I've been subbing at David's school."

"Ah! I believe I have heard your name mentioned. I'm pleased to meet you. But you look like a student yourself." He transferred the lead to his left hand and held out his right to shake hers. He looked down at Manna who was now sitting on Robyn's foot, tongue lolling happily. "But how does Manna know you?"

"David walks him in the park often. I have my lunch there sometimes. I suppose Manna might remember me from there."

Vincent nodded. "Ah, yes. Manna might have only one eye, but he has the memory of an elephant. The poor dog is missing David. He's in America, you know."

"I think David did mention that." She fondled the silky ears. "Have you heard from him?"

"Once." Vincent sighed. "He's a very independent young man."

"You must be proud of him, Mr Shaw."

"Yes, well. This year will be the test. The big one. He wants to go here." He nodded across the road to the red brick Victorian façade of Queen's University. "Personally, I'd rather he got out of this country. No future here."

His voice caught and he bent to a paroxysm of coughing.

"Mr Shaw? Are you all right?"

Vincent blew his nose. "Yes, yes, yes. Of course I am."

Robyn noted the impatient tone. She recognised that too. "How are you getting home?"

"Manna and I travel by bus or taxi these days," he said with dignity. "I had a bit of bad health and my wife won't let me walk far just yet. She's a doctor, so I suppose I have to do what I'm told." He held out his hand again and said with old fashioned courtesy: "It has been a pleasure to meet you. May I wish you well in the new term."

She shook his hand. "If you're in touch with David, give him my regards."

"I will, my dear, I will." He turned away, tugging the lead. Manna whined and looked back, his head turning to find her with his good eye.

When she reached her flat, Robyn checked her letterbox. Empty.

The state exam results were issued and many of the teaching staff appeared in school along with the anxious pupils. Robyn sat at her desk in her classroom pouring over a print-out, highlighting her own pupils. Most of them had done well, some very well. One or two were going to be disappointed. Robyn hoped to have good results to show for her short time here.

There was a knock on her door. Absently, she called, "Come in." She heard a rustle of paper. It was Angus, holding an enormous bunch of flowers. She stiffened.

"Don't worry," he said quickly. "I'm going to stop just inside the door. Honestly."

"What do you want?"

"This is a peace offering." He nursed the flowers over one arm, looking at her pleadingly. "I just want to say I've been a complete prat. I want to apologise again. I should have known I was way out of line." He reached in and set the flowers on a desk. "I don't want us to start the new term with aggro between us. Who knows? Maybe we'll have to work together."

Robyn looked at him sideways, her pen still poised over her notes. "Unlikely, I hope."

Angus held up both hands and backed out the door. "I won't bother you again. No need to say anything to the Head. You can trust me. Promise." He smiled and left.

Robyn retrieved the flowers. She stood poised over the wastebin for a moment. It was an expensive bunch, complete with bow and sachet of cut flower food. She turned and walked quickly down the corridor, down the main staircase and into the school office. It was bustling with life, dealing with the exam results, clamouring phone calls, parents and pupils. The Headmaster's secretary was loading paper into the printer.

"Here, Helen," said Robyn, "This is your lucky day."

She dropped the flowers on a table and walked out again.

When she got back to her classroom a cluster of pupils was

forming at her door. The phone was ringing in her storeroom. She answered it impatiently.

"Hallo, Rob," said Neil.

"Neil, I'm busy."

"When are you coming down to see your mother?"

"When hell freezes," she said and hung up.

Suddenly, life was very busy again. She gave up the charity shop with regret, promising to help again when she could. A few days later the teachers were all in school for a staff meeting, departmental meetings and planning. The Headmaster, after years of practice, made his speech without flinching at the regular pop of Billy Dobbin's bubble gum.

On Friday afternoon, Robyn was making her final preparations for the first week. She was returning from the office with a bundle of papers. At the top of the stairs she turned. And stopped, her breath catching at the sight of him.

He was leaning one shoulder against the door frame. His arms were folded and one leg was crooked over the other at the ankle. He couldn't really be taller? Browner? Broader at the shoulder? Not after only four weeks. And one hour. But the dusting of beard was definitely new. Slowly she walked towards him. He didn't move, just watched her from under his brows in that unsettling way he had.

When she reached him, she looked up into the hollow of his throat, brown against the open collar of his shirt. His lightly bearded face was a mixture of the familiar and the strange. Finally she met his eyes and anger ignited like a fire cracker, an anger that she hadn't known was there.

"Why didn't you even send me a *postcard?*"

He straightened and set a forearm on each of her shoulders, clasping his hands behind her neck.

"Hi," he said, low and soft. "I've missed you too."

22

S HE BROUGHT UP her free hand and pushed his arms away, turned and walked quickly into the room.

He followed her and strolled to the back of the classroom. He turned a chair round and sat astride it, arms across the back. Robyn set her papers down and sat at the desk. There was silence for a moment and then he said:

"I didn't send you a postcard because I would have had to write your name on it. I wanted to forget about you for a while."

"Really? And did you succeed?"

"No."

Robyn lifted a pen and began making notes, notes which made no sense but helped her feel occupied, made her feel as if she was busy despite this interruption. When she said nothing, he spoke again.

"And I wanted you to forget about me." He waited. "Did you?"

"I've been very busy, David. Really."

A corner of his mouth twitched. "Can I take that as a 'no'?"

"Didn't you find some nice, *suitable* American girl?"

"Loads of them. Security had to fight them off at the airport."

She caught his eye and had to smile. As his grin spread slowly, white teeth accentuated by his short dark beard, she could almost believe him.

"You'll have to shave that off before Monday," she said. "It's quite impressive."

He rubbed his chin. "Not bad, is it? I'm quite impressed myself."

"I met your father one day."

"He told me."

She pulled some papers out of a drawer and selected one. "I got the class lists for this year today. I am to take your year group for one period a week till my subbing finishes. But your name isn't on the list. Why not?"

The length of the classroom was still between them, desks and chairs neatly arranged. She saw his brows draw down, his expression darken. He stood suddenly, sending the chair crashing into the desk in front.

"What a stupid question! Did you really think I was going to sit at one of these desks for midgets, have you talk at me, walk past me?" He walked up the room towards her. "Did you really think you were going to do all that?"

She flung her pen down and stood up herself, angrily facing him. "And why wouldn't I? It's who I am and that's who you are. Don't forget it!"

"Just because you're an emotional cripple, Robyn, it doesn't make me one!" She gasped, his tone rougher than she imagined he could ever be. Suddenly his voice lowered, and his eyes locked onto hers. "And," he said, "if I forgot who I was, and who you were" – he raised a finger for emphasis – "I wasn't the only one."

She tossed her hair over her shoulder. "Well, maybe it's time we remembered." She gave a brittle laugh. "I'm used to dealing with young men with crushes after all."

His arm shot out and gripped her shoulder. He brought his face to within an inch of hers so that she could see the golden flecks in his eyes. "Don't," he breathed, giving her shoulder a little shake, "don't insult both of us."

For a moment they stood inches apart, Robyn feeling her own anger tempered by something she could not name. Then he spun away from her. In the doorway he stopped and turned, his face hostile.

"Thanks for the welcome home party."

Then he walked out.

Robyn went to the back of the classroom and carefully straightened the chair he had disturbed. She edged the desks back into perfect alignment. She smoothed a poster on the wall and repositioned a drawing pin in its corner. On her way back to her desk, she picked up a tissue she must have dropped earlier. She reached the front and carefully dropped the tissue in the bin. She noticed a window still open. She reached for the window pole. She lifted it. Her grip on it tightened. Her fingers became white. She jabbed it forwards so hard the glass shattered, a starburst of spidering lines shooting from one edge to the other.

She couldn't sleep. She lay on her back and looked at the dark ceiling, the quilt heavy on her, the room warm despite the approach of autumn. He had called her an emotional cripple. Despite the wonderful freedom of the summer, despite all her efforts, the ability to spoil anything good that happened to her was still a talent that she could not shake. She put a hand over her face in the dark. That boulder of hatred was still there, that vat of boiling anger, which spilled and burnt her and anybody who got close to her. Most people never came back to be incinerated twice. Most people.

Her mobile rang. Startled, she checked the time. Two o'clock in the morning. The name flashing on the phone was 'David'. Long ago she had changed his brief 'DS' to his first name. She pulled the phone onto the pillow and nestled it to her ear.

"Hi," she said.

His voice was tired, flat. "Robyn. I'm sorry."

"It's OK. I'm sorry too," she said into the dark.

"You've no reason to be sorry."

"Yes, I have. I broke a window after you left."

"You what?"

"I reported it as an unfortunate accident. Hopefully it'll be fixed by Monday."

"And was it an accident?"

"No."

He went quiet. She lay without speaking, just keeping the phone lying at her ear, content to wait out his thinking time. Then his voice again. "Robyn?"

"Yes?"

"Do you have any idea how alike we are?"

She rolled onto her side. "No, David, you were right earlier. I'm an emotional cripple. You're not. That's how different we are."

"When you and I were first getting to know each other... " She heard his smile as he stopped and said "Remember?"

"I do. You should have told me to get lost."

"When you and I were first getting to know each other," he repeated, "I told you that I had made choices and that you could too."

"You told me Catherine Earnshaw had made the wrong choice."

"So I did." After a moment he went on slowly: "I want you to say to me that you are making the choice, of your own free will, to stay crippled, to stay afraid, to retreat to your burrow, even – especially – when you can see light ahead."

She didn't answer immediately and he waited out her thinking. Finally she said: "I don't have the choice. It's too difficult. I can't face it."

He said almost desperately: "But you have been facing it! I have seen you. Don't give up now. I'm with you, Robyn, all the way."

"But David," she said sadly, "don't you see? You're the problem."

Another silence. Then he said: "I know what I see. I see that you and I meeting was always going to be dangerous."

She didn't answer that. A minute later he said softly: "Robyn?"

"Yes?"

"I wish you were here beside me now."

Her knees pulled up to her stomach in a reflex act of protection. She buried her face in the pillow and fought against the longing in his voice, a longing that leapt away from the safe bounds of friendship and into a land she never wanted to revisit. She felt as if she were being torn in two. He had woken something in her that terrified her. It was a feeling that was so good and so bad all at once. His voice was loaded with all that had caused her pain, all that had humiliated her, all that she felt she could never bear to hear again. Her mind was damaged. But her body had begun to tell her that it was not. It was a contradiction she did not know how to deal with.

She turned her head back, put the phone to her ear again; tried to speak lightly. "Be serious! David Shaw could have had half the women in Florida."

His reply was quick: "Maybe I could. But I came back across the Atlantic to the one woman who won't have me."

Silence. Then she said quietly: "Goodnight, David." And ended the call.

She set the phone on the bedside table and curled into a ball beneath the quilt. The phone bleeped. She reached for it again and read the message.

David had sent one word: "Shalom."

Apart from his first year, when he had been terrified, Tim had always loved the first few days of a new school year. The community exploded into life: before the serious work began experiences were shared, friendships renewed, jokes swapped, gossip traded. Along the walls of the main corridor, pupils shoaled in vibrant groups, laughing, fooling around, poring over timetables and spotting clashes before the teachers did. Screens showed off photographs of the places they had been over the summer.

Tim leaned against a radiator, happy to watch and to look out for Chloe. He looked up and down the corridor and spotted her with some other girls from her form class. She was looking cross and they were looking suitably sympathetic. Hypocrites! thought Tim wryly. The word's out that David is available again.

There was no sign of him, although he thought he had spotted a small green car at the far end of the car park. David's reply had been odd when Tim had said casually to him at the weekend, "Back to the grindstone on Monday. See you there, man."

"Yeah." David had replied. "Possibly."

Tim chewed his lip thoughtfully. Much as he liked David, he regarded him as headstrong, self-willed and, like all those cursed with charisma, used to getting his own way. He had a strong suspicion about the real reason for David's ambivalence about the new term. The guy hadn't taken his advice of earlier in the summer. If he was infatuated with Robyn Daniels, then Tim knew he would go up in flames before he would give up. The idiot might have let things get worse, not better.

Tim sighed. He hooked off his glasses and polished them vigorously with the end of his tie. In the Holy Huddle, Tim was well aware that he himself was regarded as the plump, gentle one. David was the incendiary, the spiritual bomb. Yet he was going to talk to him again, and risk an explosion.

Penny Woodford was looking terrible. Her hair was like straw, the purple ends rough and unkempt. Her uniform was wrinkled, the cuffs of her blouse dirty. She had lost weight.

One or two of her year tried to talk to her, but Penny rebuffed every approach. Last year she had been unpopular, certainly, but she had been sparky, giving as good as she got. Now there was a vacantness in her eyes, a lethargy.

Edith Braden had noticed it too. At lunchtime towards the end of the first week, she fretted to Robyn in the staffroom.

"She looks really ill. I wonder should the school contact her home, just to check things out."

"I think that'd be a good idea," said Robyn. "I've tried talking to her but she just looked through me."

Angus was sitting several feet away, absorbed in a newspaper. Robyn gave him very little thought; she was just thankful that he had given up and stopped harassing her. He had hardly spoken to her all week, and when he did, it was only to wish her a polite good-day, or to hold a door open for her.

Edith shook her head. "And another thing," she said, her face creasing with worry, "I saw David Shaw talking to her this morning. They were in an empty classroom. He's the only one she seems to be talking to. It's very odd."

Angus' paper moved slightly and he glanced across at Robyn. He raised his paper again.

"Anyway," said Edith, "he wasn't looking very friendly. He seemed almost exasperated with her. I didn't like to stare, but I was going into the room next to where they were, and I'm sure I heard her swearing at him."

"That wouldn't bother David," said Robyn, opening a yogurt.

"How would you know?" said Edith crossly.

Robyn licked yogurt from the inside of the lid. As she did so, she saw Angus look quickly at her and away again. With rapid movements, he folded his paper, stood, and left the room.

The next day, Friday, Robyn marked Penny absent.

At lunchtime, she saw David across the dining hall. He was on duty, helping the new junior pupils who were still rather lost in the size of the school. Their blazers were crisp and new and a bit too long in the arms. When she first spotted David, he was hunkered in front of an eleven year old girl, looking into her scarlet face because she had dropped her plate with a resounding crash. The floor was strewn with chips and orange juice and the entire queue was laughing at her.

Robyn knew the child would never forget the humiliation. Then David said something that made the child start to smile. He made a funny face and started to hop around like a monkey from the Jungle Book. The girl laughed and so did everyone else. David stopped the entire queue and let her choose her lunch again. Then he paid for it himself and carried it to the table where her friends were watching. Carefully he laid out her cutlery, set her plate down and placed her drink beside it. With a flourish of his hand, he gave a mock bow and pulled out the chair for her. Robyn watched as the child sat beside her speechless friends, suddenly transformed into the centre of envious attention.

When Robyn looked for him again, he was wielding a mop, cleaning the floor. The image tucked itself into her mind as she turned away.

She didn't hear from him all weekend. He had avoided being in sight of her all week. She tried not to mind. It was what she wanted after all. The summer was time out that should never have happened. He would settle into life and look back on her as a temporary distraction, a bit of an oddball.

That night she fixed the chair under the door handle and went to bed. After a moment she put a hand out to check that her phone was in reach.

On Monday morning, Penny was still absent. Robyn noticed that David was not at morning assembly. This was unusual. David never missed it as a matter of principle. Occasionally he took part.

Robyn had to attend a meeting at breaktime, so it wasn't until lunchtime that she went to the staffroom. She was hungry and ready for a rest after a hectic morning. She made herself a coffee and sat alone in a corner. Angus came and sat almost opposite to her, but at the far side of the room.

At first she didn't listen to the chat around her. It was always there, like wallpaper.

"The holy ones are the worst," said Billy Dobbin, over to her right.

Matt Harkin ambled over to him. "You are so right, Billy. All perfection on the outside. Just as bad as everyone else inside."

"Worse. Definitely worse."

Gradually, a sense of something having happened impinged on Robyn.

"Still," said someone, "it's hard to believe. He's a bit different all right, but he seems like a decent guy. But you never can tell, I suppose."

"Poor Penny. I wonder what she'll do? She's hardly likely to be back in time to do her exams."

Edith came in, her face white. She made straight for Robyn. "I knew something was up. I knew it." Her voice rose in pitch. "He's young and he's handsome, God knows, but her? How did he fall for it?"

Robyn had gone rigid. "What's happened?"

"Men!" Edith's voice was almost a wail, "they're all the same underneath. Specially the young ones. You think to yourself, there's a decent young chap. And look what happens." She threw her hands in the air. "If you can't trust David Shaw you can't trust anyone."

Robyn leaned forward, took Edith by the arms and shook her. "Edith, what's happened?"

"You haven't heard? Where have you been? Well," she said, "I suppose the pupils will only be hearing by now."

Robyn was ready to hit her. "What's happened?" she said again loudly, shaking her harder.

Edith took a deep breath. "Apparently it all happened on Friday afternoon," she said. "Penny Woodford's pregnant and she says David Shaw's the father. He's been suspended." She slapped her hands on the arms of her chair. "And Penny's vanished. Can't find her anywhere."

Robyn sank back into her chair, her breath leaving her as if a fist had slammed into her stomach. She saw Angus watching her across the room, an unpleasant grin smeared across his face.

23

LIKE INK THROUGH a blotter, the news soaked through the school. Every class was agog with it; every corner was a corner of whispers. Robyn set some work for her senior class after lunch and left them. She climbed the stairs to the art rooms. She had never been up here. She searched each one until she found Tim Thompson. With a raised eyebrow of request and apology to the teacher, she called him out. He came slowly, even his unruly red curls looking sombre, subdued.

"Tim, what happened?"

Tim shrugged, a helpless puzzlement etched on his features, his whole demeanour upset.

"It was just after lunch on Friday. He was on his way up to the library when the Head called him to his office. He just didn't come back."

"Have you seen him?"

"Yesterday. But his parents are so upset they aren't really welcoming visitors. I didn't stay long." He scuffed a shoe around and looked at her sideways. "I don't think it was me he wanted to see."

"Where exactly does he live?" she asked.

Tim told her. "Big place. You'll know it by the two big lilac bushes on each side of the gate."

"And is there no news of Penny?"

"None that I've heard."

"Thanks, Tim."

Robyn turned back to the top of the stairs. Tim said quickly: "If you see him…" He hesitated awkwardly, "…be careful what you say to him."

He went back into the room, leaving her to wonder what he meant.

She had a free period before her last class and shut herself in her storeroom. In one corner a pile of texts sat where David had put them before the holidays. The day he had told her that there was always colour, that we either find it or mix it ourselves. The day he had first touched something in her and sent the first weak ripple trembling across the surface of still water. The day he touched an injured heart with an audacity heavy with the threat of healing.

Images reeled through her brain, tumbling, indisciplined. Lying on his back on Scrabo Hill, convulsed with laughter. Frowning with concentration as he fought with a wonky screw on her door. In the cathedral, eyes closed, quiet. Looking gently up at her and telling her she was the good news, not part of the bad news. Pretending to be a giant crab and chasing her. Standing in a crowded shopping centre holding a toddler and telling two open-mouthed girls that he ate children.

She got up restlessly and paced the room, arms folded tightly. There were other images. Close conversations with Penny Woodford. Guiding Penny along a Belfast pavement, a hand hovering at her back. Deflecting the conversation every time she tried to ask about her. Refusing to recognise any gulf between their worlds.

Robyn closed her eyes and rested her forehead against a bookshelf. One other image. Last Friday at lunchtime, turning an embarrassed little girl into a star. Then bending his own back to wipe her dinner off the floor. It must have been only minutes later that the Head had sent for him.

Trust had always been a husk of a word to her. It had a dictionary definition but had no form or shape. She could use it in sentences, read it on a page, and yet have no grasp of its meaning. She had never trusted anybody; it always led to betrayal, hurt. Always.

She sat again heavily, putting her elbows on the window sill and lowering her face into her hands. Even her own mother. That was just the worst and latest betrayal. If a mother's love is not an immovable rock, if a mother's love can bend to expediency, if a mother can watch her child be perverted, sullied, terrified, and do nothing to prevent it, then who in this world is to be trusted?

Unconsciously, she touched the spot beneath her index finger where a thorn had drawn blood one day and he had laughed.

A minute after the final bell, Robyn lifted her bag and walked through the school gate. It was nearly a mile, but she found the house easily. It was about half way along a quiet, elegant avenue, one of a line of houses that estate agents called 'gentlemen's residences.' She stopped and studied it, aware that she was stepping for the first time into David's own territory, and that she had no idea how she would be received.

To one side of the front porch, a tall stained glass window spanned the height of the wall, lighting the stairs. She scanned the upstairs windows, wondering if David's room lay behind one of them.

There was the little green hatchback. She passed two other cars at the front and at the bend in the gravelled drive she looked round at the neat flower beds, the immaculate lawn with its edges trimmed and straight. A pampas grass gracefully dominated one side. Chrysanthemums splashed the ground with colour near the door, and baskets of petunias and lobelia trailed down the walls of the porch.

It was hard to believe that the small, neat woman who answered the door was David's mother. Apart from a slight likeness around the cheekbones, she had passed nothing of herself to her son. He was almost entirely a bigger, stronger version of his father.

His mother was reserved, even unfriendly, her face etched with strain. Robyn explained who she was. She lifted her bag a little. "I've brought some notes for David."

Elizabeth put out her hand for them. "Thank you. I'll give them to him."

"Perhaps I could see him for a moment? I may need to explain some of the... stuff."

Elizabeth hesitated, passed a hand across her brow. "It's not an easy time."

"I know," Robyn said quickly.

Elizabeth raked her with a look. Robyn dropped her head. Then she began to pull a folder from her bag. "I'll leave this then. But please tell him I called." She looked up again. "Please."

Elizabeth looked back into the house and then turned, her shoulders sagging suddenly. "He's in the back garden. But please be quiet. My husband is lying down. He's taken this very badly."

Once through the kitchen and out the back door, Elizabeth left her to go down the steps alone. Robyn passed a weeping cherry tree and stepped onto the lawn. The back garden was very large, neatly cultivated for about two-thirds of its length, then thickly planted in a small copse of shrubs and trees. In the afternoon light, magpies were chattering in the branches. A weak breeze fidgeted through the leaves.

She couldn't see him. Further along, the lawn elbowed to the right into a secluded corner. She turned into it, and saw him sitting on a garden bench, his head lowered. Manna lay on the ground at his feet. The dog looked up and whined. His tail brushed the ground twice and then he set his head back on his paws.

When David saw her he stood slowly, his eyes fixed on her. He looked as if he hadn't slept for days, his eyes were hollow, his hair unkempt, his feet bare. Robyn stopped six feet from him and set her bag down.

"I was a mile from you," she said. "All weekend, I was only a mile from you. Why didn't you tell me?" When he said nothing, she went on. "I called you once when I needed you. Remember? And you came. Did you think I would do less for you?"

His voice was hoarse with tiredness. "I wanted you to hear it from somebody else, the way everybody else has heard it." He took a shaky breath. "And I've been waiting to see your face."

She spread her hands. "Well, here I am. What do you see?"

He didn't speak for a moment. Then: "Tell me."

She came right up to him and reached up to put a hand on each side of his face, over the roughness where the stubble was starting to grow again. She turned his head down towards her so that she could speak to the pain in his eyes. She made her words very clear.

"You see a woman who does not believe any of this. You see a woman who did not believe any of it from the first second she heard it." She watched her words registering in his brain. "David Shaw," she went on, her hands still on his face. "I trust you."

She folded her arms round him and pressed her cheek to his chest. The strong beat of his heart was slightly fast. After a moment, his arms went round her and his own cheek dropped onto the top of her head. Behind them, Manna rolled his eye towards them and his tail brushed the leaves on the ground.

Later, when Elizabeth came to see what had happened to Miss Daniels, she was startled to find her sitting on her coat on the grass. The full length of her son was stretched out on the garden seat, his head propped on her bag. He was deeply asleep. Elizabeth turned without a word and went back into the house.

Robyn watched the clouds gather overhead and felt the air grow chillier. When the first spatters began to land, she repeated his name gently until he stirred. Even so, he was groggy, confused, looking round as he sat up as if he wasn't sure where he was.

Robyn pulled him to his feet. "Come on. You need to be in

your bed. Not out here getting soaked. Let's go in."

He leaned on her shoulder as they walked back to the house.

"I think I was dreaming about you," he said, his voice still husky with sleep.

"Was I an angel or something?"

He shook his head and said quite seriously. "No. You'd just driven my car into a gatepost and I was about to yell at you when you woke me."

They reached the edge of the lawn. "You know, of course," she said, "that I would have yelled back. Even in a dream I can be a right old shrew."

Through the kitchen window, Robyn saw his mother getting up and going towards the back door. "Listen, David," she said urgently, checking his weary face. "Are you awake enough to listen to me?"

"I think so," he said fuzzily.

"I don't care what time it is. Right now, you are to have a shower and then go to bed and sleep some more."

He focused on her briefly. "And you?"

"You need to talk to me. When you're rested."

His father appeared from the hall as they came in. Robyn noticed that David passed him without a look and without a word. Vincent had been pale when she had met him before. Now he was grey. Elizabeth went to him and took his arm.

"Sit down, Vincent. I'll make you a cup of tea." She turned to Robyn. "Thank you for coming. David appreciated it. Obviously."

"This is a nasty thing to happen, Dr Shaw. I'll do everything I can to get this nonsense sorted out."

Unexpectedly, Vincent snorted. "Nonsense is it? Do we really know that young man at all? Just when you think you can trust him again…" He leaned heavily on the back of a chair. "Years it's taken. Years. And now this." To Robyn's discomfort, tears began to well in his eyes.

Elizabeth gently pushed her husband into a chair. "What they're saying isn't true, Vincent. It's not true. When you are calmer, you will realize that. You're upsetting yourself." She turned to Robyn. "Thank you again. Please forgive me if I don't show you out."

As Robyn walked through the thickly carpeted hall, she heard the sound of water running upstairs. Thank God. Then David was unlikely to have heard his father's words. Unless, of course, he had heard them before.

When Robyn emerged from the Shaw's gate and turned back towards the city, Angus waited for one minute exactly – he timed it – before following her. He had been going to wait for two minutes, but she walked quite fast, so he emerged from the overhanging branches before she went out of sight. She had been in there much longer than he had expected. He couldn't see her face, but she kept her head down most of the time, her hair lifting and falling with the rhythm of her walk. Occasionally she pushed it out of her eyes and tucked it behind her ear. He really hoped she was devastated. He really hoped she had scratched that bastard's eyes out. He had to stifle a laugh. Play with fire, Robyn Redbreast, and you'll go up in smoke! As for Holy Joe, Angus crowed to himself, let's see you pray your way out of this one!

He followed her until she turned the corner into her own street.

The next morning Robyn received a letter. The envelope was neatly printed and bore only the anonymous postmark: 'Royal Mail'. Inside was a handwritten letter and a cheque for a high five figure sum. Immediately, she recognised the writing and a glance at the signature on the cheque confirmed that it was from her mother. She pushed it into her bag and hurried to work.

There was a pecking order in the school and Robyn knew that, as a temporary sub, she was at the bottom of it. Although she knew the Headmaster had some regard for her – she got the job after all – he would tell her nothing if she asked him outright. There was an etiquette to be observed and it didn't involve either him or his senior staff talking freely about serious matters of discipline.

It didn't stop the tongues elsewhere. In the staffroom, Edith still chaffed.

"I think I'll call and see the Shaws. I'm sure they could do with some support." She sighed. "I really can't believe this."

"Then don't," said Robyn. "It isn't true, Edith."

Matt Harkin arrived and dropped into a chair near them. "The only thing I wonder is how she's managed to avoid getting pregnant up to now."

Across the room, Billy Dobbin jabbed a finger at the men around him. "They're all the same. Do you know what I heard an honest-to-goodness Sunday-go-to-meetin' businessman say once? Owned a garage. You know what he said?" He looked around, chewing vigorously. "I saw him cheat a customer. I saw him. I said to him afterwards, I said 'I thought types like you weren't supposed to do things like that'. You know what he said?" Billy leaned forward and clapped his hands on the knees of his tracksuit. "He said 'Ach Billy, sure Calvary covers all!' "

He sat back and laughed. His cheeks distended and a huge membrane of bubblegum swelled from his mouth. It burst over his cheeks and his tongue darted out to pull it in again.

Robyn stood up and set her mug beside the sink with a steady hand. Then she walked to the door. As she passed Billy Dobbin, she stopped and looked down at him. She spoke quite calmly.

"Billy, David Shaw has more courage in his little finger than you have in your whole body. And you wouldn't know integrity if it burst all over your face."

The staffroom went deathly quiet as she turned and opened the door. As she closed it, she heard Angus Fraser's drawl break the silence. "Well! I know pupils get crushes on teachers. It's a bit rare to find it the other way round."

As Robyn walked back to her room, two thoughts were uppermost in her mind. The first was that she wouldn't be going back to the staffroom for a few days, maybe not again at all before the maternity cover was finished. The second was that, actually, Billy Dobbin was almost right. She thought of her father, the familiar quiver of anger rippling her brain. Then she thought of one sunny day in the park, of David handing her a pink rose, replete with fragrance, and telling her not to judge a whole species by one example.

To avoid the staffroom, she went to the dining hall near the end of lunchtime. The Headmaster was there, sitting at the staff table. Robyn set her tray down and took an empty chair near him.

"No word of Penny yet, Headmaster?" she asked casually, unloading her food from the tray.

The Headmaster looked briefly at her over his glasses. "I'm afraid not." He continued eating.

Robyn lifted her knife and fork. "I think David Shaw has been set up."

He didn't even bother looking round. "You don't know the facts of the situation," he said dismissively.

Robyn took a deep breath. "Is there proof?"

The headmaster wiped his mouth with a paper napkin. "Robyn, you're very young and very inexperienced, but even you should know that I wouldn't have taken such action if there wasn't at least a case to answer. Of course there'll be a proper investigation. But this is a prestigious school. One of the best in the UK. Things like this may happen elsewhere in this day and age. But they won't happen here."

Robyn kept quiet for several minutes, wondering how far she should push this. She craved more information, facts, not gossip. The Headmaster was nearly finished his lunch. She wished he was a little easier to talk to.

"Well, I hope Penny's OK," she said. She set her glass down carefully. "I'm sure David denied everything?"

"Of course he did." He pushed his plate away irritably. "But the allegation came with the support of a member of staff. And he left me no option but to suspend him on the spot, after what he said to me."

Robyn closed her eyes, ghastly foresight hitting her. With a sense of dread she asked: "What did he say to you?"

The Headmaster stood up and she thought he wasn't going to tell her. But after a moment he said: "Perhaps you should know this. It might help the staff understand my actions. Shaw leaned over my desk and told me that if I believed such rubbish, then I knew where I could put my school." He crunched up the napkin and threw it on the table. "Actually, he was more specific than that."

As he walked away, Robyn dropped her knife and fork and slumped back in the seat.

"You idiot, David!" she raged silently.

24

BEFORE HER NEXT class arrived, Robyn searched her desk for an envelope and addressed it to her mother. Then she took out the letter she had received in the morning and, unread, she tore it into tiny pieces. She took the cheque and tore it apart also. She put the pieces in the envelope, sealed it, went down to the office and dropped it into the outgoing mail tray.

After the final bell went, she stayed on for half an hour to catch up on some paperwork. There was a knock at her door. She saw Chloe's face through the glass pane. She thought she also spotted the edge of short red curls that quickly disappeared.

Chloe came in, looking strained, ill at ease. She started to talk quickly. "Miss Daniels, I've known David Shaw all the time he's been here." She tossed her head. "I've known him… quite well. I know he wouldn't…" She stopped and swallowed "…do what they're saying."

Robyn set her pen down, wondering where this was leading. "I know that too, Chloe. None of his friends believes it, I'm sure."

Chloe looked over at the door. Robyn glanced at it and just caught the edge of the red curls darting away again. Chloe was twisting her tie, a scarlet flush beginning to bloom across her cheeks. She tried again: "He doesn't…"

Robyn put her hand up to stop her. "He doesn't sleep around. I know, Chloe." She stood up and went round her desk. "Will you tell Tim something for me?" Chloe nodded. "Tell Tim that I think David's fortunate to have a friend like him. Tell Tim that I've already told David that I believe in him totally." She came back and sat again, picking up her pen. "And tell Tim that I don't need any more messengers."

Chloe stared at her for a moment, then turned and left without another word.

Sensing where David was going, Manna nosed open the door of the study and padded to Vincent's side. David's father was seated at the table, photograph albums in a pile beside him. He had opened one and was turning the pages slowly, one by one.

David approached and, when he was ignored, sat down at the table, opposite him.

"Dad?" he said. Vincent continued to ignore him. David reached across and gently closed the album. "Dad," he pleaded, "I'm here. Now. And I need you."

Vincent put his elbows on the table and covered his face. He spoke in an exhausted tone through closed fingers. "I'm too tired just now, David. I think I've had enough."

David rose and went round the table to his side. He went down on his heels beside the chair and gently removed one of his father's hands from his face so that he could see him.

"I have done all I can, Dad. What more can I do? Maybe I've had enough too." There was no response. David took his father's hand between his own two. "Talk to me, Dad."

"Tomorrow. Leave me alone just now."

Slowly David stood and backed away from him. Manna followed him, his tail low. As David reached the door, his father ordered: "Leave the dog with me."

David hooked Manna's collar and steered him back. Then he went out and closed the door.

At least David looked as if he had slept, but there was still an edginess about him, a shadowing under his eyes. Robyn knew he didn't normally say much when he was driving and was content to be quiet. He drove along the coast, turned under the railway bridge and pulled up at the sea front at Holywood, on the southern shore of Belfast Lough. He got out of the car and she followed him. With only the briefest glance at her face, he took her hand and she followed him up onto the shore walk towards the low wall that ran along the top of the large boulders that filled in the space between the wall and the sea. He stepped up onto the top of the wall and, with a little tug on his hand, she followed to stand beside him.

The far side of the lough was hidden in mist, the hills of the north side of the city totally enshrouded. A patch of darker mist hung to the east, where it was already raining. After a moment, he let go of her hand and circled her with his arm to pull her into his side. Robyn watched the fussing and squabbling of seagulls bobbing and wheeling at the edge of the water. Then her arm stole round his waist and they stood together, facing the mist, listening to the chattering of the little waves on the rocks.

They took their time getting into talk. It was as if they both needed to settle, to find a point of calm. A train droned past on the line behind them. It was rush hour, time to go home, and the carriages were full.

She felt his arm tighten a little as he spoke finally, pensively. "Where is she, Robyn?"

She twisted her head on his shoulder to look up at him. "Penny, you mean?"

"Yes. There's no answer at her house phone, although that doesn't surprise me. But she's not answering her mobile either."

"You've been trying to contact her?"

"Of course I have."

"After what she's done to you?"

"Especially after what she's done to me. I'm afraid for her."

"Why?"

It was a moment before he replied. "Because she'll be hating herself."

Robyn took this in, turned it over. "Is she pregnant?"

He shifted his feet a little. "I don't know. She could be."

A motor launch scudded past, bouncing on top of the waves. Towards the city, the ferry came into sight, ploughing its way towards the open sea. To the north-east a plane eased itself down to the City airport, hanging and humming like a giant dragonfly.

He let her go and jumped down to sit on the wall. He held up his hand for hers as she hopped down to sit beside him.

"I think you've been very kind to her," she said.

"I think I was the only one who was."

"Does she have family?"

His tone became angry. "Her mother is so legless most of the time that she's either lying in a sodden stupor on her bed, or out playing the local drunk round the streets." He stopped for a minute, his face twisting. "Her father was in prison until July. He's out now."

"Why was he in prison"

"Her father used to be a paramilitary. He got done for drug dealing." He spread his hands in a gesture of amazement. "They let him out! They let him out. Penny had seen it coming and she was terrified. He wasn't just violent to his enemies; he was an all round, all time brute to his own family too." He stood up and paced restlessly. "He came home and beat up his wife, broke her nose. Penny took her two younger brothers and hid in a neighbour's garage until the next day." He gave a bitter smile. "He's still around. To coin a famous phrase, 'he hasn't gone away, you know'. But Penny went looking for love and amnesia." He stopped in front of Robyn. "She looked for the love from me." Robyn held her breath, guessing what he was going to say. "She couldn't accept that that had its limits." He paced away again. "So she looked for it elsewhere."

"And the amnesia?"

David came back and pulled Robyn to her feet. Folding her into his arms, his voice was muffled in her hair: "That's the bit that worries me."

While they walked a little way along the sea front, she told him what the Headmaster had said. "You know what you need?" she said.

"What?"

"A tongue transplant. He mightn't have suspended you if you'd kept your mouth shut."

"James chapter three, verse six was engraved on my soul long ago."

"What does it say?"

" 'The tongue also is a fire, a world of evil among the parts of the body' ".

She looked sideways at him and gave a little skip of mischief. "Oh, I think there are worse parts."

He feigned shock. "Robyn Daniels, you're a disgrace to your profession."

She grinned, relieved to see the laughter crinkling his eyes above the dark shadows.

They shared a fish supper. David wasn't hungry, but Robyn made him eat the bigger half of the fish and most of the chips.

"You still have exams to work for and you need to keep your strength up."

He bit a chip and chewed silently before speaking again. "Robyn, I've some thinking to do about…" He glanced at her and away again. "…what I do next." Before she could ask what he meant, a thought struck him. "Do you still have the alarm I gave you?"

"Yes, I do, don't worry."

"Where is it now?"

"In my bag…"

"… in the car," he finished. "What good will it do you there? What if I attacked you? You couldn't reach it."

"David, nobody's going to attack me, don't be silly."

"Keep it in your pocket," he persisted stubbornly, catching a piece of fish as it rolled out of the paper.

"Yes, sir," she said, and licked her fingers. "Did I tell you Angus Fraser apologised? Flowers, the full works? He's history."

He told her about Florida, about the children he had worked with.

"Just like everywhere, life isn't fair. Some of them have everything and think they've nothing. Then there are the ones who have nothing, but still give you a smile that's pure gold."

"Will you go back?"

"One day at a time, my darling."

Although he said it lightly, she was shaken. They were leaning on railings and she jolted upright and walked away from him. She turned to see him watching her, one hand on the railing. Then he came towards her. The wind was blowing in from the sea, sending her hair flying around her face. His own short black waves rioted across his head.

"Sorry," he said, "that just slipped out."

"Don't apologise." She heard her own voice shake.

"OK then." His eyes ranged over every part of her face, then came to rest on her mouth. He tilted her chin up towards his. The panic rose instantly, erasing everything. Erasing his soft voice and replacing it with harsh and demanding tones. Erasing his gentle touch and replacing it with thick rough fingers. His brown eyes, their centres darkening, disappeared behind the lurching shadow of a nightmare. She beat him with her fists and ran.

She stopped under the railway bridge and hunched against the wall, her arms wrapped tightly round herself. Gradually her breathing slowed and the terror began to back off. Through the arch of the bridge, David appeared. He stopped, lifted a hand and knocked on the bricks.

"Can I come in?"

Anger, sorrow and despair tangled together inside her. She spoke in a rush. "I'm sorry. I'm so sorry. Stop thinking about me, David. This can't happen. It just can't."

He had reached her and stopped, smiling crookedly. "It's funny. Several months ago, you needed me. You were lost and lonely." He put up a hand to stop her as she started to speak. "I *know* you were. But now, the thought of being without you paralyses me with fear."

She stared at him, still hugging herself tightly, while a train roared over the bridge above their heads. When it passed, he said: "You say this can't happen. But it already has." He risked brushing his fingers down the side of her hair. "And you know it has."

Then he backed away. "Come on, it's getting dark. Let's go."

He didn't say a word all the way back. His profile was still, shuttered, as he concentrated on the traffic, his hand steady on the gears, his gaze swivelling from the road to his mirror, never once turning to her. It started to rain and the windscreen wipers thrummed through the gathering dark.

He got out of the car and came right up to her door with her. He spoke as she searched for her key. "It's over to you now, Robyn."

"What do you mean?"

He looked away for a moment, reaching for words. "I've done all I can, but I can't walk through walls. You've erected the defences. You're the one who's going to have to take them down."

She put her hand flat on his chest and looked up at him, questioning. "I wonder sometimes why you don't give up. I'm really not worth it."

"That," he said emphatically, "is blasphemy. I spent the weekend in hell waiting for you. I'd still be there if you hadn't come. Oh, you're worth it." He covered her hand. "Maybe trusting yourself is going to be even harder than trusting me."

She leaned her forehead on his chest and whispered: "Why do you always sound so much more grown up than me?"

His mood changed like lightening. "Because I'm bigger! Now get in that door before we get any wetter."

When she was safely inside, David walked up and down the street on each side of Robyn's door, looking in the doorways and at the parked cars. Satisfied, he returned to his own car.

When he drew up at the side of his own house, he didn't go in immediately. He slammed the car door and, putting his hand on the weeping cherry as he passed it, he made his way across the lawn through the near dark. It had stopped raining but the sodden trees and bushes at the back of the garden drenched him as he pushed through them. He leaned his back against the pitted trunk of a fir tree and looked up through the branches. Thin scraps of cloud brushed over the stars as he closed his eyes, allowing his thoughts to ebb and flow with the night breeze. Some little creature scuffled through the undergrowth. David stayed still, drawing peace into himself, allowing it to sink into the very pores of his skin. A pigeon churred sleepily above him, the sound travelling softly through the night.

The reality of his situation bent his soul and he could see no way out of the thicket of problems. He spoke aloud to the stars.

"How about a hand here? Things are a bit rough, you know."

His mind moved on, beginning to fill with a lovely face framed by hair flying in the wind. A mischievous grin on a mouth he would die to kiss. But she was so much more than that. She had become the anchor of his days, the companion of his heart.

He shoved himself upright, spun round and punched the tree trunk so hard he skinned his knuckles. She can't see it! Oh my God, why can't she see it? What is wrong? Despite the wet and cold, he pulled up his sleeves, clenched his hands into fists and flexed his arms.

At the edge of the lawn there was a garden shed. Quietly he pulled the bolt and searched in the dark until his hand found the axe. He brought it out into the starlight and prowled round the garden, swinging it easily in his hands. His eyes darted from tree to tree. Somewhere in this forest, there must be a tree just asking to be chopped down. He pushed through the bushes again. His eyes lit on a laburnum tree. Ha! They were poisonous anyway. Placing himself where he could get a good swing, he poured all his frustration into the muscles of his arms and swung the axe in a mighty arc. The first strike sliced halfway through the trunk.

Lying on his stomach with one bare arm hanging out of the side of the bed, David was in a restless sleep. His dreams were full of trees and seagulls, and someone was hiding from him, darting away just as he thought he was about to catch up. The sun seemed to rise and shine very brightly. Gradually he became aware that it wasn't the sun. The light in his room was on and someone was bending over him, saying his name. He pushed himself upright. Fuzzily he checked the time. What was his mother doing in his room at half four in the morning? He pushed his legs over the edge of the bed and focused on what she was saying.

She was in her dressing gown, her face creased, tears of anxiety very close. She was telling him that she had woken to find his father gone from the bed. She thought he had gone to the bathroom but he hadn't come back. She had got up and checked, but he wasn't anywhere upstairs. She had been to the bottom of the stairs also, but she couldn't hear him anywhere.

Now fully awake, David didn't patronise her by telling her not to worry. She had turned on all the lights already. He went onto the landing and methodically searched upstairs, room by room, walking round the furniture to check every corner. Every few minutes he called out, pausing to listening for a response.

Then he went downstairs and went through the study, the den, the cloakroom. He covered every inch until finally he came to the kitchen. Elizabeth had followed him. Manna's basket was in the corner by the radiator. It was empty. David thought he heard a whine outside. His thoughts racing, he checked the back door. It was unbolted.

"Mum, turn on the outside lights," he instructed urgently, pulling the door open. It was raining again, teeming onto the gravel at the bottom of the steps. Manna stood floodlit in the light from above the door. He was soaked and distressed. David felt his mother throwing a rainproof coat around his naked shoulders. He bunched the collar under his chin and went barefoot down the steps.

It was Manna who led him. Dread made his knees weak as he followed the dog along the wet gravel, heedless of the sharp stones beneath his feet. At the start of the lawn, he could see a figure on the ground. He ran. The coat fell from him and rain battered his skin unheeded. His father lay on his side, his pyjamas soaked and sticking to his body. One of his arms was stretched out towards the weeping cherry tree, his hand fixed in a grasp that had fallen just short of its target.

With trembling fingers David checked for a pulse, but already he knew it was too late. His father had gone away. As Elizabeth came running towards him, little screams coming from her, David gathered up his father's body from the soaking ground.

"Oh, Dad," he cried, "tomorrow never comes."

25

H E TOLD HER.
Robyn was reaching for her coat when her phone rang in the morning. Instantly, she knew that something was wrong. David's voice was strained and hollow, his words brief. The house was mad, he said. People had already started to call, there were arrangements to make, people to be polite to. And there was his mother. He couldn't leave her, although her sister and her husband were on their way from Fermanagh already. Meantime, a medical colleague was with her.

He couldn't talk long. Just as he was about to hang up, Robyn said gently: "Shalom, David."

There was a long pause. Then he just said: "See you," and the line went dead.

The news travelled round the senior school and the staff, but Robyn paid very little attention to the talk. Most comments from the staff were sympathetic, although Billy Dobbin was in his usual form.

"Church leader, dicky heart, learns his son's been going forth and multiplying. The old man couldn't take it, I suppose. I wonder how King David feels now."

Angus put his head round Robyn's door. "Poor guy," he said, "his trouble's don't come in ones, do they?" He grinned. He closed the door and she felt like spraying the handle with disinfectant.

Tim came to see her. "The funeral's on Friday. But it's going to be in their home church in Fermanagh. The grave's there."

"Did David ask you to tell me that?"

"Yeah." Tim's fair skin reddened. "He also said to tell you he doesn't want you to go." He must have seen the hurt written on her face. "It's not that he doesn't... I just think he needs to focus on what's happened."

"But I wouldn't stop him doing that."

Tim backed towards the door. "Yes, you would."

That night she tried a text message. Although she stayed awake a long time, there was no reply.

The day of the funeral was dry, with a strong breeze. All day her eyes kept wandering to the window as she wondered what the weather was like in Fermanagh. Gemma contacted her.

"Fancy some grub in town? I finish at five."

Robyn's first reaction was to say no, but then she decided that it would be a distraction. Gemma was a little subdued, as if she were building up to something. Robyn soon found out what.

"Do you know your mother's not well?"

"What's wrong?"

"Well, Neil was on the phone earlier. She hasn't been herself for some time, but he says she got a letter from you and now she's really depressed. He doesn't know what was in the letter, but he's actually quite worried about her."

"So Neil asked you to see me?"

Gemma looked defensive. "Yes, he did. But I would have anyway. He can't get up to Belfast just now, or he would have come to see you himself."

"Please tell him not to bother."

"This is about your mother, Rob, not Neil. What's happened between you and her anyway? You haven't been back home in weeks."

"It's a long story, Gemma. And a private one."

Gemma twisted her fork in a plate of spaghetti. "Well, she's your mother, no matter what. I just hope you don't regret this."

When they had finished, Robyn opened her bag to get her purse.

"Rob! You've got a mobile phone!" Gemma took her own phone from her bag. "Great! Give me the number. It'll make things so much easier. Why didn't you tell me?" She sat with her thumb poised.

Robyn stood up. "Sorry, Gemma, it's only for emergencies. Restricted, so to speak."

Gemma gaped. "But I'm your friend. Even if we're not going to be related."

"There's still my land line, and it has an answer phone."

Gemma put her phone away and sulked. "I don't believe you. A phone's not much good if nobody knows the number."

"Absolutely none at all."

That night Robyn was about to go to bed when her mobile rang. Her hand trembled slightly as she answered it. "Hi," she said.

"Are you in bed yet?"

"No," she said.

"If I drove down, would you come down to the car for five minutes?"

"Yes."

"I'm leaving now."

The street was a patchwork of pools of light and craters of darkness. Robyn waited at the top of the steps. There were a few people about: drunks hollering their unsteady way home; couples walking in close embraces. She recognised David's car pulling into a space a little further up the street.

She slid in beside him.

"I thought you might stay in Fermanagh overnight," she said.

He was still dressed in a suit, with a white shirt. The black tie had been pulled loose and hung below the open neck. His shadowed eyes were circled with smudges. He reached for her hand and she let it rest in his as she waited.

Finally he said: "He died thinking very badly of me, Robyn.

I tried to talk to him, but he wouldn't listen." Lamplight angled in through the windscreen, highlighting the sharpened planes of his face.

She squeezed his hand. "This is the bad time. The very worst bit. And your father loved you."

"Yes he did. And I loved him." He rested the side of his head against the window. The anguish in his voice was hard to bear. "That's what makes it hurt so much."

She waited a moment and then asked: "How's your mother?"

"Not good. But she'll cope."

"So will you."

He fiddled with her fingers. "Thanks," he said after a while.

She watched his fingers interlacing through her own, detaching, twining, gripping again. "What for?"

"For still being here."

She smiled a little. "You're not the only one who can stick around." Gently she pulled her hand away. "It's been a long traumatic day for you. Go home now."

He gave a long deep sigh and raised his head. "Thanks," he said again.

"What for this time?"

His mouth twitched slightly. "I've been surrounded by clichés for days." He mimicked voices. " 'Time is a great healer.' 'He can't have suffered for long.' 'Wouldn't it have been far worse if he'd had a terrible disease?' He touched her cheek. "You haven't come out with one yet."

"Give me time."

Longing was plain on his face as he looked at her. His hand moved to the back of her head and she felt a gentle pull as his eyes travelled to her mouth. With a quick reflex, she twisted and reached for the door handle. He released her instantly.

Despite everything, he didn't drive away until he saw that she was safely through her own door.

They met again near teatime on Sunday, on a seat under the rose walk in the park. He didn't look any better, although he was quite calm. She listened while he told her every detail of the night his father died. He told her about their rocky, volatile relationship. They respected each other but, although physically alike, their minds were very different. At one point he stopped and studied her, his mouth open as if he were about to say more, perhaps to tell her something. Then he stood up abruptly and walked across to the rose beds.

The roses were sadder now, less fragrant. The days of rain had bent the great heads and rotted many of the buds on their stems. They looked scrawny, disconsolate.

"Remember playing the guessing game with the names of these roses?" she asked, standing behind him.

"The day you bit my nose off."

"The day you didn't walk away."

He turned to her and held up his open hand in an unconscious repetition of what they had done that day. She raised hers and touched it palm to palm with his. They stood facing each other on the damp grass, hands raised together. His face was etched with stress, grief, sleeplessness, yet he held her gaze with an energy which made her catch her breath. She felt the whole world narrowing to the patch of grass on which they stood, felt the petals of an entirely new emotion unfolding in her, an emotion for which she had no name.

Always he stirred her mind. She hardly recognised the colours she now lived amongst as belonging to the same world which had once been so dull and grey. He had succeeded in stirring her body; she recognised that now. But what she felt today, eye to eye and palm to palm with him, was neither of those things. Her fingers bent through his as she searched his face as if she could find the answer there.

It seemed a long time before he dropped his hand and backed away from her. "I must go." He walked backwards for a few steps. "It's still up to you, Robyn."

Then he walked away. He took a set of steps in two strides and walked briskly along the path towards the museum and the gate. His head was up, his back was straight, and, although she watched until he was out of sight, he didn't once look back.

On Monday there was still no news of Penny Woodford. Robyn tired of keeping up professional appearances and came back to her flat straight after school. She needed activity. She turned the radio on to a local music channel, wrestled the ironing board from behind the kitchen door, and attacked a pile of ironing. At five o'clock, near the end of the news summary, there was mention that police frogmen had pulled the body of a female from the river in Belfast, near the Lagan Weir. It was thought that the body had been in the water for several days. A post mortem would be carried out later.

Robyn unplugged the iron, unease unfurling in her head.

Tim felt so much for his friend that he couldn't say anything. He sat in the den in David's grand house and blinked across at him. For something to do, he ruffled Manna's ears and put his nose down to receive a warm lick that knocked his glasses askew.

"Manna doesn't understand at all," said David. "He keeps going to the study and putting a paw on Dad's chair. He whines up at me. And I can't explain it to him."

Elizabeth came in with some sandwiches and coffee. Lines that should not have appeared for several years yet furrowed her cheeks and mouth.

Tim stood up awkwardly. "Thank you, Dr Shaw. How are you?"

The inanity of it struck him, but he had to say something. Elizabeth smiled briefly.

"Oh, you know. Still in the denial phase, I suppose." She set the tray down. "I'm going to bed, David. Remember to put all the lights out."

She bent to give him a peck on the cheek. Before she could straighten, he put an arm out and pulled her cheek to his again. "'Night, Mum. Do you need anything?"

"No, I'll be fine."

When she had gone, David said: "You know what makes me feel worse? Mum and Dad really loved each other. Sometimes I think I can't handle my own feelings and hers as well. I just want to be left to work this through on my own."

"Yeah, man." Tim ran a hand through his hair, the red curls twisting round his fingers. "Have you seen... Miss Daniels?"

"I have."

"And... um?"

"And I'm not going to say any more."

"OK, man. But we all miss you." Manna rolled over, giving Tim the excuse to bend and rub the dog's tummy. "There's something else I need to tell you. I don't suppose you've been listening to the news?"

"It hasn't been the first thing on my mind, no."

Tim sat up. "They found a body in the Lagan last night." He watched David carefully. He wasn't particularly engaging with this. "A woman's body. A young woman's body." David's eyes swivelled to his. "It hasn't been identified yet." Tim pulled a cushion onto his knee and squeezed it. "Chloe phoned the Woodford's house. Her brother answered." He put the cushion back. "He said police had called at the house and his mum had gone with them. To the hospital."

The next morning David trawled the news web sites and listened to every news bulletin. It wasn't important enough to be in a main report. There wasn't much time for meticulous detail on young women fished out of the Lagan. Eventually a few facts were available.

The body had been identified as that of Penelope Woodford who had been missing from her home in south Belfast for ten days. The post mortem had been rapid and simple. She had been alive when she entered the water, and in her veins ran a lethal cocktail of drugs and alcohol. He frowned. How could she afford the drugs?

David checked his watch. Still lunchtime. He rang Chloe. Chloe had contacts. As he expected, the bush telegraph was filling in the details. There was such a mess of drugs inside her, Penny must have been off the planet. Not only that. She wasn't – and never had been – pregnant.

In shock, David sank into a chair and asked God to be kind to Penny Woodford. She had gone looking for amnesia and had found oblivion. She did not deserve to die like that. As his shock settled, he began to get angry. A fury grew in him, rose and filled him, blazed up through his body and brain and sent him to his car and down to the school before his thoughts could order themselves into logic.

The bell for the end of lunchtime had just gone and Tim was standing at a window in the corridor with a group of friends discussing the news. Nothing like this had happened before and it was going to take a long time to talk out. Tim knew they would have a lot of questions to ask themselves in the coming months. He was already putting the hard ones to himself. Was he really such a complacent prat? Had he been so busy building his own life that he couldn't see the person next to him unravelling her own? Why was David the only one of them all with the insight to see what was going on and the moral courage to try to do something about it? They had left him to it, to pay a price which David himself could never have imagined would be demanded of him.

As they dispersed, Tim turned to lift his bag. A green hatchback lurched up to the main door and was abandoned. With surprise, and then with alarm, Tim saw David leap from it and hurl himself up the steps.

Angus Fraser was settling his class, junior brats, when the classroom door was flung wide. He opened his mouth to bawl at the intruder, and then stopped. Shaw! He shouldn't be here. The bugger's suspension might be over, but his old man had snuffed it. Shaw strode to the centre of the classroom and ordered the class out of the room.

"Hey!" said Angus.

"Out!" roared Shaw. In a shoving of desks and clatter of chairs, they fled like lemmings.

When only the two of them were left in the room, Shaw seemed to become very calm. Angus stood warily, his fists bunched, as Shaw circled him.

"How much did you give her, Fraser?"

"Get out of my room, you bastard!"

Shaw circled closer and repeated: "How much did you give her?"

Angus made for the phone on top of the filing cabinet. Shaw threw himself in front of it and yanked the cord from the socket.

"Oh no," he snarled, "This is between you and me, Fraser. Just you and me."

Angus felt fear dampening his collar. Shaw came closer, his own fists curled and rigid by his sides. Then he pulled away. Angus exhaled slowly.

"Isn't it funny?" Shaw ruminated. "Apparently Penny Woodford's story was supported by a member of staff. I wasn't told who that was. But it was the clincher. I wondered who it could have been." He spun round, making Angus jump. "Someone who was out to get *me*, obviously. Then I knew it couldn't have been any one else. Nobody else is quite such a slurry pit of lies and *pig shit*. How much did you pay her, you asshole?"

"You can't prove anything, Shaw." Out of the corner of his eye, he thought he saw a red head at the glass in the door.

Shaw's finger jabbed towards his nose. He recoiled. "You paid her enough to buy half the crack in Belfast. Plus a few bottles to mix it with." Shaw's voice became a roar again. "Didn't you? Did you know she was an addict, or was it just a lucky guess?"

Angus' head started to hum. This was the person in his way. This was the person who had succeeded where he was despised. Robyn Daniels had let Shaw put his hands on her. God, how he hated him!

"It was worth it!" he spat. "Look what's happened. Beyond my wildest dreams, *boy!*"

Shaw circled him again. "And this was all to get at me? You have as good as killed someone just to get at me?" His face suddenly stilled for a moment as a thought occurred to him. "You're not just a dirty old man, are you? You're sick, Fraser. You must be."

Angus' felt himself swell with pride. "I got Woodford, I got your reputation. And what a bonus – I got your old man too!"

As Shaw's fist flashed through the air, Angus grinned. That's right, you bugger. Hit me. That'll really finish you!

26

ROBYN WAS COLLECTING homeworks when there was a brief knock and a junior boy ran into the room, his voice squeaking.

"Miss Daniels! One of the prefects sent me to get you. He says you're to go to Mr Fraser's room now!" He gasped with the importance of his message. "*Now*, he said, Miss."

Robyn lifted her finger to the class. "None of you move. I'll be straight back." Puzzled but impelled by the urgent tone of the message, she ran down the corridor.

Angus closed his eyes to brace himself for the impact. It didn't come. Instead there was a clatter and a thud. He opened his eyes just in time to see Shaw being knocked across the room by the airborne body of Thompson. They fell into the desks which went spinning and crashing in a deafening tangle. Shaw rolled to the floor, Thompson on top of him. Thompson straightened his glasses and rearranged himself to sit on Shaw even more firmly.

When Robyn spun through the door, Angus was standing frozen near his desk. David was on the floor by the window, a chair toppled across his shoulders. Tim was sitting firmly on his back.

Angus came to life. "Shaw's a bit stressed out. Naturally." He dusted his sleeves. "I won't report this. This time. After all, there's no harm done. To me, anyway." He walked to the door and Robyn moved away from it quickly. "I'd better go and see where my class has gone."

Tim was quickly losing the battle to keep David on the floor.

"I sent them to the library, sir," he said, wobbling.

"Thank you, Thompson. I'll retrieve them." He went through the door, then put his head round it again. "Perhaps the floor could be tidied up before I get back."

When Angus disappeared, Tim struggled to his feet before he could be knocked sideways. As David rose from the floor, his face white, Robyn rounded on him, furious.

"What the hell were you doing?"

"Something he" – David pointed angrily at Tim – "shouldn't have stopped me doing."

"Well now…" said Tim.

"Were you attacking him? Were you really being so stupid?" Robyn couldn't keep her voice down.

Tim pushed the door shut. "Maybe…" he said.

David strode over to Robyn. They were inches apart, yelling. "You don't know the reason. If you did, you would have helped me!"

"Perhaps…" said Tim.

Robyn punched a finger at David. "How much trouble do you want to be in, you stupid fool? Haven't you had enough?"

"Look…" said Tim.

"I'll be in more before I've finished with him!"

"You're a walking disaster, David!"

"And I suppose you're Mother Theresa!"

"Shut up!" yelled Tim.

He pushed between them and gripped an arm of each. "Shut up for a minute!" He looked at Robyn. "Excuse me, Miss, but shut up for a minute. You're both going this way."

One volcano Tim could deal with. Two erupting at once he was going to leave alone. Especially these two. He could think of only one place where he could put them with rapidity. At the top of the main staircase, beside Fraser's room, were the girls' cloakroom and toilets. He propelled David and Robyn to them, opened the door and pushed them inside, shutting the door firmly.

He leaned against the wall and rubbed his elbow where he had hurt it in his tumble. Further up the corridor, Matt Harkin's head appeared from his classroom.

"What's going on down there?" he called.

Tim raised a hand in a reassuring gesture. "It's OK, sir. One of the juniors fell and made a bit of a racket." The noise of angry voices reached his ears from behind the door. "She's fine now," he called loudly. Mr Harkin's head disappeared. Tim closed his eyes and asked God why he hadn't made him a better liar.

Another door opened and a girl emerged. Tim realised with alarm that she was coming towards him, towards the cloakrooms. Oh, why wasn't Chloe with him? He called out:

"Go to the ones at the other end. These ones are out of order. Blocked cistern or something." The girl turned round and went the other way.

Thanks, Lord, said Tim silently. That one was a bit better.

He thought for a minute and then trudged back to Robyn's room. There was a hum of conversation as he entered. Twenty-five pairs of eyes lit on him expectantly. Something Was Going On. Tim nudged his glasses up the bridge of his nose. "Right. You've to go to the library for the rest of this period. Off you go."

As they filed out past him he asked God to give him a really good whopper to tell Mrs McKinley, the librarian, because she was going to be after his head. Another pupil was making her way to the girls' cloakroom. He panted back up the corridor, calling: "Don't go in there! I mean, it's out of order. Broken cistern. Use the other ones."

She went down the stairs instead. He looked into Fraser's room. It was still in a mess and Fraser hadn't returned. He could sort that out himself. Tim went back to the cloakroom door and listened. It was quiet but they were definitely still in there. Then he heard David's deep tone again, still raised. He sighed, wiped his brow and went down the stairs as fast as he was able. As he expected, David had left his keys in the ignition. Tim pulled them out and dropped them into the pocket of his blazer. Then he hauled himself up the stairs again to resume his guard on the door.

David looked as if he didn't know and didn't care where he was and Robyn didn't waste time on surprise. As soon as Tim closed the door she lashed out.

"OK, so you're not a pacifist. Point taken. But do you have to be suicidal?"

David came to a stop by the drinking fountain and whirled round. "You tell me. You're the one who's done the fieldwork in that area!"

She gasped. "You bastard! And why are you so mad at Fraser anyway? He hasn't been near me in ages."

"He's been a lot closer than you know. And anyway, can't you believe there might be other reasons apart from you?" He stopped. "Except there aren't."

"What the hell do you mean?"

He moved round the room, banging the cubicle doors. "You're not to go within half a mile of that freak. He's sick. Do you hear me?"

"Don't you dare tell me what to do. I've had enough of that. I'm certainly not going to take it from you!"

"Damn it, Robyn, You don't know what he could do."

"Now you're being melodramatic."

He came towards her. "You've heard about Penny?"

"Yes."

"He paid her." His voice rose in a fury again. "He paid her to say what she did." He stopped, his breath coming in rapid beats. Robyn looked at him in disbelief. He spread his hands.

"And now she's dead. What if it had been you? What if I turned on the news and heard that..." He spun round and leaned his elbow on the tiled wall. He ran his hand through his hair and closed his eyes for a moment. His voice was dredged from a pit of exhaustion. "Robyn, have you any idea how tired I get of trying to be good?"

She put a hand out to him but he shrugged away. "You're worn out, David. You've been through so much. Things will look different..."

He flung his hands in the air suddenly. "Bingo! Things will look different in the morning. There's the cliché at last!"

She flared up again. "Don't be so bloody cynical! You've just been saved from assaulting a teacher by the best friend you'll ever have. You're far too young to be screwing up at the rate you're doing it!"

He thumped the wall. "And what are you? Methuselah? What's your excuse?"

"I don't need excuses..." she began furiously.

"Bullshit! You're screwed up big time. And when you mess up your own life, you mess up every other life that touches it." He flung a hand in the air. "Come on, English student! Repeat after me: 'No man is an island entire of itself'... Come on, what's the rest of it?"

" 'Every man is a piece of the continent, a part of the main ...' "

He broke in again " 'If a clod be washed away by the sea, Europe is the less...' "

"Shut up! And I didn't mess up my own life. Somebody else did that for me!"

He strode the length of the room to stand in front of her. "And you're going to let him away with it? For ever and ever, amen? Because it was a man, wasn't it?" He waited, his face close. "Wasn't it? How thick do you think I am, Robyn? I've got a brain and it has worked overtime on this." He stormed back to the far end of the cubicles and swung round again. "You've got to face it. You've got to take out whatever happened, look at it and say this will not control my life."

She flung her hand out. "Stop sounding like such an expert on life skills! I'm not stupid either. You've messed up too, but you've never told me about that, have you? So stop acting all self-righteous with me."

"Of course I messed up! Why do you think I know about the cage you're in?" He raised his arms and then dropped them to his sides in frustration. "Oh Robyn, you've been rattling the bars so loudly this past while. Step through them." He stretched out one hand towards her. "Step through them to me."

She went quiet. "David?" she asked slowly. "Why are we so angry with each other?"

He put his back to the tiled wall and slid down it until he was hunkered on the floor. His fingers ruffled his hair and his expression was one of total fatigue. "Because there's nothing else left to be." His head swivelled up to her. "Fire burns. But so does ice."

"What do you mean?"

"I mean that I can't be friends with you. I thought I could, but I can't. Just before my father died, I had decided to leave this school. Coming here at all was a stupid idea. So expulsion would be pretty pointless." He stood up slowly. "Look what's happening to us. I have fought with you. I have prayed for you. I have laughed with you. I have tried to stay only what you need me to be." His voice dropped. "I can't do it any more." Robyn was shaking so hard she put a hand on the wall for support. "Do you know how long my parents had together?" he asked. "Twenty-four years. And it's over like that." He snapped his fingers in the air. Then he took her by the shoulders and shook her. "It should have been longer," he shouted. "But at least it was twenty-four years more than nothing!"

"My parents were married for twenty-six years," she shouted back. "And it was twenty-six years too long!"

Total silence descended while they stood immobile, eyes locked.

Then she hissed, "Let go of me!"

He did. He released his grip and spread his hands wide on each side of her for a moment. Then he turned and opened the door. "Stop making excuses and start making choices." He cocked his head in mock thoughtfulness. "Or is that where we came in?"

She flung the door shut after him with all her strength.

Tim flinched. The cloakroom door banged shut so hard it shook the wall. Thank God there was no glass in it. David went past him so fast Tim's curls lifted in the slipstream. Then from the bottom of the stairs the outside door crashed against the wall as David went through it like a missile.

Tim took off his glasses and polished them vigorously on his tie. Something was going to have to give with those two before the whole school ignited. He pushed his glasses on again, sighed and tramped down the stairs, reaching into his pocket for the car keys as he went.

In the foyer he gave a token push to the office door and said without stopping: "David Shaw doesn't feel well. Permission to take him home? Thank you."

David was sitting behind the wheel, his fingers just beginning to register that the keys weren't there. Tim opened the driver's door.

"Shove over."

"The keys. Someone's taken them."

"I did, man. Now shove over. There's no way I'm letting you drive home. I've more respect for the citizens of this city."

David looked at him and then something in him seemed to

collapse. He moved across. Tim settled himself and found the ignition. He wobbled the gear stick.

"Where's reverse?" David put it into reverse with his right hand. "Thanks." The car jolted backwards and stalled. "Sorry. It's been a while." As he steered carefully down the driveway, Tim looked across at David. "Why are you mad at Fraser anyway?"

David sank further into the seat and closed his eyes. "Just drive," he said.

That night, David saw the fox again. This time there was no moonlight and she slid across the lawn in the dim shimmer of the street lamp. The great seed heads of the pampas grass rose to rock gracefully in the breeze. The fox snuffled under the fronds, stopping every now and then to look around and nibble any titbits too slow to escape her flicking tongue. David watched her trot to the hedge and slip through it, the white tip of her brush vanishing like a snuffed candle.

He put his head down onto his arms. What if she couldn't do it? What if she slipped away like the fox, graceful and cold? What would have been the point of it all? What would be the point of anything?

He heard a noise and raised his head. From his mother's room came the sound of crying, rhythmic sobs of anguish and loneliness, the metronome of a desolation for which there was no comfort this side of the grave. He sat and listened, feeling himself turning to stone.

27

PENNY'S FUNERAL WAS a wretched little affair. The hearse drew up at the crematorium and she took her place in the queue to be consigned to the furnace, ashes to ashes, dust to dust.

Her father was there, surrounded by hard men who had thrust their biceps into suits for the occasion. Her mother was sober, but with the air of one for whom this was a brief and painful interlude inserted into a life of much more preferable states. Her nose still bore the mottled remnants of a bruise. The only ones who seemed genuinely sorrowful were Penny's brothers.

Robyn looked round at the number of staff who had come. There were a few, including the Headmaster. This chapel must be full of uneasy consciences. Many of her classmates had also come but, by the time the service started, Robyn could not see David.

As they filed out, dutifully looking at the few wreaths, Robyn saw David's unmistakable figure disappearing from the colonnade. He had been there. He must have slipped in at the back and was leaving equally unobtrusively. She should have known. He had tried to hold out a hand to Penny Woodford in life; he wouldn't desert her in death, even though it was the second funeral he had attended in less than a fortnight.

Robyn turned to speak to someone, a question chipping at the back of her brain. She knew his every line, every changing note of his voice. She could tell what mood he was in simply by the way he walked towards her. She knew how his eyes could light with anger or dance with mischief. He never bought her a sandwich with mustard in it, and he never left her alone until she was safely inside her door. And yet today he had ignored her like a stranger. Is that really all there was left to be?

The calls of Sunday afternoon golfers came over the hedge onto the quiet paths of the cemetery. Robyn stood beside her father's grave and stared at the headstone. Some lines from Wordsworth came into her mind: "And have I then thy bones so near, And thou forbidden to appear?" She shivered. Those words were far too flippant for her current emotions. God forbid that he should ever appear again.

She sat down on the black marble of the grave surround and then stood up again. Even that was too close. She wandered round to the back of the derelict church and looked out over the hedge to the golf links. The last time she had been here had been with Neil, when he was so proud of the new headstone, wanting to show it off.

It had been many days since she had thought of Neil. Was she the same person as the one he had brought here that day, early in the summer? He could have been a refuge of sorts, if she'd desired that. She didn't desire that any more; she wanted the colours of storms and lightening, the excitement of a world to discover and the courage to discover it.

He wanted to be a guardian. She didn't want that. She wanted no chains, no closed doors. She wanted the liberty to be hurt and to decide her own healing.

He had been authoritarian. She would never bend to that again. She wanted to walk with someone who wanted to walk with her, beside her, talking, listening, laughing, crying.

Above all, he had been a child, a silly child throwing tantrums when he didn't get his own way. The grass rustled and a blackbird flew up onto the top of the hedge. It opened its throat and began to sing. She kicked at a nettle and sat down on the grass. A realisation shot through her like a laser. Age isn't about how much time has passed since you were born. It's about how much you've grown up.

And how did she know so clearly what she wanted now? Clouds built overhead and the breeze strengthened, blowing her hair in unheeded tangles as she sat for a long time without moving, thinking about just how she knew.

Finally she became aware that someone had come round the corner and stopped behind her. She turned and stood slowly.

"Hello, Robyn," said her mother.

Robyn was shocked. Her mother's hair had lost its groomed look; it was long and without shape. She wore no make-up and her coat was baggy over her bones.

When Robyn didn't speak, Anne said hopefully: "Were you coming to see me?"

"No," said Robyn. She moved to go past. "I have a bus to catch."

"You came for some reason."

Robyn kept walking. "Maybe I came to see if he'd written an apology on the headstone." Then she swung round. "Why did *you* come?"

Anne shrugged helplessly. "Maybe for the same thing."

Robyn turned away again. "Then we're both disappointed."

Her mother followed her to the front of the church and called out as she walked quickly down the avenue towards the gate. "Robyn, Onion's dead."

Robyn slowed to a stop. Without turning she asked: "What happened?"

"He went too far one day. I found him on the main road. There was hardly a mark on him. It must have been just a glancing blow. Neil helped me bury him. He's just at the back door, near the roses."

Robyn stood for a moment remembering the last hug she had given him, the purrs squeezed from him the day she had left her mother's house for the last time. He was the pet of her adolescence, the soft refuge, the warm round weight on her knee in the evening.

Behind her, her mother said: "So now, you see, I don't even have a cat." Robyn turned slowly. Anne held out a hand. "Even if you never forgive me, Robyn, please don't end up like me. A lonely old woman." Her voice rose in urgency, pleading. "Some of the things you said have haunted me. Don't let him do to you what he did to me." She clenched her fist and shook it as she spoke. "Fight him, Robyn. Fight him."

"You didn't."

Anne dropped her head. In a low voice that was close to breaking, she said: "I wish to God I had. Regret is a life sentence." She looked up. "Don't pass it on yourself."

Robyn looked away across the forest of headstones. Traffic rattled past on the road beyond the gate. She looked back at her mother.

"As I said, I've a bus to catch."

She walked away, leaving her mother standing alone.

That night, tired from the long bus journeys, a memory stirred and Robyn pulled the volume of Beowulf from her bookcase. She flicked the pages until a fragile, translucent petal fell from them. It had been pink and still held a hint of colour, but it was dried and pressed to tissue, smooth as fine silk.

She ran it between her fingers, conjuring up the selfish, odourless red rose and the fragrant pink rose; the day she had decided to accept a dangerous friendship and nothing had ever been the same again. The day the petals had scattered from her bag and she thought she had thrown them all away until she found a last one in her slipper. She raised it to her cheek and held it there. Then carefully she smoothed it back between the pages and returned the book to its shelf.

On Monday morning the Headmaster called a special assembly for Penny. The senior school filed into the hall in unaccustomed order. Robyn looked for David. He would have to come to this, even if he had left the school. She saw Tim Thompson a few rows from the front. Chloe was on one side of him. He was keeping a seat on his other side. Then, just before the Headmaster started to speak, David entered and looked around for Tim. His long grey jacket and dark tie stood in sharp relief in the sea of uniforms. He was different. He had always been different.

Robyn turned away, feeling winded. As his eyes had searched for Tim, they had briefly caught her own. Had he even paused before continuing to sweep the hall? She didn't think he had.

Edith was beside her. "David's taking his mother back down to Fermanagh after this," she said. "To her sister's. I called with Elizabeth last night. She's finding it very hard. She said David had suggested it. She shouldn't have come back at all."

"Was David there when you called?"

"I think so. But he didn't appear while I was there. Apparently the Head asked him to take part this morning. To do a reading, I think. His choice. It's the least the Head could do. I hope he's given him an apology too." Edith sniffed. "I never believed a word of it."

Chloe sang a solo. As always, there was an innocent sweetness to her clear, untrained voice. She stood quite still in the centre of the podium and took a deep breath. At first her voice was soft, dejected, the melody sad. She sang of how life just doesn't seem to make sense sometimes.

Robyn looked at David. He was leaning forward, dark head bent low. As if he had told her, she knew he had picked the song. Chloe's voice rose in strength as the song ended on a note of fragile hope for the future. When she finished, there wasn't a sound. David left his chair and went to the podium. He was carrying a book, but Robyn didn't think it looked like a Bible. He set it down and gripped the sides of the lectern firmly.

Always lean, he was now gaunt. His skin was stretched taut across his cheekbones, his collar loose at his throat. The slow look he directed around the hall seemed to hit every person, every pair of eyes, every conscience. In the long silent minute that David surveyed the assembly, no-one moved. Even Billy Dobbin stopped chewing. David turned right round to look at the Headmaster, seated behind him. Then his gaze travelled back again, considering the room for a second time. Robyn wondered if anyone else could tell, as she could, that this wasn't accusation. He was thinking, thinking deeply.

Then he opened the book and began to read. Robyn smiled a little. John Donne had obviously stayed in his mind. In a strong voice reaching to the very back of the hall he spoke firmly: "Death be not proud, though some have called thee mighty and dreadful, for thou art not so."

Robyn put her head down and let his voice envelope her. He was reading this for Penny, and he would honour that. But how could his father not be uppermost in his mind? The father who had not lived to see his son vindicated.

Tears began to gather, threatening her lashes. She hadn't cried for years. And it had been David who had so nearly coaxed them out before, as they stood in Down Cathedral in the thunder storm. Then, she had felt touched by a tenderness that had been missing all her life, a simple holding, companionship, understanding. And what made it so different was that the link between all of these was respect. It didn't occur to him to treat her with anything other than respect. When he found out she didn't like spiders, he didn't tell her not to be silly. He just made sure he caught every spider that came close. He had never even shortened her name. Not once.

Because she had always felt herself to be worthless, damaged goods, born in the memory of a terrible day and profaned where she should have been safest, she simply didn't know what to do with deep, personal, intimate respect from another human being. She hadn't considered herself worthy of it, hadn't recognised that she could accept it, revel in it. Most of all, it hadn't occurred to her that she was whole and free to return it, deeply, personally, intimately.

She brushed her eyes and looked up. He was just finishing, not reading any more, just speaking from memory, holding his head high. Like a declaration of defiance, his voice lifted. "And death shall be no more; death, thou shalt die."

As he stepped down from the podium, Robyn felt the strange emotion stir within her again, the one she had felt in the park as they had stood, palms touching. The final petals of it unfolded and she recognised it at last.

He might already have walked away. She had to reach him.

When the assembly finished, she struggled through the clumps of pupils, subdued clumps but just as solidly in the way. Then someone wanted an absence note signed. Then Duncan Maguire, the head of Geography, stopped her and said that, as Angus Fraser was off for a few days – he didn't know why – he was down a teacher for the field trip. Sorry it was short notice, but could she go? It would be good experience for her, he said. The school bus was leaving after lunch tomorrow and she would only be needed for the one night. Between prefects and teachers, he had plenty of cover for the rest of the week. She said she would see him later and stumbled through a row of chairs to reach the exit.

Which way would he go? She ran through the foyer and burst through the main doors in time to see the green hatchback disappearing through the gates. Against the rules, she ran to her room. Pupils were beginning to line up at her door. She told them to wait quietly until she called them, and shut herself in her storeroom.

Phone to her ear, she paced the length of the room, biting her nails and willing him to answer. At last he did. And suddenly she found speaking very difficult. He sounded as if he was outside, and she heard a car door shut. He must have just arrived home.

"Hello," he said, his tone guarded.

"David," she said.

"Yes?" he said.

"I want to see you."

Silence.

"David, I really want to see you."

She heard him take a deep breath. "Sorry, I'm away for the rest of this week."

"Where are you going?"

"I'm staying overnight in Enniskillen. Then they want me to go up to the school hostel to help with the Geography field trip. I volunteered before… all this. I'm told," he added dryly, "it'll do me good."

"So you won't be back till the weekend?"

"No."

There was a knock on the door and Edith Braden put her head round it. Instead of leaving when she saw Robyn on the phone, she came in and waited.

Robyn turned her back. "I'm going on that too. For tomorrow night anyway. I'll see you there."

"What?" he said sharply.

"I'll see you there," she repeated firmly and hung up. "Well, Edith, what can I do for you?" she asked, but she didn't listen to the reply.

At break time she sat beside Duncan Maguire. "Yes, I think I can manage the field trip for one night. I'd just need to get cover for two classes."

"Great. I'll sort it. Thanks, Robyn."

28

A TWO HOUR journey seemed double that in a school bus full of fifteen and sixteen year olds. Robyn made herself concentrate, doing all the things she was supposed to do. It was the first time she had any responsibility for a trip like this and she wanted to do it well, despite her preoccupations. She checked off names on the register; she ticked off the boys in the back seat when they became too rowdy, bantering them back to humour. Half way there, the driver had to stop and Robyn got off the bus to rub Kerry Jones back while she was travel sick behind a hedge.

At last they were winding upwards round the narrowing roads, finally finding the lane that led to the hostel. The bus filled the lane from hedge to hedge and, as branches scraped across the windows, Robyn saw a small lake on the left, visible through the trees in the darkening evening. The driver steered them through the narrow gate, past the trees that partially obscured the front of the building, and round the gable to a yard at the back. Beside the kitchen door was the green hatchback.

The pupils tumbled out and sprinted for the dormitories. First ones there got the best bunks. Duncan followed them in to ensure that, at the top of the stairs, the boys went to the right and the girls went to the left. Robyn lifted her overnight bag and stepped into the kitchen.

David was at the cooker, stirring a huge pan of soup. He looked tired. The warden of the hostel, whom Robyn later learnt was called Jane, had set out the long tables for an evening meal. She was still there, cutting bread. When he saw Robyn, David left the soup and came round the nearest table.

"I assumed," he said, "that you were serious yesterday."

"Of course I was serious."

"So," he continued, "I'll show you the room I've kept for you."

"When did you get here?"

He reached for her bag. "Lunchtime."

"What do you mean – the room you kept for me?"

He led the way up the stairs. "There are three rooms you could have. One is best."

Excited noise came from both right and left. David took a key from his pocket and opened a door just across the landing at the top of the stairs. It was a small plain room with a single bed, bedside table, wardrobe, and washbasin.

"Why is this room nicer than the others?"

He set her bag on the bed and walked to the window. "The other rooms are shared. And it's the view. Look."

The room was at the front, its window facing west. A tree loomed out of the dusk on the left, its branches almost touching the building. Through and round it Robyn saw that the sky was already a deep orange above a landscape of shifting clouds. Like ships in mist, they drifted across the gold and pewter space, gilded with all the tones from yellow to the deepest ochre.

"See up there?" David pointed. "That bit's just the colour of Tim's hair."

She smiled. "So it is."

The lake was visible from here too, and she could make out a narrow path that ran from the patch of lawn, over a stile and down through the dense undergrowth of trees and shrubs.

David backed away. "There's your key." He set it on the bedside table. A bell shrilled through the building. "Supper's ready," he said, turning to the door.

"David." He stopped but didn't turn back. She came up behind him. "I was also serious about saying I want to talk to you."

"Why?"

He wasn't making this easy for her. "I've been thinking a lot since… you chewed me up and spat me out."

Hungry pupils were passing by on the landing, rattling down the stairs to the kitchen. Some curious looks were directed through the doorway.

David spoke over his shoulder. "After supper, I think the pupils will be given some background to the fieldwork tomorrow. There should be time then."

"OK," she said to his back.

There was a washing up rota to organise, rules to be emphasised, fire drill to be explained. It was nine o'clock before the group was gathered into the large lounge for a talk about the work they had come to do.

Robyn hung up a drying cloth and wiped the ledges, slotting the last knives and forks, scissors and spoons into their places. Where was he? She was trembling like a teenager. He had a barrier around him, a defensive force field. The irony of the role reversal did not escape her.

The evening was mild and dry as she walked outside, round to the front of the hostel. There was some light but the moon wasn't full.

"Do you want to walk down to the lake?"

David's voice came from near the front door, under the tree that spread up past the window of her room. Torchlight suddenly flared in his hand. His talent to materialise out of nowhere was as acute as ever.

"OK."

Duncan Maguire's voice called from inside the front door. "David? Would you mind getting me the flip chart? I forgot to bring it in."

It was obvious from his tone that he was well aware David was no longer subject to his orders. He was doing Duncan a favour by being here at all. David handed Robyn the torch. "I won't be long. Wait for me here."

She stood on the dark patch of lawn, sleepy churrs coming from roosting birds. Occasionally the dart of a bat cut past from shadow to shadow. The bushes whispered in air that carried the sharp smell of pine cones. Above, the clouds were iron grey now against the night sky. She decided to go over the stile. It was fairly new and sturdy. Once on the other side, she shone the torch through the bushes, following the track. She looked back. There was no sign of David yet. She wandered on to the first bend to see what was beyond it. Just past the bend, the torchlight picked out some feathers on the ground, half hidden under a hawthorn. She walked the few steps to it and crouched to see what it was. It was a dead…

Her hair was wrenched hard. She cried out in pain and fell backwards. A rough hand pulled her hair taut, twisting it. The torch bounced away into the undergrowth. Fingers clamped across her mouth. A face lurched over her. Angus Fraser.

"It's time, you whore," he snarled, shaking her.

Shock streamed through Robyn's body. Dissolved into a desperate struggle. She twisted, jagging her cheek painfully on the rough ground, but her hair was so firmly clamped that her skin was standing out on her temples. She tried to bite the fingers over her mouth but he moved too quickly and his hand gagged her mouth shut. She heaved with her legs but he placed a knee across her ribs until all the air was gone from her lungs. When a knife flashed in front of her eyes, fear turned from hot to cold. She thought of the alarm David had given her. It was in her bag. Her bag was on her bed.

"Not a sound," he instructed, tilting the knife where she could see it, before slowly removing his hand from her mouth.

Robyn's mind jolted around in panic as Angus yanked her to her feet and bent her under his arm. He dragged her, stumbling, falling, further away from the hostel, towards the lake. Branches whipped painfully across her face. Had he just got lucky, thinking she was out on her own? Did he know David would be looking for her? Did he intend to attack David too? She knew what he intended to do with her.

Fir trees bordered the lake and the needles made the ground soft underfoot as Angus flung her against a tree trunk, jarring her painfully. Stars were helping the meagre moonlight, reflecting off the water to glint in Angus' pale eyes and on the thick gold chain around his neck.

He waved the knife in front of her face. It was a penknife, but a large one, and honed. He seemed to calm down, now that he had got her in his control. He began to touch her face, stroke her hair like a hungry man who has imagined a meal for many days. That was when Robyn realised she was at the mercy of a madman.

He dropped the knife and with both hands behind her head, brought all her hair round her shoulders to the front. He lifted it in both hands and buried his face in it. Robyn began to feel sick. She braced her hands against the trunk behind her and jerked her knee up hard. He dodged and caught her leg, tossing her sideways onto the ground.

She fell heavily on her side, skinning her cheek on a root. He knelt over her. "You'll not do that to me again, you bitch." He rolled her over onto her back. His hand gripped the collar of her blouse and ripped it from her shoulders.

Robyn began to leave her body. It was a trick she had learnt many years ago, a coping strategy, a way to believe this was not happening. She hadn't had to use it recently. She hadn't thought she would ever need it again. But with the ease of a lesson well learnt and never forgotten, she went limp and travelled away, far away.

Impatiently, David went to the school bus and flipped up the side luggage compartment. By the yard light, he hauled out the flip chart easel and the bag of notes and maps which Mr Maguire had also forgotten to bring in. He carried them to the lounge, set up the flip chart in the corner, dug out the marker pens and left.

He picked up another torch from the shelf beside the front door and stepped outside. He was trying not to think about what she might say to him. It was easier that way. An owl hooted as he looked for her. He swept the beam from one side of the lawn to the other. He would have seen her if she had gone back into the house. She must have gone on ahead. He threw his leg over the stile and jumped down, picking his way carefully over the rutted track. Round the first bend something in the undergrowth caught his eye. He pushed through the bushes. It was a torch, still lit, but tumbled askew in a tussock of grass. A large moth fluttered in and out of the line of light.

He swept the torchlight over the ground. The grass had been disturbed, tossed. At one place, the ground was ploughed up in a line, as if a heel had been scored through it by someone being dragged along.

The hair stood up on the back of his neck. He started to run. Then something told him to stop running and to go quietly. Something told him not to shout her name. Stand still. Stand still for a minute! Listen! Stand still and listen! He braced his feet against the ruts, and snapped off the torch. He stopped breathing and honed his ears to the night. In front of him, towards the lake and slightly to the left, a handful of birds clattered from their roost, squawking their alarm as they rose out from the branches.

He clicked on the torch again and sped towards the spot, urgency making him sure-footed. The first thing he saw was a pair of white shoulders pressed into the ground. A man was on top of her, roughly pulling and tearing at her clothes. A knife lay on the ground. Robyn looked as if she were already dead.

Strength shot into his muscles, a blinding power took him across the space in a blur of speed. His first blow sent Fraser spinning into the undergrowth. David braced his feet for another lunge, glanced quickly at Robyn. He couldn't see her clearly.

Fraser pulled himself out of the bushes, his fists raised. David didn't wait for him. Anger, disgust, frustration, and grief poured out of him in a pyroclastic surge, to concentrate on incinerating this monstrosity once and for all.

Before Fraser could react, David was on him. He swung his right fist hard into his jaw and sent him sprawling back onto the pine needles. Fraser lay winded for a moment then flipped over to scuttle on all fours towards the knife. David reached it just as Fraser's hand covered it. He brought his foot down onto Fraser's fingers so hard he felt the fingers snap. Fraser crawled to a tree trunk and pulled himself up, feeling his jaw, blood pouring from his mouth and one finger jutting askew.

Still seeing through a red mist, David shot out both hands and gripped him by the shoulders. Angus held up his undamaged hand in a gesture of surrender.

"Hey, stop, stop! OK?" he said through thickening lips. "Look, why don't we do a deal?" Desperation drenched his voice as David took aim. "There's only the two of us here. Why don't we share, eh? You can even go first."

He didn't see the warning in David's bared teeth. The next blow broke his nose, bone and cartilage mashed into his face.

David took his slumped body by the chain around his neck and dragged him, strangling, across pine needles, tree roots and stones to the edge of the lake. He threw him on the ground, half in and half out of the water, his face submerged between two rocks. He lifted one foot and put it on Fraser's head, holding it under the surface. The cold shock brought Fraser round and he began to struggle. David held his foot firm and unyielding, watching the bubbles rise round Fraser's ears.

He looked up at the stars. It should have been a beautiful night, by a peaceful lake, under an autumn sky. As if a hand brushed his arm in warning, the red tide ebbed and he knew he had to stop. Robyn. He must go back to Robyn. He lifted his foot and, taking Fraser by the ankles, pulled him out of the water. A trail of blood from Fraser's nose glistened colourlessly in the faint light as he spluttered and coughed.

David spun round, a thought attacking him. The knife had been beside Robyn, but when Fraser had reached for it, she had not been there. His torch was flickering as he picked it up and swept it urgently round the bushes and trees. He called her name but there was no reply, just the faintest lapping of water, the tiniest rustle of leaves and the occasional groan from the water's edge. David called again and shouldered through all the nearer undergrowth. She was gone.

He ran back up the path, calling, stumbling, his mind refusing yet to contemplate what this had done to her. In the hostel kitchen, several drawers had been pulled out, one wrenched so hard it had spilled onto the floor. Cutlery littered the tiles and ledges.

He leapt up the stairs and found two girls outside Robyn's door, their faces worried, puzzled.

"Is she in there?" he demanded.

"We think so," said one. "We heard banging in the kitchen and then this door slammed. It's locked." She looked at David curiously. "Were you with her?"

Duncan Maguire came up the stairs. "What's going on?"

David tried the door. "Robyn? Let me in. Please, Robyn. Let me in."

He didn't care now, and wouldn't care later, what the others thought. He rattled the door handle. Then he stopped, his mind working fast. This would be adding to her terror.

He backed away from the door and motioned the others to do the same.

"Nobody," – he sliced a hand downwards for emphasis – "nobody but me is to go into that room."

More pupils appeared at the top of the stairs, mouths open. He turned to the teacher, his eyes imploring. Duncan met his gaze for a moment and then he nodded.

"Right, back downstairs everyone. Show's over and I haven't finished the briefing for tomorrow."

Briefly, in the kitchen where Robyn wouldn't overhear, David told Duncan what had happened. "I'm going to get into that room if I have to take the slates off," he said. "No matter how long I'm in there, don't let anybody, anybody, come in."

He waited as Duncan's face drained to ashen white. Then the teacher nodded and made for the telephone to call the police. The signal was poor here; he would have to use the land line.

Outside, David looked up through the branches of the tree and saw that the light was on in Robyn's room. He had no torch, so he searched the ground by the faint light escaping from the curtain edge at the lounge window. He found a stone and brushed soil from it, hefting it experimentally in his hand. Satisfied, he pushed it into his shirt and leapt for the nearest branch.

He swung himself up through the tree, the branches becoming thinner, more supple, less supportive, as he shifted his weight with quick, quiet efficiency. When he was level with the window, he worked his way as far as he dared along a branch and stretched across to grip a drainage pipe which was fixed to the wall beside it. It was old and rusty, powdery on his hand. He pulled on it carefully, so that the branch swung to the window and he could look through.

Robyn wasn't visible anywhere. But the bed had been moved.

It had been pulled across the door, totally blocking it. Even if the door was unlocked there was no way it would open. She had barricaded herself in.

But it was what was strewn on the floor that stunned David into shock and immobility. Hair. Strands of it. Lumps of it. Bunches of it. Her beautiful dark hair, shot through with pine needles, was lying like skeins of discarded thread across the room. One twisted clump had blood at the root. The last piece, its ends splayed like the spokes of a spider's web, lay at the door of the wardrobe. The door was slightly open, trembling on its hinges.

David made himself harden to steel. He examined the window. It had a conventional opening, with a latch and bar on one side. Thank God for low budgets. This hostel was well overdue for an upgrade. The pipe was grating, slipping against the wall.

David reached for the stone and raised it in his free hand. He called out: "Robyn. I'm going to break the window." He waited but there wasn't a sound. He swung the stone back and called again. "I'm going to break the window now."

Glass splintered into the room. Working fast with one hand as both branch and drain pipe weakened, David knocked out the jagged edges with his closed fist and reached for the latches, flicking them up. Still holding himself close to the window by gripping the swaying pipe with one hand, he swung both feet up and in one movement knocked the window open, slid his legs across the ledge, let go the pipe and grabbed for the window frame. He dropped onto the carpet of glass on the floor.

He stayed where he was for a moment. "Robyn?"

Still no sound. He tried to ignore the clumps of hair, stepping over them as he moved towards the wardrobe. When he reached it, he stopped to listen, then slowly pulled the door open.

She was curled in a tight ball at the bottom of it, rocking herself to and fro, to and fro. Her jeans were torn and her arms were scratched and bleeding. The remnants of her shirt were hanging like rags from her grazed shoulders. Her face was hidden in her arms where they hugged across her knees. What was not hidden was her head. David's knees buckled and he sank to the floor.

29

THERE WAS NO one to hear the crashing of branches, the snapping of twigs, the alarms of startled birds as Angus staggered through the bushes. Shaw had nearly killed him! He had really nearly killed him! Fear and indignation writhed crazily through his body as he stumbled along, his intact hand covering his mouth and nose. Blood poured between his fingers and mingled with the soaked cuff at his wrist. He found the fence beside the road and his shirt ripped as he threw himself under the barbed wire. He lurched down the laneway to a track that disappeared to the right, from starlight into darkness. He found his car where he had left it, hidden in bushes. He collapsed across the bonnet and yelled out as his broken fingers twisted under his weight.

Hands slippery with his own blood, he reversed the car. Pain shot through his fingers as he worked the gears, found the headlight switch. Back on the narrow lane, he accelerated sharply, slewing round the corners, slicing the hedges, until he reached the road. He put his foot down heavily on the accelerator, roaring downwards, round the corners which curved down the hillside. His whole head throbbed. The steering wheel was slippery as he tore at it one-handed.

The fox loomed like a ghost, an exquisite sculpture in the middle of the road. Her muzzle pointed straight at him, her nose and pale chin catching the shine from the headlights. One front paw was raised, her brush low and motionless. Angus gasped, wrenched the wheel to the left, felt a massive jolt. The bonnet rose and a tearing noise ripped along the side of the car.

The fox put her paw down and her nose lifted to sniff the air. Then she trotted to the side of the road where shuddering bushes bracketed a gap in the hedge that hid the steep rocky drop on the other side. She looked over the edge, her nose quivering. With a couple of sharp snuffles into the air, she turned her back and trotted across the road. She slid into the undergrowth, the white tip of her brush vanishing like a snuffed candle.

David sat cross-legged on the floor and looked at Robyn. He felt courage drain out of him, leaching into the night and making him want to crawl away, away to some peaceful haven where nothing would be asked of him ever again. He could not cope with this. He was not equipped for this. He was mentally, spiritually, emotionally and physically near the end of his endurance.

It was only for a moment. He banished the weakness and stretched out instead for the wisdom that he was going to need. He closed his eyes. When he opened them again, his mind cleared to a crystal calmness.

Her head was a mass of stubble, some longer tufts still poking from behind her ear. In one place he could see that she had hacked into the skin surface. Blood was oozing from the wound. He could not tell if she knew he was there. He heard some noises from the landing and immediately shut them out of his mind.

"Hey," he said to her, "I can break windows too."

No response. She continued to rock to and fro. He reached out a hand and gently touched her shoulder. Her head came up and her hand lifted towards him, a hand which wielded a pair of scissors, held like a dagger. There was an ugly gash on her cheek. Recovering fast, he trapped her eyes with his own and willed her not to look away.

"Robyn, Angus has gone. He's gone. It's over. I'm here now. And you trust me."

Holding her gaze, he poured all of himself into those dark pools of fear. "You told me once you weren't afraid of me. You told me you weren't afraid of me at all." He held out a hand, but didn't touch her this time. "Trust me now."

She was beginning to listen. He could sense a slight change, as if the tide of panic had been halted, even if it had not turned. Her face looked smaller, vulnerable, like a familiar picture that has been ripped from its frame.

"Remember the day you told me you trusted me? I'll never forget it, Robyn. Not as long as I live. It was a big thing for me to hear. But it was an even bigger thing for you to say. Wasn't it? Is there any reason why you would stop trusting me now? Is there?"

He waited to see if she would answer. Her body had stopped rocking, relaxed a little. The hand with the scissors had drooped between her knees, and still she watched him, her eyes starting to blink, to flicker.

David started to talk again, gently, softly, talking about things they had done, conversations they had had, things they had discovered about each other. As he watched, blood trickled down her ravaged head and began to creep across her shoulder to drop down her back, visible through the torn material. His throat choked with all that he really wanted to say and yet instinct told him to hold back, wait. Not now, not yet.

He unfolded his legs. "Robyn, you might want to stay here forever, but I'm going to want out some time. I don't want to have to go back the way I came. You did a good job of barricading the door." He rose to his feet slowly. "I'm going to move the bed out of the way." Her eyes were following him. That was good. "I'm not going away. OK? In fact I'm not leaving here unless you come with me. I'll be straight back."

The bed was old fashioned and heavy. There was a clump of hair on the quilt. Briefly he brushed it with his fingertips, then lifted it to set on the bedside table. He put her bag on the floor, one end of the unused alarm he had given her visible beneath a red purse. Then, as quietly as he could, he turned the key in the door to open the lock. When he turned back, she had moved and was sitting with her feet on the floor between the doors of the wardrobe. She had put down the scissors, but her arms were back round her knees, her eyes still huge above the cheekbones accentuated in her frameless face.

David went down on his heels in front of her. For a long minute he held her gaze, unable to say any more, moved beyond words by what he was seeing, what he was feeling. Then slowly he lifted up his hand, palm open towards her.

"Shalom, Robyn Daniels," he whispered.

It all happened in one swift second. She flew into his arms. He caught her and stood, scooping her up in both arms onto his shoulder as her own arms went tightly round his neck. Jesus! he breathed, holding her, rocking her, relief making him weak.

When he could speak his voice was shaky. "Well, hello. I thought I was going to have to get in there with you. And I don't think I would have fitted somehow."

He tried to look down at her but her face was buried against his neck, her arms pulling herself closer, tighter. Blood was streaked across his shirt where her cheek had brushed his chest as she reached for him.

His head began to spin. The sea. He heard the sea as if it was raging at his feet, pounding, wild, brutal. Clear as a descant above the waves was the sound of crying, slowly diminishing, desolate weeping, fading away, draining into the sounds of the sea, until only the storm remained. David closed his eyes and staggered slightly. Not now! No, not now! With rigid determination, he pulled himself back to the present.

"You need that head fixed." He hugged her and chuckled slightly. "You always did, my darling." To his delight, she responded with a little movement against his neck. He put her down on the bed, gently disentangling her arms, and pulled the quilt round her. He stooped to picked her up again and with a struggle managed to reach for the handle and open the door. Duncan Maguire stood on the landing.

"I'm taking her to hospital. I'll phone you."

Duncan nodded. "The police may want to talk to her there."

David swung Robyn to his side and started down the stairs. "They can wait," he said.

It was a long drive through dark countryside and he took his time, making no sudden movements. The headlights slewed along the hedges as he negotiated the bends down the hillside. Not far from the hostel, the lights jumped across a gap. David noticed it but gave it little thought.

The next hours were a blur. Amongst all the questions, tests, doctors, nurses, wheel chairs, trolleys, swishing curtains and rattling needles, one bright, electric moment stood out for David. When she was asked for the name of a contact person, she gave his name. She was confused. She must be. But he said nothing.

For some time he was banished to a chair in the waiting area. He rang the hostel and checked in with Duncan. The reception was poor and broken. He was about to hang up when Duncan asked, "David, is Robyn Daniels the reason you've left the school? There have been rumours."

"I'm done with rumours," he replied, too tired to think. He thumbed the call to an end. Then there was nothing more to endure but the interminable waiting.

Later in the night he stood beside Robyn's bed in one of the wards. She was asleep, under sedation. The doctor didn't think any lasting physical damage had been done. He confirmed that, although she had been violently assaulted, she had not been raped. Her hair would grow again, except perhaps for one small area near the crown of her head.

As for her mental condition, the doctor would not make an assessment. David looked at her cleaned and bandaged head, the doctor's words etched on his memory, pieces of a puzzle slotting into place.

"I see she has marks on her lower arms." He had looked at David questioningly. David nodded and the doctor continued: "Taking that into account, and bearing in mind the way she has responded to questions we have asked, her reaction to this attack reminds me of another case I saw some years ago. In that case, the woman had a history of sexual abuse in her childhood." He touched David's arm sympathetically. "Terrible thing. She's lucky to have you, young man. Much will depend on you." Overworked, he had left wearily to see to his next patient.

A nurse pushed through the curtains and checked Robyn's pulse. She looked at David. "She's going to sleep for a while. Why don't you get some rest? The day room's just down the corridor." She smiled. "Not many people use it in the middle of the night."

"Are you sure she won't wake?"

"Not for quite a while."

With all his soul, David craved solitude. He was running on empty, his mind, body and spirit sapped of strength. Along a corridor lit by dim night lights, he pushed open the door of the quiet room. Inside, he stood still in the darkness, feeling the silence falling over him like a blessing. Then he sank into one of the chairs and leaned his head back. As he relaxed, he felt for the first time the bruising on his right hand.

He closed his eyes, stilled himself, settled. His mind opened, desperate to find and draw on a reservoir of love and peace and strength that he needed so badly.

Robyn woke some time in the early morning. Soft light filtered round from the nurses' station. She could just see it by shadows on the ceiling and through a tiny gap in the curtains that were pulled around her bed. She knew there were other beds around her, could feel the presence of other bodies. There was a rustling as someone turned over, muttering.

She seemed to be filled with a total calmness, floating in airy comfort on the pillows piled behind her. Her memory was clear; she had forgotten nothing of what had happened, but it was far away, nothing to do with the tranquillity that enveloped her now.

She moved her head slightly, feeling it scrape and bump on the pillow, jagging painfully. Tentatively she explored her scalp. Tufts alternated with stubble and in one place, a sorer place, she felt strips of bandage holding the skin. She felt her right cheek. It was covered with a pad of gauze.

No regrets, none. Peace draped itself around her, tucking itself between her fingers and toes so that she felt cradled, rocked, innocent as she had never been as a child.

A man was seated beside her bed. She sensed this slowly and without alarm. His body was thrown forward, cheek resting on his arms crooked on the covers. His face was turned away from her, but even in the dim light she knew who he was. She would know that wavy black hair anywhere, recognise the curls licking the pale glimmer of his neck.

Softly her hand stole forward and, light as a kitten's paw, brushed the springy waves. His right hand was flat on the sheet near her, emerging from beneath his sleeping head. His knuckles were bruised and cut.

Her hand settled on top of his. She remembered how he had reached through the terror, the panic. This time it would have been the end. She could not have coped, could not have fought it without him. And he was still here. She smiled. Something nibbled at the edge of her memory. Slowly she tried to grasp it, turning after it as it slipped away.

She saw David's head rise slowly and turn towards her. Her mouth was still curved in a smile but he didn't answer it. Instead, he looked down and, very deliberately, placed a slow, gentle kiss on her hand where it lay on his. It was the first kiss he had ever touched to her skin.

He raised his head again and she saw his deep eyes fix on her face. He spoke softly. "I love you, Robyn".

"Yes," she said, her eyelids closing. "Yes, I remember now." Her voice began to trail away. "I wanted to talk to you."

David twisted his hand to hold hers and was still keeping watch as she drifted away into sleep once more.

30

R OBYN WOKE WITH a start. Someone was poking something cold into her ear. Immediately she tensed and knocked the hand away, pushing herself to the far edge of the bed.

"It's OK, pet. You're in hospital. I'm just taking your temperature." A nurse with a worn but kindly face smiled at her.

Memory came flooding back. Robyn put her hand to her head, her cheek, ran her fingers over her shoulders. They felt rough where grazes had been cleaned and left open to the air. She lifted the bed cover. She was wearing a nightdress that didn't belong to her.

The nurse lifted the chart from the end of the bed and wrote on it. "You took a pretty good hammering from some bastard. I think they'll want to watch you for twenty-four hours anyway." She snagged the chart back in its place and tucked the pen behind her ear. "Did you know the guy who did this?"

There wasn't a trace of sedation left in Robyn's system. The shock of returning memory was being replaced by a jumble of emotions. Anger, fear, amazement, relief. And a dim recollection of dreaming about David.

"Yes, I knew him."

The nurse pulled her forward and thumped the pillows behind her with some force. "They ought to cut the balls off him when they catch him." Then she grinned. "Maybe give you the scissors, eh? You look as if you can use them."

"I must look a sight."

"It can be tidied a bit. You've been lucky. No lasting harm done. And you've the bones for a short hairdo. Maybe you've done yourself a favour." She ran a practised hand over the covers, smoothing, tucking. "Look on the bright side. The beast could have done worse." She leaned her knuckles on the side of the bed. "And if ever you get tired of that boyfriend, there's a queue here already." She bustled away, chuckling.

Where was he? Her bed was in a corner next to the corridor, and the curtain was still partially pulled round it. She swung her legs out. She was shakier than she realised. She wanted a shower. There was a ridiculous thick, striped bath robe across the low chair next to her locker. She had no soap, nothing of her own with her. But that was not going to stop her from standing under clean, fresh, warm running water. She could dry herself on the bath robe. It looked like a towel anyway.

She stood carefully. Her head felt odd, light. She felt exposed. There was nothing to swing across her face when she wanted to hide. She must have been doing that all her life. She put her head up in a little movement of defiance. Time to get used to a new view on the world. She pulled on the bath robe and walked barefoot with careful steps into the corridor to find the showers. Then she stopped.

David was coming through the swing doors. He had a carrier bag in his hand. When he saw her, he slowed. Then he smiled slightly, his eyebrows raised in a cautious question. Her expression must have satisfied him because he dropped the bag and opened his arms. Without hesitation, she walked into them.

Back in the ward, she sat on her bed and pretended to criticise everything he had brought. It was a way to cope with the electricity of the emotions that sparked between them, an odd jumble of the familiar and the unexplored. Something had changed, pivoted, altering the future, realigning the past. Combined with the residual shock in her system, it was making her jumpy, looking for ways to be normal, everyday, mundane, until she could tunnel through to a time when she would look at him and listen and talk and work this thing out once and for all.

"A blue toothbrush! Didn't they have any pink ones?"

"So?" he said. "Blue ones clean your teeth just as well as pink ones."

"And that's not mint toothpaste."

"I'll remember in future. Mint it is."

She rummaged further down the bag. "Hmm. The facecloth's OK."

"One out of three ain't bad," he said.

She held up a bar of soap. "No shower gel then?"

She squealed as both his hands went round her neck. He brought his mouth close to her ear.

"You," he said very low, "are being a little bitch." He shook her slightly as his face moved across her vision and his mouth arrived at her other ear. "And I take that to be a very good sign."

He released her and she stood up, lifting the bag. She tossed her head but there was no hair to toss. "Well, seeing you didn't get me a toilet bag, this" – she rustled the bag – "will have to do."

He sat in the chair and leaned back, stretching out his legs and putting his hands behind his head. "Are you going to have a shower or are you going to scold all day?"

Suddenly she felt weak, strength going from her legs and she sat again. "David, do you think they've found ...?"

His expression hardened. "I haven't heard anything overnight. My phone battery's done. But I'll find out later." He reached for her hand. "They'll get him. Don't worry. They'll get him. What's left of him."

She was quiet for a minute, looking at the floor. Then she lifted the carrier bag a little. "David, you're the most thoughtful person I've ever known."

He leaned forward. "That'll do for now." He sat back again and looked around. "Now scram. I'll probably get thrown out of here soon. If you're not back by the time the breakfasts are brought round, I'll eat yours."

Robyn washed her bruised body with care, removing the gauze on her cheek to examine the gash which was still raw and angry. Would there be a scar? It wasn't a long cut, but it was quite deep. The memory of Angus Fraser's brutal hands was fresh and horrible. And yet... and yet... Also strong was the brush of David's breath on her uncovered ears, the timbre of his voice, low and close.

She raised her face to the falling water. How was it that, the morning after being attacked, she was standing in a shower recognising as never before the goodness in another man?

Something decisive had happened to her yesterday. Something unexpected, even perverse. Her mind was sorting, shifting, clearing out old concepts, old fears. She wasn't a worthless person. Someone would fight for her! She knew now about goodness and integrity and unconditional love. It was new and glorious and breathtaking, shining in magnificent relief against the ugliness of its opposite.

She stepped out of the shower and looked down the length of her body, right to her toes. She took the bathrobe and rubbed the condensation from the mirror. Raising her hands high above her head, she turned slowly, looking at every part of herself. She was bruised certainly. Her head looked very peculiar.

She thought of the extraordinary young person who waited not very far from where she stood. He respected her. He had fought for her.

She began to dry her skin carefully. There was bad and there was good. She had experienced the bad. She wasn't going to be a prisoner to it any longer. Her heart was healing.

She would be leaving tomorrow morning, provided she showed no further ill effects of her ordeal. When David asked if she wanted to contact any of her family, she said 'no' so quickly that she saw his sharp flicker of surprise.

"No point in worrying anybody," she explained.

"Worrying me's OK, of course?"

She grinned and wrinkled her nose in mischief. "Of course."

He made a grab for her foot which dangled over the side of the bed near him as he sat in the chair. As he held it, all the fun left his eyes. He ran his hands along her foot, examining it intently. His thumbs traced the little veins deep under the skin of her instep. His fingers moved to cup the curve of her heel. His other hand folded over her toes, warm and gentle.

Mesmerised, her breath catching in her throat, she watched the top of his dark head bent in total absorption.

"Stop, David," she whispered.

He paused and looked up like a man coming out of a trance. His eyes had darkened, his emotions free on his face. He looked around and at last seemed to realise where he was. One last time he ran his hands slowly along the sides of her foot, from her ankle to her toes. Then he relinquished it carefully. Robyn felt her foot become cold as the heat of his touch left it.

He sat with his head bowed, hands loosely grasped between his knees. Tentatively, Robyn reached out and touched his hair. A memory stirred. When David felt her touch, he reached up and pulled her hand down between his own. He held it for a moment and then looked up at her. Holding her eyes he lifted the back of her hand and gently kissed it.

Memory flared again. "It wasn't a dream, was it? Last night?" she asked, her voice unsteady,

Still watching her, he turned his mouth into her palm. "No," he said. "It wasn't a dream."

David took a deep breath in the silence that followed. He was still holding her hand. Then his mouth crooked in a lopsided smile.

"Maybe I should go back and get your stuff. Another night without shower gel and you might start chopping off fingers."

Robyn retrieved her hand. "You need to sleep for a few hours. You can recharge yourself and your phone at the same time. And bring me any news," she added.

He looked puzzled. "For someone who's been through what you have, you're remarkably perky. You're better than I dared hope you'd be."

She touched his cheek. "You've no idea, have you? No idea that it's all about you. You change things. You make a difference." She dropped her voice. "Penny knew that. And your father knew that. Deep down he must have known that. And if he didn't," she went on, "he does now."

Pain filled his eyes as he propped his elbows on his knees and covered his face. His voice was muffled. "I hope so."

He was still haunted, hurting, the pain in easy reach. Gently she pulled his hands aside. "You must tell me about him some time. I'd like to get to know him."

He sat without speaking, and she waited out his thinking, as she had become so accustomed to doing. A doctor and the nursing sister swung into the ward on their morning rounds. David gathered himself and stood up.

"Right. I'd better go and sort out a few things." He rubbed his jaw. "The stubble's growing."

She touched her hand to the side of her head. "I hope mine will. I must be a phrenologist's dream."

One of his eyebrows shot up. "Phrenologist?"

She waited a moment, grinning. Then she pointed a triumphant finger at him. "Ha! You don't know it!"

"But I will by tonight!"

"You will come back tonight?"

He backed away. "I'll be here."

"And David?"

"What?"

She felt almost shy. "Maybe I know a lot of words. But I haven't the words to thank you."

He looked at his feet as a slow smile spread across his face. He looked up at her from under his brows, his eyes twinkling. "You'll have to think of something else then."

The mid morning traffic was heavy as David headed out of the city. He stopped for petrol, propping himself against the car to watch the gauge spinning round. Out of the corner of his vision, an ambulance sped by on its way to the hospital. Beside him as he waited to pay at the counter was a tray of beanie toys, little felt rabbits, bears, and monkeys filled with beans that moved under his fingers as he picked through them. He decided on a rabbit.

As the road rose up the hillside towards the laneway to the hostel, David slowed round a long bend. On the other side of the road, just beside a gap that had been torn in the hedge, a police car was pulled in as far as it could onto the narrow verge.

He drove past carefully. He hadn't gone far before a thought bloomed in his head and the hairs started to prickle on the back of his neck.

Only the warden, Jane, was there when he pushed open the door of the kitchen. She was anxious for news, distressed at what had happened. There was no news of Fraser, although the police had called early, wanting to take statements. They would probably call at the hospital later. Duncan Maguire had made a full report to the school and two other teachers had arrived to enable the field trip to continue.

"I tidied the room," Jane said. "It's all here. Mr Maguire said he'd take it to her tonight." She pointed to a corner next to an old sofa where she had put Robyn's holdall and shoulder bag. Her red coat was thrown over them. Jane paused, then she opened a drawer and pulled out a small, flat parcel of kitchen foil. She held it up uncertainly.

"I wasn't sure what to do with this." Silently, David took it from her. She went on: "The room had to be ready for the new chap who came. They're fixing the glass some time today."

David eyed the little pile in the corner. "Sorry about that."

"What else could you do?"

David lifted Robyn's belongings.

"I'm going back later. I'll take these to her."

"But Mr Maguire ..."

David opened the back door. "Tell him I've got them."

He opened the boot and set the bags and coat in carefully. He turned the foil parcel over in his hand. Then he unwrapped one end and glanced at the contents. He closed it again and tucked it inside his shirt. There were still traces of dried blood across his chest.

A ginger cat appeared from the front of the house and stopped when she saw him. She sat and licked her paw. The air was damp but it had not yet rained. How could everything look the same? Not even a day had passed since he had almost committed murder.

He slammed the boot shut and walked to the front of the house. After a quick glance at the tree and the broken window, he jumped over the stile and pushed his way along the path to the lake. Here were a few broken twigs. There, the score of her heel furrowing through the grass.

Down by the lake, he walked round looking for signs, markers in the light of day to confirm what had happened in the dark. It occurred to him that the police had probably been here already.

At the edge of the water, he looked at the stones where he had held Fraser's head down with his foot, jamming it with all his strength onto the gravel bed. He walked further along until he came to a clear stretch of grass extending from a stand of mountain ash. He crouched and sat, arm resting on one bent knee. A gentle breeze rippled the water. A moorhen paddled by, busy and oblivious.

He needed to process all this. At last, he allowed the pictures to scroll in his head. Robyn on the ground, Angus on top of her. Robyn curled in a tight ball in the bottom of the wardrobe. Robyn flashing a pair of scissors at him. Robyn flying into his arms. On and on they came in a reel that would join the others stored in his brain for ever. When he came to the picture of Robyn that morning, stepping barefoot into the corridor as he came through the door of the ward, he paused the film.

Above her bare feet and legs, she wore a pink nightdress that was too big for her. Over that was a hospital dressing gown, a towelling creation of blue and white stripes. The sleeves came down over her hands and the long belt trailed on the ground behind her. Her face was white, sculpted, stark. A large gauze bandage was taped over her right cheek. Her head was an untidy jumble of tufts and strands, hacked and chopped in a frenzy.

She had looked like a scarecrow on a bad day. And he had never loved her more.

He threw a twig into the water and watched it bob in a circle of ripples. He had always been slow to catch fire. Tim used to tease him about it. He got to his feet restlessly. At the water's edge he kicked a pebble far across the surface and heard the moorhen clatter away in fright. From the first days of knowing Robyn, really knowing her, curiosity had become delight. Delight had become need. He had now reached a desire that he had never experienced before, a conflagration that, far from destroying the curiosity, the delight and the need, seemed only to enrich and inflame their colours.

He didn't know how to deal with it.

A powerful longing to see his father again hit him like a dagger. His head went back, a gasp escaping him as the raw sense of loss punched him once again. Robyn had talked about his father in the present tense, talked about getting to know him. He could love her for that alone.

He might have tried to talk to his father about this. His adolescence had been overshadowed by the edge between them, but recently he thought they might have come to understand each other better. Except he knew what his father would say. He could hear him, see him. "It's lust, lad. Pure and simple," he would admonish. "Have a cold shower."

No, he couldn't have talked to his father about this. It would have started another argument. Dad, he said in his head, it's not lust, it's not simple – his mouth curved – and it's certainly not pure.

And Robyn? The foil parcel of her hair was warm against his skin. He loved a woman who had just been assaulted, and who, he was now sure, had been cruelly damaged in childhood. The thought hurt him more than he could bear. She might still run away as she had before, graceful and cold. But today? Today he had sensed a change in her, sensed that the ice was almost gone.

He wished Tim were here. He slipped his phone from his pocket. Even if he could get a signal, the battery was totally flat. With a tight smile, David looked up at the sky. "I suppose that just leaves you," he said aloud. "I hope you're being particularly understanding today."

He settled his feet apart on the shingle, pushed his fingers into his pockets and closed his eyes. His mind and body still, he emptied his heart to the sky.

31

JANE FED HIM. David hadn't thought about food until a double helping of shepherd's pie steamed in front of him. He was briefly alone in the kitchen while he polished the plate clean. He prowled to the fridge and, head thrown back, drank a pint of milk straight from the carton. Before Jane returned, he hid the empty carton deep in the rubbish bin.

Sleep was attacking him and he had his foot on the stairs when he heard a car pull into the yard. A policeman snagged the latch and entered. The officer pulled out a chair.

"We think we've found him. Sit down." He drew a driving licence out of his pocket and opened it, pushing it across to David. "That him?"

David glanced at the photograph. "Yes."

The police officer took it back and returned it to his pocket. "He's dead."

David stared at him.

"His car went off the road. We found it – and him – at the bottom of a hill about a mile away. Lot of rocks about. He didn't have a chance."

David pictured the gap torn in the hedge. The thought he had as he drove back this morning had been right. He also remembered seeing it last night as he drove Robyn to hospital.

"Did he die instantly?"

"The ambulance men thought he hadn't. He wasn't wearing a seatbelt so he was thrown out of the car, but it looks as if he'd crawled off a bit. He was really bashed up."

"Did they say how long he'd lived for?"

"No, they didn't. Why?"

"No reason."

"There's more. Our men entered his house in Belfast. They found enough. You don't want to know. He was a sick guy."

David stood up. "You haven't told Robyn this yet, have you?"

"No, but…"

"I'll tell her."

"I have to speak to the teacher in charge."

"He'll be back later." David had turned to the door, but he swung round again. "I'll tell her," he repeated firmly.

He plugged in his phone, setting the alarm on it for two hours time. He lay on his bed. Angus Fraser was dead. And he might still have been alive when he had driven past the spot last night. If he had known, he could have called for help.

Would he? He held the question up and looked at it. Then he put it down again and turned onto his side. His last thought before he fell asleep was of the warm foil which still nestled against his skin.

Two hours later he stood under a refreshing shower. He held his head to the water to let the foam run out of his hair and stream down his body. His right hand ached and the knuckles stung in the soapy water. He looked at it, flexing the fingers, recalling the splintering disintegration of flesh and bone as his rage had powered into the man's face. Now he was dead. David's only emotion was relief.

Robyn had given her statement to two police officers. They were sympathetic, but she felt restless afterwards. Surging through her was a desire to celebrate being a survivor, to shrug off victimhood, to find out what it was like to take wings and fly.

A nurse had trimmed the tufts on her head into something that passed for neatness. The afternoon dragged. She tried to read a magazine. She talked to some of the other patients. But her mind and heart were full and restless and she couldn't settle. Near teatime, the door of the dayroom opened and a nurse put her head round it. "Robyn? You've a visitor up in the ward."

He was back already! Eyes bright, she spun round the corner. It was Neil who rose slowly from the chair, his jaw dropping when he saw her.

Robyn stopped dead, her pleasure draining away.

"What are you doing here?'

"Rob! What on earth happened? Who could do that to you?"

"The hair? Oh, I did that to myself."

Neil slumped back into the chair. "They told Gemma you'd been attacked."

Robyn sat on the far side of the bed. "Who's 'they'?"

"The school. Gemma rang looking for you and someone told her you'd been attacked and were in hospital. She rang me. And I came straight up."

"You haven't told my mother?"

"Not yet, but…"

"Don't tell her, Neil. She's not to know."

"Were you attacked? I mean, they said… were you…?"

Robyn interrupted impatiently. "I wasn't. Someone rescued me."

Neil brushed his hair off his face. Robyn looked away. "Why did you cut your hair off? You look like a skinhead. How could you do that to yourself?"

"With scissors."

"But why?"

Robyn was tiring of this, and irritated to see him sitting in the chair which had been filled by David. She didn't like the person she became when Neil was near.

"It seemed like a good idea at the time," she said. "Now, I'm afraid I'm expecting another visitor."

"I've only just got here!"

"I'm going to be fine, Neil. In fact I'm going to be just great. "

"Well, I suppose your hair will grow again." He spread his hands wide, incredulity overcoming him. "How could you do that?"

"By the way," Robyn said, "the cut on my face was caused by being hurled on the ground. The grazes on my shoulders were caused by being dragged over stones and pine needles. And I've other bruises, caused after my clothes were torn and ripped off me. And they haven't caught him yet. But, yes, I'm sure my hair will grow again."

Neil stood up. "I can see I'm not welcome."

He regarded her for a moment longer and then turned on his heel and left the ward. Robyn pulled her pillow onto her lap and punched it. Then she stood and walked rapidly after him. She caught up with him just as he went through the swing doors to the foyer.

"Neil!" He turned, looking almost sulky. "I was never the one for you. Never. But I do want you to be happy."

Robyn heard a lift door opening, saw Neil's eyes dart away and fix on someone behind her, felt an arm come round her waist.

David and Neil locked eyes, then Neil turned away. "Good luck to you," he said as he stepped into the lift. The doors closed slowly, obliterating him inch by inch.

Robyn looked up at David. "I wonder did he mean it?"

He swung her towards the ward, her bags in his other hand. "I've something to tell you."

She curled up against her pillows, her knees pulled up sideways to make room for him to sit facing her on the edge of the bed. He looked wonderful; fresh and crisp, his hair shining. He reached for her hand.

"They found Fraser."

She stiffened. "Where?"

"His car went off the road not far from the hostel. He was found near the wreckage. Robyn, he's dead."

Her hand flew to her mouth, her eyes wide. "Dead?"

He sat without speaking, letting her take this in.

"Angus Fraser is dead?" she repeated.

"Yes."

A feeling washed through her so strongly that she gasped.

"I'm glad. I feel glad," she said, her eyes wide.

"So do I." After a moment he added, "Let's leave him behind. He's gone."

Robyn was puzzled again by the sense of a deep well of wisdom in him, a young man just starting on his adult journey yet with a maturity beyond his years. What was it Edith had said way back before the summer? He knows who he is and he's comfortable with that. To be with him was to be accepted, tranquil, superbly human. And yet he knew deep hurt and great anger. She was utterly fascinated.

His gaze roved over her. "You look better. You've a neater skull cap now."

He touched the strips of tape which now held the cut on her cheek. She felt his fingers go to her shoulder and brush across the grazes there. He stopped abruptly. The ward was filling with visitors, loud with chatter. He stood up and tugged her to her feet.

"Come on," he said. "You and I have business to finish."

Hand in hand, they left the ward and along the side corridor past the day room, past the bathrooms and showers right to the semi-darkness at the far end. Here were the consultants' rooms and a secretary's office, all now deserted and locked for the night. In an alcove, four plastic chairs had been placed, two on each side, to make a waiting area. A few leaflets littered a small table. The vinyl tiles were cold on her bare feet.

"This'll have to do," he said. He swung round and let go of

her. "I believe you wanted to talk to me."

She reached up and held her palm against his cheek. There was tension in him, trembling through his body, detectable through the tips of her fingers. Her words stumbled a little, fluency deserting her in the unfamiliarity of what she wanted to articulate, tripping over the hope and the fear and the doubt and the uncertainty that swirled in her strange and newly softened heart.

"I think... I mean... I would like to..." She took a deep breath and then unleashed a storm of unstoppable words – "I think I might feel about you the way you say you feel about me but you have loads to do yet, you've to go to university and have lots of new experiences and meet lots of new people, and meet other girls and get a job and I'm just someone you met one summer and liked for a while and anyway a relationship like this is way out there and I'm not sure that we could make it work and ..." She stopped, gasped a breath. "...that's what I wanted to talk to you about."

He froze. For thirty seconds he was immobile. Then, with a little smile, he reached for her. His cheek came down carefully onto the top of her head and his whisper caressed her exposed ear, the gentlest of breaths. "Yes, Robyn. Yes, we'll talk."

After a moment, he pulled his head back and, very gently, tilted her chin up. There was the uncertainty of youth in his look. She felt the lightest brush of his lips on hers, tentative, cautious. He stopped and his eyes, inches from hers, asked the question.

She whispered, "Do that again."

He did.

"Let's go away," she said, low and longing.

"Anywhere you want."

"I used to stand on the shore of Belfast Lough, looking at the ferry going to Scotland, and wish I was on it."

"You shall go on it, if that's what you want."

"Tomorrow?"

"If we can," he said. "Now be quiet."

The long belt of the striped dressing gown trailed after them when they finally made their way slowly back. The main light was out in the ward. Robyn slipped off the dressing gown while David pulled back the bed cover. She climbed into bed and lay on her side. He pulled the cover over her and bent to kiss her goodnight, confident at last.

"We'll make it work," he whispered. "We'll talk and we'll make it work. Now close your eyes. You must count to twenty before you open them."

Puzzled, she did as he said. When she opened her eyes he was gone. On the pillow beside her was a little felt rabbit.

32

IT WAS A long drive the next morning, but finally David left her at her flat to change and pack and went on to his own house. Robyn passed the dental surgery and mounted the stairs slowly. She was shaky, felt like a stranger. She turned the key and opened the door. This wasn't a haven any more. It was a prison.

She walked into the tiny sitting room and looked at the chair, the bed, the table, the bookcase, the yellow cushions. She hated them. This was a place of fettered wings and a wounded heart, a place of guilt and shame, a place to shrivel and grow old. David had called it her burrow. It was more than that. It could have been her grave. She pulled her suitcase from the top of the wardrobe. She would never live here again.

David knocked on the landing door an hour later. His face was white. She drew him in.

"You should have let me go with you," she said.

He held onto her. "There wasn't time. But the place was cold, so cold. And empty." She felt him shiver. "There were yellow hairs on Manna's spot on the rug."

"But your mother will be back. And Manna."

"I rang her. She's happy I'm going away for a bit. And she will be back. She said so. She sounded better."

Robyn hesitated. "Did you tell her about me?"

"Not yet. I told her I was going with a friend."

She pulled away and held him at arm's length. He swung away and lifted her case. "Come on, let's get out of here."

Robyn followed him and slammed the door without looking back.

On the small section of open deck on the ferry, David stood with Robyn and watched the shores of Belfast Lough slip past. His visit home had been even harder than he had admitted to Robyn. His father was everywhere, seeming to inhabit the house even more because there was no-one else to fill the space. Both his parent's cars were still in the drive.

But what had been hardest of all had been passing the weeping cherry tree. In his mind's eye he saw it there now, alone in the empty garden of the empty house. It seemed like a betrayal all over again.

He looked back over the receding city, the hills, the smoke, the cranes of the docks, the high rise flats, the new developments along the waterfront. He loved this city. In a sudden surge of emotion he swung Robyn round into an embrace so strong she gave a squeal of protest.

"Robyn," he said close to her ear as the engine note rose and the white wake churned, taking the ferry out into the open sea, "wherever you and I have come from, it's where we're going that matters. The only thing that matters."

After a moment of silence, he heard her voice muffled against his jacket. "Can I breathe now, please?"

He held her out from him, laughing. She put a hand to the side of her face in a sweeping gesture, then dropped it again.

"I keep forgetting I've no hair. But it's funny," she pondered. "It's good being able to look at things without hair getting in the way. There's a gale blowing on this deck, but my eyes are clear. I can see everything."

"You're a new woman. And I can see your face properly now."

"But I need to let it grow a bit."

He ran a hand lightly over her head. "Two inches. I'll hide the scissors till then."

Robyn recognised the hotel from a tourist brochure. It was the one she and Gemma and their two friends had stayed in after their exams. David phoned. One of the private cottages in the grounds was available. He booked it.

They arrived in the early evening. It was a cool but dry autumn dusk as they followed directions around the hotel drive to the back and found their cottage. There were several together, but each one had its own front door and porch. There were only three rooms: sitting room, bathroom and bedroom.

In the door of the bedroom Robyn stopped. David went past her and put her bag on the bed.

"Fight you for the sofa," he said.

She grinned, tension evaporated. "Race you to the bathroom!"

The green dress with its scooped neckline and cap sleeves, the defiant symbol of her embryonic independence, had travelled well. She clipped on daisy earrings and looked at herself in the cheval mirror in the corner of the bedroom. She had regretted the purchase back before the summer. When would she have an occasion to wear it? she had scolded herself. She smoothed the pale green lace inset at the fitted waist above the graceful skirt, angled her head to see the effect of the earrings on the stark jut of her cheekbones. She had allowed one narrow strip of bandage to stay on the cut. David's voice sounded impatiently from the hall.

"Are you ready yet? I'm going to start eating the furniture soon."

She opened the door, self-conscious. He looked round. She stood still. Then he came towards her and set his hands on the lace at her waist. She felt the warmth of his palms through to her skin.

"I'm sorry I was so long…"

"I'm not," he said. Holding her loosely, he brushed each corner of her mouth with his. When he lifted his head she smiled up at him. Unlike Neil's kiss in the park weeks before, this time the wine was very pleasing.

The hotel was a converted hunting lodge and the dining room was wood panelled and elegant. They were on their best behaviour. David had had a quick shower and his hair glistened in the subdued lighting. Robyn linked her fingers under her chin and watched him as he examined the menu. She started at the wave on the top of his head and traced every inch of his face. His long black brows, his dark lashes lowered and moving slightly as he read, his fine nose, the cheekbones smoothing to the slightly rougher skin of his jaw. She was contemplating the point of his chin when he looked up.

"Happy?" he asked.

She just smiled, her eyes bright.

As they ate their hors d'oeuvres, she said: "There are some good looking waiters here. Spanish, I think."

He bit a prawn. "Any more remarks like that and we move out tomorrow."

As they ate their main course, he said: "This was a good idea."

"I'm full of them," she said.

Over dessert, she took his right hand. "Battlescars."

He flexed his fingers. "They still work anyway," he said.

Over coffee, he reached for her wrist and turned it over. He ran his finger down the faint scar. "So who did it to you, Robyn?"

She pulled her hand away and crumpled her napkin. "Shall we go now?"

He held her eyes for a moment, then pushed out his chair. "OK."

33

A CRASH REVERBERATED through the cottage. It pulled David from a deep sleep. He sat up, his legs cramped from the inadequate length of the sofa. The thick curtains were slightly open, allowing a faint flush of moonlight to steal across the room. He clicked on a lamp and swung his legs to the floor, calling. There was no reply. Heedless of the chill on his body, he went into the hall.

Dark memories twitched in his brain, memories of the night he had been woken to look for his father. Irrational fear made his knees weak. As he pushed the door of the bedroom, he saw the glimmer of her body standing beside the bed. He turned on the light, keeping the dimmer switch turned low. On the floor in one corner lay one of a pair of bedside lamps. Its cream shade was bent askew and pieces of glass were mixed in with lumps of the shattered base.

Robyn had the other lamp in her hand. She jerked the flex from the wall and hurled it violently after its pair. With a deft movement, he caught it in mid-air. One lamp they could explain. Two might look like vandalism. Alarmed, he set it out of reach.

"Robyn, what's the matter? What's wrong?"

Her voice was taut with rage. "He should have loved me. He should have loved me!"

"Who should have loved you?"

"My father. He should have loved me the way yours loved you!"

He spread his hands in a helpless gesture. "I'm sure he did…"

"Oh no, he didn't!" she cried. "He twisted me, he corrupted

me, he made me believe I was a bad person." Her voice lowered. "I used to look at the other girls in my class and think, well, they're OK." She spread her hands wide. "But I'm not like them. I'm worthless. Born manacled to ghosts. I don't have to be cared for. I just have to be used. "

Shock cut through to his marrow. "You mean it was your father?"

Rage flared, white hot. "Yes! You know the one?" She jabbed a finger at him. "Daddy. The one who buys you sweets and helps you with your homework." She paced across the room, stopped beside the bed. She leaned across it, challenging him. "You know, I used to go to church and I used to think the big holy guy who said 'When you pray say: Our Father,' had never met mine! Either that or God was a filthy bastard!" Her chin jutted. "Does that shock you?"

"No, it doesn't shock me at all." He crooked a smile. "In fact, it sounds just like you." He saw her shiver. "You're freezing." He pulled the quilt from the bed and draped it round her shoulders. She looked up at him, her eyes huge.

He took her face between his hands. "Tell me."

She was silent. Then she opened the quilt and hooked one side of it up round his shoulders, including him in its warmth.

"Hey, that's good," he said, closing the edges round them both to make a warm cocoon.

They went back to the sofa, their bodies wrapped tightly together. And there, her face hidden against his neck, she told him. Everything. From the age of four until she lay on the bathroom floor at the age of fourteen, trying to find the only way out that she knew. She spared him nothing. From early fondling until her father began to come into her room in the night. On and on she went while David froze in horror, nausea churning the pit of his stomach.

Finally she stopped. His arms were still round her as fast as ever, her head still nestled against his neck. But he was totally unable to speak. As the silence stretched into minutes, she lifted her head and looked at him, her eyes frightened.

"David? Please don't hate me."

Galvanised into action, he pressed her cheek to his, his words coming in a rush. "How could I ever hate you? Little wonder you ran away. Little wonder you were prickly." His voice shook. "I know it happens. I knew something like this must have happened to you." He spoke through gritted teeth. "But I've never seen the pictures before. I've never heard the cruelty, the evil, twisted, bloody barbarity." He pushed himself forward, turning to face her. "And I never knew anyone could be a survivor of that and yet be as magnificent as you."

He tried to gather her close again but this time she resisted, her hand firm against his chest.

"You have to know it all, David. You have to know the kind of woman I am." She took a shuddering breath. "He got dementia. In the end he was in a home. I found myself alone with him one day. He didn't even recognise me by then." She paused, a thought amazing her. "I got up and went over to him. He was thin and wasted. I stood there and thought about what I could do to him if I wanted. I thought about it. And thought about it. Rehearsed it in my mind." She closed her eyes and raised her face to the ceiling. "I looked down at him, an old helpless shell of a man. And the urge to kick him, to beat him, even to kill him, was so strong I was terrified. I turned and ran." Her voice rose again, furious. "That's what he made of me. A woman who could hate so much she could kill!" Both her hands clenched into shaking fists. "It's been a black weight in me for so long."

He took her chin in his hand and made her look at him, his voice quick, urgent.

"Everybody's a killer if the need arises. I know what you felt. I could have killed Fraser the night he attacked you." He put a hand on her shoulder and shook her a little. "I nearly did. But neither of us actually did it in the end." His mouth twisted. "But if your father walked in here now, he'd be dog food in thirty seconds."

"There's such a rage in me. It fires out at all the wrong moments. Sometimes I don't even know it's going to happen. I did it to you. I nearly lost you." She put her head on one side. "I nearly did, didn't I? You were going to leave me, you were going to walk away. I forced even you to think about it. You started to ignore me."

"Ignoring you was a temporary survival strategy. There was so much going on in my life, I had to do something to take control, to cope, just for a little while. Can you understand that?"

"Yes, but it would have broken my heart."

"My own was getting a bit frayed round the edges." He stroked her cheek. "But I would have been back. I would never have given up on you. I was much too afraid of you giving up on me."

He settled back on the sofa, tightening the cover round them both again.

She turned into him, her face hidden, her voice full of pain. "You've always waited for me, accepted me just as I am." He felt her hand go up to his neck. "When I woke earlier, I came in here and watched you sleeping."

"Did you indeed? Spy."

"And I remembered the night you phoned me when I was in bed. And you told me that you wished I was beside you then."

He remembered that very well. The need to talk to her, to see her, to touch her, had been a piercing ache.

"And I couldn't deal with it then," she went on. "I couldn't bear being that vulnerable, giving up my self-possession for anyone. I never wanted to belong to anyone who would have power over me ever again."

"And now?"

"Now?" He felt her body responding beneath the warm cover. "I watched you sleeping, knowing that now I'm so totally vulnerable. And it petrified me." She started to shake against him. "And then suddenly I was choking with anger. Choking with it, blazing with it. It's like something just exploded."

A thought struck him. "Your mother?"

The question hovered. Then she said: "She knew. She knew all along."

His breath left him in a rush as his head went back. "Jesus!" he whispered. Tremors of a fury of his own rippled through his body. He pulled her tight against him. "I'm not afraid of anger. Sometimes it's a dagger to kill the devil." He closed his eyes, trying to bring his spinning emotions under control. "And you couldn't tell anybody." It was a statement.

"No," she whispered.

He went on. "You couldn't tell anybody because no-one would believe you. And because, even if they did, you didn't want anybody to know. You didn't want people pointing at you in the street." He paused. "Am I right?" She had gone very still, listening. "You didn't tell anybody because he threatened you and because you believed him. You thought you really were a terrible person and that it was all your fault."

He went quiet while she lay tense against him. Then he said softly, with absolute certainty: "But most of all, you didn't tell anyone, right up to tonight, because to say it is to make it real. To say it happened is to remember it happened and to know it happened. And that's unbearable."

She was still and silent. Years ago she had grasped the fact that at last she had the power to say no. It kept her safe, away from all the pain and humiliation and guilt, all that Angus Fraser had wanted to visit on her again. Don't go near the roses and you'll never feel the thorns.

But this unusual, fathomless person was more complete than any she had ever known before. Age had nothing to do with it. Her whole universe was lit by a different sun. Streaming along its beams came a new power, the power to say yes.

David felt the change in her like a tremble in his own body. Despite his unique depth and insight, he was also young and very tired of trying to be good. Finally, he crossed the limit of his endurance. He slipped off the sofa, bringing her with him onto the deep pile of the carpet. He was on fire in seconds, answering the little cries of desire already coming from her throat.

"I told you," he breathed against her ear. "*I told you.* You and I meeting would be dangerous."

She cried.

Still lying on the carpet, he tugged cushions from the sofa to put under their heads. He pulled the whole length of her against him, holding her while she wept as if her heart was breaking. A calmness descended on him, an assurance that this was, paradoxically, good. He lifted a corner of the quilt and mopped her eyes. With only a slight hesitation, he wiped her nose as well.

"Hey," he said, "I think we can get away with the lamp. But we won't even try to explain the state of this quilt."

He stroked her back gently as he listened to the melt waters cascading from her, dead water stirred to a purging torrent of atonement. Once, he twisted to look up at the window though the partly open curtains. He could see the sky. Fingers of the dawn were beginning to splay above the clouds, lacing their edges with the promise of early gold. He turned back. Why did I have to look up at the sky? A voice had started to speak insistently in his head.

No, he thought, putting his hand on the back of Robyn's head and pressing her into his shoulder. *No, I can't. I can't tell it, I can't make it real. No!*

She was starting to speak through gulps, her sobs subsiding. "When your father died, you needed so much more from me."

She wiped her nose with the back of her hand and he wiped her hand with the quilt. It was too far gone to worry about now. She pulled back a little and he saw the wet fringe of her lashes framing her eyes. He flicked his tongue out and tasted salt. She held his face between her palms. "And you have things to tell me. I know you have."

He felt as if she were scouring his soul.

No! I can't. Living it once was enough. She has more courage than I have. Don't ask me.

She waited, tracing the contours of his face with her thumb. Still she waited. The little piece of transparent tape was peeling off her cheek. How had it lasted this long? They'd need to find a new piece. He reached up and tapped it back carefully. As his hand moved away, she caught it.

"David?"

He didn't want her to touch the raw parts of him. He was strong, *he* was there for *her*. No-one had yet peeled him down to the last, hidden layer.

Finally, she brushed his cheek with her lips. "When you're ready, I'm listening." She sat up and pulled her knees up to her chin. "I've always hurt people who might have got close to me." She dropped her forehead onto her knees. "Neil had an accident on the way home one night. I said I wasn't responsible for it. But maybe I was, partly." She extended a hand in question. "If he'd been killed, how could I have lived with myself?"

As if he had been kicked, David rolled away from her. After a silence, he felt her move, felt her hand on his shoulder.

"What's wrong?"

No!

Gently, she rolled him onto his back. "You trust me, remember?"

She took his hand and twined her fingers into his, pulling his hand up into the air. He watched as she opened her fingers. He opened his own and matched hers. Felt the soft pressure of palm on palm.

"Shalom," she whispered.

He closed his eyes and felt a breeze touch the innermost layer of his being for the very first time. He forced the words from his throat.

"I need to tell you about Abi," he said.

"Abi?"

"My sister."

34

Mayo, West of Ireland. Ten years ago.

ANGELS COULDN'T POSSIBLY be as noisy as Abi, David thought. Legs pumping like pistons, three-year-old Abigail Elizabeth Shaw was running round this stranger's living room as if she owned it, over-excited and over-tired. Her pink dress with the blue cornflowers round the hem flew in all directions as she climbed onto a chair and threw herself off again, arms spread pretending to fly. Her shoulder length hair was wavy like her brother's, but unlike his, it was a silken gossamer blonde. People were always stroking it and predicting that it would darken as she got older.

Ever since her blue eyes (where had she got those?) first opened on the world she had been making a noise. He couldn't understand how his father could call her his little angel several times a day. That was when he wasn't calling her his little miracle. No, Abi was neither an angel nor a miracle to her brother.

David didn't fully understand, but he knew that his mother and father had been married for several years before he was born and that it had been another six years after that until Abi arrived. His father took him to the hospital to see his mother and his new sister. He had peered into the little cot and looked at this tiny pink thing with the screwed up face and stubby wrinkled fingers.

She wasn't what he thought of as a miracle. Miracles were when the sea parted, or blind people got their sight back, or sticks turned into snakes, or dead people came to life again. Certainly not a tiny, messy, noisy person who got all the attention that he used to get.

Although she had become mildly more interesting as she had begun to crawl and then graduated to toddlerhood, life as it was before Abi had never returned. Sometimes his mother would be too tired to talk to him. Sometimes his father would spend so long reading bedtime stories to his little miracle that David would have his homework done and put away before Vincent reappeared.

"All finished, David? Well done. You're a bright boy."

It was all finished, but he would have liked to share it, to talk about what he was learning. It seemed to him he was doing well at school with very little effort and it puzzled him. There was nothing in the world that didn't interest him and he felt like a sponge, greedily absorbing all knowledge, all wonders that were put in front of him. Sometimes he would have liked the reassurance that he wasn't doing anything wrong. He flew through any new work. He was devouring books while some of his classmates were still struggling with words. Was this because he was good at bluffing and would he be found out one day?

But now it was holiday time and they were making their annual journey to their summer cottage out in the west of Ireland. If only they hadn't met these people, David thought. They seemed to know his mother. They had insisted that the Shaws stop off with them for tea. They had a bungalow overlooking a wild, rocky stretch of the Atlantic coast. They had no children of their own and spent all their summers here.

Close to the bungalow, they stopped above the spectacular cliffs of the coastline. They stood in a line on a grass verge in the blustering Atlantic air to gaze down at the sea boiling around the jagged outcrops and abandoned needles of rock that formed the arms of an isolated cove. David was mesmerised. His father lifted Abi and held her tightly, her hair tossing like a broken cobweb as she gazed round-eyed at the shear, harsh faces of the land's edge. Seagulls were buffeted like confetti in the wind. David's mother was keeping him close to her side. He had his ninth birthday some months before and he wouldn't let her hold his hand, but he didn't mind being wedged securely against her. He fixed one gull in his sights and followed it, feeling his heart soar and wheel along with it, exhilaration in the tilt and swirl of wing and tail, abandon in the rise and fall, near and far of the squalling cries ripping into the wind.

He looked up at Abi, still in her father's arms. With a quick jerk of her head, she looked away from the sea and down at her brother through the blonde wisps whipping across her face. Her thumb was in her mouth, a sure sign that something had seriously moved her. David smiled at her. Like a burst of sun, a smile lit Abi's face, her mouth spreading around her thumb. David had a sudden sense that maybe there were things they might share as she grew older; that inside her head, Abi was indeed made of the same stuff as himself.

When they were fastened back in the car, Abi whispered to her brother: "Adventure."

She said it perfectly. Once she got a word, she got it right. This was a new word that she had grasped and she understood it very well. She had heard stories of the brown hen going for an adventure across the farmyard. She had heard about the spotted puppy going on an adventure through a busy town. Her blue eyes sparkled and David thought of the stormy beach, the power and the glory there would be in standing down there alone in the roaring wind, a small atom, the solitary audience of a mighty drama.

Now however, in this strange living room, she was noisy again. It was so late they were going to stay here overnight. Abi the aeroplane landed in the middle of the room, and David covered his ears and waited for someone to take her away and get her ready for bed. But she wasn't ready to go.

"David, David! Watch me, watch me!"

Ignoring the four adults in the room, she held her dimpled arms in front of her until she was sure her brother was watching and then rolled her short length into a somersault. Her little bottom went up in the air and the skirt of the pink dress with blue cornflowers blossomed on the floor round her upturned head. She landed on her back, her hair askew over her face. She scrambled up, lost her balance and fell over again, landing effortlessly with a tiny bump.

"I can turn over!" she cried in triumph, bouncing up again onto her short legs. The pink hairslide slipped further round to her ear.

Her mother's friends owned a cot because they had a niece who came to stay sometimes. Abi complained about being put in a cot. She wasn't a baby any more. In her yellow pyjamas she jumped up and down in a fury, rattling the rail and demanding to sleep in the bed on the other side of the room. But her brother was going to sleep there, and she was stuck, her little fingers unable to manipulate the catches on the rail.

Later, when she was asleep, David heard the adults laughing about this, about how Abi wanted to sleep in the bed. He said nothing, but it occurred to him for the first time that perhaps sometimes Abi was jealous of him.

When he crept into the room later, his sister was fast asleep. He changed and, just before slipping into bed himself, he stood beside the cot and studied her. He still couldn't think of her as an angel or a miracle. But maybe, maybe, as an ordinary sister, she might grow up to be just about OK.

He pulled the strange bedclothes up to his chin and turned his mind to the mysteries of different houses and how odd and exciting it felt to be in someone else's. He turned over and saw the light slide across the wall as the door opened quietly and his mother came in. She ruffled his hair.

"Are you all right, son? Are you warm enough?"

"I'm fine, Mum. Can we go to our own house tomorrow?"

"Yes, tomorrow. Now sleep tight." She bent to kiss his forehead and smiled. Still smiling, she went to the cot and stood with her hand on the rail watching her sleeping daughter, a small hump under the blanket, a dynamo recharging.

Then she went out and the light crept back across the wall as the door swung behind her. David tucked the blanket under his chin and closed his eyes. His last thought before he went to sleep was of tomorrow. He always remembered that.

He woke in the very early morning. He could hear the sea. Slipping out of bed he went to the window. He discovered that it looked out onto the front, towards the sea which was just across the road at the bottom of the long drive. The light was the sharp, cool, damp light of an hour when only the very earliest land birds were beginning to stir, when most people were still in their deep summer sleep with hours to go before the first yawns and stretches and the realisation that day had stepped in the window unnoticed.

That was the Atlantic Ocean out there. David pressed his small nose to the glass, feeling drawn to the whistling wind and the stunted trees bent like old men to the prevailing wind. In this place, the sea paid no notice to the fact that it was summer. Storms could harry the coast at any time and with very little warning.

The power and the glory! Bewitched beyond resistance, David began to pull on his clothes. He was as quiet as he could be, but as he slipped on his shoes he heard a rustle from the cot and looked up. Abi was standing, the cot clothes rumpled and her eyes bright with vanishing sleep. Her chubby fingers were fastened round the rail.

"Adventure, David?" she whispered, seeming to understand the need to be quiet.

"No, Abi," he whispered back. "You've to go back to sleep."

"David going out!" she accused, giving the rail a shake.

"Not far, just to the garden. I'll be straight back."

"Abi go too!" she demanded, her voice beginning to rise, petulant.

"Don't be silly," he said scornfully. "You're too small."

It was the wrong approach. Abi inhaled deeply and opened her mouth wide. David flew to the cot and put his hand over her mouth.

"Shut up, Abi! You'll spoil everything."

She waited until he removed his hand and then repeated with a stubborn set to her chin: "Abi come too. Adventure!"

"You can't! You've no clothes to put on."

She pointed to a chair. "Clothes there."

"You've no coat."

"Coat out there." She pointed at the door.

"No shoes."

"Have shoes! Have shoes!" She jumped up and down and took a deep breath, her face red.

"All right, all right!" David said, annoyed.

He fiddled with the latches on the cot rail and finally managed to lower it. It was a nuisance and a fidget, but with her enthusiastic co-operation Abi was dressed quickly. There was a further hold-up when she whispered that she had taken off her night-time pull-ups and wanted her potty. David waited, expecting his father's voice to pin them to the floor any moment.

The bolt on the back door gave his fingers some difficulty but finally it slid back with a slight clunk. Then he discovered the door was also locked with a key. He looked round the kitchen ledge and went straight to a ceramic jar in the shape of a tomato. He reached up to the green leaves of the lid and found the key.

At first he held Abi's hand tightly, but the dawn and the gulls and the wind and the trees and the sounds and the scent of the crashing sea made the restriction unbearable. Soon she was running free with the wind and David was running too, high spirits and wonder warring for space in his soul.

Abi had stopped at the bottom of the drive. Some of the gusts were so strong they made her stagger. David had found her elastic hair bobble and tied her hair back so that it wouldn't get in her eyes. She stared at the other side of the narrow road, knowing that she mustn't go onto a road alone. That rule had been embedded in her so firmly that she wouldn't disobey it.

David ran down the lawn and jumped across a flower bed. It was the longest jump he had ever made and he didn't touch a leaf as he sailed over. He swung round and trotted to Abi. They were the only people alive in the whole world! Abi put one arm round his leg and pointed across the road.

"Over there. Look down."

More than anything, David wanted to do that too. He remembered looking down at the thundering breakers in the cove the evening before and the thrill it had given him deep inside. He took Abi's hand.

"You're not to let go of me. Do you understand, Abi? I mean it."

He felt her fingers tighten in his. "Abi hold tight," she said, nodding for emphasis.

On the grass above the cove, he made her sit down well back from the edge so that there would be no possibility of her running away suddenly. She kept tight hold of his hand and they sat together speechless. Gulls screamed above and below them. The sea thundered onto the headlands on each side, spray rising high, tossed backwards, upwards, occasionally spattering the air around them in the strongest gusts. The smell of salt and seaweed stung their nostrils. The rocks seemed to live as the spume gushed over them, foamed towards the stony beach, then sucked away again, licking across the boulders, running in frothy rage in the gulleys between.

Abi put her thumb in her mouth. Then she looked up at her brother with eyes like blue china. Speaking round her thumb, she asked: "God?"

Even at the age of nine, David's sense of the spiritual was keen. With a surge of pleasure, he realised that this sense was in Abi also. He smiled at her and squeezed her hand.

"Yes, God," he answered.

To his right, David could see that the cliff face leaned backwards and made a more gradual slope down to the inlet. With some care, he might have been able to slither down, but it was out of the question for Abi. How he would have loved to confront those breakers! To stand before their might and feel the wind rip through his hair as they crashed and foamed towards him. The power and the glory!

They had to go back. He would be skinned alive if his parents found out what he had done. With a sigh he said, "Come on. We have to go back. And don't tell Mum and Dad about this. They'd be very cross."

Briefly, he let go of her hand as he pushed himself up from the grass. She didn't let go of his. He let go of hers. At that moment a large gull swooped down close above their heads and sliced over the cliff edge.

"Bird! Big big bird!" Abi squealed. And ran after it.

At the same instant that David shouted her name, she was gone. He flung himself forward onto his stomach, horror almost taking him over the edge after her. In his nightmares or caught unawares in the daytime, he could always replay every blow on her body as he watched the cliff tumble and toss her like a ragdoll from outcrop to ledge to boulder. He knew she was screaming but above the roar of the wind and the sea, he couldn't hear her.

Her body jarred to a stop on a narrow ledge about ten feet above the stones of the beach.

Unlike the searing, indelible memory of Abi's fall, David never fully recalled what he did then. His next clear memory was of scrambling sideways across from the shallower slope of the cliff. Of seeing her lying still, her body shaped as it shouldn't have been shaped. Of frantically yelling her name. Of seeing blood on her head and her coat.

The next vivid picture burned on his brain was of gathering the tiny body into his own childish arms, feeling her bones shift where they shouldn't have shifted. Over most of her head her gossamer blond hair was sticky and red. The elastic bobble had hung on, but it was red and sticky too. Her arms were floppy and he had to hold onto them, hold them in to her side to stop them trailing over the ledge.

He had to get her back the way he had come, but one look at the perilous jagged rock that he had crossed hardly knowing he was doing it, told him that it would be impossible as long as he carried Abi. He tried to remember watching his mother taking a pulse. He placed his fingers on Abi's wrist. There was a faint flutter.

"Hang on, Abi, hang on!" he urged desperately.

He would go down. Somehow he would get down. He was shifting her slight weight to test his footing over the edge when he looked below. The breakers were slavering up the cliff face towards him. The tide was coming in and there was no way down except into the maw of the sea.

He sat holding his sister in his arms, her blood smeared across his chest, her crushed head supported in the crook of his arm. The sea came closer, at one point snapping at the edge of the precarious piece of rock where he sat frozen in body and mind. He kept checking the thread of pulse, told himself it wasn't getting weaker.

He prayed.

Once, he moved slightly, shifting her weight. He was startled to look down and see her blue eyes open, staring at him. A spume of spray soaked them and when it receded, she was still looking at him.

"Abi?" he said.

Even as he watched in desperate hope, the shine left the vivid blue, the colour flattened, the spark went out. He buried his head in her little blood-soaked coat. He was wet to the skin, cold to the marrow and a hundred years old when he realised that his sister had died in his arms.

Later, he knew he had crouched there for two more hours before they were found. He became numb and dangerously cold. The power and the glory were in the brutal beauty all around him, the boiling Atlantic, the squalling gulls, the defiant needles of rock.

Abi would be forever a little child. For ever and ever, amen.

He would never be a child again.

35

AVID WAS SITTING on the edge of the sofa. He leaned forward to set one arm loosely around Robyn's shoulder where she sat on the floor at his feet. Her chin rested on her arms, folded along his knee. That he would have to carry this burden always, stunned her to silence.

"If it had been winter, I would have died too," he said finally.

As the silence lengthened, his thumb rose to touch her cheek.

"You're the only person I've ever told about Abi. Even Tim doesn't know." He took a shaky breath. "Funny. It got easier as I told it. I didn't think it would. I've always been too frightened."

"Frightened? You?"

"Oh yes. Me."

Across the car park, the early staff were already arriving at the back door of the hotel. There was a question she had to ask, but she wasn't sure how to ask it. She tried.

"David, I was close to giving up. If it wasn't for you, I might have. Yet you've dealt with this and me as well. You're a very, very strong person." She looked up into his brown eyes. He waited for her questions patiently, as if he knew there would be many. "How... how have you lived with this? I mean ..." She shrugged, perplexed. "I'm covered in scars," – she touched her cheek and smiled a little – "I mean metaphorically, not just real ones. But you're not. You're an amazingly effective human being. How?"

"You think I've no scars? It would take years to count them! But seriously, think about it. What way leaves you with the fewest wounds – making peace with the past? Or making war with it?"

She let this sink in, taking it deep into the empty spaces within herself, the places that used to be filled with hatred and hopelessness, and that were now open to love and wonder. So many questions surfaced and swirled in her head and she would ask them. But now wasn't the time, and it certainly wasn't the time for platitudes. She stood and gently tugged him to his feet.

"I don't deserve you," she said.

"On the contrary. I've always thought we richly deserved each other."

She rumpled the quilt under her arm and pulled him towards the door. "You're coming to the bed and you're going to sleep."

Cold air nudged its way in as Robyn opened the front door an inch to swing the 'Do not disturb" tab onto the door handle. David was in bed before her. He was quiet but his eyes followed her as she pulled back the covers. His arms opened and she slid into them. Curled up with him, warm against him, arms and legs twined with his, she listened while his breathing slowed into sleep, the rhythm of his heart tapping against her cheek.

As she grew drowsy, her last thought was of little Abi. Would her hair have darkened to the near black of her brother's? Exhaustion captured her before she could topple into a crater of questions which could never be answered. It hadn't crossed her mind to wedge a chair against the door.

When she woke, David had gone from her side. She yawned and stretched. She had never before woken to such peace of mind. She pulled on her bathrobe and went in search of him.

He was in the sitting room, by the window, absorbed in a book he had found. He had pulled on a pair of jeans and sat with his ankle across his knee, the book balanced on his leg. He was so engrossed that at first he didn't hear her. She glanced at the open page.

"I see Ferrari and Jaguar are more interesting than me," she huffed.

He looked up and laughed, snapping the book shut. "A mere time-filler until you decided to wake up. Books don't go to sleep on you."

She went to him and wove a kiss into the unruly waves on his head. "I seem to remember you doing quite a lot of sleeping yourself." She indicated the window, where the evening was already dimming to darkness. "We seem to have missed out a whole day."

He stood and gripped her shoulders. "I tell you what we've missed out on. Food! Do you realise how long it's been since we ate?" He screwed up his face and bared his teeth. "Just as well you woke up. You might have been dinner!"

She patted his stomach. "I'm so scared," she said calmly. "You should have eaten the biscuits on the hospitality tray."

He held up two empty shortbread wrappers. "Been there. Still hungry."

"Looks like we'd better visit the dining room then, before the situation gets out of hand."

They didn't say very much as they ate. Robyn enjoyed the surroundings, the people, the hum of conversation. She took particular delight in watching David's food disappear into him at speed.

As he scraped the last of a crème brulée from the dish, she asked: "Where are you putting all that?"

He grinned, licking the spoon. "Hollow legs."

The night was chilly as they left through the main hotel foyer.

"Let's walk," Robyn said. "The grounds are lovely even in the dark."

The light from the hotel faded as they crossed the wooden bridge and found a bench facing the stream. They sat side by side, not touching, taking their time to settle into each other's

314

silence. The starlit night smelled of grass and water, the air drifting lazily, the sounds of the hotel far away across the lawn.

"David?"

"What?"

"Abi."

"Yes?" Only a breath of hesitation.

"Is your father buried in the same grave?"

They were both still looking straight ahead. "He is."

"Is that why you didn't want me to go to the funeral? Because I would see her inscription? And people would mention her?"

"It was one reason. But the reason I gave Tim to tell you was also true."

Another silence.

"It must have been specially hard for your mother. To see the grave opened again, I mean."

He looked away. "She has scars."

Robyn touched his knee lightly. "It must have been dreadful. Just after…"

He took a deep breath and turned back to her. "It was. At first they were thankful they hadn't lost both of us. But it became clear very quickly what had happened. The cot side was down. Abi couldn't do that herself. She was dressed. She couldn't do that herself either." He gave a tight laugh. "Anyway, I told them it was my fault."

"You were a child. Why are you still so hard on yourself?"

He looked surprised. "I couldn't be hard enough on myself."

She let that go. "I'd like to visit their grave."

"I'll take you. On one condition."

"What's that?"

"That you take me to your father's."

She stiffened. "Why?"

"Because you need to be sure that all the anger is gone. And you need to forgive him."

She stood up and whirled round on him. "Don't preach at me! Who do you think you are?"

He was quite calm. "You know exactly who I am."

She walked away across the lawn to the deeper darkness of the trees. Behind her, he was silhouetted against the hotel lights. She walked round the trunk of an oak tree and leaned against it. A car purred along the road beyond the hedge.

She could never forgive her father. The very memory of him still turned her stomach. How could David suggest it? In that quiet way he had, he appeared beside her.

"I know what I'm talking about." He dropped onto his heels. "My mother ended up in hospital with a nervous breakdown. I went to pieces as well. I was sent to school, but I wasn't really there. I had to repeat the year. There was no moving on, no forgiveness, for a long time."

Robyn touched his arm. "Forgiving yourself must have been the really hard bit," she said.

His head was bowed, his voice so low she bent to catch his words. "I haven't yet. Not really. It still goes on. Every day. Every single bloody day."

Robyn put her hand on his shoulder. "Did Abi look like you?"

He pulled a stalk of plantain. "Some people said she was beginning to." He chewed the stalk and she waited, knowing there was more. "My father forgave me, but he found it very difficult. Even more so than my mother. It was always between us. He had prayed for a miracle, and she happened." David pressed his fingers into his eyelids, his voice bitter. "But I was able to reverse a miracle. How's that for power?" He stood and walked a few paces. She followed. "The night he died, I was all screwed up and I needed to talk to him. He was looking at photos of Abi. I had disappointed him again. And he spent the evening with Abi. Not with me." His voice was hard, final. "Forgiveness has to be unreserved. Otherwise it's a canker. It taints your life."

316

"My father's dead," she said. "How can I forgive him? He's beyond it."

He took her shoulders and gave her a gentle shake. "But *you're* not. It's two way. There's giving and receiving. All you have to do is give it. How or where or if it's received isn't your problem." He thought for a minute and then held her out from him to see her face. "And your mother's not dead, is she?"

She pushed him away, her expression hard. "She may as well be." She walked round the tree. When she faced him again her chin was up, her eyes accusing. "Have you forgiven Angus Fraser?"

He replied instantly. "No. Not yet. I can't even think about it. But I'll have to face it some time." He threw out his hand in a helpless gesture. "I didn't say I didn't have work to do as well."

She turned her back to him to look out across the dark lawn to the lights on the drive near the hotel entrance. He came up behind her and his arms stole round her waist, his head bent to her cheek.

"I need you, Robyn," he said softly. "You know the worst of me and love me anyway. I need you now more than you need me."

It didn't matter where they went. The next day, in a field somewhere – anywhere – they lay on their stomachs, heads together, like the hands of a clock pointing to a quarter to three.

Robyn twirled a buttercup, tickling his nose. "When I asked you if you'd chosen colour, you said 'eventually'. I know why you said that now."

He rolled onto his back and studied the clouds. "Living in Enniskillen, I'd often heard about the Remembrance Day bomb. We used to pass the war memorial with the doves on it. One for each person who died." He paused, thinking. "So many bad things have happened to so many good people. I remember hearing of one man burying his only son. He'd been murdered. Pointlessly. He was in tears. He said 'Bury your hatred with my son.' " David rolled onto his stomach again. Robyn picked grass out of his hair. "And it hit me one day. I must've been about eleven. Bad things happen to good people. But turn that round. Good people can make bad mistakes too."

Robyn sat up, leaves sticking to her clothes. She pulled her knees up to her chin. "Yes," she said slowly. "I think I know what you mean. Just because of what you had caused to happen, it didn't make you a bad person."

He spat out a piece of grass. "So I decided to fight back. I was going to be who I was meant to be." He sat up. "When you get blown off course, you can choose to stay lost – " he raised a hand above his head "– or you can reach for heaven and steer by the stars." He looked away across to the road where they had left the car. "But I couldn't bring Abi back."

They sat in the middle of the field, two figures in the grass, still and quiet. Hoping it would work. Making it work.

David turned on his mobile phone. He had been keeping it switched off and checking it for messages occasionally. There was a text from Tim. David grinned and showed it to Robyn.

"Where r u, u big moron? Ring me," Tim had sent.

David thumbed back, "Talk later."

They were swaying idly, side by side on swings.

"I suppose," said Robyn slowly, "that's what you were trying to get Penny to see."

"Get her to see what?"

"That she could row herself back. Like me." She gave herself a little push with her feet and leaned backwards. "Just because someone has made you a victim, you don't have to be a victim for the rest of your life."

He stopped swaying and stood up. "Vicious circles can be broken." He put his hands in his pockets. "But I failed her too."

She hung forward in the swing, her arms round the chains. "You mightn't have succeeded. But you were the only one who tried."

He kicked a pebble. "The vicious circle was just too tight." He leaned against the metal upright of the swings. "It taught me something though."

"What?"

"All she needed was for someone to care." He scuffed the ground. "But caring can come too late."

The next afternoon they spent in the deep comfort of a sofa in the hotel lounge. David rang Tim. Tim didn't waste time.

"Are you with La Daniels?"

"Yea."

"Is she all right?"

David glanced across at Robyn, at the sparkle in her eyes, her sculpted cheekbones.

"Tim wants to know if you're all right," he said to her.

"Tell him you've kidnapped me and I'm desperate to be rescued."

Before David could speak, Tim said sharply, "I heard that. This isn't funny. When'll you be back?"

"I don't know. A couple of days maybe."

"You need to get back here, Davey. You need to sort yourself out. What are you going to do?" His tone was fizzing with exasperation and more than a little anger. "You've decisions to make before you mess up big time." There was accusation too. "And a few people want some explanations about what you've done. You shouldn't be away right now, man. Whatever the reason," he added.

"I hear you. How're things there?"

"OK. Plenty of talk about what happened. Everyone's still in shock. They've got a sub in for Fraser's classes. He was buried yesterday. The Head went. Nobody else did. Apparently there were only three people there."

There was a silence. Then Tim said: "I don't expect you'll mind. Chloe and I have got together."

"You and Chloe?"

"You're not the only one with hormones."

"It's just…"

Tim broke in. "You know, for someone who has more brains and balls than anyone else I know, you can be as blind as a bat sometimes. And you're doing it again now. Get back here. Reality's waiting for you." He waited a beat then added "Both of you."

When David ended the call, he sat in thought, tapping the phone on his chin.

"Everything all right?" Robyn asked.

"Tim and Chloe are an item."

"At last. I thought they were ideal for each other."

His brows climbed. "Did you?"

"Tim's carried a candle for Chloe for a long time. You were in the way." She cocked her head. "Didn't you realise?"

He didn't answer that. "I don't think he approves of you and me."

"A lot of people won't."

"Too bad!"

Youthful impetuosity was still part of who he was. She replied carefully.

"Let's take a day at a time. We've a lot of thinking to do."

He leaned back. She could see he was not entirely happy with that but he said nothing. She watched his face become thoughtful again, his eyes unfocussed. She had got to know this look and kept quiet.

"Tim said Fraser was buried yesterday." He looked sideways at her, watching for her reaction. There was none. "He said there were only three people there. One of them was the Head."

After a moment, she said: "That's sad."

He leaned forward. "Yes, it is sad."

"But do you care?"

He looked round. "Do *you* care?"

She flicked her fingers round her ear, a vestige of the old gesture. "I think," she said carefully, "that it's sad that there are people whose lives are twisted and wasted like his was. And Penny's."

He extended his palm. "It puzzles me. Why can some people come through hell and find heaven? And why do some people stay in hell?"

"Maybe it depends on who they meet when they're in hell. You had your own strong personality and a loving family." She took his hand. "As for me, you took me by the scruff and dragged me out."

"I wonder where Fraser came from? What made him what he became? It's not just what people do. It's why they do it. Understanding makes forgiving easier." He was quiet for a while and she leaned against him, stroking his fingers where they had settled back on her shoulder. His thoughts surfaced again. "It reminds me of the main thing I learnt in the year after Abi died. I was sent back to school, but it seemed pointless to me. It didn't matter what I knew. That just seemed so one dimensional."

"Knowledge is breadth. Reason is depth."

He went on. "So I began to look for the how and the why in knowledge. That way I found heights and depths, peaks and bunkers. And life wasn't lukewarm any more. It wasn't grey." He gave her shoulder a little squeeze. "That's when I found the colour again."

"Finding it's one thing," she said. "Becoming a prism that can make it dance on others is very special."

She had hit a chord. "Yes! That's it, exactly!" He let her go and stood up, agitated, pacing to the window and back again. "This world matters." His eyes were sparkling, alive. "Being there. Reaching up to heaven and bringing a piece of it down to earth. Bringing eternity into time for people who badly need it here and now. It's like the roses in the park. It really stuck with me what you said that day. We need to leave an impression in the air around us. Otherwise we're pointless."

His mood flipped again and he pulled her to her feet and into a tight, smothering hug. Then he found her lips and kissed her deeply, confident and happy with her now. Familiar responses tingled through her. He pulled back, leaving her dizzy.

"Hey," he whispered.

"What?" she breathed, her eyes still closed.

"When's dinner? I'm starving."

They were trying to compose themselves for sleep. They weren't succeeding. Robyn lay across the rumpled sheets, her head on David's stomach, her fingers drawing little circles on his chest. His eyes were closed, his hands relaxed across her back.

"David?"

"Mmm?"

"How are you going to do your exams?"

"College, I hope. Where I should have gone in the first place."

His eyes were still closed. She eased herself over him a little. "What are you thinking?"

He opened his eyes. They were clouded, far away. "I was thinking about a cherry tree."

"A cherry tree?"

"One you've seen, but you wouldn't remember."

"Where is it?"

"In my back garden. When we moved to Belfast, my parents planted it specially. We call it Abi's Tree." He moved one hand to the back of her head. His voice was unsteady. "Dad died beside it. It's a weeping cherry. And it's all alone at the moment."

Robyn stayed still, quiet. Then she rolled to his side. She opened her arms and he turned into them, urgently, desperately, his composure fracturing at last. She stroked his hair gently. In the middle of happiness, grief hooked in from the side, abrupt and crippling. She moved a little to ease him on her shoulder and cradled him until finally he slept. And for a long time afterwards.

They woke together. Just by the way he looked at her, Robyn knew what was in his mind.

"It's time to go back." she said.

"Yes," he said.

As the ferry ploughed back across the waves towards home, they sat side by side at the prow window, looking ahead. When the first smudge of land blurred the horizon, they reached out at the same moment to link hands. David lifted her fingers to his lips and held her gaze.

"So do you think we can make this work?" he asked.

"Yes, David, I do believe we can."

Contented, he turned his eyes back to the window, to the sea, to the land, and to the future.

Epilogue

IN DRIVING RAIN, Robyn stood beside David on an isolated hillside in Fermanagh. On his other side a little whine escaped Manna as he checked his master's face with his good eye. The flowers on the grave were faded, windswept. It added to the sense of desolation. The white headstone still bore just one name:

"Abigail Elizabeth, aged three years and six months."

David stood hunched against the wind, his hands deep in the pockets of his coat. Robyn put her hand on his back where the rain was making dark patches across his shoulders.

"They gave you their forgiveness, David." She stepped back. "Accepting it once and for all is up to you."

She clicked her fingers and Manna slipped round to her heel. She walked away to the car, leaving David alone. He would come back to her when he was ready.

This cemetery was different. An orderly town graveyard with headstones in neat rows. David parked the car outside the gates and Robyn led him to the black marble of Matthew Daniels' impressive surround. Manna stopped ten feet from it and sat down obstinately. His head was low; his eye followed them anxiously. He would not go any closer.

In the centre, on top of the white pebbles, was the flower urn. It was empty. David stood beside her.

"Can you lay the ghost?" he asked gently.

A tremor went through her, from her head to her toes. David left her briefly. When he came back, he was holding a stone the size of his palm. He held it out to her.

"You could still hit him. Do whatever you have to."

She took the stone and turned it in her hands, looking from it to the headstone with its proud lettering.

She raised the stone. Took aim. Flexed her wrist. Took aim again.

Then she lowered her hand slowly and opened her fingers. The stone fell to the ground with a dull thud. She walked away to the hedge where some dandelions flowered amongst the nettles and brambles. She tugged a few stalks and came back. Lifting her arm high, she threw them at the headstone. The golden flower heads bounced off the marble and fell across the white pebbles beneath. Robyn's lip curled.

"There you are, you pathetic bastard. I forgive you. But where you are, I'd say that's the least of your worries."

Then she walked away. David didn't follow her until she sat heavily on another grave surround, further down the path. She heard him stop in front of her.

"David," she said.

He dropped to his heels. "I'm here."

"I think," she said slowly, "I'll go and see my mother soon."

A moment of quiet stillness. Then they stood, turned and walked side by side down the path and out through the cemetery gates. Manna followed, his tail rising happily. They would never return.

Never again.

Author's Note

Telling the story of David and Robyn has been a labour of love for me. I hope I have done justice to their rocky passage towards a future that could be better than the past.

They struggled with so much that cast a blight on their lives from their earliest years. Perhaps, especially from Robyn, there is a message here that vicious circles can be broken, that the past need not define us forever. As David says at one point: "When you get blown off course, you can choose to stay lost — or you can reach for heaven and steer by the stars."

Sadly, there are also those, as in David and Robyn's story, who do not make it out of the vicious circle, those whom society lets down or even worse, just simply doesn't notice. There must be many who, from their conception, have life's odds stacked against them.

As in this story, there are too many bad people alive today. We hear about them, their deeds and ideologies every day. But I reflect on the undeniable truth that there are many good people too, celebrated and uncelebrated, famous and anonymous.

And I take hope from that, hope in all the people who, like David, are persistent and patient, with an inextinguishable spirit of goodness and kindness. They do exist and I am privileged to be related to a few!

On a less serious note, if you have enjoyed this story, it would be massively helpful if you could leave a review on Amazon. It all helps work those mysterious algorithms! Thank you!

Sheila Turner Johnston
September 2020

Also by Sheila Turner Johnston

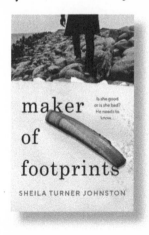

"This is one of those rare books that touch the soul – a story of irrevocable change, tragedy and indestructable love."

Meeting him was easy. It was knowing him that burned bone.

Paul Shepherd is dangerous. He crashes into Jenna's life like an asteroid into an ocean. Willful and exhausting, he stirs feelings that make her confront all that has kept her safe – and bored.

Relentless and determined, he needs Jenna with a desperation she does not understand. Jenna discovers that, although she can try to hide from Paul, there is nowhere to hide from herself.

But he is married…

What do you do when you discover you are not the person you thought you were?

Visit https://bit.ly/2RKwlfu to hear the author read from Chapter 4.

www.sheilaturnerjohnston.com

 @SperrinGold   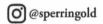 @sperringold